Siren in the Wind

Louise Dawn

To sign up for Louise Dawn's newsletter, go to:
http://www.louisedawnauthor.com

For my sister, Colleen.
Thanks for diary snooping as a kid and being
the sole fan of my weird scribblings.
Your encouragement got me here.

◊ ◊ ◊

Also, for my sweet parents.

◊ ◊ ◊

Some final thanks to my fine military/law enforcement friends,
who put up with my endless research and nagging.

To stand serenely in raging storms while others turn and run.

Prologue

New York.
Three Years Ago.

Liberation was just a few steps away. Today they'd finally be free. Sharon watched the shoppers spill out from jammed escalators. Long wait times fueled the oppressive atmosphere in the mall. Black Friday posters scattered throughout the pandemonium added to the frenzy.

Arisha tugged at Sharon's jacket, staring up with solemn eyes. "We need to find a seat, Mamma."

She ran a hand through her daughter's thick black hair. Sharon despised her own wispy blonde hair and always kept it trimmed in a neat bob. Reaching down, she picked up their two small suitcases, nudging Arisha forward. "Then find us one."

The packed food court gave them few options. A man and woman situated nearest the terrace railing cleared their table and Arisha ran up and waited. The lady smiled. Her little girl captivated people, with her mother's delicate features and her father's Iranian ancestry. Sharon stepped up, and the woman's smile faltered. Her gaze skimmed over Sharon's abaya with censure. Sharon was used to a daily dose of anti-Islamic sentiment and mentally shrugged it off. The world was at war, and the Americans knew it. The couple moved on, and Sharon scanned the bustling mall below.

It was an unusually balmy day for November, and the heating in the crowded mall ran high. The man's broad girth resulted in a warm bucket seat, and Sharon hid her disdain. First-world greed was leading to more obesity. The smell of charred burger hung in the air, making her stomach roil. It was nerves, and she had every right to feel rattled. Today was a big day. The men were coming to take them away.

"I'm thirsty, Mamma," Arisha said.

Sharon shoved her purse into her daughter's hand. "Quickly get a drink and please, my love, don't go far."

Arisha dashed through the crowd.

Sharon yelled at her disappearing back, "Please do not run!"

Ignoring the noisy kaleidoscope of screaming children, yelling parents and people dashing about, Sharon wiped at the sweat clinging to her brow. This is what it had come to. The feverish air rippled with fresh energy as he stepped up from behind.

Sully had come. Her savior. Her rescuer. Her destruction. Was Sully's team with him, led by the capable soldier with the icy eyes? She couldn't let that man see her. It felt like he'd seen into her soul the one time they had met and if he looked at her now, he'd know.

◊ ◊ ◊

The slight stiffening of her delicate neck and the rise of her head were a good indication that Sharon knew he'd arrived. Simon "Sully" Cook squeezed her shoulder as he assessed the environment. Arisha made her way back to the table while gulping down a drink. He glanced down at their packed bags and slid into the seat opposite Sharon Nasari, of New Zealand descent, the current third wife of Abdul-Habsid Nasari.

Abdul Nasari was a suspected terrorist and a wife beater. Sharon was ready to blow the extremist whistle on her husband's sleeper cell. Cook had approached her twelve weeks ago. Winning over her trust had taken perseverance.

After a particularly harsh beating ten days ago, she'd finally reached out, promising to testify against Abdul. They were preparing the warrant, but Abdul wasn't the primary target. They were chasing a significant player known as the Sandpiper, who held no allegiances to any extremist group. A businessman who sold arsenals of terror to private organizations and collapsing regimes in East Africa—An arsenal that included training camps, suicide bombers, and weaponry.

Her hollowed-out cheekbones looked harsher than when he'd seen her three weeks ago. Sharon was young enough to be his kid. Anger surged when he thought of one of his daughters trapped in a marriage with a sadistic monster.

Abdul had spotted Sharon in Istanbul when at the tender age of seventeen she'd traveled through Europe on a student holiday. He'd pursued the kid aggressively and hadn't stopped until she was an indoctrinated wife. They'd climbed up the terrorist watch list after moving from South Sudan to the States three years ago.

Sharon had a tough road ahead. They required intel but first needed to relocate the mother and child. She was terrified and had asked to meet him on Black Friday—the busiest day of the year—feeling safer in the massive crowds where she could easily get lost, terrified that Abdul might suspect something and find her. They'd all get lost together. The priority was getting her to the South Side entrance where they could hustle them away.

Sully had brought along another agent, Mike "Stone" Stretton. Sully and Stone arrived ahead of the rest of the team. Sharon had changed the meeting point at the last minute. Sully knew he'd broken protocol, racing ahead, but the urgency in his gut outweighed the risks. Besides, the rest of his men were just a few minutes behind.

Stone stepped up and leaned in. "I'm sorry, Sharon, but I'll need to check that you're clean."

"After all we've been through, you still do not trust me." Her smile was wooden. "Go ahead."

"It's just a formality," Sully reassured her. Sharon raised her arms and Stone felt around her waist before turning to the luggage.

"Where's the rest of your team?" she asked.

Sully smiled into her eyes. "Not far off. Relax, we've got this. You'll soon be free of Nasari."

Sharon glanced down at her clenched hands and spread them out on the cold plastic surface. "Of that, I have no doubt."

Sully glanced around uneasily. There was no intel indicating they were compromised, but something felt off. Hot little hands closed around his left biceps, causing him to whip around.

Little Arisha looked up shyly. "Hello, Mr. Sully."

His heart warmed. "Angel, are you ready for a great adventure?" He forced himself to smile into her sweet face.

Something flickered in her eyes that unnerved him. She knew more than a little girl her age should know. A child that young shouldn't have such sober eyes. What had Arisha seen in her young life?

Sharon pulled Arisha into a chair. "Habibti, sit quietly and play your Candy Game."

Pulling out her phone, Arisha smiled lovingly at her mother.

Through his earpiece, he heard the teams checking in, approaching from the wrong level. That was his fault for rushing the meet.

Sully spoke into his comms. "We're on level two. At the food court." He turned to Stone. "They're approaching from entrance five, but they're still on level one. Intercept them."

Stone disappeared into the throng of shoppers as Sully leaned forward. "You'll be starting your new life and I'll be here for you. Do what I say, and we'll get through this just fine."

Sharon glanced over the balustrade at Sully's team moving towards the escalators.

"Time to go." Sully bent over to retrieve the bags.

Sharon grabbed his sleeve, the look on her face stopping him momentarily. "You are family to me, you've been there for me in the darkness, and you will always have my heart."

Sully glanced across as the team moved onto the escalator. They'd spotted him and looked pissed. Stone waited at the top. "Not now Sharon, later we can—"

Sharon continued talking, "But you can never have what's in my head."

What did she just say? Her manic smile revealed the fanaticism. Instantly Sully knew. Sharon Nasari had played him for a fool. Everything slowed as adrenaline kicked in. He looked at Arisha playing her game and realization dawned. Hot hands. The kid wore a bulky jacket, too thick for that crowded day in the mall. She wore a fucking suicide vest. The phone lay flat as her tiny finger hovered above a flashing dot on a black screen, before descending. The small cubicle impeded his scrambling lunge.

Through the roaring in his ears, Sully heard Sharon's last words, "Sandpiper sends his regards."

White heat flashed, then came the blackness.

◊ ◊ ◊

London.

Heading back to Dubai as the first-class galley slave suited her just fine. The galley was where Joey could avoid passengers on the busier flights. She threw herself into the set routine as soon as she stepped onboard. Safety checks, loading ovens, pouring champagne, prepping hot towels, checking the ovens—the list was long. It was always a rush.

Joey had spent the past three years working a first-class cabin. Aircrafts and airline companies might have changed over her brief career, but the job was primarily the same and being organized was key. Her two colleagues manned the deluxe cabin with grace.

Ahlam Airlines handpicked the girls from thousands of applicants to serve the UAE royal families. They had to possess beauty and, more importantly, intelligence to sustain polite conversations with privileged passengers. Aside from royal personnel, cabin attendants looked after foreign diplomats, prime ministers, politicians, and celebrities. Joey could serve passengers along with the best of them, but lately preferred the quiet routine of the galley.

She stepped into the cockpit and gave the Captain and First Officer their morning coffee before racing back to kitchen duties.

Sarah glided past to hang a jacket. "Joey, when you get a second, Three Alpha wants to say hello, he says he knows you."

Joey stuck her head out of the curtains and caught an exotic whiff of expensive perfume. A group of local women dressed in designer robes blocked her view as they gathered in the cabin, chattering loudly in Arabic. Joey greeted them warmly and helped to stow their carry-ons. The aisles were crowded, and she couldn't see past the first row.

There was too much to do before push back. "I'll check later, thanks Sarah."

The first few hours were always busy. Joey sent out all six courses for lunch with precision, ensuring the food was hot and the service impeccable. After clearing the last round of Arabic coffee, Joey breathed a sigh of relief, removed her apron and squeezed into a compact lavatory. She stared at her reflection, barely recognizing the sleek mannequin looking back. Another flight, another dollar. She enjoyed her job but lately felt a little worn down and well, just a little lonely. Throwing herself into work wasn't working. Raking up a few escaping tendrils and with a quick lipstick swipe, she was back in the cabin.

Three Alpha's seat was empty; instead, Joey came face to face with a peregrine falcon perched on a small wooden stand. Falconry was one of the oldest traditions in the United Arab Emirates, dating back at least two thousand years to when tribesmen used falcons to hunt and capture their food. It was now one of the favorite pastimes of the wealthy. Arabic airlines allowed the birds onboard, as long as they wore hoods and were tethered to a glove or a pole perch.

"Not to worry, Habibti, she is friendly." Joey swung around as the passenger stepped through the business class curtain. His spicy scent enveloped her immediately.

"*As salam alaikum.*" The Arabic greeting rolled off her tongue belying the fact that her insides quaked.

"*Wa alaikum salam.*"

The falcon wasn't the source of her nerves; she'd seen enough of them on board in her five-year career of Middle Eastern flying. Instead, it was the man cloaked in a white robe, standing in the passage, his hands clasped in front of him.

Khalid Al Juhani.

Her roommate had introduced Khalid to Joey, and now she

ran into him everywhere. They hung out in the same circle of friends—which seemed odd, given that he was a wealthy Saudi, in comparison to her humble self.

Khalid bowed. "My apologies, I was stretching my legs while talking with my friend in business class." He quirked a smile. "I needed to walk off that delightful but long lunch."

The meal had been a lengthy affair; it was a first-class perk. Joey tried to relax; she never understood why he made her uncomfortable. Khalid had impeccable manners along with a handsome and kind face, in fact, he came off as being a wonderfully groomed vision of perfection.

"I'm glad you enjoyed it."

He bowed again, this time playfully, and gave her a small wink. "Compliments to the chef."

Joey smiled. "I'm not the chef, I just warm up the food."

"I think a little more goes into it than that. I know how hard you ladies work."

Wow. Nothing like complimenting a girl's work ethic to get her all warm and fuzzy inside.

Joey studied the beautiful bird perched beside her as Khalid stroked a wing.

"I just bought her in London for sixty-five thousand pounds. She'll be an excellent candidate for falcon racing."

Joey gaped at the kestrel. "That's one expensive bird."

Khalid laughed. "Hopefully she's fast enough to be worth it. Besides that, she's really pretty. What can I say, I have a weakness for a pretty face."

Khalid was good at flirting. Joey was not and smiled politely.

"Good luck with her and have a lovely flight. I'll make sure that Sarah looks after you."

"Wait! Habibti—Josephine—I would like to ask you something."

Joey turned back.

"I'm having a get-together at my home in Sharjah on Saturday and I'd be honored if you would attend."

A get-together. Joey had been around Dubai long enough to know that when a man like Khalid mentioned a "get-together," it was probably a formal party hitting the five-hundred-guests mark.

Her stomach rebelled. "Khalid, I am honored but I—"

"Please say yes. You would not have to stay long, and some of your friends will be there."

Joey hesitated. She wasn't the wild partying type and preferred curling up with a good book. Khalid's eyes glowed with warmth. What the hell. She lived in one of the most exciting cities in the world, and she was acting like a bloody recluse. With a renewed determination to break out of self-imposed hermitude, she graciously accepted.

"Thank you, Khalid. I cannot refuse such a gracious invitation."

"Habibti, I promise you an unforgettable night."

Chapter One

Johannesburg. South Africa.
Present day.

Abby lowered herself into the water, welcoming the fluid embrace. Adjusting her goggles and tugging the back of her swimming cap down, she pushed off. God, she loved this, therapy for the soul. Soon she'd be warmed up enough to slide into an effortless rhythm and then the meditation would begin. The distant noises of the gym were drowned out by even breathing and the water sliding smoothly over her skin.

Lap one. The tension rippling through Abby's body craved release, and she pushed harder, cutting through the water with efficient strokes. Laps flew by as muscles burned. Quiet was how she liked it, and even though the rest of the lanes were empty, it was one of those days where it was impossible to unplug.

Abby avoided peak times at the gym—early mornings or late evenings—especially during the week with screaming kids or swimmers jostling for lanes. Off-peak suited her just fine, all on her own. Always alone. Her mind worried over the design work she'd recently lined up as laps flew by.

Jeez, Abby, relax, don't think about work, don't think about anything. She threw herself into lap forty-one with determined strokes.

◊ ◊ ◊

Max Andersen couldn't take his eyes off the graceful swimmer. She swam alone. Seven o'clock on a wintery Sunday night meant the gymnasium was virtually empty, making his job harder to blend in. The upper level overlooked the Olympic-sized pool, and Max chose the treadmill in the darkest corner.

The pool's length spread out below. His hoodie was pulled down. That, combined with the scruff on his face, should keep him safe from prying eyes. Abigail Evans swam her fifty laps on a daily basis. She was a good swimmer and made it look easy, slicing cleanly through the water. Her long, lean strokes were hypnotizing.

Routine was dangerous, and Max knew her routine well; he'd been trailing her for the past three weeks. Soon they'd meet, and Abigail's world would change forever. Steadying his pace, Max fell into a comfortable run.

Johnny's voice rang in his ear. "We're set. Evans will meet her friends at that Italian joint, called La Coraggio, tomorrow at 1900 hours."

"The one at the strip mall near Edengate?"

"Yes, sir."

Max smiled wolfishly. "I'll be ready."

Game on. Lap forty-two.

"Hey, you!"

Max lost a step and glanced at a pert blonde bouncing onto the machine next to him. *Jesus.* The woman just wouldn't quit. This was the third day in the row that she'd approached him. Politely turning her down wasn't working, now she was a nuisance. Ordinarily, Max wasn't rude and back in the States this babe would probably be his type, but he was working, and his prey was the long-limbed brunette swimming below.

"Would you mind pacing me?"

Max gave her his best "Fuck off" glare and told her bluntly. "You wouldn't keep up."

She ran a glittery talon down his arm. "God, I love your accent. It's like so different, and your eyes are so damn cool. Scary but sexy gorge."

Lap forty-three. Where was Evans? Max paused the treadmill and subtly leaned over the front, checking if she was situated below. She was no longer in the pool, eight lengths shy of the usual fifty, probably headed to the change room. Damn. Max's teammate, Donnie, climbed off a bike and moved towards the exit. As Max stepped off, Miss Pink Spandex stepped up. The girl was persistent; he had to give her that.

"Don't be so rude. I've been nothing but super nice to you." Her huge lips glistened. A heady combination of self-tan, cloying perfume and berry lip-gloss assailed his senses.

Max ran a hand through dirty blond hair. "Sweet cheeks, I like my gym buddies a little rough around the edges. Lose the fake nails, the lip gloss, and those ratty extensions, and maybe then we can talk."

Her mouth fell open. Max gave her a wink and slipped past.

"You're an asshole!"

Max ignored her shriek of rage; he was on the clock. Abigail never fussed in the change room, always leaving within five minutes of her swim, with damp hair, old sweatpants, and a worn cotton shirt.

Max muttered quietly. "Donnie, are you in position?"

"Confirmed. I'm not the one cuddling gym bunnies."

"Screw you. I'll follow Evans home. Grab us some supplies at the store."

Max barely had enough time to make it to his truck before she exited the gym. He couldn't lose track of Evans for one minute. The stakes were too high.

After getting the all clear, Max slipped into the apartment complex two minutes after Abigail. In order to fly under the radar and to maintain cover, one of the guards at the gate—Timothy—was on Max's payroll.

The condos, set out in rows, were small but comfortable. Many South Africans chose to live or rent in a complex for security reasons, surrounded by electric fencing; guards manning the gates and regular patrols reduced the fear of hijackings or burglaries.

Abigail lived in a ground unit that led out to a small garden. She worked from home with a freelance graphic design business and did quite well for herself. Max's team chose an apartment opposite hers on the upper level to use as their base. Their place was sparsely furnished, stuffed with just enough random crap to keep them under the radar. It smelled slightly of stale fast food and musty socks. The shuttered windows hid the equipment clicking and beeping in a corner.

They were a four-man black ops unit, part of a larger task force called Mobile Intelligence Team. Divided into six (four-man) teams assigned to hot spots around the globe, operating under Joint Special Operations Command. A tier one taskforce, so newly elite that they were described as the ghosts of JSOC. Their main objective was precision targeting of high-value targets. To gather intel, track down, find and kill extremist leaders in high-risk nations. Officially Max's deep reconnaissance hunting pack was referred to as Mobile Intelligence Team: Two (MIT2) and their focus was the Central and East African region. This didn't rule out the unique flexibility of their teams. When on the hunt, they moved into neighboring regions, relying on fellow MIT teams and indigenous allies for support.

Erik "Maximus" Andersen was the team leader and loved his job. After twelve years of service, Max was a military lifer, first serving as former US Marine MARSOC and then enhancing covert skills for MIT2 as an interrogation and language specialist.

His given call sign was Maximus, known for pushing limits and using his intellect to the "max." The current mission would solicit all his skills. MIT2 had been pulled down into Southern Africa, chasing down a target that could lead to one of the biggest takedowns in East African extremist history—capturing Khalid Al Juhani, also known as the Sandpiper.

Max toed off his sweaty sneakers at the front door. "This place stinks. Where's Slater?"

James "Johnny" Cane scribbled in the surveillance log. "In the shower."

"He's always in the damn shower. That peacock smells better than Kim fucking Kay." Max headed towards the monitoring station. "Text Donnie to get some extra cleaning shit while he's out, like some good old-fashioned bleach. This place needs a soaking."

Slater sauntered into the room. "Are you in OCD mode again?"

"Don't start with me, you're the untidiest asshole of the bunch."

"Yeah? I just used your razor to shave my dick. My gift to you."

Max chuckled as he shoved Slater out of the way, bending to pick up a discarded newspaper. "Well there goes that then."

"Sharing is caring," Slater said while pulling on his socks.

Max rolled his eyes. "You're going to be sharing my boot when it's up your ass if you don't wash those filthy dishes marinating in the sink."

"Go sit in the dark and think about herrings," Slater quipped, alluding to Max's Finnish ancestral roots.

"I'll beat your ass with a herring if I don't see a clean kitchen."

Sighing dramatically, Slater moved towards the sink. "Another fine day, ruined by responsibility."

Slater was a former Green Beret, a sniper and the force protection specialist on MIT2, responsible for their safety logistics and assessing environment. He was the funny dude in the bunch, the king of one-liners. He was also just as laid-back as Johnny, a former Ranger and the team medic. Leave the two of them together for the afternoon, and it looked like a nuke had gone off in the apartment.

After a quick tidy, Max moved towards the station. "It's my turn, take a break."

Johnny glanced over his shoulder and griped, "By the way, Evans is goddamned baking again!"

Max grinned. Since arriving in the country, Johnny had been assigned to befriend Lizette Steyn, a close friend of Abigail Evans. His laid-back demeanor and special ops ASOT training gave Johnny the skills to not only easily befriend assets but also convert potential targets to assets in the field.

MIT2 needed to infiltrate Abby's tiny circle of friends, but so far it hadn't worked. Johnny kept moaning that he was moving slower than pond water, eventually upping his game with Lizzy through seductive flirting. He'd almost met Evans once at a birthday bash, but she'd pulled out at the last minute. The rest of the time Johnny was dragged to Lizzy's family barbecues—called *braais* in South Africa—where he'd stuffed down plenty of good food. Johnny packed on a few pounds and the former Ranger knew it, placing himself on a high protein diet. He was now one grouchy son of a bitch.

"Who does that, exercises like a demon possessed and then comes home to bake?"

Max shoved Johnny aside, which was no small feat—the man was built like a boulder. "The cake is probably for her client coming in tomorrow morning. Move your tree trunk ass out of my way and take a break. Go. Eat a carrot." Max settled in, adjusting the monitors. Thanks to their equipment, MIT2 had a clear view of Evans's entire apartment. Surveillance covered every inch of her place. They could hear a mouse pee if they wanted to. Not that Abigail Evans had mice, her home was immaculate.

Many could get drawn in by her classic beauty, the light olive skin and glossy brown hair were a throwback to her Italian roots. Her nose was aquiline straight and her lips naturally full. Max wasn't affected by beauty. He'd known many model-esque girls in his younger days.

The last few assignments all involved beautiful women who betrayed their countries. Sometimes that brittle outer shell was just that, but Evans was shaping up to be a Rubik's cube. Her energy and those direct eyes unsettled him. This type of surveillance was a drip, drip, drip information operation, and learning the target's tells and giveaways took patience.

Max had a talent for reading people—one of the reasons he worked for MIT. Many called him a walking lie detector but no one could be a human lie detector. In Max's eyes, anyone who bragged that they could do that was stupidly arrogant. The human psyche was layered and complex, and detecting deception was challenging.

Max had studied human psychology, and had also touched on anthropology, anatomy, physiology, communications, zoology, linguistics, language, and grammar as just starting points in examining how *Homo sapiens* behaved under pressure. Establishing a baseline of how the target behaved naturally in their environment, without duress, was the first step, observing tells that might come up on a daily basis.

For the past thirty days, he'd focused his energy on the cool lady currently lining a loaf tin a hundred meters away. It was a viable possibility from all the intel that Abigail Evans was a sleeper in an international terrorist cell. Her name had been flagged a couple of times through extremist networks, linking her to suspicious activity in the Middle East.

The intel clashed with some of his readings, but her profile still matched that of a sleeper. Isolating herself, no family ties. Working from home, allowing herself the freedom to plan her work schedule. She was also damn guarded, wary of strangers.

He had no sympathy for an American who betrayed their country and hiding in Africa wouldn't save her. Max would be the first one to shove her on a plane destined for Washington. Being a female wouldn't earn her brownie points either; he knew plenty of women who sold out their loved ones for money or infamy. He was a cynical bastard, but it got the job done.

◊ ◊ ◊

Abby pottered around the kitchen, feeling lighter after her swim, loving the buzz she got from exercise, plus the added benefit of keeping trim. It meant she could happily bake without indulgence guilt looming. Not that she exercised for appearance reasons, she craved the spiritual aspect, taking her mind off the constant worry and prepping herself for whatever lay ahead.

She hummed while peeling bananas for the loaf mix. She wasn't the best baker but learned as she went along. A British roommate taught her the basics a few years ago. Her mom had never taught her. Growing up, they were always traveling, working in remote villages in distant countries, and there was never any time to bake cakes; her parents had enough time, though, to beat her until she bled. She vowed she would never go back to that life.

She'd run away at sixteen, happy to work at fast food spots while attending art classes. Finding her way to a life filled with light was the goal, and she'd become a nomad. Until that terrible night… Abby knew she hadn't been the first. She wasn't a fool. How many women had come before her? How many were out there now, waiting?

In the early hours of the morning when she woke from the terror-swamped nightmares, Abby wondered who could save her. But whenever she woke, she knew her path was the righteous one. The key was remaining in control, and jittery hands were unacceptable. Instead of sieving the dry ingredients, Abby set the flour aside and tidied up the small mess trailing the counter. Some might call her a perfectionist, but since escaping her chaotic childhood she'd always strived for order. As a teenager, she'd foolishly convinced herself that she controlled her destiny, but she now knew better.

The waiting was the worst. They'd make contact soon. Six weeks ago, Abby had received an anonymous tipoff that terrified her. She wasn't sure how or where it would happen, but she was as ready as she'd ever been.

The cell phone on the counter rang.

◊ ◊ ◊

Chime music filled the room.

"Incoming!" Max barked, and Johnny took the seat next to him.

Max observed Evans as she looked at the readout, taking a deep breath.

"Hi, Kris."

Adrenaline flickered. Slater moved towards the monitors. "Who is it?"

Max's answer was to the point. "I'm guessing it's the boy scout. Kris Muller, her childhood buddy."

"Holy hell. That's a surprise. Things are about to get real interesting."

Chapter Two

Johnny and Donnie left to trail Evans to her rendezvous with Muller. Once Abigail Evans stepped out, Max snapped up the opportunity to switch out a microphone in her bedroom that had fuzzy sound quality. Max slipped through Evans's gate into the immaculate garden. Delicate paving ran along the neat flower beds. Rose bushes lined the wall. He'd watched her many times fussing around among her plants. The result was charming.

Her dark porch made breaking in easier. It was late, and he was also glad she'd drawn the curtains before she left. Nothing like a nosy neighbor spotting him through the windows once he was inside.

South Africa posed more challenges when it came to breaking and entering, so Donnie had acquired a copy of her keys from her bag in the gym locker. In Johannesburg, windows as an entry point were ruled out due to the hefty security bars crisscrossing them. Max clicked open the door mechanism before opening her sliding security gate.

The smell of banana bread cooling on the kitchen counter assailed Max's senses, and his stomach growled in response. Martha freaking Stewart, he thought as he stared hungrily at the homely loaf. Johnny was right, this assignment sucked ass.

Except for Johnny Cane, his team currently lived on takeout. Max couldn't remember what a home-cooked meal, never mind a freaking home-baked cake, would taste like. His job was his life and most of it was spent maintaining a low profile in small villages and arid mountain regions in East Africa, eating MREs or local food. Max stuck to a healthy diet whenever possible, but his bachelor lifestyle back in the States wasn't exactly conducive to domestic bliss. It usually consisted of kicking back with work buddies—most of whom were single.

"Perkele." It felt good to swear in Finnish. Even though he was born and schooled in America and spoke with a Midwest accent, Max still spoke Finnish on occasion with his first-generation immigrant parents.

Leaning against the counter, he massaged his forehead. The guys were finding this assignment a little more psychologically challenging and it was up to Max to keep them on track. This series of investigations involved sleeper cells made up of young women. It wasn't as if they weren't used to dealing with suspects who were women. Over the years they had taken out or detained female bombers, extremist bodyguards—hell, coerced wives and mothers clutching AK47s. But the team had never been faced though with the possibility of moving in on an "All American girl" who'd betrayed her country.

As far as Max was concerned, a terrorist was a terrorist; there were no gray areas. You were either with or against them. His men wouldn't hesitate to take out any threat when it came down to it. Max felt a measure of unease but not for the same reasons. Nothing added up. The energy was off—something was missing.

He had no idea how deeply Evans was involved but red flags littered her profile. Just glancing around her place, there were no obvious links to any loved ones. No family photos or albums.

She'd cut ties with anything or anyone that mattered, that was what scared him the most. Evans might be readying herself.

Max took his time prowling through her perfectly put-together home, going over every detail. He'd been here twice before when they set up surveillance but always took his time getting a handle on her core energy.

Personal space spoke volumes when profiling a suspect; self-image left a footprint in the suspect's home. A well-ordered color palette of pale greens, blues and creams rolled through her apartment and complemented the white walls and clean tiles of the space. The pale blue Persian rug that dominated the dining space looked expensive, and her lounge was lined with a beige sofa set decorated with pastel green throws. A subtle scent of vanilla hung in the air.

He confirmed that Evan's piece was still strapped under the sofa. Donnie had found the weapon on their initial search. It wasn't unusual for a woman living alone in South Africa to keep a gun for protection. Max always kept a close eye however for any additional weapons that might have found their way in, possibly through her suspected network. So far it was just that one small Glock 19.

Next was her art studio. She had converted the first bedroom, on the left, into a workspace combining an artsy area with an office. Max stared in reverence at her latest canvas of a dense forest. He'd watched it gradually take form through the surveillance but standing in front of it rocked him slightly with rising anger. The woman had raw talent—why in God's name would she throw such potential away and blacken her soul by collaborating with terrorists?

Max sat at her desk and ran through recent activity on her laptop. Nada. A MIT2 camera faced her laptop so Max wasn't surprised. All she'd been working on over the past few weeks were design materials for her business. If she communicated with her cell, there was another channel. Again, no evidence of personal photographs or social networking links, not even a personal email account. It was all business. After studying her sketchpads and scrapbooks, Max pressed his earpiece.

"Status?" He heard Johnny shift.

"They've just ordered drinks. Nothing as yet."

"Where are you?"

"In the van. Reception is loud and clear. We have a clear visual. You can analyze the footage later."

They'd planted listening devices on both of Evans's handbags. Thank God she wasn't a handbag freak but instead was practical and low maintenance when it came to accessories.

Max left Johnny to do his job and headed to her bedroom to fix the equipment. Her perfume lingered. Delicate, creamy. The white bottle sat on her dresser—Juliette has a Gun: Sunny Side Up—Max bet his bottom dollar that Evans would find a way to re-purchase this scent. She had only one, which meant this was a signature scent.

His eyes landed on the small statue sitting in front of the mirror. The only knickknack on display. It meant something to her. A small replica of the ancient Hellenistic sculpture called the *Nike of Samothrace*, depicting a figure of a woman fighting against a strong sea breeze, draped garments flowing in the wind. The pose drew him in, evoking a graceful balance between fierce motion and steadfast stillness. Possible parallels to Evans were disturbing. He turned it over, noting the Louvre sticker pasted underneath before placing it back and finally reaching behind the white dresser for the microphone.

◊ ◊ ◊

What the hell was she even doing here? This was foolish. Abby glanced around the darkened sports bar. She needed to tread carefully when it came to Kris. She'd run into him a month ago while doing her weekly grocery shop at Edengate Mall. Kris had crushed her to his chest, his warm tears wetting her neck. Never thinking she'd see him again—convincing herself that he'd remained in the Middle East—the reunion pushed her off-kilter, and she'd elected to tell Kris an altered version of her story, leaving out the vital parts. Abby wasn't sure if he'd believed her but hadn't given any indication otherwise. Now they were meeting for a second time and Abby felt foolish for coming. Guilt made people do stupid things.

The truth about that night could never be revealed. What she'd become. A murderer and a coward. Shame made it hard to breathe and yet her heart was warmed at the prospect of seeing him again. They'd become childhood friends when her missionary parents stayed on his aunt's game farm in Botswana for six months. Thirteen-year-old Kris immediately became a big brother to an awkward ten-year-old. Much of her time was spent learning about conservation and, through Kris's encouragement, Abby developed a love for the African bush.

Her family eventually moved on to South Africa. Their strong friendship had endured the distance, writing letters back and forth and eventually Skyping. Even after Abby ran away from her family, she'd always tried to meet up with Kris over their vacation times.

When a twenty-one-year-old Abby traveled to Dubai to work as a flight attendant, Kris was working in Botswana as a game ranger. A year later he joined her, landing a prime job as the head game ranger for one of the sheik's desert lodges. Everything had been an adventure. Snatched time off was spent traveling with friends and partying it up in the city and desert camps. All innocent fun, until that fateful evening when things had changed. The night she'd fed the love of Kris's life to the wolves. The night she'd turned her back on their longstanding friendship.

And there he was. Winding his way to the table with his trademark confidence. Kris was now part of an elite anti-poaching unit and currently traveled throughout Southern Africa, protecting rhino and other endangered species from extinction. The rugged game ranger—God, he was attractive—the tall, dark and handsome vibe suited him.

Her heart warmed. Why had they never dated in the past? Maybe subconsciously they'd never wanted to risk the friendship. For her, the time had never quite felt right. Dubai had changed them both. Kris had started dating her roommate, Megan Jehani, and he'd grown distant. Abby had hung out with their circle less and less. The final twist of fate had ultimately thrown them apart.

"You okay, Cricket?" Kris asked.

Abby rose and smiled at the nickname Kris had bestowed on her on the farm, all those years ago. She never liked the nickname, but Kris had tagged her with it when a huge cricket had jumped down the back of her neck, causing her to shriek uncontrollably while doing the highland fling. Needless to say, the name stuck, just like her absurd fear of crickets and grasshoppers. Orthopterophobia. She could deal with snakes and spiders. Just not crickets or anything that looked remotely crunchy or spiky. Abby shuddered.

Kris pulled her in for a bone-crushing hug, intense emotion

rolling off him. Abby wanted an escape. *Stop it. This is Kris.* A rare moment to be saved, cherished, taken out and examined later when she was all alone again. He pulled away slightly and gazed into her eyes as hands cupped her face. She tamped down the urge to squirm.

"Still so beautiful. When I saw you in the mall, I nearly had a heart attack. For the past three years, I thought you were dead. All along, I thought you were dead." His eyes swam with confusion. "Why in God's name would you just disappear like that?"

"Take a seat, let's talk."

They ordered drinks. Abby ordered a Coke. Her stomach couldn't bear anything stronger.

With restless energy, Kris gestured towards the door. "There's a great Indian place next door. Should we grab something?"

Shaking her head, Abby placed her hand on his. "This is fine, I can't stay long."

Kris smiled softly. "Remember those hot nights, that Indian place with the outside courtyard we'd go to? Best kept secret in Dubai. The three of us—Meg loved that spot. I forget that you pretty much hated it, except for the butter chicken, which you ordered every time. You were never a fan of Indian cuisine."

Abby smiled. "I preferred the Persian place on the creek. I think that was Meg's favorite spot too, made her a little homesick. She loved those kebabs, said they reminded her of her mother's Persian cooking." Her eyes filled with unshed tears.

"This is hard. I'm so sorry, I'm an idiot."

"Please don't." A tear spilled over. "I'm the one who should apologize."

His eyes looked empty, his face dull. The responsibility for those deep scars lay with her. "Hell, yes, you should. You just disappeared—walked out on me—I lost both the women I loved that night. I fucking needed you. What in heaven's name were you thinking?"

Abby couldn't bear to see her old friend this way, berating herself for the thousandth time. "I wasn't thinking."

The waitress returned, and Abby took a long sip of the Coke. She should've ordered a glass of wine…or a truckload of tequila shots. Typical Abby, always the control freak.

"Please give me something," Kris begged. "Anything. I need to know what happened that night. Were you there, when the accident happened? Were you in the car with Meg? I've tried to investigate but the case is shut up so tight. They wouldn't even let me see Meg's body because we weren't fucking married. They wouldn't let me near her." His face twisted with buried grief.

She swallowed hard. Kris could never know the truth. Time for a little more Abby-style deceit. "I left the party just twenty minutes after her and arrived just after the accident happened. The car was surrounded by police, who extinguished the flames. When I saw Meg's red shoe next to the car, I fell apart. I couldn't stay there so I just ran. I was in complete shock."

Squeezing his hand on the table did little good.

"God, I just wish I'd been there, I was called away to help with the birthing of a foal. One of the prince's breeding mares went into labor." Stroking her hand, he asked, "I know Meg was meeting up with you at the party. Why didn't you leave together? For God's sakes, she was your flat mate."

"I left with…left with a man I met at the party."

Disbelief flooded his face. "I don't believe you. You're bloody lying—you would never have a one-nighter."

Abby felt her face flush. "I wanted to live a little. Big deal. It was a foolish decision to stay with him instead of going home with Meg." Real emotion rose to the surface. "After that night I just couldn't face the reality of her death. I couldn't go back to the apartment and be surrounded by all Meg's stuff. A few days before, Meg asked me why I looked so unhappy living in Dubai, why I didn't start fresh. I'd been running for so long that I forgot how to stand still. But after the accident, I ran like a coward. That's who I am. I couldn't face you and I doubt you'll forgive me and that's okay. "

Abby could barely see straight. Everything seemed out of focus. She hated deceiving one of the few people who'd been there for her and who loved her for who she was.

Kris's glare held suspicion. "You just never bothered to drop me a line to say, 'Hey, Kris, by the way I'm alive and safe.' The car was an incinerated mess. I'd wondered if you'd died in the car with her, the police gave me nothing. I searched for you for so damn long, it was like you dropped off the planet."

"I'm sorry."

"Bullshit. If we never ran into each other at the mall, would you ever have contacted me? Even your own father has no clue where his daughter is."

"You spoke with my dad?" Abby leaned back in disbelief.

"Yes, I spoke with your wonderful father." Kris's mouth twisted. "That's how damn desperate I was. The bastard said you'd died."

Kris ran his hand through his hair in frustration and stared at the ceiling.

The truth clawed up her throat. So many times she'd had to pull herself back from finding him and rushing into his arms. It was now too late; she was fully committed to her cause. If Kris knew the truth, he'd never look at her the same way again. Abby ran her finger through the water vapor clinging to the sides of her glass. Strobe lights filled her vision. Everything was too hot.

Feeling bilious, she took a deep breath and got to her feet. "I'm not the same person you knew. I'll destroy you. Walk away from this—from us. Our friendship is over."

"Stop being so dramatic, that's a bloody bitchy thing to say and I've only just found you again."

She carefully bent to pick up her bag and scrounged up some notes, barely making out what they were.

"I've got this," Kris said.

The pounding in her head threatened to bring her to her knees. "I literally have an epic migraine coming on. I need to leave. "

He grasped her arm. "You're not escaping, I won't let you disappear again."

Abby didn't have the strength to fight. Her vision was now completely blurred out, and bar furniture seemed to jump in her way.

"Let me help, you cannot possibly drive like this, let me take you home." They made their way into the parking lot, Kris guiding her with a reassuring hand.

She absolutely couldn't let him know where she lived. Abby shook him off as she got to her car.

He growled in frustration. "God, you're so damn stubborn. I'm staying in the Kruger National Park for a couple of weeks on a rhino protection assignment. We'll damn well talk when I get back."

Abby ignored him. It was over.

Kris yelled as she backed out. "Text me when you're safely home." With a vague wave, Abby crawled out of the parking lot. Driving like this was not the wisest move but she had to get out of there. The migraine had excellent timing.

That was the last time Kris Muller would see her face. Self-hatred tasted bitter in her treacherous mouth.

"Pull back, she's heading home."

Max slid out of her wooden gate. "Already?"

Donnie yawned. "It was a disastrous little date. Basically, he cried, she lied and now she's driving home like a drunkard on crack."

Max paused on his way up their stairs. "What the hell are you talking about, control freak Evans is fucking drunk?"

"Nope. She's come down with a migraine. Definitely some ape-shit driving happening. She looks like crap, as white as a damn sheet."

Max slipped in their door. "I'm back at base and I want to see that footage."

Chapter Three

The following afternoon, Abby pulled into the strip mall and chose to park on the periphery of the frantic lot. Although there was a spring chill in the air, the late afternoon was pleasant. Due to the warmer weather, people spilled out of crowded cafés onto the pavements, La Coraggio was the busiest of the bunch. The Italian community loved the place, and the result was a boisterous, laid-back atmosphere with incredible cuisine. Honestly, she loved it too. Abby had an Italian grandmother, vague memories of a warm, loud lady enveloping her in happy hugs. Although her grandmother passed away when Abby was four, she felt a sharp pull towards her Italian roots. Abby was told growing up that she was the spitting image of Granny Lucy.

Lucy had been married to Grandpa Noah for twenty-four years when she'd died suddenly of a heart attack. Abby's father, Jimmy—their only child—turned in an extreme way to religion. A couple of years later, frustrated with his son's constant tirades and Biblical lectures on sinning, Noah moved away. Abby remembered Noah clearly, often curling up on his big lap, and hearing that gruff laugh rumbling through his chest. He would jump out from nowhere and throw her over his bear-like shoulders, spinning her in circles until she was dizzy with giggles.

She never saw him again.

The happy times left with her grandpa's disappearance from her life. As a teenager, she'd dreamt of running away from her father and his severe beatings and finding her grandpa. Would Noah know what a monster his son had become? Was he still alive? Luckily Abigail saved herself a long time ago from that life.

A smudge of yellow paint drew her attention, and Abby rubbed it off her wrist. The hands of a grubby artist. Abby grumbled at the spots of dried paint crammed under closely clipped nails. Tough luck, fancy manicures were a waste of time when slapping paint on a canvas on a weekly basis.

She grabbed her handbag and took off her sunglasses, only to slam them back on. Remnants of the migraine still lingered from the night before, the ebbing sun way too bright for her light-sensitive eyes, but this night was important. Abby hadn't seen Lizzy in a while, and after loads of soppy texts and phone calls about the new man in her life, Abby thought it was time to meet the "dashing" specimen. If for no other reason than to assess the risk to her friend's lovely heart.

If it weren't for Lizzy, wild horses wouldn't drag her out on a Friday night. There'd be other Americans at dinner. Lizzy had invited them from her Facebook page, Americans in Jo'burg. Abby took a deep breath and clambered out of her car. The lively atmosphere in the café made her smile. Lizzy waved frantically, and Abby carefully maneuvered through crowded tables to the faction gathered on the far side of the outdoor piazza.

La Coraggio was a simply decorated café with little fuss. People came for the incredible food and great conversation. Red cloths hung off casual white tables, fairy lights decorated the railings and hung from the roof. Sounds of a televised soccer game flowed from the bar area, and men shouted over the game in Italian. Abby's stomach growled in response to the delicious smells wafting out of the kitchen.

Lizzy could only be described as a bouncy ball of blonde energy that swept Abby up in a sweet-smelling hug, her Dutch roots evident in her sparkly blue eyes and vivacious smile. If you could combine bubble bath and rays of sunshine into a happy little package, you would create a Lizzy.

"Why is there a pink streak in your hair?"

"It's just temporary. It goes with my Cyndi Lauper vibe." Lizzy waved a fingerless laced glove. No one pulled off the retro vibe as effortlessly as she could. Her faded denim jacket looked like it had just been tossed off the runway.

She babbled, dragging Abby the rest of the way. Lizzy had spent most of her childhood in Santa Barbara and still retained that buttery Californian accent. "Holy Shiblets! You're meeting my sexy man. He's like a chilled version of Jason Momoa."

"Who the hell is Jason Momoa?" Abby asked.

Lizzy rolled her eyes. "You know, Khal Drogo, Game of Thrones. But John is much sweeter, he's a big teddy bear." Abby still had no clue, not having time to watch telly or the iconic television series that everyone raved about. Lizzy waved a hand in the air, bangles jangling. "Okay, so don't be mad, my friend, but we've organized a delicious little—well, maybe not so little—surprise for you. John has the nicest, hottest friend who's here, and you'll absolutely love him."

Whoa… Before Abby had time to dig in her heels, they were at the table. Wrenching her hand out of Lizzy's iron grip was next to impossible. Sheez, how strong was her little friend? Her glare met Lizzy's innocent smile, and Abby whispered, "Sweetpea, what have you done?"

"Relax, Rain Man, it's just dinner. Besides, there's a whole group of us. Have some fun for a change." Lizzy stuck out her tongue and swung Abby around for introductions.

Lizzy knew better. Abby would never allow a strange man anywhere near her world. Damn her meddling friend. Abby would gobble up her food and quickly excuse herself.

John stood, waiting to shake her hand, and Abby took an involuntary step back. Big and tall didn't begin to describe the brawny giant standing before her. Lizzy hung off his arm like a tiny flea, barely reaching his broad chest. He could squash her little friend like a bug. Her eyes traveled up to his. John's kind eyes crinkled in welcome—that was unexpected.

Lizzy toed her leg, and Abby shook his large hand.

"A fellow American. I've heard so much about you." The soft-spoken mannerisms contrasted with his towering physique. Abby shot her friend a dark look. What had she told him?

"I told him that you're a talented graphic designer and the loveliest friend a girl could have."

Ah hell. Abby couldn't stay mad. It wasn't her friend's fault that her life was so screwed up. Lizzy took that as a green light, promptly leading her to an open spot. On the way, Abby greeted Lizzy's other friends. After slipping off her sunglasses, she went back to skewering John with an assessing stare. Lizzy threw her arms around Abby's neck and whispered, "Turn around, buttercup."

She turned to scowl, but all that registered were disturbing moonstone eyes. A lightning-quick assessment of the threat revealed an athletic built demigod, head lowered as he glanced at her from under his brows. He watched her with such stillness and yet she sensed tremendous icy energy swirling beneath the facade, ready to suck her in. Those deadly eyes ramped up his jarring intensity.

"Ab-cakes, Max Hansen works with John. Max, this is Abby Evans. She's a fellow American, and my rock in this crazy country."

◊ ◊ ◊

Max Andersen used Hansen as a cover name. A background check by potential targets revealed a fully developed Max Hansen entity in the field. Max expected her reluctance—gaining her confidence or trust would almost be futile given what they suspected she was. Now as Evans stood in front of him, Max saw a glimpse of something else, uncertainty or interest maybe? Couldn't be, but he could try his level best at charming the fuck out of her. Give it the old heave-ho and see where it led.

Evans was distractingly flawless in person. He'd seen a dated photo in her file and observed her at a distance but this close...sooty lashes framed ivy-green eyes and her skin glowed. A refreshing and mutely elegant tall drink of water. Dark blue jeans molded her ass beautifully, a white blouse clung to perfect curves. Two delicate gold chains adorned her slender neck, tangled and fighting for rights to her exquisite cleavage. He clasped her hand firmly, and the jolt of awareness was unexpected. Her hand jerked indicating she had felt it too. *Fuck.*

Evans shifted. "Um, excuse me?"

His gaze shot up and collided with hers. "Did I say that out loud? Double fuck."

The corner of her mouth quirked, and she slid her hand out of their electric grip. Lizzy flitted off to grab menus, as they stared awkwardly. Time to play.

Evans slipped past, and Max touched her hand with the back of his. She froze, and he leaned in, speaking above the din. "Here's the thing. I was caught unawares, just as you were. John told me about the blind date as you walked in. I'm not looking to hook up in any capacity—work is my priority." Max stroked his thumb over the edge of her wrist, feeling a tremble, she liked that. "You're beautiful." His warm breath feathered her ear. "But I'm no idiot; I see you have no desire to meet someone. How about just a friendly meal and you need never see me again."

Max let go. Her pretty lips parted, and her tongue darted out to lick a shapely lower lip. His eyes tracked the movement and rose to hers. Desire flashed before her walled serenity slammed back in.

"Max, is it? Thanks for clearing that up. Now, if you'll excuse me." She politely smiled and headed to the ladies' room.

Max paused to get his shit together. He'd deliberately tried to rattle her and succeeded, yet his own reaction pissed him off. Her silky skin and delicate scent drew him in, and that look in her eyes...

"Yo, Max, you gonna order or what?" Johnny yelled over the table.

Max lowered himself onto the bench as Johnny shot him a questioning glance.

◊ ◊ ◊

The toilet cubicle felt safe, super safe. Abby had never been this shaken by a man and in such a short amount of time. One minute of conversation and she was ready to toss all caution to the wind.

Breathe, Abby. Don't think about him. Focus on getting home and preparing for the mission ahead; you don't need or want a man. Especially not a man like him. There's no future for him in your existing world. He'll end up very dead. Abby took another minute before heading back.

Max sat next to her open seat, his capable-looking hands playing with the paper from his straw. Her stomach did a flip. Abby slid in and opened a menu, studying it solemnly. She knew La Coraggio well and occasionally grabbed a bite to eat during the week when the place was quiet. Still, the menu gave her an excuse not to look to her left, at that rugged profile and sensuous mouth with that nibble-inducing, full lower lip.

Max glanced over at the menu she held up like a shield. Abby surreptitiously hid a stained fingernail.

"What's good here?"

Max's deep voice jarred her out of her reverie.

"Everything," Abby answered. *Your sexy, rippling, very male forearms…*

"Yeah, but what would you recommend?"

Abby gnawed on her lip. *Just answer, and he'll quit.* "The vitello or the polpette."

"Come again?"

"The veal or the meatball pasta. They also have excellent lamb chops on the specials menu. You can't go wrong with any of their pizzas either."

He skewered her with a killer smile. Jeez, talk about Nordic god dimples. He was leaner than his wrestler-built friend John but just as lethal looking. *Wowser.* Abby took a slow breath and leaned over to chat with Lizzy.

◊ ◊ ◊

She'd effectively dismissed him. Max wasn't a natural flirt, but for him that was a first. Evans's unflappable demeanor was a definite challenge.

Once everyone had ordered, Max tried his hand again, asking her what she did for work and for fun. Evans's terse answers would have any man running. Max plugged on, smiling, touching her arm, staring into her eyes. Evans concentrated on the dish in front of her, and fair enough, it looked sumptuous. Tagliata beef filet baked in the oven—with garlic, rosemary, and balsamic vinegar. It wasn't one of her recommendations to him—gee, thanks. His meatballs were great, but nothing compared to the juicy steak gracing her plate. He was staring morosely at Abby's dish when she surprised him with a question.

"Are you from the Western states? We have a similar accent."

"Yeah." Max purposely didn't elaborate. "But I'm sure both of us have also taken on some local African slang over the months of living here. Can't be helped."

"Do you work with John?"

"I run my own business as a subcontractor. John and I have worked together on many occasions."

"What do you do?"

He took his time, wiped his mouth with the napkin before placing it back in his lap. His cover story could stand up to intensive background checks by the enemy. "I provide protective clothing to military and police around the world."

"Like uniforms?"

"Boots, uniforms, gloves, helmets… Clothing needs to be climate- and situation-specific, designed for a particular use. For instance, fire-retardant boots for riot control and protection against Molotov cocktails. Kevlar gloves that may vary in the field. Lighter bulletproof vests that still offer full protection."

She played with the stem of her wineglass. "Interesting. I guess you've served in the military?"

"I did. I left two years ago."

"Were you Army? Navy?"

"Army but nothing too glamorous. I never really served in the field. In layman terms I provided and built security for all US assets and bases that enemies might want to target. You could say I was a security expert."

He watched carefully for any reaction. A shift in posture, turn of her hand, any suspicious eye movements. Khalid would love to get his hands on a US security expert who'd supposedly built clandestine military facilities. A perfect honey trap to lure Khalid out of hiding.

Evans smiled. "Well, good for you and thank you for your service—you may not have served on the front lines but I'm sure you've made a difference." A skinny dude on the other side of her asked a question and Evans promptly turned away.

Nothing. Zippo.

Terrorists could mask body language but never fully hide their tells. Max was an expert on spotting ticks and nuances. Was Evans that good at masking her interest? He exchanged a look with his team member, who'd also picked up on her flawless delivery. Evans could be biding her time, possibly contact him for a date, set him up as a mark.

She'd be signing her death warrant along with the rest of her terrorist cell.

◊ ◊ ◊

It was time to leave, but Max's fierce stare whenever he spoke kept Abby anchored to her seat. He kept touching her hand and even used his thumbnail to rub off a smidge of acrylic paint on her knuckle. The man used his hands a lot and not in a fidgety way. Nervous energy was not a synonym for Max Hansen. His movements were conservative and deliberate; that exacting control made her feel safe. She hadn't felt safe in a long time.

Abby stared out into the night, beyond the noise and the

laughter. Time to stop pretending, time to stop flirting. The last time she flirted with a man, it had almost gotten her killed.

His magical fingers touched her again. "Are you okay?"

She turned to his handsome face with a heavy heart. "It was lovely to meet you, I wish you luck in your military clothing business." She squeezed his hand, not wanting to let go. "Please keep safe and tell John to treat Lizzy right. She's a chatterbox, but she has the biggest heart."

Max squashed a smidgen of guilt. The fallout would most likely crush her friend. Max failed to establish a strong enough connection. He swore softly as Lizzy and Johnny said their goodbyes. There were other ways to run into her; they'd adjust the schedule.

Clenching his jaw, Max forced himself to remain seated, mentally going over where he'd gone wrong. The hum in the café worked on his nerves. Needing space, Max shifted dinner plates. There, lying under a napkin, were her aviator sunglasses. She'd worn them on entering the restaurant. Evans didn't seem like the type to forget things. Were they purposely left behind or was it an innocent mistake? With only one way of finding out and hoping to catch the elusive Evans before she left, Max picked up the shades and headed for the exit.

Chilled air whispered through Abby's silken shirt as she made her way to her little Ford. The sweet night was a small memory to tuck away. Thoughts of Max made her want to turn back, instead she wrapped her arms closer, grimacing at her tiny car sitting desolately at the back end of the lot. Abby opened the door and was slammed forward. Her head bounced off the edge of the car roof, and an arm pulled her up against a hard chest as a gloved hand muffled her scream.

"Not a word, bitch."

The gravelly voice was hot on her neck. The brutal stranger licked her ear, and revulsion made her lightheaded. Blood trickled from her hairline. *God, was this a hijacking?* Terror made her squirm. He twisted her with such violence that an elbow cracked painfully against the car. Wedged in the door with no room to move, Abby searched for an opening. A knitted balaclava hid the assailant's face and beneath it, black paint masked his features. A black hoodie covered the rest. Something snicked and pricked her side. Vision tunneled as the horror slammed home.

"Move or scream, and I'll gut you like a fish." He wiggled the knife for good measure. "We're going for a little ride." He unclamped her bruised lips.

"The car...take the car..."

His erection pressed against her thigh. "I don't want to ride the car, sweet thing. I want to ride you."

Rubbing against her, he shoved his face into the side of her neck, biting down hard. At her yelp, the knife nipped her stomach. From a distance they looked like lovers, making out. No one would suspect a thing. If they drove to a second location, she was as good as dead. Abby wanted to throw up all over the hideous mask. Through the haze of adrenaline, she remembered the Taser tucked into the inner bucket of the door.

The knife slid up as she purposely collapsed, and her attacker was forced to readjust. "My head—I think I'm going to vomit."

"Stand up, now." His hand gripped her hair. Abby closed her hand around the Taser and rammed it deep into his balls, pulling the switch. The brute howled, stumbled back but didn't collapse. Car keys lay somewhere on the ground. Abby shoved past and freedom lasted only a heartbeat. He dragged her back and wrenched the Taser away, before shoving it into her side. Agonizing pain had her collapsing onto the asphalt.

"Fucking bitch! If you're going to use a Taser, get a stronger one next time."

Chapter Four

Where the hell had she parked? Max made his way through two rows of vehicles before shoving in his comms.

"Where's Evans?"

Donnie's voice barked in his ear. "It's a clusterfuck, someone's just jumped her."

Max stilled. "Where?"

"Back of the lot. North side. Should I break cover?"

Max took off. "Negative. I'm closer. Be ready in case I need you!"

He moved soundlessly, spotting the distant figures. Was the son of a bitch her contact?

"Are they having a meeting?" Max barked.

"Not unless the agenda includes sexual assault and bashing her head in."

Anger gushed. The fucker was dead. Could she have parked any farther away?

The bastard dragged Evans up by the hair, and all hell broke loose. Max choked on impotent rage, pushing his limits in a full-out sprint. They were gonna watch Evans die. The fucker rammed something into her side. A knife? She collapsed like a wet rag, and her head bounced off the tarmac. Exploding with wrath, Max tossed the sunglasses aside as a van pulled up. Max dimly heard the exchange as he narrowed in.

A gruff voice yelled from the van. "What the fuck happened!"

"Change of plans," the perp answered, picking up a knife off the ground, then dragging Evans towards the vehicle.

Not on Max's watch.

The driver yelled out, "Behind you!"

Max brought the attacker down hard, wrestling the knife away with a few deft moves, but the son of a bitch was quick. Military training. He tried to flip Max over. Max countered the move. The bastard kneed him in the ribs and reached for a black object on the ground. Taser—too late, Max shifted sideways, and it glanced off his arm, the pain paralyzing for a brief second. His opponent used the advantage, bucking him off. As Max flew back, the fuckhead expertly rolled away and dived into the van. Tires squealed as the vehicle raced away.

Lying on his back, Max swore up at the night's sky. Team members yelled through comms, checking if he was okay and he gave them a quick thumbs-up. Slater appeared a few feet away, breathing heavily. Max gave him a brief nod, and the Ranger disappeared into the shadows.

Rolling over, Max stumbled towards her still form. Blood covered that beautiful face. Max swept back her hair, first checking for life, then for injuries. Gash above her temple, a knot forming on the back of her head. He ran his hand down and around her waist, feeling for the stab wound. Donnie spoke, "He jabbed her with a Taser, not the knife." Max let out a breath. Evans whimpered and stirred.

"Stay still, sweetheart, I'm calling an ambulance."

Evans grabbed at him, trying to focus. Max stroked her cheek before pulling out his phone.

"No. No. Please. No ambulance. I'm fine…fine, I swear it." Shoving his hands away, she pushed herself up. "I need to go. Help me, help me get out of here, please!" Panic fueled her frantic desperation.

With a sinking heart, Max knew why she avoided the authorities. No red flags for Miss Abigail Evans, who couldn't be caught before completing her mission. The violent urge to shake sense into her wouldn't help. If Evans was indoctrinated, she wouldn't stray from her macabre task. Feeling ill, Max let go and she stumbled. He turned his back, as Evans staggered around, gathering her belongings.

A small crowd grew, as a mall security guard headed their way. *Grow some balls; this is a way in.* He'd help Evans but refused to analyze the twinge of relief at the prospect of spending more time with her. Fuck that. She was nothing more than a target, one planning a despicable act. Pivoting around, Max was appalled to see her seated in the car, trying valiantly to slip the key in the ignition. He opened the door and knelt down.

"I've got this." Max covered her shaking hand. "I'm driving."

With a gentle nudge, he drew her out and guided her to the passenger side. A couple of witnesses saw the tail end of the fight and the security guard pushed for answers. Max told the guard it was a mugging, and he was taking her to the hospital. Rent-a-cop asked her a few questions and she answered woodenly.

Max ignored the man's grumblings, as he secured her seatbelt and gently cupped her face. The translucency bothered him. He checked the head wound; bleeding had almost slowed to a stop. She needed a decent medical, but it was nothing he couldn't handle for now. If she deteriorated, Johnny would conveniently drop by. Or a visit to the ER was on the cards.

"Abs, I need your address."

A blank stare. Max waited and asked again. He knew where she resided but couldn't give the game away.

After licking her swollen lips, Evans whispered it, and he sprang into action, swiftly moving around to the driver's side and activating the GPS as cover. Max cranked up the heat, checking the rearview mirror for unwelcome tails. The team would take care of any, and maybe get answers to this mess.

His mind raced as he floored it towards the freeway. This wasn't a random hit or a hijacker taking a chance. If it was planned, what the hell was the motive? Why injure or kill a useful operative? Had she betrayed Khalid? Was she trying to escape the cell? Hope surged. Max moved on to other possible scenarios and quickly dismissed the possibility of another elite team moving in. A trained professional might snatch the target but wouldn't sexually assault her.

MIT2 needed details on what the bastard did to her. The nature of the attack pissed him off.

Evans sat ramrod straight, trying to hold herself together with a gargantuan effort. Any other woman would be a blubbering mess. Max hoped she'd release some of that robotic control that defined every aspect of her life. He could handle the hysterics. As adrenaline levels dropped and the body relaxed, it was a natural process to release emotions. Evans needed that good cry. As a soldier, he'd learned to deal with the aftereffects of adrenaline and trauma over the years and developed other coping mechanisms but understood the body's natural need for release.

The world excluded her from all color and sound. Abby sat in an anesthetized bubble as the city flew past in a blur. Her brain couldn't stay in tumble dryer mode. *Think, Abby.* Was her cover blown? Were they coming for her? She knew they would; it was just a question of when. The attacker took his time hurting her. Why would he do that? She couldn't remember much after the bastard Tased her. She'd been vaguely aware of Max charging into the melee. Was he hurt? Why would she agree with a strange man driving her home? Max saved her life, but now he was involved, and that was the last thing she needed.

The adrenaline wore off. Her head pounded in time with sore muscles. Abby straightened her legs to relieve cramping pains. Those had to be the effects of the Taser.

"Where do you hurt?"

"I'm fine."

"Bull-fucking-shit."

The expletive had her shrinking back.

"I'm sorry, I didn't mean to swear, I should be taking you to the ER. Your head is pretty banged up. There's a hospital two blocks from here."

Max drove fast, Abby grabbed the seatbelt as he rounded a corner. "I feel tender, but nothing's broken. Are you okay?"

He looked at her like she'd grown an extra head. "I'm fine. Why don't you want to go to a hospital?"

"Bad memories." She knew he didn't believe her and that was okay. He hardly knew her. It was far from a requirement that he know all her dirty secrets. "Pain pills and a first aid kit are all I need."

The assessing look he gave almost made her squirm, but she already felt more grounded. *Breathe in. Breathe out. You're fine. You've been through worse. You're fine.* The mantra played over and over in her brain, sedating frayed nerves.

◊ ◊ ◊

Evans handed Max her key card to access the complex. Once in the carport, he helped her out of the car. Awareness of her fragility added to the simmering anger. Max didn't want to feel protective or responsible. This was a convenient way into her guarded life. All that mattered was getting to Khalid, and Evans was the golden ticket. She tried to brush him off at the gate to her yard. *Not happening.* Max grabbed the house keys.

"I'll patch you up. When I'm done, John will pick me up at the gate."

"I can take care of myself." She stumbled, would have fallen if Max didn't grab her around the waist, leading her up to the front door.

"Just like you're walking all on your own?" He unlocked the layers of security and guided her in.

"Not my sofa. I don't want bloodstains. The guest bathroom is down the passage to the right. There's a first aid kit under the sink."

Max guided her to the toilet and pulled the kit out, dreading to see what it contained. Most civilian outfits were useless. They included generic items like burn cream, cheap Band-Aids, small stretch bandages and maybe a tube of antiseptic ointment.

His fully stocked military-issue kit—sat in his room, just a hundred feet away. If she didn't have supplies he could work with, he would make an excuse to run out to the pharmacy and pick up supplies across the lot. But hers was a well-stocked box. It shouldn't surprise him. Every facet of her life was well organized. Why would she need such a large kit? Max filed the question away for later analysis and grabbed the iodine.

A dark smudge on her neck caught his eye. Brushing her hair back revealed a rapidly bruising bite mark.

"The son of a bitch bit you?"

Jumping at his voracity, she nodded.

"Shit. Jesus. Shit." Max was up and pacing the small bathroom. "He fucking bit you!"

Putting his fist through the wall wouldn't calm the raging anger. The only release would be pounding that sick bastard's face into solid concrete over and over again. Evans's cowering forced Max to bring himself back down.

"Just give me a moment, sweetheart. You're safe with me. I just need a moment." For the next minute, the only sound in the small bathroom was uneven breathing as Max leaned on the sink and dropped his head. Finally, he looked in the mirror, meeting her wary regard. "I'll plug the slice on your forehead, but first I want to examine that neck. A human bite can lead to infection."

Kneeling down, he gently ran a finger over the injury. The individual teeth marks were obscene, but the bruised skin wasn't broken.

"I don't think you'll need antibiotics. You'll need to keep an eye on it."

"Sure." Evans's voice lacked any substance.

Her eyes showed no signs of a concussion. "How's the headache?"

"Manageable."

"Any nausea, dizziness?"

She shook her head.

Max asked a few basic questions, checking for alertness. He then donned gloves and cleaned the wound just below her hairline. She barely flinched, which surprised him. That had to sting. The gash wasn't as deep as he initially thought. Glue would work. He grabbed the Vetbond, stood up and pulled her head towards his abdomen.

Evans recoiled. "What are you doing?"

"Easy. I'll need to squeeze the wound closed to glue it. If you lean against me and tip your head back, I have a better angle."

Max knelt down and addressed the guarded look in her wide green gaze. "I swear I'd never hurt you. Abs, I can help. Let me do this. I need to do this."

◊ ◊ ◊

He kept calling her "Abs"—rolling off his lips in that low growl—and it did something to her insides. Sitting opposite this striking man in her tiny bathroom was so intimately surreal, and his guiding attitude spoke to her desire to restore order. Maybe if she allowed him that control until she regained her equilibrium, it wouldn't be so bad. Except his dynamic capability unnerved her. Anyone who was this well rounded was too good to be true.

"You have experience as a medic."

Her statement seemed to surprise him. "I initially trained as one in the military. I still attend refresher classes. You never know when you'll need it."

His answer was adequate and would do for now. Blood rolled down her forehead. The quicker she got patched up, the better.

"Heck, let's do this. Impress me with your medical skills but if I end up looking like Frankenstein's monster, I'll kick you in your rock-hard ass."

"Yes, ma'am!"

Max grinned as he rose. He gently dabbed at the gash and guided her head towards him. Holy hell. Those incredibly defined abdominals beneath his shirt were heavenly against her cheek. Max tipped her head back as his fierce eyes concentrated on her hairline. It hurt when he pinched the gash together and the glue burned like the blazes, but all Abby noted was the radiating body heat comforting her cool skin.

"Don't move. It needs to dry."

How long had it been since Abby had basic human contact? Someone holding her with affection. Touching another solid human being felt so damn fine, she never wanted it to end. Her throat burned. *Not now. Please not now.* Max made eye contact as humiliating tears spilled over.

"Oh, crap sweetheart. I can't move yet, and I can't let go; the glue hasn't set."

Abby couldn't slam the floodgates shut and couldn't speak or move without messing up the glue. Silent tears rolled as Max cradled her with his free hand, swiping gently at her cheek.

"You're safe now. Cry it out, sweetheart. Just cry it out."

She never took her eyes off his. This grim stranger's bleached eyes touched her soul. Minutes passed as Max soothed her with kind words. When he could finally move, he slid onto the floor, pulled her into his arms and scooted against the wall.

◊ ◊ ◊

Jeez. Talk about moving at warp speed. They had only just met and here he was, sprawled on the floor with Evans—no Abby—sobbing in his arms. Max eased through her defenses like a buttered asshole yet couldn't imagine being anywhere else. The cold space felt cramped, and his leg numbed under the weight but hell, she fitted him in all the right places. Way up in his personal space, Abby's soft breath tickled his neck, and that ethereal scent hit him straight in the kahunas. Woodsy elegance. Vanilla sandalwood with that hint of coconut.

Max took target analysis seriously; working in the Middle East and Africa for many years, he'd learned about vices. A flutter of robes could unleash an opulent, beckoning trail of scent. The

Middle East had the biggest spenders per capita on luxury perfume in the world; the locals purchased a new bottle every couple of months.

Then came the layering. Throughout the Arab and North African regions, both men and women approached fragrance ritualistically, layering on various oils and even infusing their clothing and hair with smoky incense before spraying perfume.

If vanity played a role, wealthier suspects like Khalid were advocates of exclusive clothing brands, body lotions, designer shoes, perfumes. If you knew what they couldn't do without, then the game was on. When wealthy terrorists evaded surveillance, it was possible to track their digital footprint, and custom-made perfumes were good footprints for high-value targets.

Much to the team's horror, Max had taken his men to an institute of perfumery for a month to learn the basics about fragrance structure and tracing complex compositions. The taskforce had a global network of perfumers and technicians that assisted MIT teams in tracking orders. Virtual tracking had led to the location of more than a few elusive extremist targets.

But no one smelled as good as Miss Evans, and he pulled her closer. Those somber eyes undid him as he'd glued her gash. An unblinking stare stacked with fear and hurt... Max was in fucking trouble. Abby was a suspect in an international terrorist cell. It was sheer dumb luck that he'd landed on this cold-ass floor with the target snuggled in his arms and his expertise wasn't to blame; it was all on the dickhead, the piece of shit that attacked her. He'd send a thank-you note later. Maybe stuff it down the unlucky bastard's throat when Max found the son of a bitch and shot his balls off. Fucker bastard.

Abby shifted in his arms.

"You're hurting, sweetheart. We need to get you tucked up in bed."

She stiffened.

"Relax, I'll just help you to your bedroom."

"It's not that." Her voice sounded husky from spent tears. She cleared it as she pulled away. "I'm sorry. Oh hell. I'm never this clingy. I'm— Wait, let me get up."

Shifting his weight, he pulled her to her feet. His leg tingled as nerves sprang to life.

◊ ◊ ◊

Leaning on a hard-looking stranger was a sign of her desperate state and Abby knew it needed to stop, but not tonight. Tonight, she aimed all her energy towards reaching her bed. She was grateful for Max's assistance as he covered her aching limbs with a fluffy duvet and brought her some pain pills.

Abby muttered her thanks and asked him to swing the security door shut on his way out.

"I can't leave," Max said. "I can sleep on your sofa and monitor you through the night."

"Thank you, Max, for saving me. Although I'm grateful, I don't know you and I cannot trust in someone I've just met. You need to go."

He didn't move, instead those iced-over eyes assessed her as he stood at the side of her bed. Abby groaned and raised herself up. She didn't want a strange man in her home while she was vulnerable. Before she could climb out, Max laid his hand on her shoulder. "I don't want to upset you. I don't know if sleeping with that head injury is the best idea. Here's my number." He pulled out a card and laid it on the side table. "Call me if you need anything."

"Thank you but I promise my head feels fine. Will you get home okay?"

"I'll send John a text. Do you mind if I ask Lizzy to message you tomorrow?"

Abby mumbled a yes into her pillow. Then he was gone. She heard the front door slide shut. The clanging of the garden gate closing meant that she was finally alone and safe, yet her dreams were filled with faceless attackers and a ghostly knight, fighting at her side.

Chapter Five

The noon sun filtering through the shades caused Abby to stir. Bruised muscles made rolling out of bed an ordeal; the head wound was tight and sore. Carefully covering it with a shower cap, Abby jumped into the hot spray. The steaming water helped a little, but it still took time to pull on a loose black T-shirt and a pair of grey leggings.

One brewed cup of coffee later, and Abby was sitting on the front patio, warming herself in the pale sunlight. The soft breeze and chirping birds calmed her rolling anxiety. She wasn't ready to analyze what happened, who the masked man was. All she could handle at that moment was the creamy cup of caffeine and the simple sounds of nature.

She ignored the desperate need to phone the one person that mattered most, just to hear his beautiful voice. Her brain kept poking her—*just use a burner phone—it'll be a quick phone call, a minute tops. There's no danger; no one will know.* Abby knew better; she had to stick with the plan, and with the schedule. Soon she nodded off under the warmth of the sun, so when the latch on the front gate clicked, Abby spilled coffee down her shirt. Rising quickly and brushing off the wetness, Abby turned to see Max stalking down her garden path.

"What are you doing here?" Abby demanded.

"I came to see how you're feeling, if you survived the night." He winked at her as his mouth turned up into a slight grin.

Oh boy. That Hollywood smile could strike down a girl. It rubbed her the wrong way, and she folded her arms over her damp shirt. "If I survived the night. Nice. You sure know how to charm the ladies. How did you get in?"

"I drove in behind another car, the gates were open."

"You shouldn't be tailgating, you'll get fined for that. So what? You sat outside the complex waiting till someone drove inside?"

"No, sweetheart. I'm not a psycho. It just so happened that another car was ahead of me when I pulled up. Otherwise, I would have rung your apartment number." Max turned serious. "I've offended you. I can leave if you want."

"Next time you decide to drop in, call me first. I don't like strangers just showing up."

"Is that what we are? Strangers?"

"We only just met last night. I hardly know anything about you."

"Yeah, we've only just met. Call me crazy, but after what happened last night, after what we went through—Abs, that was fucking intense." Max dragged a hand over his mouth and took a breath. "I hardly slept a wink worrying about you. I feel a stronger connection then I would with some random woman I went on ten dates with. Maybe the basis for these feelings stems from pure adrenaline, but I sure would like to make sure you're okay."

Dammit. How did a girl say no to that? The annoying part was that he was right. There was a connection. He'd seen her at her most vulnerable, not only that but he'd rescued her like a freaking knight in shining armor. Risking his life to save hers and, oh God, he'd been so achingly sweet with her. Holding her, rocking her… Abby at least owed him a cup of coffee.

As they stared at each other, she reached a decision. Giving him a brief nod, Abby turned towards the house. Max followed.

◊ ◊ ◊

Max expected the grilling. Walking into Abby's property without warning put her on edge. If only she knew that he'd merely walked over from his team's apartment a few hundred feet away. Abby had just invited a wolf into her pasture. The past night's events provided a convenient gateway, a smooth insertion, into her world.

Max hadn't been lying about everything. He'd been worried about her health, the head injury being a cause for concern. He should've insisted on waking her intermittently throughout the evening. Instead, Max stared at the monitors for the rest of the night, watching her sleep. As he trailed her to the kitchen, he noted her stiff gait. The woman was hurting.

"What would you like to drink—tea, coffee, water, juice?" Abby asked.

"Coffee sounds good. No sugar. No milk."

Abby checked the coffee maker as she eyed him. He leaned against the counter, knowing he took up too much space in the tiny kitchen.

"I have cake. Would you like a slice?"

Max had watched her baking a chocolate cake on the cameras the day before, and his stomach growled in response.

Abby's mouth turned up. "I'll take that as a yes." A capable hand pulled long hair over a shoulder.

His eyes drifted back to the blackened bruise that obscenely marked her pretty neck. The perp bit her deliberately. Why? For his own sick pleasure?

Abby laid out the plates and mugs before pouring coffee. She took her time, her movements composed. She apparently didn't feel the need to talk, instead falling into a comfortable silence. He enjoyed watching her move around the kitchen—that is, until she pulled a huge knife from the knife rack and walked towards him. Max tensed, eyeing the weapon.

She looked at him oddly. "Do you mind scooting over? The cake is on the counter behind you."

Of course. Shit. He shifted slightly to the left, and she cut into the spongy bit of heaven smothered in dark frosting. Her warm scent mingling with the smell of cocoa made his dick stir. *Hell no. Down, boy! She's a target. An attractive target, but still a target.*

Abby loaded the plates with mountainous slices of cake and handed him the largest serving. "Let's eat on the front deck. I need the fresh air," she said, licking a drop of frosting off her thumb.

His cock bucked in response. *Holy chocolate crumbs.* Grabbing his coffee, Max headed back out. Again, they sat in silence. It didn't bother Max. So many people these days were insecure, always trying to fill space with bits of themselves. Bragging or competing for airtime with fellow humans. The silence spoke to his hunt for inner peace. His foot dragged a nearby chair closer and Max propped up his legs, settling in for the afternoon—or for however long Abigail Evans allowed him within her range.

The cake tasted incredible. A trace of cinnamon ran through the velvety frosting, melting on his tongue. Kids played in a yard nearby, their shouts carried over the neighborhood. A dog barked. A truck rolled past. Eventually, the surroundings grew quiet, and all that was left was a cool breeze blowing through the trees.

Max was almost done with his coffee when Abby finally spoke. "Thank you for fighting for me last night. For saving my life."

"Don't thank me. It's what anyone would have done."

"Bull. You risked your life—he had a knife and could've done some real damage."

"Angel, I'm a big boy and I'd never turn my back on someone in need. It's not in my DNA."

They sat quietly for a moment more.

"Do you have any idea who would hurt you?"

She rubbed a bruised elbow. "I'm pretty sure it was random. You know, with the high crime rate in Johannesburg."

That was a lie. Abby knew more than she was telling by the slight rise in her tone and her folded arms. Max was surprised to note that she was a pretty bad liar. Her tells weren't at all subtle; he mentally recorded her body's betrayal as he replied.

"You didn't want to file a police report or go to the hospital. Are you on the run from the law?"

"I can't do this." Abby scooted her chair back.

Max touched her arm reassuringly. "I just want to know what I'm getting myself involved in. Whoever attacked you saw my face and may have followed us. They may even know where you live."

Abby visibly blanched, pausing in her escape before sitting back down. "I can't talk about this, but I doubt it has anything to do with last night." She pinched the bridge of her nose as Max waited.

With a deep breath, she told him. "There's an ex-boyfriend I'm avoiding. He's a little unbalanced, but he has no idea where

I live. He's a powerful man and has connections, so if I go to the police or a hospital he might find me."

Now that was an odd one. Looking at her body language, there was some truth wrapped up in there somewhere, but it still didn't make sense. Abby had no history with ex-boyfriends. In fact, as far as he knew, she avoided men in general.

"What happened last night, before I got to you? What did the bastard say?" Max asked. "Did he say what he wanted?"

Abby shook her head. "I assumed it was a hijacking and asked if he wanted the car. He said no, he wanted me."

Max sensed that Abby was telling the truth in this. It still didn't make any sense as it wasn't a lone attacker who saw a pretty girl and took a chance. There were two or more well-trained perps with a getaway vehicle. But why the sexual assault?

"It was really hard to pick up, but I think he had an accent."

"What kind of accent?"

"I don't know. He tried to speak with a South African accent, but it sounded off. Like he was trying too hard."

A South African accent was notoriously hard to pull off. Most foreigners got it wrong. Most professional actors got it wrong, making it sound Australian when in fact the accent stemmed from original Dutch.

"Excuse me for a second." Abby disappeared into the house. A short time later, music drifted through the doors. She played this piece often. It meant something to her. The song featured a Japanese flute with frogs croaking and chirping in the background. He'd googled it; the piece was called "Soliloquy to the Frogs." Max settled into the chair.

The song was on repeat and halfway through the second round, when Abby emerged with a cup of what looked like chamomile tea. "If you want more coffee, help yourself."

"I'm good for now," Max said.

Sighing, she stretched out her legs and sank back into the cushions.

"Sore?" Max asked.

"A little. I just took something."

"Good. I may need to apply more glue. Can I check your head?"

Abby shrugged, and Max scooted over. He ran his thumb gently over the injury. No sign of infection. It looked like it was holding, but he might add more Vetbond to the site just to be safe. The music floated in the breeze. Max decided that he liked the soothing melody. His phone buzzed in his pocket. An incoming text.

"Can I use your bathroom?"

Her head moved faintly towards the door. "Go ahead. You know the way."

Max used the toilet break as an excuse to check his phone. A coded text from Johnny confirmed their meeting that afternoon with a South African contact named Mandla Nkosi.

Max knew of the contact and had a highly classified dossier on Mr. Mandla Nkosi and his intricate African network. Nkosi originated from the Xhosa tribe, one of the most prominent tribes in South Africa, and the ruling government majority.

His wealthy parents sent him to London for schooling. Like Max, he was a hyper polyglot—a student with a high language learning aptitude, he effortlessly took to new languages. At nineteen, Nkosi was recruited by British Intelligence. Undisclosed activities with MI6 and the Secret Intelligence Service had rounded Nkosi into a formidable operative. At thirty-two years of age, upon his return to Africa, Nkosi assisted the US in the capture of a number of elusive terrorists.

Mandla Nkosi was now a covert leader in an African partner nation, working together with the US and the United Kingdom. He conducted joint investigations and countered the growing threats of terrorism in the Southern African region. His web extended all the way up into Angola. There wasn't much that got past Nkosi. Max hated to admit that he needed him. A clean, quick operation was preferable, without involving local parties, but Max required extra eyes and ears to defeat Khalid's vast network. If Khalid or any of his minions snuck into South Africa, Max needed to know.

Abby was in the kitchen when Max walked up the passage. She loaded the dishwasher with precision.

"I apologize, I have a meeting to get to."

Rising gracefully, she smiled. Max rarely saw her smile. Not on camera or off. The innocent gesture was an unwelcome surprise, and his stomach did a nasty flip in response. Her smile wavered, and Max internally shook himself. He wasn't a player and his blunt attitude was getting in the way. *Use it to your advantage, you dunce!*

Abby wiped the sink with a damp dishrag. The damn kitchen sparkled with cleanliness, unless there were teeny tiny crumbs only visible to her X-ray vision.

"Thanks for the cake. It was delicious." Arms folded, Max took a step towards her.

"It's a pleasure. Anything made of chocolate is always delicious," Abby said shyly. She pulled at a corner of the dishrag with her thumb.

Max stepped up. "Take a compliment. You're a good cook, but yeah, chocolate does make everything better."

Abby smiled again at that.

Emboldened, Max moved right up beside her. "I enjoyed the relaxing afternoon."

Max traced the shell of her ear with his thumb before pulling her in with a tender kiss to her forehead.

"You're a sweetheart, Abs, and damn brave. Hell, you're also still shaken up. You need to rest." Abby opened her mouth and Max cut her off. "How about lunch tomorrow? My treat, to make up for the incredible slice of cake."

"I don't think that's a good idea," Abby said huskily.

His proximity affected her. Max used that to his advantage by grabbing her hips and pulling her close. His hard body pressed her to the counter. Her widening eyes meant that she could feel his erection against her belly.

"I like you. Hell, I fucking want you, and I know you're not looking for anything serious, so why not keep this light?"

"What do you mean?" she whispered.

"Let's enjoy each other a little, have some fun. I'm leaving in a couple of months anyway so there are no strings and no complications."

Uncertainty flashed, so Max pressed on. "I never do this. I haven't been with a woman for a long while. I'm a workaholic and don't have the energy for a complex relationship. I feel something with you, and it's warm and delicious. Fucking delicious," Max said, rolling his hips.

Her groaning response had him capturing her mouth. Max took his time, nibbling those full lips. When she opened for him, he plundered her warm wetness that tasted like chocolate. Abby's hands slipped under his T-shirt, and his dick grew in response. If they kept this up, he was going to lose his load.

The incredible chemistry was not ideal for the job, but he could use that to their advantage. He'd use her to find the Sandpiper. The thought doused his desire like an ice bucket, and Max pulled away. It wouldn't get that far. The quiet kitchen amplified their ragged breathing.

Resting his forehead against hers, Max said, "I'll pick you up at noon."

Abby's hesitation had Max holding his breath. Finally, she replied. "This won't be a couple of months, a couple of weeks maybe. I've got too much on my plate, and I don't want anything getting in the way. I call the shots."

Max grinned, nuzzling her neck. "Yes, ma'am."

Melting into him, Abby sighed. "I mean it."

Her words were muffled, as he nibbled the side of her mouth before giving her a final kiss. His other hand traced the bite mark. "Put some ice on this."

◊ ◊ ◊

Abby's legs felt like jelly as he walked out. Max Hansen's intensity in the kitchen was suffocating. Hell, if he'd lifted her onto the counter, she would've opened herself up to him. Just thinking about those defined hips nudging open her legs made her want to squirm. Abby never squirmed. There was no way she was about to start now. So big deal, he was a hottie. Abby slammed the dishwasher door a little more firmly than was called for. So what if he kissed her like she was made of porcelain and hot lava at the same time. So what if she could imagine his thumb stroking something else besides her neck. Those languid, firm strokes. A cool shower was what she needed, and it would kill two birds with one stone. Soothe aching muscles and calm raging hormones.

Five minutes later, Abby was under the spray, about to close the shower door when she caught a glimpse of herself in the mirror. Rivulets of water ran over her breasts, running down between her thighs. She traced the stream from her lips to her neck where Max had touched her. Her hands drifted further down, imagining his lips running over her flesh. Her mirror image looked wanton. When had she last touched herself? Years ago maybe. Her hand slid between her thighs, nudging her folds apart. She swirled a finger over her clit.

◊ ◊ ◊

Donnie and Slater ran out to grab lunch and would be back for base duty by the time Max and Johnny left for the meeting. Johnny jumped in the shower, and Max replaced his friend at the monitors, grabbing the headphones. Glancing at the screens, Max saw Abby pulling clothes out of a drawer, before wandering into the bathroom. He'd give her privacy. The dossier before him had his attention. Mandla Nkosi was apparently competent, but Max had to ensure the team's safety.

Max was playing a dangerous game with a suspect. Fucking a target was stepping over the line, and his team had never resorted to that. Yes, Johnny was dating Lizzy, but hadn't taken her to bed and wasn't planning to. Max was eager to play hardball with Abby, to ignore his moral code for a couple of reasons. They were running out of time. Khalid was becoming more elusive, and his suicide network was strengthening. Abby was the closest link they'd had in years. She was also hot for him and the pull was strong. Yanking her out of her comfort zone was the quickest way to get under her defenses.

The physical assault on her the previous night was ugly, and Max hated that she was injured, but it opened a normally bolted door. Her vulnerability would be exploited. Max felt like a shit but if she was a card-carrying jihadist terrorist, then he didn't give a flying fuck. Playing with the big boys might just get her flayed.

Glancing up at the screen, Max stilled.

Abby was showering with the effing door open—wide open—as in "I can see her gyrating goodies" open. *Holy freaking hell.* The heavily frosted glass meant that all you would usually see was a blurred-out shape. When Abby changed in the bedroom or bathroom, Max always looked away. The rest of the team were good at not gawking, not that you could see a whole load of detail, as the images were generally grainy. But this...

The bathroom camera had an excellent view of the action, a fuzzy but beautiful angle, and Max was mesmerized. Abby ran her hands down her wet body. Her fingers found her pussy, and she stroked herself as round breasts strained upwards. Max was instantly hard, feeling like he could fell a tree with his dick. *Shit.*

Abby turned and rubbed her tits against shiny tiles while spreading her legs. Her ass raised up as her fingers worked her clit. His dick swelled even more, throbbing in time with her moans; he'd never wanted to fuck a woman so badly. A cold sweat broke out as she rubbed her nipples up and down the slippery wall. Rounded ass cheeks started to clench as her climax built. What he wouldn't give to suck on those wet nipples, to shove his dick inside and slam her against the wall... *Jesus. Stop.*

Max swiveled the chair, about to rip off the headphones when she screamed his name. Over and over, coming with his name on her lips. Glancing back nearly made him come. Max cursed, knowing he'd never soon forget the sight of Abby orgasming in a shower, a glorious wet dream permanently stamped into his brain.

Chapter Six

A battered taxi blared its horn as it forced its way in front of them, ignoring the rules of the road and veering over the pavement in the process. Anton Vorster slammed on the brakes.

"Shee-it!" Johnny white-knuckled the door handle in protest.

TIA, buddy, this is Africa. Hell, this wasn't just Africa. They were heading into Hillbrow, an inner-city neighborhood of Johannesburg riddled with gang activity. Hillbrow was known for high levels of population density, unemployment, poverty, and crime. Max glanced out the back window of the Jetta. It was a Saturday afternoon, and activity littered the streets. Gangs of men huddled on street corners, arrogantly watching over the scurrying locals. Anton pulled up at a light. Street vendors and beggars tapped at the windows, jostling for their attention.

"Fok off!" Anton yelled, waving an aggressive window washer away.

Anton was a neutral contact who would get them in Mandla Nkosi's door. He worked for Nkosi on occasion, renting out his SF skills. Max was no stranger to working in dangerous cities— places that made Afghanistan look like utopia—and he bore physical souvenirs as proof. Hillbrow felt about the same, that keyed-up heightened awareness. Being surrounded by wolves waiting for any sign of weakness. Towards the end of Apartheid, Hillbrow was named a grey area where people of different ethnicities lived together. However, due to poor planning, its infrastructure could not cope with the rapid population growth. An exodus of middle-class residents in the eighties left in its wake an urban slum. Fast forward to present day, and it was a dangerous cesspool of drugs and poverty.

"Are you sure we can trust this Nkosi guy? He hasn't exactly taken up residence in the best part of town."

Anton glanced at Johnny. "Mate, he chooses to live here for that very reason. Nothing goes on without Mandla Nkosi knowing about it. Don't worry, he has men watching our six on every street corner for the next five blocks."

"No offense, buddy, the only one watching my six is my teammate." Max reached over and squeezed Johnny's shoulder.

"Want me to turn the air up?" Anton fiddled with the vents while swerving around a jaywalker. *Jesus, that was close.*

"*Perkele.* Just get us safely in and out of this damn ghetto."

"Is there a reason we're doing this on a Saturday?" Johnny asked.

"You sound like a bunch of girls, all pink on the inside. Mandla's a busy man and this is the only time he'll see you. Let me guess, Big John, you're not a fan of crowds?"

"Which operator is a fan, you fucker?"

Anton laughed. He was enjoying this. Max would bet that the tough mother was a regular visitor to this part of town.

Anton Vorster's hardness resulted from the brutal life he'd lived as a South African Special Forces Soldier—also known as Recce—ruthless warriors who instilled fear in their enemies. For many years, Recce was ranked as the best trained unit worldwide. Now many of the Former SF men found themselves unemployed.

Some turned to mercenary work. Max knew of Recce fighting the Boko Haram in Nigeria and had also run into them in Sierra Leone and Iraq. Others had been killed or captured in shadowy corners of the world. The lucky ones like Anton found work with consultancy firms, covertly aiding the government and wealthy clients by protecting their assets. Max didn't entirely trust Anton—not many men earned that right—but he did respect the hell out of him.

His mind kept drifting back to Abby touching herself in the shower. He'd been with a fair number of women in his time, yet that was the most erotic moment he'd ever experienced. Abby's throaty moans echoed through his brain. The way she'd shouted his name. Shit. There was no way he'd allow his dick to get his team into trouble and fucking a target would get them into a tank load of it. A target. A terrorist. A traitor.

"Heads up, we're here." Anton braked suddenly and swung into a parallel space with little room to spare. They exited the vehicle and immediately stood out like damn glow sticks. Although they dressed to blend in, the three tall warriors screamed *operator*. Max surveyed the urban chaos; hostile curiosity littered the street. He ignored the stares, scanning for potential threats.

Anton knelt to greet a street child. "*Sawubona baba.*"

Max recognized the tribal greeting spoken in Zulu. Anton handed the child a package, which Max presumed was food. Judging by the strung-out look in the boy's eyes, if Anton gave money, he'd spend it on glue or weed.

The child replied, "*Yebo, Sawubona.*"

The rest of the conversation was lost to Max. The skinny kid was an informant and the exchange probably pertained to the meeting, so Max bit his tongue. Four men sized them up from across the street, gang-affiliated judging from the clothing. Street vendors yelled among each other. A family looking down on their luck scuttled by. A Bob Marley wannabe ambled past strumming at a guitar that had seen better days. Two stocky men chatted in Russian and Max eavesdropped.

"I want my merchandise."

"You'll get it."

"Tell Alexei if I don't get it tonight, I'll be mailing pieces of him to his pretty wife."

The Russian mob operated openly in South Africa; it had been that way for over two decades. Hearing them loudly going about their business demonstrated the Wild West mentality that was the embodiment of Johannesburg.

Max forcibly blocked out the felonious conversation and focused his attention back on the four thugs now crossing the street. Johnny casually repositioned himself, preparing for potential hostility. Anton straightened. Max felt for his piece. Instead, Anton nodded at the gang leader and ushered Max and Johnny towards the nearest alley. The gangsters followed from behind, watching their backs. Max released a breath. *Gee, thanks for the heads-up.*

"Friends of yours?" Max asked under his breath.

Anton smiled. "Something like that."

"You slick bastard. What did the kid say?"

Anton led them to an old apartment block probably built in the 1920s. The once beautiful facade was crumbling, and the alley stank of piss and rotting waste. Three steps led up to a side door.

"He gave me the all clear." Anton punched in a code, and the door swung open. His four "friends" casually took positions facing the street. Johnny and Max followed Anton into a dark passage. Seventies wallpaper peeled off the walls, and the carpeted stairs were caked in filth. The term *slum lord palace* came to mind. Hitting a second metal door, they emerged into an antiquated lobby encased in cheap wooden furnishings and old metal turnstiles. A fucking huge gatekeeper guarded the elevators. Armed to the hilt, he could barely stand upright with all that freaking hardware. Beady eyes challenged them to make a move.

Johnny sniggered, and Anton elbowed him. "Jackson, my good man."

A deep growl emerged. "Fuck you, Vorster. What do you want?"

Anton spoke out the side of his mouth. "I kicked his ass in the ring last week, guess he's still a little sensitive."

Stepping up to the goliath, Anton parried and punched. "Gotta move fast, my big friend, otherwise, you'll lose out on the moola!"

"Screw you, I'll rip your white-boy head off if you keep that up."

Jackson suddenly grinned, and his surly demeanor evaporated. He grabbed Anton's shirt and attempted a headlock maneuver. Anton countered the move, jabbing and dancing to the side.

"I'd love to kick your ass all day, but Mandla is expecting us."

"Whatever, asshole. Get your skinny ass up there before I snot slap you."

He nodded at Max as they wound their way through a turnstile and boarded the oldest elevator in Africa. Once the doors finally slid shut, it shuddered upwards. Cables groaned and Johnny gripped the handrail.

"He's Mandla Nkosi's security detail? Seriously."

Anton shot Max a sideways look. "Jackson and Mandla grew up together. They're from the same tribe. Mandla saved his friend from drowning when they were kids. So, Jackson has it in his head that he needs to return the favor." Anton chuckled. "Jackson appointed himself as Mandla's bodyguard, and Mandla just accommodates his wishes. It's easier that way. But to answer your question, nope. Mandla has a separate detail."

The elevator convulsed once before stopping. The doors creaked open, and Anton wasn't kidding. Five men moved towards them as two others hung back. They moved with practiced ease, indicating excellent training. All their handguns were at the ready. The room was staggeringly elegant, nothing like the slum conditions below. The muted walls and comfortable furniture scattered throughout the foyer complemented the fresh aroma of lemon and rosemary.

The lead guard stepped forward. "Vorster."

"Jones." Anton nodded. "We have an appointment."

"I know. We'll need to frisk your new colleagues. Weapons?"

"Yes."

"Hand them over."

Johnny smiled dangerously. "Not gonna happen, bro."

Jones glared at Johnny, and Max reinforced his buddy's statement.

"We don't know you. No offense but if the shit hits the mercenary fan…"

That pissed Jones off. "We are not mercenaries. Vorster, talk to your Yankee friends."

"Mate, you know I never give up my piece. Check with your boss."

One of the men tapped his earpiece and rattled something off in Zulu as a standoff ensued, all Stonehenge-like.

"Stand down, boys." Mandla Nkosi stepped around his security team and grasped Anton's hand warmly. The man had an immediate presence.

"Comrade. It's good to see you again."

"Hey, brother," Anton replied.

Dressed casually in black slacks and a crisp white shirt, Mandla exuded confidence. The white shirt contrasted with his ebony skin. His lean form radiated strength. As Max shook Mandla's hand, *polished* and *refined* were words that came to mind, but both meant shit in this world. Mandla would be a useful asset or thorn in his side. If Mandla got between him and Khalid, he was as good as dead.

"Keep your weapons, Anton has vouched for you, but my men will still perform a search."

They checked clothing and shoes—both physically and with scanners—looking for listening devices. After a thorough pat down, the men pulled on their boots.

"Please, gentlemen, follow me." Mandla walked ahead with Anton, leaving Max and Johnny to file in behind.

His airy office was lined with floor-to-ceiling windows. The view of the Johannesburg skyline was impressive. Max walked over and tapped on the glass—bulletproof, which didn't surprise him.

"Mr. Andersen, please take a seat." Mandla stood behind an oak desk, gesturing to the luxurious leather chairs in front of him.

"I gather this room was swept." Max referred to listening devices.

"Twice a day and no one enters without being thoroughly vetted. We also have surveillance-blocking technology throughout the building."

Max nodded once. He eyed the security team as he took a seat. Johnny remained standing. Silence descended as the two seated men weighed each other up. With a soft knock on the door, a petite woman bustled in carrying a tray of refreshments. Biscuits and tea. How very British.

"Help yourselves." Nkosi waved his teacup. Max poured a cup and selected a small biscuit as a gesture of politeness.

"Nkosi—"

"Please. Call me Mandla. I hate formalities." Mandla ignored Max's raised eyebrow. "I've heard good things about MIT. Rumors are, thanks to MIT2's loyal work, there are six notorious Isis leaders behind bars."

Max kept his expression neutral as Mandla continued. "I'm sure you've reviewed my file. But you don't know me, and I don't know you. We have little time to establish trust. I need to reassure you however that I work closely with the STF."

The STF was an elite police tactical unit of the South African Police Service. It consisted of ninety operators based in all major South African cities. Their tasks included resolving hostage situations and combating urban and rural terror.

"Colonel Andre De Beer, who heads up the Johannesburg division, will be here shortly."

That made the partnership easier, but Max would still need to negotiate their stay.

Nkosi narrowed his eyes. "You're a quiet one. You're analyzing me—picking me apart—when it's me that should be putting you and your team under my microscope. You could possibly incur violence in my country and, if my information is accurate, you're expressing an interest in one of my citizens, along with gathering intel on an extremist gunrunner. Khalid Al Juhani."

Impressive work, Max thought. The man seated before him had an even broader network than Max first calculated. No mention however of Khalid's suicide bomber recruitment network. Classified information too high up the US covert ladder.

"What makes you think that we're watching a South African target?"

"I'm not a fool. Evans's name came up as a person of interest."

Max stiffened. "By whom? No one except MIT knows she's here and it took all our resources to find her."

Mandla leaned back. "You forget that I worked for the British Government. Evans got one of our agents killed."

A frisson of anger ran through Max. Fucking MI6 was sticking their nose in where it didn't belong. "Tell your English friends to back the fuck off. If they screw with this operation and any of my MIT2 members get hurt, I'm coming for your Limey friends with my entire arsenal of weapons, tied up in a gift of bullshit red tape and a decade worth of paperwork. Their shot-up asses will be bandaged to a desk for the next decade. Do I make myself clear?"

Nkosi's brows drew together. "If you're targeting a South African citizen, especially one involved in the killing of a British spy, I'll need to know if she's a viable threat."

"We're figuring that out. Don't forget that Evans has dual citizenship, she's American born," Max replied.

Nkosi tapped his fingers together, his smile calculating and his gaze direct. "I'm only one man. I use my limited time on this planet to protect my beloved country against both foreign and domestic threats and will happily die for that cause. I don't care for anyone else higher up in the food chain. My vision for South

Africa is all that matters. Is the government failing in many aspects? Definitely. For sure. Does that mean that every government official is corrupt or not doing their job? Perhaps. Perhaps not. Should I step back from my role in the country's future, a role that ensures that my rainbow nation is safe and that there is equal opportunity for all? I'll never do that."

The passion and love for South Africa shone in the man's eyes. Judging from his past work history, Mandla didn't seem like the double-crossing type. Patterns were a good indicator. Relying on patterns of behavior did not mean that people never stepped out of their role or acted out of character, but that was the exception and not the norm.

"You've worked with two of our teams in the past," Max said.

Mandla nodded. "I have. MIT1 and MIT4."

"Are you still willing to help the United States wherever possible?"

"Rivers of blood will not be allowed to flow freely through my country, and a trickle of blood has begun. Hijackers, thieves, and murderers are killing our South African people. I will help to staunch the flow. I will fight to make my country safe and whole." Mandla paused to sip his tea. "Do you remember the 2010 FIFA Soccer World Cup, held in South Africa some years ago?"

"Vaguely. I'm not a soccer fan. American football is more my thing," Max said.

"Now that's a black mark against you." Mandla chuckled as Max smiled. "Anyway, that was the first time that I worked closely with a US covert team. We stopped an imminent threat to the games, catching a four-man squad holed up in a beach house in Durban. Caught the bastards red-handed with suicide vests lined up on the living room floor. That was when I knew that I was making a difference helping to prevent the mass murder of hundreds of South Africans. My life path took a different turn."

With no red flags flapping in the wind, a solid alliance seemed likely. Mandla Nkosi would be a useful partner in the war against the Sandpiper.

Max asked a question which had been on his mind. "Have you had an increase in terrorist threats of late? I know there are regular bomb threats here, but most have turned out to be bogus."

"South Africa hasn't had a major terrorist incident. But that does not mean that it won't happen. There are too many unknowns, the threat level is rising rapidly. The Southern region is a cauldron of corruption, violence, and beauty."

Max agreed. Too many countries ignored growing indoctrination within their borders and only realized the extent of the problem after the wake of their first terror attacks. Better to be proactive before extremists established strongholds. The challenge was identifying sleepers hidden among good citizens. Mandla's incredible network was formidable in nipping extremist cells in the bud.

Max placed his cup down. "Working together requires a certain level of transparency. I'll bring you up to speed on what MIT2 has on Khalid, if you promise to watch our backs and feed us any intel that comes your way."

"I'll do one better, any resources that you require are yours. Between the STF and my team, you have reliable operatives as backup and access to our resources. Understand that if your team screws this up, I'll deal with Khalid and you won't like my methods. If Khalid Al Juhani steps onto my soil, he won't be stepping off."

There was a knock on the door. "Sorry to interrupt, sir. Colonel De Beer is here to see you."

"Show him in."

The colonel was well trained and competent. A seasoned soldier who, after talking with Max at length, offered his assistance willingly.

Mandla folded his hands. "Now that the dick-measuring contest is over, let's get on with this. Anton and Johnny, please have a seat. Max, brief us on what you have so far."

An hour later, after the five men had run over the operation, Mandla led them one floor up and showed them around his facilities. To say it was impressive was an understatement. There was a detention center, interrogation rooms, a well-stocked armory and an analysis room. Bigger sharks backed this baby, Max thought. The equipment looked spook stamped; there was no doubt that the CIA had their hands in this African pot. He didn't give a fuck who Big Daddy was, as long as his team stayed safe and uncompromised.

Chapter Seven

It was a casual date, and *casual* was the keyword. Abby messaged Max, telling him that she only had time to grab a quick bite. Grocery shopping was on her list for the day, aside from the design work needing her attention.

Abby refused to do the candles and roses thing with Max or any other man for that matter. *Casual* was her new favorite word. Casual dates, casual necking on the sofa, casual sex, especially when it came to a man as intense as Max. Hell, one more glance from those laser eyes and she'd climb all over that rock-hard body.

Casual dating had never been Abby's thing, and that was why she was staring at the third outfit she'd tried on in the space of five minutes. Her new neon-orange-and-white Nike sneakers were paired with dark blue jeans and a white Taylor Swift 1989 T-Shirt. The soft, worn T-shirt was one of her favorites, her lacy white bra subtly peeked through the thin white material, giving a hint of girl-next-door naughtiness.

"It'll do," Abby muttered as she threw a lipstick and deodorant into a worn leather bag.

The ring tone from the front gate indicated that Max had arrived. Abby gave security the green light and jogged through to the front sitting room to grab her keys. *Stop acting like a freak. You can do this. You're casual Abby. Just chilling and hanging loose.*

By the time Max opened the front gate, Abby felt more in control, until she saw him in a navy-blue Henley shirt matched with blue jeans. He wore the jeans well. The sweatshirt, molding his hard chest in all the right places. Abby swallowed. *Holy crumpets.* She could thoroughly watch him walk to her gate and back over and damn over. And then she spotted the small bouquet of wildflowers held so carefully in those capable hands. That kicked the casual vibe to the curb. Damn.

"Hey, Abs. Are you okay?"

Abs. He called her Abs. Nope. She was not okay. Just a puddle of pudding melting all over her sitting room floor.

"Hi."

"I know they're not much compared to the flowers in your garden, but I thought of you when I saw them." He thrust the bouquet forward.

Oh no, you don't, mister. It's not going down like this. Just two people, hanging out, grabbing some grub, even if one of them looked like he'd been sculpted from quartz.

She hadn't said anything and Max stared at her oddly. Abby lunged for the flowers, muttering her thanks while racing for the kitchen and flinging them into a vase in record time. Max stood awkwardly in the other room, and Abby took three calming breaths before rejoining him.

"Ready to go?" she asked.

"You look pretty."

"Thanks. Just doing my normal day-thing, you know how it goes. Chores, errands, chores…" She sounded like a chump, Max still offered her a smile as he led her to his car.

◊ ◊ ◊

She was adorable and clearly nervous. He kept reminding himself that this was a job and not a first date. Never a first date with a woman like her. One who might be planning on eradicating innocents with the blink of an eye. There was no doubt that Abby was hiding something and there was no denying that she was a person of interest on the militant network, but his gut said that this was more complicated than simply uncovering a sleeper. The more he investigated her, the more complicated she became. The puzzle pieces were getting jammed up. Were they wasting time? No, Abby was involved with Khalid Al Juhani; it was just a question of how.

As Max drove the new rental they'd acquired, he deliberately stretched out his free hand and ran a thumb over her ear before playing with her shirt sleeve, running his fingers along the fabric and brushing the top of her arm with the back of his hand. "I can see you as a Taylor Swift fan. That shirt looks damn good on you." Max ran his hand down her side before returning it to the wheel. "Abs, where are we heading? Edengate Mall?"

"I do my weekly shop there, so we might as well get lunch at the same time."

"I know a great place just a block away. It's a little cozy, and the service is good," Max suggested.

"Cozy?" she asked.

"Yeah. Cozy. Quaint tables, set out in a small courtyard."

"Quaint?" Abby quipped.

"Are you going to repeat everything I say?"

"No." She smiled. "It's just that, well, I didn't expect the word 'quaint' coming out of your mouth."

They stopped at a traffic light and Max leaned in. "What's wrong with the word 'quaint'?"

His eyes ran over her lips, and she licked her lower lip in response. "Nothing. You're just—I don't know—very male. It sounds weird. Such a pretty word, coming out of your masculine mouth."

Abby gasped as he pressed a kiss to her lips. Her warm lips were heaven. "Wanna see what else my masculine lips can do, or maybe my masculine tongue?"

Heat flared in those emerald eyes. A car horn blared and Max grinned, pulling across the busy intersection. Making prim and proper Abigail Evans wriggle in her seat was fun. It also served another purpose by distracting her. She wasn't thinking about protecting secrets when Max turned on the charm. She was thinking of him touching her, stroking her, licking her. Hell, he was thinking about it too, but Max wouldn't give them any breathing space; he'd slip into all her private places, mentally and physically. Abby would be putty in his hands.

◊ ◊ ◊

A sweet-talking, lady-killing Casanova took up all the oxygen. Abby's nether regions were having a party while her head ran in panic mode. Her brain obsessed over the thought of his mouth nibbling at her panties. Was it hot in here? Maybe the seat warmers were on? Nope. It was just her panty party gaining momentum, making her squirm again. Abby cracked the window and sucked in cool air. Grinning at her move, Max swerved expertly into a parking spot.

"What?"

"Nothing."

"No, what's that smirk for?"

"Feeling warm, Abby?" Frosty eyes ran conceitedly over her body.

A flush slid up her neck. No one ever made her blush. That in itself made her mad. Was he purposely messing with her? Screw him.

As she reached for the door, Max grabbed her arm. "Shit, I've upset you. That was inappropriate and rude. I'm more of a gentleman than this."

"You're fine. I just need air, and I need food."

"No. It's not fine. My mother would box my ears if she heard what just came out of my mouth on a first date."

Abby smiled at that. "She sounds fearsome. But this isn't a date, it's just lunch, and there's nothing wrong with a little flirting. I'm just not used to the flirting thing. I pretty much suck at it."

Max chuckled. "It's not possible for you to suck at anything. You're gorgeous, look at you." He traced her jaw with the back of his hand. "And…" he continued, "I'm about to kick my own ass for not opening your door. Stay where you are, and I'll come around." He circled to the driver's side.

Abby wanted to believe the sweet words that fell so easily from his mouth, but she wasn't perfect. Not by a long shot. *Cowardly* and *deceitful* were a better fit. Still, it felt nice to be put on a pedestal, even if it was by a sexy man who was a stranger yesterday and would soon be a stranger again. The trouble was that Max felt the opposite, familiar and safe, two qualities that would lead to their mutual downfall. Casual is what this was, and casual was what it could only ever be.

The restaurant was quaint and the food tasted delicious. How had she not known this place existed? The easy-going atmosphere and the glass of wine had her sinking into her chair. Max chatted about his family back in the US. His father was a rancher in Wyoming, his mom was the warm matriarch who kept his large family of siblings together. His pops always grumbled that the place was never quiet but secretly loved having friends and family over. Like Abby, his mom loved to bake. Max enjoyed visiting, he lived an hour away from his family. Then it was her turn. Abby knew it was coming. Wasn't that how it worked, I tell you mine, and you tell me yours?

Max looked at her expectantly. Abby played with a crumb on her empty plate. She could choose the path of least resistance, tell him her parents were lovely people who lived in some remote spot on the planet. He didn't need to know about her hard childhood or the monster in her closet called Dad.

Max was the man who'd held her on her bathroom floor as she'd sobbed. The man who'd patched up her head with gentle hands. The man who'd kissed her like she was a spun-glass ballerina. No one had ever treated her with such tenderness. They'd known each other all of two days and yet she instinctively knew that Max was a mighty fine man. Her biggest secrets were still hers to keep, but she'd give him a glimpse of someone she'd hoped to become. A woman who overcame the odds and came out stronger.

Decision made, Abby took the plunge. "I didn't have your idyllic childhood. I'd lie if I didn't tell you how envious I am."

Max considered her words.

"The first memories were good ones. My parents lived in my grandparents' basement in New York. We weren't wealthy, but my family was happy in a super loud kind of way. That was due to my Italian grandmother and, even though I don't have vivid memories of her, I have a vague sense of her energy. She passed away when I was four. It destroyed my father and my grandpa. Lucy was still so young, had a heart attack one morning while cleaning the stove. After a year of mourning, my dad—Jimmy—

barely came near the family and my mousy mother barely emerged from their bedroom. She wasn't exactly maternal. Grandpa Noah rocked me in this giant rocking chair that I'll never forget, singing me Italian lullabies. Noah also fed and changed me when my parents were doing God knows what."

The waiter came by, and Abby ordered a cup of chamomile tea.

Max spoke up. "So, what changed?"

"My father. Jimmy came home one evening carrying a pamphlet from a new church in the area called The Unity of Light. It wasn't quite a church at the time. More like a youth meeting held in someone's basement once a week. Jimmy started spouting religious quotes, saying he'd found his new path and would lead his followers towards the light of God."

Abby scraped at her thumb as she considered her next words. "At first, Noah was happy for his son, praying that my father would find peace in religion. Pretty soon, it became clear that the meetings damned all other congregations or sects. Jimmy chose to build his first church in a secluded wooded area far from any city. He first moved us to Colorado, calling it the land of light. His followers made the trek, and so did Noah, out of concern for me. Over the next couple of years, Jimmy kept pressing for Grandpa to convert and Noah refused. Eventually Grandpa left. My father blamed me for it, said that I was a naughty brat that destroyed everything in my wake."

"Goddammit. I'm sorry Abs."

She shrugged away the old hurt, remembering that day. An eight-year-old mind never forgets seeing her grandpa pack up his truck and give her the tightest hug in the world, while sobbing into her neck. For years she'd wondered if Jimmy was right. Did Noah get tired of looking after a lively kid after her parents had checked out? Did he leave because of her?

Blinking tears away, Abby rushed to finish her story. "Anyway, Jimmy had a falling out with his congregation, and we moved to Northern Idaho to start a new parish, where Jimmy wrote a small bible outlining his warped beliefs."

Max frowned. "What kind of beliefs?"

"If you fall ill, it's the devil who's come a-calling, infecting you with his evil. So the solution is to beat the devil out while confessing your sins. One winter, I fell ill with a severe bout of flu and was beaten with a belt and locked in the basement. I was nine years old and spent three days down there. "

Max looked furious. "What did your mom do?"

"She stood by, like a good little pastor's wife, believing that my father was a prophet, here to save humanity."

"Those fucking monsters."

"One of their devoted followers came over for tea on the third morning and heard me coughing. My mom tried to clean me up before they could lay their eyes on me. Didn't help though, I ran raging temperatures and spent two weeks in the hospital with pneumonia."

"Child services didn't take you away?"

She met his angry stare. "There wasn't a whole load of evidence to go on. Technically the witness hadn't seen me in the basement and only my butt and lower back showed bruising from the beating. The small-town police officer who stopped in was part of the congregation. He said there was nothing wrong with a good spanking every once in a while. It makes for healthy young folk."

"Ass-wipe," Max growled.

"Yeah. That was just the tip of the iceberg. According to prophet Jimmy, any book but his bible was seen as the devil's work including school books and the actual Bible. Of course, television, the radio and computers were also Satan's tools."

"Sounds like freaking North Korea. Were you allowed to go to school?"

The North Korean comment made her smile. "Yes, but just so that Jimmy could look normal in the community. I shake my head at him now but at the time it was a living hell. I had no friends, no life or choices in anything I did. I hid library books in a hole I'd dug out behind wallpaper in my room. Jimmy found them eventually and a two-day stint in the basement was the result. When he spanked me he usually used his belt but, in that instance, a cane was his weapon of choice."

Max stroked her arm. "I want to find him and beat the living shit out of him."

"If anything, it made me more determined than ever to escape that life, even though it wasn't all bad. We traveled to other countries. Jimmy used his influence to set up a second church in South Africa. I got to stay in some interesting places, and it gave me the travel bug."

"How did you escape?"

"I left when I was sixteen."

"Do you keep in touch with the bastard?"

Abby gave him a bitter look. "Would you?"

"If it were up to me, I'd bury the dickhead after putting a bullet between his eyes." The tension in Max had Abby bracing for his next words. "Did he hurt you in other ways, Abs?"

Abby knew what he meant and shook her head. "Not like that, but it doesn't make me hate him any less. It was always about Jimmy, always concerned for himself. His path in the world was the most righteous, his greediness and how others saw him. It was never about his wife or child. I haven't seen them since the day I left. I lived in Southern Africa from eleven to sixteen years of age. When we went back to Idaho for a six-month stint, I ran away to Utah, completing my last year of school while working nights. My father runs a growing cult. That's the only way to describe that community of brainwashed zombies. I'd rather die than give that power back to Jimmy. My father now runs five global locations, so I guess he's doing well for himself."

Abby ignored Max's unblinking concern as she played with a loose thread in the tablecloth. Storm clouds hung low, darkening the courtyard.

"Leaving my family at such a young age forced me to be resourceful; there were no safety nets to fall back on. I didn't have the white-picket-fence childhood that you grew up with, but I think I'm doing okay."

Thunder rumbled as Max threaded his fingers with hers. "You're more than okay. You're amazing and just so you know, I don't know of many people who had a white-picket-fence upbringing. My parents are a fluke, but we still had our difficult times—nothing compared to having Kim Jong-un as a father—but challenging nonetheless."

Abby chuckled. The wind picked up, blowing up leaves around the courtyard. Max looked dark and mysterious in the shadowed light. Her heart fluttered.

"I love your hands." He played with her fingers.

"Are you crazy? You like utilitarian grunge?"

Max chuckled. "What's wrong with a little paint? They're neatly manicured and tell me who you are. Creative…" He stroked her index finger. "Hardworking…" He circled a ring finger. "Intangible yet strong." He drew her little finger into his mouth and pulled it out slowly.

Holy Cannoli. Abby sucked in a breath; Max placed her hand back on the table. The fire in his eyes matched her raging hunger, and she looked away.

The waitress cleared their plates.

Max stroked a foot along her calf. "So, what did you do after you left, Abs? You said you had the travel bug? Where did you go?"

That was where her secrets began. Playtime was over. "A story for another time. Should we get out of here? It looks like it's going to rain."

Max kissed her palm. "I'll grab the check."

◊ ◊ ◊

It didn't bother Max that she'd raised her walls up at his last question; that fitted with her profile. What didn't fit was Abby opening up about her relationship with her family. The file they had on Abigail Evans never included details of abuse. From the intel they'd gathered, Max profiled a teenage Abby as a rebellious pastor's daughter, leaving the restrictive nest and thumbing her nose at her small-town missionary parents. When questioning the Idaho community, they'd called her parents "saints." Saying what do-gooders they were. How sad they were when Abby had left the protection of their church and the light of God. Some of the intel hinted that The Unity of Light had worrying cultish quirks, but overall the followers kept to themselves and stayed out of trouble.

Max had a problem on his hands because this new information changed things. Abby hadn't run to the Middle East as a spoiled, lost, small town girl looking to make her mark. She'd run there as a determined survivor willing to fight for a new future. She was now a square peg that Max was trying to fit into a round hole.

The heavens opened up as they ran to the truck. Max grabbed Abby's hand, hearing a giggle as she tripped, grabbing his waist and twirling in the rain. Max couldn't take his eyes off her. Jesus. The now transparent white shirt clung to her tanned skin. A lacy white bra stood out beneath.

"The rain makes you whole, doesn't it? It's freedom!" Abby shouted with sparkling eyes.

She was like a fucking glowing angel. An angel that suddenly gave a whoop and pressed her lips to his. *Holy cow.* A warm, wet female smelling like vanilla and spring rain filled his arms. Dragging his mouth away, Max hustled her into the vehicle. The downpour screwed up his comms unit, and Max slipped it into his jean pocket before climbing in the truck. They were effectively alone, and Max felt the buzz.

"That was fun. I love cloudbursts." Abby grinned and then turned serious. "Whenever a storm blew into Idaho, I used to run out to my neighbor's field and sit in the mud, feeling the rain pelt my skin."

Max paused before starting the truck. "That doesn't sound wise. Lightning is dangerous and kills around fifty people per year in the US."

"I know but the storm was an escape. It made me feel like I mattered, like the heavens reserved their potent beauty just for little old me."

"Now why do you have to go and say something so profound?" Max pulled a sodden lock of hair off her cheek.

The fogged-up windows encased them in a veiled sanctum where only the sound of their breathing filled the space. Her rounded tits rose and fell with each breath; drops of water ran down between them. Abby bent towards him; those incredible mounds were too close. Her hand ran up his chest as she climbed into his lap. Too damn close.

"This isn't a good idea." The air felt hot. Steamy. Her body heat surrounded him as Abby shifted her hips on his lap. "Fuck."

"Kiss me," she murmured.

Her serpentine eyes held him captive for long moments. The small, intimate space made him want to look away, but before he could move, her mouth was on his. They were alone for this minute, and Max took full advantage. His hand gripped her tangled hair and dragged her close, mating his tongue with hers, rubbing his hard cock against her mound. She tasted so good. He gripped her wet jeans as Abby dry rode his crotch.

Moaning, Max dragged up her filmy shirt and shoved her breast into his mouth. A nipple covered in lace puckered as he sucked. He pulled the delicate fabric down and ran his tongue around the taut nipple. God, it was so damn beautiful.

He nipped and she whimpered. He was going to shoot his wad, in this truck, just by sucking on Abby's breast. What the hell was he doing? Losing control, that was what he was fucking doing. *Pull back, buddy. Pull the hell back.* With one last lick he drew away.

"You're amazing." His voice was husky with need. "But I'm not taking you up against a steering wheel in broad daylight, at least not the first time I have you."

She kissed him, then shot a wry grin as she climbed back into her seat. "It wouldn't have got that far, honey. I'm so not that easy."

Max burst into laughter. "Well Miss Prissy, it's getting damn cold, and I can see goose bumps. Besides, you can't just run through the mall in your wet tee. Most of the men—including me—wouldn't get a damn thing done. You'll have to wear my jacket."

◊ ◊ ◊

The shopping part of the date was fun. What was not to love? Abby wore a large Arc'teryx coat that smelled deliciously like sexy male. The owner of the said jacket grinned as he held up a box of cake mix.

"C'mon, Abs. I love red velvet cake."

Her eyes narrowed. "Not on your life, buddy. If I make you a red velvet it will be free of that artificial red dye crap—not to mention all those preservatives."

"Now, now. Don't be a cake mix snob. I'm sure you've stashed away some of these babies in the past."

"You cheeky bugger. I bake my cakes from scratch!"

Max laughed. "Did you just call me a cheeky bugger?" He pretended to be offended.

"Did you just accuse me of being a fraud baker?" Abby shot back while looking for cocoa powder, shoving the shopping cart at him.

"Well," he said as he walked backwards, "I've only tasted just a teeny, tiny slice of a cake you've made. I would need to do more sampling, to make up my mind."

Abby raised her brow. "Make up your mind?"

"On whether you have mixes stashed away somewhere, or if I'm tasting the real thing…made with actual butter and all that."

Hiding a smile, Abby asked. "And just how many of these cake slices would you need, to make up your mind?"

Max pretended to think. "I'm thinking…at least ten."

"Ten!" Abby snorted.

"Well, there's chocolate, red velvet, Black Forest, Boston, carrot cake—"

"You lost me at carrot cake." Abby wrinkled her nose.

"What the hell is wrong with carrot cake?"

"Yuk! Buy yourself a ready-made version because I ain't making it, buddy. Oh, and if you want me to bake you ten whole cakes, then get ready for me to put your lardy ass to work in my yard because it'll take months to shift all that sugar."

"You're a funny girl."

"A funny girl who hates carrot cake," she shot back.

Max's broad smile made Abby feel all warm and gooey inside—those dimples were way too sexy. It felt good to laugh with someone. Abby hadn't done that in a long, long while.

Chapter Eight

After unlocking the sliding door, Abby turned to Max who fiddled with the ornery latch on her front gate. It was rusty and needed oiling.

"I can fix this for you," Max called out. "Do you have any aerosol oil?"

"Nope, I can buy some tomorrow."

"Leave it to me. I'll grab you some." He jiggled the latch back and forth.

Her hands slipped into the deep pockets of his jacket, male scent surrounding her. Was she really doing this dating thing? Butterflies fluttered when she thought of him coming in for a coffee. Forget coffee, she wanted to shove him up against the wall and...wait. Abby's fingers closed around a small metal disc, which she pulled out to examine. A weird round battery thing with a built-in speaker. Where had she seen that before? Abby racked her brains. At Lizzy's home, a few months before, they'd watched an episode of "Dates from Hell." It showcased a stalker who'd placed something very similar in his victim's apartment. Abby's heart somersaulted, and she thrust the sinister device back where she'd found it.

Son of a bitch. Trapped in her yard as Max dusted off his

jeans. Was he a psycho serial killer or had she finally been discovered? Why would he need a listening device? Ambling up the path, Max shot her a sexy grin as a crazy mix of terror and anger flooded her veins.

He paused. "What's wrong?"

Not again. Never again. The patio table near Abby held a bowl of fruit. Instinct pushed her to grab an apple and launch it like a professional pitcher. The hard fruit found its mark, slamming into his left eye. Max swore, staggering back and then moved with incredible speed, throwing himself forward.

Abby hurled herself inside, trying to slide the door shut. Out of time, she chose a deadlier alternative. Max scrambled, grabbing her through the half-closed door, before shoving through. With practiced ease, she dove across the floor, flipped to her side, slid to a stop and snatched the firearm out from under the sofa.

◊ ◊ ◊

Shit, damn, shit. When had Abby made him? Max had faced scarier criminals—hardened terrorists—and was about to be offed by Snow White who, by the way, handled the gun like a pro. If Max survived this, the boys would be ribbing him for years. He'd underestimated her in every way. Easing down to his knees, Max raised his hands. Abby had no idea how close she was to having her last breath; his men would take her out.

"Put the gun down. Now. I fucking mean it." He spoke carefully. "My sniper has eyes on you. Your pretty head will explode like a melon."

"Who are you?" Hands shook as she aimed the weapon at his chest, scaring the shit out of him.

"Easy on the trigger, sweetie. If you shoot me, you're dead. I'll say it again; I have men watching you."

"The hell you do."

The outside light flicked on and off.

"That's my sniper…on your patio."

Abby's eyes glazed over in defeat. Max hoped that was surrender, but her sudden calmness scared him. "Do it then. Shoot me."

Max gentled his tone. "We don't want to hurt you, we just want to talk."

"I won't give you a thing."

He doubted that, had heard many hardened men say the same thing. A few rounds with Max and they cracked like babes. Her next words shook him.

"I wanted you to be the good guy. You were a white knight even though there's no such thing."

Looking like a deflated doll, Abby lowered the gun and slid it over. Slater stepped inside, his unwavering weapon trained on her. Abby automatically rolled over and extended her hands, turning her head away. Why did Max feel like he'd just kicked a puppy? Screw her. She'd done this to herself.

Max's legs felt like rubber, and his eye throbbed. "Search her for weapons or explosives. Check my jacket in case she slipped something in."

"You mean aside from the creepy surveillance bug in your right pocket?" Abby muttered.

Shit. Rookie fucking move. He'd slipped the broken device into his pocket the previous night when he'd swapped it out…and forgotten to remove it. Now that really pissed him off—Max never made asshole mistakes.

Donnie entered and cautiously moved through the house looking for new surprises while drawing curtains against prying eyes.

Slater patted her down, and Max couldn't resist engaging. "If you want to shut a man out of your home, sweetheart, move a little faster and don't give the game away until you're behind locked doors."

"Still got the job done though, didn't it?"

Abby ticked him off. "I'm not the one lying on the floor."

She mumbled something that sounded remarkably like "greedy bastard" under her breath and Max stilled. "What was that?"

His team knew a still Max was a dangerous one. Slater sounded a warning. "Easy, brother."

"Fuck you," Abby said, her eyes drilling daggers into him.

As Slater swung her to her feet, Max got up in her face. "What. Was. That?"

"How much did he pay you?" she said through gritted teeth.

Was she referring to Khalid? "Johnny, get the equipment."

Johnny stepped out the front door. Max turned to the dining area and searched under the furniture. All clear. He dragged the table to the side and arranged chairs in a semicircle facing a single one. The first round was about to begin.

◊ ◊ ◊

"Get the equipment." Max had said that. What equipment? Would they torture her? Would these men abuse her in her own home? Max grabbed her arm as the other mercenary pushed her ahead. They removed Max's jacket and shoved her into the chair. Abby folded her arms defensively over a still damp shirt. *Don't show fear. You're braver than that.*

Max stepped into the bathroom, presumably to check his eye. He was going to have a hell of a bruiser and Abby did an internal victory dance.

Who were these rough men? Max apparently wasn't a garden-variety stalker, and his gang had done this before. John – the little worm – was part of their deceitful A-team. It had been an elaborate set-up. Little Lizzy had no idea that her new boyfriend was a lethal gun-for-hire. The man called Slater stood before her, a good-looking bastard, too pretty for the likes of her. Compact, tanned with a slight cleft marring his perfect chin. An etched dimple completed the picture as his eyes settled on her feet.

Abby bristled. "What are you damn well smiling at?"

"That awkward moment when you're wearing Nikes…and you can't just do it."

Abby's mouth fell open as she glanced at her sneakers. He joked at a time like this? Righteous anger surged. "You think this is funny. I am so going to kick your ass along with your moronic mercenary friends."

"Yeah?" he answered, still grinning. "Then just do it."

John walked past ignoring Abby's hate-filled gaze. "Quit it. Max will geek out if you keep that up."

"I can't have a little fun?" the playboy asked.

John set up a tripod for the digital camera lying on the table. "Max almost got his head blown off by Catwoman, and now you wanna ass around?"

Funny Boy sobered and went over to help her friend's cockroach boyfriend. Max stepped back in the room. The eye was starting to swell. *Nice.*

"Who are you? Mercenaries for hire?" she asked.

Max looked disgusted with himself that a slim woman almost bested him. Pinning her with a cold stare, he casually took the seat opposite, yet there was nothing relaxed about the man. All his movements were measured as he weighed her up. Bile rose, and the probability of projectile vomiting all over his stony face seemed imminent.

"We could ask you the same question."

This ruthless man scared her. Gone was Mr. Charming Pants. "You're a deceitful rat. You made me believe that you cared!"

◊ ◊ ◊

Max schooled his expression. Abby seemed genuinely affronted, like a bossy teacher. Her courage was admirable, but if Miss Prissy didn't come clean, she'd be shitting her pants.

Abby folded her arms. "I'm not giving you anything."

His heart flipped at that small statement, confirming what he secretly feared, that Abby had something to give. It looked like she was a card-carrying, vest-wearing terrorist wannabe. What a fucking waste. Johnny gave a thumbs-up; the video was rolling. Max placed a second recording device on the table.

He'd start the interview with an initial rug pull. "Here's what we know about you...Josephine Abigail Evans."

Her eyes widened a fraction.

"Do you prefer Josephine or Joey?"

"I prefer Abby."

"You went by your given name—Josephine—up until three years ago when you dropped off the map."

Abby didn't respond.

"Born in New York to Jimmy and Priscilla Evans. Your parents moved to Colorado when you were five and then a few years later relocated to Northern Idaho.

"Your family did missionary work in Africa. You lived in Botswana during your tenth year and resided in South Africa from ages eleven to sixteen, receiving dual citizenship. Your family returned to the States. You left home, worked odd jobs and eventually moved to the United Arab Emirates to work in the airline industry."

"Nothing new there. I told you most of that," Abby said.

"We confirmed your story twenty-four months ago through your family and friends."

"You spoke to my father?"

"Not me personally. Now let's get to the meat and bones of this interview. Khalid Al Juhani."

Abby's already blanched face drained of all color.

"Khalid made contact on numerous occasions. We have a list of dates and times for all of your meetings. A lunch date at the Shangri-La Hotel. A get-together at the Dubai Yacht Club. You also met Khalid at a café in Paris. An agent following Khalid observed the sit-down. Your last encounter was at a party at his home in Sharjah, and it led to your disappearance. You spoke with Khalid in his gardens before entering his home. Surprise, surprise, you conveniently dropped out of sight. Shortly afterwards, Khalid went underground. Escaped to Somalia."

Abby sat, hands folded like she was hosting guests for afternoon tea. Max wanted to shake that serene attitude out of her.

"Here's your predicament. You're hunkered down in the middle of a radical hurricane that will tear you to pieces. Now, you may be squatting there voluntarily, wanting to contribute to the destruction, or you were yanked into the melee, seeking an escape."

"I have no clue as to what you're referring." The look in her eyes said differently.

"We'll see about that. You'll be relocated to a US holding facility, where I doubt you'll see the light of day for a very long time."

Abby sat back. "You're with a government agency."

Silence met her remark. Max pulled out a folder and handed

over the first photograph. A pretty brunette with freckles scattered across her nose, posing for a selfie, strawberry lips pouting.

"Jane Williams. Born in Glasgow." Max handed Abby another image of destroyed bodies in a courtyard, making her flinch. "She walked into a food market in Istanbul three years ago wearing a suicide vest. Thirteen people killed. Fifty injured."

Abby stared at the carnage. Max pushed the third photograph into her hands, of a beautiful blonde holding a camera while backpacking. Sparkling eyes stood out on a tanned face as she laughed at whoever took the shot.

"Clara Jensen. She was Danish and targeted the Three Kings Parade, a religious festival in Madrid."

Abby stared at the macabre image of death and destruction— festival decor stained with blood, buildings blown to smithereens. Max paused before handing Abby the first of the final pair of images. The tension in the room ratcheted up. This was personal for MIT2. The infamous woman in the picture responsible for the worst bombing in American history.

"Do you recognize her?"

"The Black Friday bombing." Abby's voice sounded rough with emotion.

"Sharon Nasari strapped a suicide vest to her child, and this was the result." Max placed the last photograph in Abby's cold hands. He'd specifically chosen that image to gauge her reaction.

"Oh God." Abby rocked forward, her eyes glued to the horror.

The press never received this gruesome CSI image of dead children that haunted his nights, primarily because Max had been there; so had Slater. Both men had left their respective Special Forces careers, had just completed their MIT Training and were assigned to support the Joint Terrorism Task Force in tracking links to the Sandpiper. Until their first deployment, they'd worked with Sully's team as well as the FBI. Slater had watched their six that day, trailing behind the rest of the team. He'd avoided injury and was the one to apply a tourniquet to Max's quadriceps after shrapnel sliced up Max's thigh. Slater still dealt with PTSD from the incident. Cradling dying children in a mall bombing would trigger a tsunami of trauma for years to come.

Max exchanged a glance with the man who'd saved his life as emotions threatened to flood the room. "A kid's playroom was situated beneath the food court where Sharon Nasari was sitting. The explosion not only destroyed families on the upper level but collapsed on the children beneath."

The tear rolling down Abby's cheek did nothing for Max, she could be playing them. Max searched for other tics.

"Sixty-three people dead. Twenty-two of them all under the age of ten. Slater and I were on a combined task force who'd just arrived when the bomb went off. One of my colleagues—his name was Sully—died in the blast."

"I'm so sorry," Abby broke in. Max watched her carefully.

"Another teammate was in the direct blast zone across the way; the explosion blew his arm off."

"Did he survive?" Abby asked, concern burning her gaze.

Stone's life would never be the same, but his kick-ass attitude demonstrated courageous balls of steel. "He's a tough bastard. What do you know about the Black Friday bombing?"

Abby looked confused. "Just what was shown on the news. Sharon and her husband—I forget what his name was—were part of ISIS."

Max corrected her. "ISIS claimed responsibility, but Abdul

Nasari worked for Khalid, who sells terror services to the highest bidder regardless of their religious beliefs or agendas. Capturing Abdul would've led us to Khalid, who also runs a suicide bomber network, recruiting foreign girls working in the Middle East. The syndicate lures them in by offering a lavish lifestyle. The side effect of the luxury is attending propaganda classes. The girls who come to rely on Khalid are married off to his fighters who physically and psychologically beat them into submission."

Something flickered in her eyes, and Max narrowed in as he continued.

"Those who don't conform are threatened or violently discarded. There's been a rise in female suicide bombers forced to wear vests in key cities around the globe. Many women are from the West; it's easier for them to blend into Western cities."

"How does that relate to me?" Abby asked.

"Khalid recruited you the very same way. Just like the other women, you disappeared the very night you were recruited. Except you got a British agent killed and we've been hunting you ever since."

"I'm not a murderer. I didn't kill anyone." Abby crossed her ankles. "Besides, I would think to have a successful convert, they'd target a woman with hidden insecurities and low self-confidence, desperately searching for a spiritual purpose in life. A natural submissive not familiar with indoctrination."

Donnie pulled at his goatee. "And your point is?"

"That woman is not me."

Max's mind considered the information she'd laid out. On paper, Abigail Evans fitted the bomber profile, but her core personality was all wrong. There was a difference between being submissive and being reserved. What stood out was Abby's quiet strength. Khalid liked working with damaged goods. Women who desperately sought a savior, as he ground them into nothing before rebuilding them into puppets of horror.

Abby had firsthand experience of a religious fanatic. Her father. It didn't take a genius to see that she'd avoid other cult movements at all costs. Max had been coming at this all wrong. Her father's punishments and constrictive rules hadn't destroyed her psyche; they'd only made her stronger.

What was the truth behind that fateful night in Sharjah? He needed answers. The game had changed, but he couldn't tip Abby off that he might just agree with her assessment.

His smile was cold. "You're quite the expert then."

She flushed. It was such a faint difference in skin tone that Max knew his men wouldn't pick it up.

"Are you willing to bet your young life on that flimsy theory? We have open files on Khalid, and I'm wondering how you play into his life. Our government doesn't look kindly on Americans who turn extremist."

Her throat moved as she swallowed. *High stakes, Miss Evans.*

"Abigail, tell me what happened in Dubai."

Max purposely used her middle name. Reestablishing the relationship was vital. Max then remained silent. A state Abby usually thrived in. She uncrossed her legs, weighing the options.

Make the right choice, sweetheart, his mind screamed silently, *come clean.* Pulling the truth out of a target was a delicate operation that took patience and skill. Some folded quicker than others. So many factors played a role—the degree of integrity they had, what was at stake, and any personal losses that might occur through a confession.

The kitchen clock ticked away. Max's grim stare never wavered. The team waited, knowing how he worked. Abby finally slumped in the chair.

Bingo. First step.

Chapter Nine

"Before I begin, I'll need a cup of tea." Abby made a move to get up and Max's solid form caged her in. How fast did the guy move?

"Sit. Down."

"Relax, Flash Gordon, it's just tea."

"You think this is a joke?"

Abby spoke slowly. "It's been a long day. I'm tired and thirsty. If not tea, would you get me a bottle of water from the fridge."

"On it," the fourth man answered. Stubble and a goatee made him look dangerous, yet he looked like the quieter one in the group. His movements were measured. Efficient. Abby was sure he was the brownnoser of the team. Not that he looked any less dangerous.

"Donnie, get me the rest of the files at the same time."

Mr. Goatee unlocked her sliding door and moved out silently.

"Umm. The water?" Abby asked.

"He's getting it."

"Max, there's bottled water in the fridge. You've seen it."

"You'll have your water shortly. Sit down."

They were getting water from somewhere else. Another apartment? A car?

She tried again. "Why don't you just grab—"

"Sit. Down. Please."

Abby persisted. "I just don't understand the difference between the water in the fridge and bottled water from wherever—"

"Jesus!" Max swore violently, and Abby jumped.

"Why so chatty all of a sudden. Do what I say and sit the hell down!"

That must be his "I'm the commander of the world" voice. Max felt formidable, crowding her back into her seat. John—or whatever his stupid name was—gave Max an odd look.

John then turned to her. "We won't allow you or any team member to touch food or water in your residence."

Abby looked confused, so John elaborated. "Explosive devices can come in tiny packages, and then there's the possibility of hidden toxins in the fridge…"

It took her a moment to register what he was saying, her mind swirling with the implications. Tainted water. Suicide by poison.

"Who does that?" she wondered aloud.

He raised an eyebrow. "Ever heard of kill pills'? Cyanide capsules?"

Mother of God. People did that. These men thought that she was capable of ambushing them in that way or sucking it down herself.

Max moved through the house. They seemed antsy, as if they expected to be ambushed at any second. John never took his eyes off her. Abby sat dejectedly, waiting for her water, wondering if this would set a precedent for the rest of her life. Sitting in a holding cell surrounded by armed men, begging for water between interrogations. These hardened warriors had to help her. She walked a thin line but would tell them as much of the truth as she could. The rest she'd hold close.

◊ ◊ ◊

Pausing in her bedroom, Max ran his hands through cropped hair as he repeated his motivational mantra. *She's nothing to me, just a bitch who betrayed her country.* There was a history between Khalid and Abby—her name tagged in numerous interceptions meant something. She was a means to an end—capturing the Sandpiper fucker who'd murdered his teammates. *Keep your head in the game and control the interrogation.*

Johnny stepped in behind him. "Everything okay, bud?"

Max smiled coldly. "Never better. Got her just where I want her. I take it the boys are back." He turned to push past—the searching look in his friend's eyes pissed him off.

Johnny propped himself against the door jamb with hands shoved into front pockets.

"What? Say it," Max said.

"Not sure what you mean."

"Don't screw with me. Just say it."

"It's different when it's a woman. I know we've had to deal with many female terrorists over the past couple of years. I know it sometimes can get to us. Just reminding you, that's all. Women are soft. Feminine. Teary-eyed. But above all, they're as smart as hell and can be just as manipulative as any man. You taught me that." Johnny turned to leave before saying, "Hell. Sharon Nasari taught us that."

The last comment was an icy slap. "I fucking know what I'm doing."

"You're one of the coldest motherfuckers I know." Johnny

nodded towards the kitchen. "But so is Evans—no one gets through that armor. Don't let her be our downfall."

◊ ◊ ◊

Abby concentrated her efforts on opening the water; the tight cap wouldn't budge. The Slater-Goatee duo flanked her, focusing on every move like she was James bloody Bond, ready to launch a choreographed attack on the two Stormtroopers. Damn cap. Screaming like a banshee and flinging the water bottle across the room would show these Neanderthals how scared she was—no, correction, how petrified out of her wits she was.

Abby willed her hands to stop their fine trembling. She'd handled far worse in the past. One step at a time. The first step—opening a freaking water bottle.

"Will either of you fine gentleman please open this for me?" She jammed the bottle under Slater's nose.

He looked down at her as if she was a worm. Alrighty then. She could picture him strolling down the beach wearing a banana hammock while throwing a teeny tiny ball for his girlfriend's Chihuahua—a high-maintenance ladies' man did nothing for her. Her lips twitched. He twisted it open and shoved it back in her hands. The charm fairy was apparently not home.

"Thank you, kind sir."

Max and his traitorous sidekick were back in the room. Max took his seat opposite, before flipping through a thick file. Was that all the information he had on her? Was her life that interesting? Composed and wholly in control, Max placed it on the table behind him before returning his focus.

Abby refrained from gulping down water and instead took a few long, slow sips. Max's eyes focused on her throat as she swallowed. A tingle of awareness raced through her body. Max felt it too. She saw the briefest spark of awareness before he shut it down. Human after all. If she shared some of her story with him, perhaps exploited that attraction, maybe he could save her. Save them all.

He started to talk, but Abby held up her hand to stop him. *Let me tell my story.* Max skewered her with cold eyes, probably used to pulling out fingernails to get at the truth. She rubbed her thumb over a pale pink fingernail; he wasn't getting near them today. She blocked out the men and instead focused on her story. She'd only ever told it once, but never in detail. Her mind wandered back to that simple time where she was forced to close the book on the last vestige of innocence.

"Girls flock to the Middle East—to work for the airlines—for many different reasons. Some want to party, some want to marry a wealthy local Muslim, some want to save money, it's tax-free. Others—like me—want to travel, to be inspired by other cultures. I jumped at the chance of becoming a flight attendant to visit all the great art galleries and museums."

"Running from your father and your many daddy issues didn't have anything to do with it?" John examined his fingernail as he raised the question.

Ouch.

"Maybe when I arrived, but pretty soon I fell in love with the traveling aspect of the job. I craved knowledge about world art and history and enrolled in art lessons. The first year was spent concentrating on myself and finding who I was meant to be." Abby fiddled with the label on her water bottle. "That's when Meg walked into my life."

Max leaned forward. "Megan Jehani. London born. British mother and Iranian father."

"Meg moved in when my previous roommate moved back to Russia, and she refused to let me hibernate, cooped up with my artwork. Instead, she dragged me out for dinners, to clubs, for crazy walks on the beach at five in the morning. We watched so many sunrises on the soft sand after a crazy night out. She was a flaming ball of energy. Men trailed after her wherever she went." Abby smiled. "Then Kris flew over to Dubai. Kris is a friend from—"

"We know who Kris Muller is."

"Of course you do, on paper. Kris was like the brother I never had, and I was blown away by the mere fact that he'd traveled halfway across the world to join me in Dubai. He always had my back. For Meg, it was love at first sight. Kris is a good-looking guy. Why not, right?"

Max looked irritated. "How does this relate to Khalid?"

"It relates. Kris and Meg started dating. At first everything was fun. The three of us hung out, but things changed. It got awkward, and I felt like a third wheel. They started hanging out with a racier crowd. Wealthy locals and their leeches. Kris worked for a couple of the sheikhs, looked after their game farms and accepted invitations to all their events. I went to a few but felt uncomfortable. Kris kept pushing me to come along, and I eventually gave in and went for lunch at one of the fanciest hotels in Dubai, the Shangri-La. That's when I met Khalid."

Tension in the room spiked.

"He was smooth and persistent, constantly inviting me out but I never accepted. I saw him next when a neighbor took me to the party at the Yacht Club. Khalid arrived just as I left, and we barely said hello."

"You gave him your number though. There are records of phone calls," Max said.

Abby shook her head, "No. Kris gave him my number."

Max narrowed his eyes.

"I'm not the type of girl who freely gives her number out to a man I've just met. Kris looked after livestock and game for many wealthy locals in the region and encouraged me to build connections, told me it would help my art career someday. Khalid called me a few times, and I was nothing but polite."

◊ ◊ ◊

Abby stretched her back and resettled. Her discomfort was evident. Tough titties.

"And yes, I saw Khalid on a Paris trip but didn't plan on it. I ran into him at a café on the Champs Elysées."

"You just happened to run into him," Max said.

"It's the truth; I remember thinking what a huge coincidence it was. In Paris of all places. Khalid kept saying it was as if God willed it to be so. That's what turned me off whatever game he was playing. It was something my father would say. I knew he'd likely tracked me from the hotel. I was a little freaked out but flattered that he'd gone through all that trouble, thinking he just wanted to take me out...like on a date."

"You don't deny having lunch with him?"

"We ate together, but it felt staged. Did your spy stick around long enough to see me leave Khalid at the table? I spent the rest of the day sightseeing."

The agent left to meet with an informant, but Abby didn't need to know that.

"You never spent the night with Khalid?"

Her eyes flashed with anger. "I'm not that kind of girl. I worked a flight back to Dubai that same evening." Abby paused to gather herself. "I may have been young, but I've never been easy."

That fitted with her profile.

"A few weeks later on a London flight, Khalid sat in my first-class cabin with his peregrine falcon. He invited me to a party at his home. I was reluctant but threw caution to the wind." Abby chewed her bottom lip. "Biggest mistake of my life. I knew that the minute I walked in."

"Did you see something suspicious?"

"No. It was all glamour. A massive outdoor cocktail party with a live band. Hundreds of people hung around the gardens. It was very racy...shallow."

"Why did you stay?"

"To be polite and it was a long drive, and I'd paid the taxi driver a lot of money, arranged to have him pick me up in two hours. I went looking for Meg or Kris."

"According to our intel, you weren't alone for long. Khalid met you in the gardens."

"He did. He was very charming."

Johnny opened his mouth as if to say something. Max held his hand up, sensing her unease, knowing she was bordering on revealing a hidden truth that had drastically altered her direction in life. Abby took a deep breath, gathering herself. To tell the truth or to deceive? *Careful, lady.* The sudden haunted look had no right to reside on her beautiful face. Her eyes reminded Max of many soldiers he'd served with, who'd seen the horrors of war.

"I'll tell you my sad story. My life is over. Khalid will find me. If by some miracle I survive, well, then I guess I'm the property of the US."

"You believe that Khalid is looking for you."

"He's intent on killing me. I don't work for him, I never have."

"That's hard to believe. Khalid offered you a job that night, and one of our informants overheard him. A job offer in Paris. You walked into his home to sign the papers and conveniently disappeared. Not the first of Khalid's girls. The problem is that these girls turn up in the darnedest of places, with a suicide vest strapped to their chest."

◊ ◊ ◊

Abby ignored the accusation and allowed her mind to wander back to that night. The last night of her life as Josephine.

Guests hung out in the ornate gardens at the back of Khalid's mansion. A sculptured fountain of a leaping Arabian oryx dominated the landscaped shrubbery. Winding pathways sprinkled in fairy lights added to the ambiance. Champagne flowed, and waiters maneuvered through the crowd.

Joey's black dress clung to her damp body as she escaped down a pathway, finding a quiet bench nestled under some palms. A small breeze whispered across her brow as she admired the view below. The golf course running across the bottom of the garden rolled out with palm trees flanking the green on either side. The tinkling of a nearby stream calmed her nerves. Not sure how long she sat there, Joey got up to leave.

"Josephine." Khalid stepped out of the shadows.

"You knew I was here?"

"I myself was escaping the crowds."

"But those are your guests."

His robe rustled as he stepped closer. "Indeed, they are. I have a secret that you are now privy to. I sometimes need to escape. Some of my guests, let's just say, are a little pompy."

Joey stared at him blankly.

"How do you say that word…pimpus? Pampus?"

Joey giggled. "Do you mean 'pompous'?"

Khalid turned to face the view. "That is exactly it. Pompous."

Joey bet that a bottle of his peppery perfume that clung to the breeze cost about the same amount as her car.

"So, Habibti. Do you like my golf course?"

Joey's eyes widened incredulously. "This is yours?"

"A man has to own a golf course."

"Do you play?"

Khalid grinned. "I'm too impatient." He winked at her. "I have a temper, and the golf clubs come off second best."

Joey smiled. "So why build it?"

"Plenty of guests ensure that it doesn't go to waste; besides, I like looking at the green."

It stretched out into the horizon.

"You want to say something," Khalid said.

"No, I'm good."

"Say it; I have a thick skin."

She doubted he had a thick skin in any sense of the word. His fine dusky skin gleamed in the moonlight.

"Tell me what you're thinking," Khalid pushed.

Here goes. Honest Joey. "Maybe you're a tad bored?"

Khalid looked sideways, and Abby rushed to explain. "There's only so much one can do with the money spent building a golf course you'll never use… I'm sorry, it's none of my business."

"No, I agree. I'm young and still foolish." He folded his arms. "What would you spend it on?"

"If it were for myself, I guess I would travel to an artist's retreat—like in Italy—where I'd paint and hang out with fellow artists for six months. After that, I'd build an art therapy center for children." Joey mapped out her ambitions in her head.

"That's a noble dream." Khalid bowed slightly to her. "You put a playboy like me to shame."

"I never meant—"

Khalid held up his hand. "Don't apologize. Your passion is a joy to see. What drives me is not so pure. I have beautiful things because I'm trying to prove my worth to my father and build a legacy for my children."

"I'm sure he's very proud."

"No. He's a holy man and sees me as the black cow in the family."

"You mean the black sheep." Joey knew the toll it took living with a devout father. They stared out over the green in companionable silence. "How many children do you have?"

"Three daughters but I want a son to carry my name. I currently have two wives."

Joey hadn't seen any trace of his family in Dubai. "Your wives are not here tonight."

"This is not a clean environment for my family. For now, they live in Morocco. I have many homes in many countries that they can select from."

Joey didn't understand what he meant by a "clean environment," but she felt comfortable with the fact that he was married. Perhaps Khalid just wanted to be a friend.

"Joey, does your job make you happy?" Before she could answer, Khalid pushed ahead. "This restlessness you have, it's not just about tonight. I guess you've had it all your life? You are still finding yourself. You want to believe in something greater than who you are."

Joey swallowed past the lump in her throat. No one had ever taken the time to know her well enough and give her such advice. Here was a new acquaintance who knew more about her than she knew of herself. Feeling flummoxed, she plopped down on the bench. "I like my job—I enjoy the traveling—but yes, I want so much more, and I know it will come."

Khalid turned back to ponder the view. Joey stared at his regal back, pondering her own life dilemmas.

"I admire you. You're not like the other girls in the airline business, you have a solid head on your shoulders." Khalid sat down and leaned towards her in earnest. "Come and work for me."

Joey looked at Khalid as if he were mad.

"I have an extensive business network with offices all around the world and need someone with common sense. You could work anywhere you want. Paris, Rome, London—you name it."

Joey shook her head. "Khalid, I can't just—"

"No, listen, I'll pay double what you earn here. Choose an art school to attend in Europe, and I will pay for your studies and an apartment. I'll even build an art therapy school in your honor, all providing you prove yourself to me. There's a position available in Paris, a good base to start from."

"Why would you offer this?" Joey hovered in an alternate universe. "And what would I be required to do?"

"Be there for whenever I need you. I'll provide you with a tutor who will teach you about my world and the importance of what I do. You'll attend group meetings and meet some of the people that I help. I work with those who have lost their way, persecuted communities. This world is a cruel place, and I'm trying to make it better. It may take time, but you'll eventually believe in something great, greater than one person could ever be."

In the blink of an eye, her life path was altered. She thought of all the possibilities. She could attend an art school... Khalid handed her a brighter future on a surreal silver platter.

"Khalid, I don't know what to say."

"Don't say anything. I'll give you a couple of minutes to think it over. If you say yes, we can go inside and draw up a contract."

A couple of minutes. Was he dang kidding? "I need more time. Maybe a day or so?"

"I have other people I'm considering for this position, some with impressive resumés. This is a chance to change your life and change this world."

◊ ◊ ◊

Abby told the story in a detailed manner, Max believed that everything she'd said so far was accurate. He rubbed his brow and pushed down the rage. These bastards recruited women by subtly playing off insecurities and pretending that they'd make their dreams come true. Stashing the girls in a strange new country with 24/7 guards who watched their every move, brainwashing them with propaganda. Some of the girls bought into it. Others who rebelled, disappeared for good. Max had some idea of what Abby and Khalid's conversation entailed from the intel in her file. She'd just confirmed it. What happened after that conversation was what Max needed to find out. He checked the tape recorder and took notes.

"I don't know what I was thinking—no, I do know. A silly dream of hanging out with fellow artists, who understood me. Of not being anywhere near my father. I could make a real home for myself—flying can be a lonely life if you have nothing to come home to, but I was stupid. You can run from yourself but can never hide." Abby looked up. "I said yes."

Heaviness seeped into Max's bones. Abigail Evans had made a deal with the devil.

"Khalid led me inside." Abby's brow creased. "I remember

feeling numb and questioning my decision. A thought kept intruding: you never get something for nothing in this world. By the time we entered a sitting room leading to his study, I had cold feet. Khalid took me on a quick circuit, showing all his falconry trophies. He kept asking if I was okay and must've seen the uncertainty. I said that I thought he was a lovely man and appreciated his offer, then I turned him down. He seemed disappointed but asked me to stay for a quick drink. After leading me back to the sitting room, Khalid handed me a glass of Pepsi, mentioning how warm it was outside. He said he'd tend to guests and would return shortly."

Max pulled out a sturdy sheet of paper and handed it to her. "It's a blueprint of Khalid's house."

"You mean palace?"

"Please concentrate, highlight where you were situated in that house, at each point of your visit, as we go through all the details."

◊ ◊ ◊

After repositioning the map, Abby cast her mind back to the layout, scribbling and circling on the page. Then she continued with her story.

Abby remembered the layout of the mansion like it was yesterday. The large sofa in the sitting room had engulfed her. She gazed in awe at the marble, gold and crystal luxury. The Persian rug beneath her feet felt thick and expensive. Gold curtains draped the windows in heavy splendor, and a massive grandfather clock ticked quietly in the corner. The room felt cool against her sticky skin. Joey felt happy with the decision—better to slowly save money. One day she would get to fulfill her dreams, all on her own, beholden to no one.

Feeling sleepy, Joey lay back and admired the intricate mural covering the ceiling. It depicted an ancient battle with wild-eyed men riding bareback on stallions, wielding giant swords. The enemies in the painting resembled crusaders. Her eyes wandered back to the Arabic warriors. A fearsome man positioned at the front of the foray looked remarkably similar to Khalid, who must've posed for the dramatic piece. She giggled at the vanity of the garish artwork.

"Joey, is that you?" Meg stood in the doorway holding a stack of folders. She looked stylish in a white shirt, flared navy skirt and flaming red stilettos.

Joey grinned at her friend. "You look amazing! I want— no, I need—those red heels."

"What are you doing here?" Meg said, stepping forward.

"What am I doing here?" Joey asked. "What are you doing here? Why are you carrying those files? Do you also work for Khalid?"

Meg rushed into the room, throwing the paperwork onto a coffee table. "What do you mean by 'also'?" She had a strange look on her face.

"You won't believe this, girlfriend, but Khalid offered me a freaking job!"

"Bollocks. When?"

"A few minutes ago."

"You need to leave. You can't work for him."

Joey tried to push herself off the huge couch, but her arms felt heavy.

"This is a cock-up." Meg looked panicked. "I'll tell Khalid you felt ill."

"I'm having a quick drink with him. He's quickly seeing to some guests."

"I need you to stand up." Meg grabbed her arm and tried to pull Joey off the sofa.

Joey pulled her arm back, and it took effort. "Wait. You work here?"

"Luv, it's a long story and you need to hurry." Meg grasped Joey's wrist again, this time tugging hard. Pulling her towards the study.

Joey felt weird and giggled. "We're going the wrong way, silly."

"There's a private passage in the study that leads out to the gardens," Meg said.

"Whoopsie daisy!" Joey tripped and grinned at her friend.

Meg grabbed Joey by the shoulders and shook her. "Focus. Did you let Khalid believe that you had doubts about working for him?"

Joey loosely nodded her floppy head. "I said nopey nope to the job."

Meg frowned. "Luv, you're not thinking clearly. Get a cab as quickly as you can. Your legs won't hold out much longer."

Joey felt the first stirrings of panic—she did feel odd like she was floating out of her skin. "But Khalid is a friend."

"Trust me, he's not your friend—he's an evil tosser."

Panic seeped through the fog. "Meg, come with me…please."

"Bugger it, I can't. I'll need to cover for you, otherwise we're both in big trouble." Meg felt along a bookshelf and pulled a latch. A door swung open. Stairs led down into a dark concrete tunnel.

"How did you do that?"

"Go!" Meg pushed her forward.

Joey stumbled, landing on her hands and knees at the bottom of the stairs. Her limbs quivered and gave way. The concrete floor felt cool against her cheek. Dust tickled her nose;

something brushed against her face as shiny black shoes—peeking out beneath white fabric—stepped into her line of sight. Her eyes slowly traveled up to Khalid's face.

His predatory gaze zeroed in on Meg. "Using my tunnel without my permission? You've been a very naughty girl."

Khalid turned and spoke in Arabic. Two men materialized, stepping over Joey, before grabbing Meg and shoving her back into the study. One of them looked like the Incredible Hulk. Joey tried to scramble back, but her legs refused to work. Khalid roughly dragged her into the room.

Meg babbled as excuses fell from her tongue. "Joey wasn't feeling well, and I thought it best if she went home to rest..."

Khalid dropped Joey like a sack of potatoes and walked up to Meg. "Shut up, you stupid whore." Khalid slapped her, straightened his clothing and wiped his hand as if it was sullied. "How long have you worked for me as a volunteer assistant?"

"Two years," Meg muttered.

"Repeat that."

The hulk grabbed her roughly by the neck.

"Two years. It's been two years."

"I trusted you with my business, with my secrets. How many girls have you helped behind my back?"

"None."

"Liar!" Khalid spoke softly. "Four girls have disappeared from my properties within the past year. I think you've been a little turncoat, Miss Megan."

Joey trembled so hard that her teeth rattled. Her heavy limbs refused to cooperate, and her brain felt muddled. Meg worked for Khalid?

Meg looked petrified. "Mr. Al Juhani, I swear—this is the first time—Joey's my friend."

Turning to his desk, Khalid opened a wooden box and pulled out a syringe. "Break her arm."

The brute wrenched Meg's arm back with a sickening crunch, and her agonizing screams filled the room.

Oh God, oh God, oh God. Nausea rolled through Joey, she tried to drag herself towards her wailing friend.

Khalid issued final orders. "Tape her mouth shut and take the deceitful bitch upstairs to one of the soundproofed rooms. I'll deal with her later."

The massive thug grabbed Meg by the hair and the other monster slapped tape over her pain-filled sobs. Meg's anguished eyes rolled back as they dragged her away. Joey kept crawling towards her friend, knowing it was futile.

"Where are you going, little one?" Khalid knelt beside her. Something pricked her arm. "I'll give you just the right amount so that you'll remember me in your dreams, my sweet Josephine."

◊ ◊ ◊

Abby stared blankly ahead. Dry-eyed and trembling.

Jesus. Max had a suspicion of what would come next. She needed a break. He needed a goddamn break. He'd wanted the truth, and here it was in all its ugly glory. Abby was no longer considered a target. She was reclassified as a vulnerable witness. Technically the term was an intimidated witness.

This wasn't an interrogation, it never truly was. It was now an interview. The suppressed anger rolling off the rest of the team matched his own. Khalid was a monster, and they'd seen his handiwork. Experienced it firsthand, but to hear it pour out of Abby's mouth drove the depravity home.

Max knelt beside her. "Abby, let's take a break." He reached out and touched her clasped hands.

She jerked. "Don't touch me. Don't you dare, you have no right."

"How about I make you some tea."

She smirked cynically. "Now I'm allowed to drink my tea? Aren't you scared, soldier, that I'll poison myself?"

"Abs." Max locked his gaze on her.

She stared for a long moment, assessing, judging. Her eyes reflected a wild mix of pain, confusion and desolate sadness that struck him to the core. No woman should ever have that look in their eyes.

"Let me finish this. Then do with it what you will."

Max understood the determination to finish, but it would be easier for her if they broke up the interview into smaller bites. "How about a twenty-minute break to start?"

Abby shook her head.

"Is there someone I can call to provide support? Anyone that you trust?" Max asked.

"There's no one. I'm on my own in this. The story of my life, right?"

◊ ◊ ◊

Squeezing her shoulder, Max rose smoothly. Cool air replaced the subtle warmth, where his firm thigh had rested against her leg. That sudden yearning stemmed from her current state of fear. Her desperation to have someone on her side. Abby scoffed at the realization. She never had and never would need a man. Josephine Abigail Evans was a savage island.

The men settled and watched her expectantly. *Oh God.* She'd get through this. *All things pass, baby girl.* Abby forced her mind back to that gruesome night.

Khalid was right—she'd remembered. Distant fuzzy memories

of pain and violence. An endless loop of screaming agony, of lying paralyzed as Khalid played his depraved games. She'd surfaced from the nightmare feeling disorientated and weak.

Joey cracked open her eyes as something slid up her leg. A hand. Bile rose as she took stock of her dangerous predicament, definitely splayed out on a bed. Wrists and ankles throbbed in time with pain searing through her abdomen. Her lower back felt like it was on fire.

She pulled on her left arm and felt no give. A man with a rifle slung over his shoulder perched beside her, facing her legs. She was naked, tied to a giant four-poster bed. His filthy hand squeezed her inner thigh. She tried not to shiver; she lay on a cold, wet mattress yet it felt like flames licked her skin.

Hearing a door open, Joey closed her eyes. Someone ripped his hand away, shouting in Arabic. Waves of nausea had her hunkering into the mattress. Khalid's spicy perfume tickled Joey's throat as terror as she'd never known before shattered her soul. Khalid switched to English and shouted, "She's mine, you piece of filth! You dare touch her? I leave you to guard her for two minutes."

The guard spoke nervously in Arabic.

"Once I'm done, you can have what's left," Khalid said. He pushed the man out of the room.

Joey willed herself to relax. Khalid stood over her for so long that Joey wondered if he'd left but didn't dare move. Her mind screamed with revulsion as the bed dipped. So help her God, she'd fight the brute every step of the way and sink her teeth into his smug golden flesh; it would be her last act on this earth. Joey knew he'd forced himself on her drugged body throughout the night, sobbing inside with the realization. Someone knocked and entered the room.

"Khalid. We have a problem with one of the guests. He's drunk."

Khalid froze and rested his head in the crook of her neck. "I'm busy. You dare to interrupt me for this?"

"My apologies, sir. It's the Russian envoy's son. He broke a vase in the courtyard and is requesting to see you."

Khalid swore and shoved off. "These guests are like spoiled children. It's time for my guests to leave. Guard this door, you enter this room and touch her, you'll die, understand?"

The door closed, footsteps echoed down the passage. Joey counted to thirty before peeking through eyelashes. The room was empty. The guard stood on the other side of the door. If she didn't escape, she would die in this evil palace.

Silk scarves secured her limbs to the four posts with not much give. The left scarf had slightly more length, and she strained her body towards it, twisting her wrist. By the condition of her wrists, it was evident that she'd fought throughout the night. Seconds felt like minutes, but she finally reached the material with her teeth, ripping until the final threads sliced through and her arm ripped free. Feeling elated, she freed her other wrist and sat up to work on her ankles.

Joey froze, staring at the pool of blood staining the mattress. Where had it come from? There were no apparent injuries. Pain radiated from within, and then she knew. Khalid.

Horror washed over her as she swung her legs over the side. One of Meg's red shoes lay next to the window. Joey whispered her friend's name, wobbling to her feet before stumbling over something. Not something but someone. The stench of urine and death slammed home as she stared into Meg's unseeing eyes. *Oh God. Meg. No, no, please no.* Joey scrambled back, stifling moans with her hand. Meg lay broken with limbs pointing in obscene directions. Her head sat at a crazy angle.

Joey vomited. The retching turned into uncontrollable sobbing. Shuffling in the passage shook her out of her grief. *Move or die*. She stumbled around looking for clothing. A wardrobe stood open. Panic urged Joey to run, but she'd attract too much attention running naked through Sharjah. Abayas—the traditional black robes for Arabic women—hung in the closet. She pulled on a black dress.

Please Lord, let the window be unlocked. Joey frantically grabbed at the latch, and it swung open, warm air flowing in. The window sat one level up from the ground, on the opposite side of the mansion. The grounds were dark, and the revelry could barely be heard. There was no ledge; the best bet was an olive tree twisting up from the ground. Could she jump that far? No question, it was going to hurt, and it surely did. Joey's wrist snapped on impact as she bounced off the trunk, landing on the grass below.

Abby paused in the telling of her story and couldn't meet the men's eyes. It wasn't about shame—well some of it might be—it was just so violently private in every way.

Max studied her intently, like he was drilling down into her soul. She sensed movement to the left and flinched in response.

"Easy. Easy." John placed a glass of chocolate milk into her shaking hands.

When had he gone to the fridge?

"Drink this and here's a cookie. Have a cookie."

"I'm okay." Her voice shook.

"It will help with the shakes," John said.

Abby glanced around the room, noting the other two Stormtroopers shuffling uncomfortably. Max was still staring in that unnerving way. She nibbled the chocolate chip cookie she'd baked earlier and studied the floor at her feet.

◊ ◊ ◊

Max had to push her and felt like a douchebag, but ultimately it was in her best interests. The sooner the interview was over, the sooner she could rest. Her energy was flagging, and she'd be of no use to herself or his team if she toppled over from exhaustion. Who could blame her—in the space of a few days she had been attacked, injured, lied to, and now forced to talk about the most traumatic experience that any human could endure.

Icy rage ate at his hardened shell. Max was one tough mother. His career had shown him how sick and twisted human beings could be, the evil tortures they inflicted on others. He'd grown accustomed to switching off from the destruction he faced. But Evans got to him, slipping under armor. Those doe eyes swamped with tragic emotion as she told her story held him fucking captive as the black hatred rose. He believed her; no one could pull off a performance of that caliber, although some came close.

He'd corroborate it with facts, and she'd better hope to God that she had evidence to support her violent tale, or he wouldn't be able to protect her pretty ass.

"How did you escape from the property?"

"I aimed for the tree line running along the perimeter wall. My legs barely held me up, I headed in the vague direction of the exit; there was a guard house and boom gate. Shrubbery nearby provided good coverage; thankfully the guard's radios were quiet. When a hummer slowed down to exit, I ran alongside as it drove through the gate, diving into roadside bushes. I then used the dark as cover. It felt like I'd been running for hours and kept collapsing. I woke in an olive grove and heard an engine. The olive and palm tree farmer who found me took me back to his house. He didn't speak English. His wife did though." Abby smiled sadly. "She climbed in the truck, holding my head in her lap. I begged them to take me straight to the embassy."

"There's nothing on file indicating you went to the US Embassy."

"We drove to the South African Embassy as I have dual citizenship. Khalid knew I was American, but I never mentioned that I'd lived in South Africa for five years as a teenager. He's a powerful man with connections—the first places he'd look would be the hospitals or at the US Embassy. The South African route was safest."

Abby continued with her story. "They barely had enough money for gas. I promised to pay them everything I had if they could just take me there. The embassy staff were amazing. They transported me to a local clinic used for official medical checkups. When I was well enough to travel, they flew me to Johannesburg, where I stayed in the hospital for just over a week. I later found out that Meg's body was discovered in a burned-out car on the side of the road. The papers said it was a car accident. Khalid must've had police officers on his payroll. There were even so-called witnesses to the accident that supposedly killed her."

Abby stared with haunted eyes. "I debated coming forward, but at the end of the day, I hid like a coward even though I was responsible for her death."

Max summed up all she had told them. He knew about the cover-up. Two roommates, one dead and one missing. Except Megan Jehani hadn't been what she'd seemed: she'd infiltrated Khalid's circle as an MI6 agent. Her death had triggered investigations from multiple agencies. Khalid had a mother of a target on his back.

Time to play devil's advocate. "Let's examine your story from a different angle. Interesting that you chose the South African Embassy. The US has more power to get you the right help and protection in a foreign land but, then again, they would demand a full investigation. Lots of paperwork and resources that could expose Khalid's network. Maybe you didn't want questions raised about your activities? Risk any exposure? It's on record that you met Khalid many times. Something went wrong in his office that night. Perhaps Megan Jehani went looking for her friend and stumbled on your dealings with the devil. She freaks out, is murdered. Plans get adjusted. The easiest location to hide is in a place where you have citizenship. Khalid slaps you around a little and bingo; everything is tied up in a neat little package." Max ignored the visible pain passing over Abby's face. He had to be a thorough bastard, couldn't afford not to.

Abby spoke softly, Max leaned in.

"Slaps me around…" She huffed out a dry laugh. "If that's the term you want to use for what he did to me." She rounded on Max as her voice gained strength. "Thirty internal stitches from the rape. Khalid found creative ways to violate me."

Max inwardly flinched.

"A broken wrist, cracked ribs and a concussion—I must've fought back at some point and got my head bashed in. Multiple contusions all over my body. I still have a few of the scars. Oh, and let's not forget the branding."

The what?

"I'll give you the names of the doctors who treated me, both at the clinic in Dubai and at the hospital here. They have my records."

"Wait, what did you say about branding?"

Abby snapped as anger ignited tears. "Screw you for making me do this."

Gone was calm and in-control Abigail Evans. Emotion now ran the show. He always congratulated himself on manipulating the interview towards this point—except now he just felt guilty for making her relive that abhorrent nightmare. The truth screamed out at him from every pore. He had his answer; Abigail Evans was innocent, but really at what price?

Abby shot up, Johnny moved in, and Max held up his hand. Her burning gaze raked over Max with contempt before she turned her back to him. He heard her unbutton her jeans and slide the zipper down.

What the freaking hell. Max rose as she slowly pulled down her jeans then paused. At a glimpse of rounded ass cheeks, for the first time in his life, Max felt a warm blush creep up his neck.

"Abby," he croaked.

Slater stepped forward. "Sweetheart—stop—what the hell are you doing?"

"I'm not your sweetheart," she spat, before turning back to Max. "Look at my back."

She raised the soft T-shirt. Perspiration broke out on the back of his neck as Max took in that gorgeous ass half molded by tight jeans. And then he saw it. Rage slammed in, rocking him back.

"Do you see it?"

"Yes." Max turned away.

Abby pulled up her jeans and the shirt fell into place.

Fury clogged up the room.

"It means *whore*."

"I know what it means." Max growled the words. Abby's lower back was branded. Arabic lettering stamped into flesh. The scar stood out starkly against her creamy skin and was now seared permanently into Max's brain.

"They branded me after drugging me. I remember feeling the

injury when I first woke, but the agony of internal injuries overrode all else. I only saw the blistering two days later at the hospital."

Slumped shoulders made her look achingly vulnerable. Max had a ridiculous urge to take her in his arms, but the job came first.

"We're done for tonight. Two men will stay with you until we can sort out this mess. Don't put up a fuss, pull a fast one over on us, or you'll find yourself on the wrong end of a firing stick."

Abby nodded once.

"I'll need to check out your story, and we need proof. You will provide that. Get some rest and stay out of our way, you're still under heavy surveillance. If you endanger this operation in anyway, you're done. You cannot tell Lizzy about us, we are a black ops team. No one knows we're here. Do you understand?"

"Yes."

The team gathered in the kitchen, Abby hadn't moved. Max gave out orders, glancing her way as she clenched and unclenched her trembling hands. They'd put her through the ringer, and she'd come out the other side bloody and bruised but still standing.

Chapter Ten

Max struggled to keep his eyes open. Four in the morning and his team had finally settled. Abby was told to sleep in her living room with a team member present, until she was cleared. Slater sat on Abby's other couch on watch duty. Her apartment needed a thorough search and they'd take their time. After crashing in the guest room, Donnie would lead the search when he woke. Both Max and Johnny took turns with guard duty from across the way.

Instead of resting, Abby curled up and quietly sobbed. Max rubbed his forehead tiredly. The soft weeping drifting through the speakers drove him up the goddamn walls, and Slater looked to be in the same boat. Max felt like a son of a bitch for forcing her to tell them about her ordeal. Abby had likely never shared the full story with anyone, and now she'd told it to a room of strangers.

Khalid would pay. Nausea threatened every time he thought of what that evil bastard did to her.

Did Abby know of the surveillance in her apartment, that a group of men had access to her most private moments? Close surveillance was needed in case they'd misjudged her. Max knew within his gut that she was a victim caught up in Khalid's web, but he always covered his bases. Until there was definite proof that she was telling the truth, they'd be cautious. Her medical records from Dubai would be in his hands by late morning.

The mind map he'd been working on for the past year lay in front of him. After updating the file on Abby, Max filled in some of the gaps. His fingers folded a piece of paper over and over as he ran over the intel.

Why was Khalid so determined to track her down? Intel indicated that he was narrowing in on her location? Josephine Abigail Evans had been hiding from Khalid for almost three years, yet the dust hadn't settled. Khalid's people were actively looking for her. Was he obsessed with her? The one who got away? Did he want to teach her a lesson for escaping and thwarting his sick plans that night? Had Abby unknowingly taken something that belonged to Khalid, or perhaps seen someone in Khalid's network that she shouldn't have, and how did this tie into the attack at La Coraggio? They were related.

Abby finally fell asleep. Max sensed that she knew more than she was telling. *Get some rest, sweetheart, because the second round starts tomorrow.*

◊ ◊ ◊

A new sofa was on the cards. Maybe she'd buy a cushy lounge sectional set. Abby was still sore and bruised from the attack, but holy hell. One torturous night of feeling sorry for herself while huddled in the corner meant that she was shuffling to the kitchen like an old lady. Mr. Lover Boy shadowed her every move.

"Give me some freaking space," Abby grouched, turning to Slater's looming form before continuing. "I'm making a cup of coffee. That's all I'm doing, making damn coffee. Sit down quietly in the corner like a good little Stormtrooper, and maybe I'll make you a matching cup."

A grunt was all she received. Abby ignored the grumpy oaf as she muddled around the kitchen. Donnie and John systematically searched her home looking for God knows what. Were they expecting an Uzi-clutching Sylvester Stallone to be hiding under the bed? Tuning out the giant warriors rifling through her space was key to her sanity. She stood on the edge of a mental abyss—one small shove, and she'd break into a million pieces. Abby stared glumly out the window as the percolator started to bubble.

Slater suddenly chirped, "Perkatory."

Abby jumped. "What?"

"The anguished, prolonged period spent waiting for a fresh cup of coffee to be ready. That's called Perkatory."

"Pfft. You're an ass."

Slater's bleary eyes sparkled with humor. "But I got you to smile."

Abby pursed her lips to stop the grin. Maybe Mr. Banana Hammock wasn't so bad. Bless the man, exposed to her pity party for most of the night. Any man's worst nightmare. Abby couldn't stop those humiliating tears. Slater had made her a cup of tea, covered her with a throw and tuned the telly to a "Friends" marathon. That was super nice of him.

"Sorry for the crying fest last night. You were very kind."

The man winced. "It's nothing. You didn't want a bunch of strangers seeing you that way. It was a tough night."

"Well, I appreciate it." Abby squeezed his arm.

Max stepped into the kitchen and glowered at Slater. "Abby, can we talk?"

Her heart stuttered. This was it—she might be on the next

flight to some US facility. She couldn't leave. Not now. It would destroy her world and her biggest secret. Whatever it took to convince Max to let her stay, she'd do it.

The bruise on his cheek was angry, and his face looked drawn. Abby guessed that he'd spent the evening going over her story. Well, welcome to the exhaustion boat, buddy. The only member of the team that looked somewhat rested was Donnie, who dashed around like an Energizer bunny. Good for him.

Despite the fatigue, Max was very male and very virile. Damn the man for looking so good. Her traitorous heart did a small flip as he cupped her back, leading her to a dining room chair.

◊ ◊ ◊

What was with the sudden familiarity between Abby and Slater? They were here to do a fucking job, not to get all touchy feely. Max would kick Slater's ass if he looked at her sideways. The foreign possessive surge when it came to Abby was unwelcome. She might no longer be a target but was still a person of interest, and a tangle of complications when it came to catching Khalid.

"I have copies of your medical records from Dubai and from the follow-up visits at the clinic in Cape Town. The South African Embassy in Abu-Dhabi released your travel records along with your statement."

"You believe me?"

"The evidence backs your story." It did a whole lot more than back her story. *Shit. Jesus.* After flipping through the records, photographs and the documented rape kit, the fragility of her broken body was etched into his brain. In his career, Max had seen some sick shit, but this took the cake. What he wouldn't have given to have been there that night in Sharjah. To have killed Khalid before he'd lain his putrid hands on her.

Instead, here they were. Abby's tangled hair and chunky bathrobe did nothing to hide her natural beauty. Dark circles hinted at her crying jag, yet her thickly lashed green eyes were starkly beautiful against that luminous skin. Open windows to her brave soul that hid nothing. Not the pain, not the horror and not the fear. *Shit and hell.* She was a landmine to a man's heart.

"So where do we go from here?"

Gritting teeth against her frailty, Max answered, "We haven't decided. Sending you to a debriefing facility is the next step."

"I don't want to go."

"You have no choice. The debriefing will take anything from a week to six months. After that, you can choose to return to South Africa or remain Stateside. If you come back, you're painting a large target on your back. If you stay in the States, the witness protection program will be the best option."

Abby paled; her next words took Max by surprise. "Let me help. Khalid wants me, I can lure him out of his greedy hidey hole."

"This isn't a game. I cannot one hundred percent ensure your safety. Besides, why would you want that? I'd think after what you've been through you'd jump at the chance to disappear."

"Except if I vanish, I'm just delaying the inevitable. Do you think I'd trust you or the powers that be to protect me? I've relied on myself for so long, and that's not about to change. I won't leave until Khalid is either dead or locked away in a deep, dark corner of the world. You'll have to drag me kicking and screaming onto that aircraft because I'm not budging."

"We could do that, you know. Remove you forcefully from South Africa."

She swallowed nervously.

"But for now, we're in a holding pattern. I don't have the

power to keep you here if Command is determined to pull you Stateside. I can submit my recommendations along with my reports, but at the end of the day, it's not up to me."

"I understand. When will you know?" she asked.

"I'm not sure. I promise that as soon as I do, I'll be the first to tell you."

They were alone in the dining room. Slater had grabbed a coffee and gone over to the other apartment to rest. The other men were in her bedroom.

Abby bit her lip before asking, "Why did you lead me on, pretend that you liked me? There were other ways to get me to open up."

"I won't apologize. We needed a quick insertion into your life. You were a suspected terrorist. I'm sorry I hurt your feelings, but it is what it is."

"*Insertion* being the keyword. Do you make a habit of sleeping with all your targets to get information?"

"That's not what I said. I wouldn't have taken you to bed. I've never resorted to that. We planned to confront you today."

Abby snorted. "What about Lizzy?"

"What about her?"

"She's a human being, you know."

"Johnny isn't sleeping with her and doesn't plan to. She's your best friend and the best cover we had. For all we knew, she was just as involved in his network."

"John might as well be sleeping with her. Her heart's involved. Do you think that makes it okay? Just because he hasn't screwed her doesn't mean that she won't be devastated by the betrayal."

Max's jaw ticked. "I won't defend our actions. Lizzy will also need protection. Khalid will find ways to get to you. Since you've cut ties with your family, your friends are the next obvious targets."

Closing her eyes, she nodded. "Will John be reliable protection?"

Max reassured her. "In his career, Johnny has rescued many hostages and protected high profile leaders. He's the best there is."

Silence descended as Abby appeared to mull over Max's words. He could almost see her mind ticking over as she sorted through the chaos of her new world. She traced a grain pattern in the wooden table.

Finally, she spoke. "That flirty man who took me on the date wasn't really you, I see that now."

"We've gone over this, Abby."

"I'm looking forward to getting to know the real Max."

That threw him. Was she freaking kidding? Max was sure that she wouldn't want anything more to do with him. "There's no need, this is all business."

Abby stood. "I disagree. I have a feeling we're going to be spending a lot of time together. You know my secrets. It's only fair that I know at least one of yours," she said, stepping into the kitchen.

"Careful, sweetheart. That's third-degree burn territory you're wandering into."

Smiling cynically, Abby poured some coffee. "Excellent, my kind of territory and I've got the scars to prove it—I'll feel right at home."

Abby then situated herself in front of her computer for the rest of the day. Max and his team went over the apartment with a fine-tooth comb while a remaining team member watched her work. Intel needed revising, looking at new angles and potential scenarios. Throughout the day, Abby only emerged twice. Once to go to the bathroom and once to grab a cup of tea. Max insisted that she eat and forced a couple of slices of pizza down her throat.

◊ ◊ ◊

Five new graphics projects lay on her desk. If she sat twiddling her thumbs she'd go insane. The men took turns keeping an eye on her progress. As long as they stayed out of her way. Max was avoiding her—maybe he was just busy sorting out the tangled web of complications that was her life. He had no clue. That was just the tip. She wasn't letting him sail near the glacial mass that was her dangerous life, refusing to be the iceberg to his *Titanic*.

Anger swelled every time she thought of the smooth play he'd made for her head and her heart. He could simmer in his Bat Cave for the rest of the mission for all she cared. Except her fate was in his hands and, like it or not, she had to play nice, at least for the moment.

By the following morning, the agitated tension had Abby pulling out her yoga mat and shoving a strength and flexibility DVD into the TV unit. As she wasn't allowed to go swimming, this was the next best thing.

"Can I join you?"

The quiet voice behind her made her drop the remote control. Jesus, these big men moved like freaking ninjas.

"For the love of Christ, Slater, don't sneak up on a girl. You'll get a black eye for your efforts."

Slater snorted. "Yeah, like that's gonna happen. I'm not Max, sweetheart."

Abby's mouth quirked upwards at Slater's dig. Yep. Mr. Banana Hammock wasn't bad at all.

"So, can I join? I need to get my gym quota in for the day."

"You sure you want to work out to a stretching video? It's not the hardcore action-man stuff that you sleep, breathe and eat."

"Just play the damn thing, and let's get on with it."

"I don't have an extra mat, so the tile floor is your new friend."

"Yeah, yeah. I've worked out on far worse."

An hour later Abby sat down on her mat for a cooling-down session.

"That wasn't half bad!" Slater grinned. "That chick has some good moves."

Abby ignored him as she turned on music. A Buddha Bar tune drifted through the room. She grabbed a couple of pillows and threw them on the floor. Lying back, she got comfortable, placing one beneath her head and one under her knees. Finally, she took a slow breath.

"What are you doing now?" a meddlesome voice asked.

Abby cracked an eye open. "Trying to meditate?"

Slater looked horrified. "Do you want me to break out the green tea and a bag of weed while we're at it?"

"Live a little. Give it a try."

"No offense, Evans. You're serene and all, but you don't strike me as the 'think the flowers, feel the flowers, be the flowers' kind of girl."

Abby grinned, then grew serious. "I don't do the typical cross-legged, flowing pants, humming-ohm stuff. But I occasionally use relaxation exercises. My therapist taught me how. It's helped me through some of my worst moments."

"Oh damn. I'm such an ass, I'm sorry."

"Give it a go; it won't get all weird and Zen-y. Grab a throw pillow."

Slater stared at her before hunkering down and getting comfortable.

"Close your eyes and still your body."

"What if I have an itch?"

Abby rolled her eyes. "Then scratch it."

Slater scratched his family jewels causing Abby to giggle. "Let me know when you're done."

Another couple of seconds and Slater settled himself. "I'm good."

"Okay." Abby softened her voice as she led him through a visualization. "Breathe in slowly. Breathe out slowly. Relax your muscles. Feel them sinking into the floor. Breathe in slowly. Breathe out slowly."

Once in a rhythm, she continued, "Close your eyes and imagine a candle flickering in a small, dark room."

"What kind of room is it? A holding cell? An interrogation room?"

Slater's seemingly serious question had Abby holding in a chuckle.

"It's just a room. I don't know. A tiny log cabin?"

"How dark is it?"

"Slater! Focus! Now, imagine that whenever you breathe in, the flame moves towards you and whenever you breathe out, it flickers away. Focus all your energy on the flame."

Abby breathed in and out for a few moments before Slater cut in.

"Theoretically, how close am I to this candle? Am I sucking the smoke into my lungs? Is that a sensible thing to do?"

A pillow thumped him in the face. "Ouch!"

"Get your anti-buddha ass out of here."

"Hey!" Slater laughed as another soft missile flew his way. "You do realize that you're assaulting an agent and that comes with dire consequences!"

"Yes, sir! Agent Doofus! Now move your butt, I need to roll up my yoga mat."

Their friendly rapport was interrupted by a scowling Max rapping on the glass door. "Open up. Slater, quit clowning around."

◊ ◊ ◊

Max turned to Abby. "I'm getting a set of house keys cut for each member of the team. That's not negotiable."

"O-kay. Do you need my keys, for the locksmith?"

"Nope. We already have a copy I can use."

"I don't even wanna know." Abby bent to roll up the yoga mat.

Max pulled Slater aside. "Can we talk?" They walked out to the patio and Max rounded on him. "How's Kathleen doing?'

"Kat's just fine. Why do you ask?"

"You're still dating her?"

"You know I'm still fucking seeing her."

"I know you're having relationship issues."

Slater bristled. "What's your point, sir?"

"Don't screw around with a target, especially one as vulnerable as Evans."

"I'm not screwing with her; she needs a friendly face at her back."

"She's off-limits, and I'm warning you, act like a damn professional or next time we'll have more than words." Max stepped back inside. "And corral the rest of the team; we need to chat with her."

Ten minutes later, that chat turned into a heated debate.

"Today is already Wednesday. I have three appointments lined up. I'm not hiding away from life while you all decide what to do with me."

The four men reflected identical stances. Arms folded, legs planted firmly and grim expressions to match.

"And glaring at me won't change my mind. I'm leaving in thirty minutes to meet my first client. She's opening a preschool and needs a logo and signage. It's a big contract that I refuse to give up."

Donnie spoke. "You do realize if you end up dead, getting the contract is pointless."

"Agreed. I may be dead tomorrow," Abby shot back. "I may be on my way to God knows where, or I may just need to continue living my life, paying my rent and earning my dues. Sitting here stewing, however, doesn't get us any closer to capturing Khalid."

"There is no 'us' in this equation," Max said.

"Then there's no Khalid. We know he's hunting me. Without me, you're screwed."

"My team knows he's after you, the latest intel indicates movement, that the elusive fucker is closing in on your stubborn ass. Question is, why do you think he's hunting you?"

"I have no idea. Because I'm the one that got away?"

Liar. Max gritted his teeth. Finally, he said, "What are your client's names and where are

we meeting them?"

It was obvious that she was mentally cheering her progress. She still looked wiped out. Getting brutally attacked followed up by an interrogation was a lot of duress for any person to go through. Max didn't like Abby being in the general public until they had a clear directive, Khalid might already have a team on the ground in South Africa. Max was still awaiting additional intel on the cell's movements.

Abby gave him the names. "Rosie Fisher. We're meeting at

ten o'clock at her preschool. It's in Kensington, twenty minutes away. I then have a lunchtime appointment with Levi Bakal. He has a Jewish bakery called Geshmak Goodies, which he's renovating. I'm creating a new vibe and logo. He's persnickety and changes his mind every week, but it's a good little contract."

Oh, he was persnickety all right. While she'd been under surveillance, Abby had met the diminutive man on two occasions. He was crusty, stubborn and difficult. He'd already ripped apart two of Abby's logo designs, which pissed Max off. The logos were beautifully clean, modern and sleek, and the ass gnome had treated them like filth. Abby had the patience of ten Italian saints.

"Blowhole," Slater coughed into his hand.

"Yeah," Abby agreed, "he's a little crabby, but he's a client and I've dealt with worse."

"Who's the final client?"

"Wayne Jacobs needs a workbook designed for a presentation. Max, I don't need you breathing down my neck when I meet with my customers."

"That's not up for debate; I'll be along for the ride. Max Hansen is now your new nap buddy."

"Nap buddy?" she gasped.

"You know, your boy toy, your man slam, your pooky bear…" Hiding a grin, Max turned his back on her face of horror and glanced at his team. "Let's get moving, Hardy Boys; we've got work to do. Oh, and Evans, get some glow on. You look as pale as linen. You'll need to look like a woman in love, not like someone who's just lost their damn dog."

Her fury at that last comment had Max running for the door. Cool-headed Abigail Evans was as mad as a trapped hornet. Men scattered as insults flew their way, but at least Abby now had some color to her cheeks.

Chapter Eleven

Levi Bakal's bakery seemed as dull as dishwater. Fair enough, he'd just bought the place, but it was clearly in disrepair and would not be in use in the foreseeable future. It was the first time Abby had seen the actual bakery, and she was shocked at how much Levi needed to do before it was functional. The crumbling wallpaper revealed water damage on the far wall. The place smelled musty and looked filthy. Kitchen equipment in the back would need replacing. What was Levi thinking?

Abby tried to ignore the brawny dolt sticking to her like glue. Oh, she'd prettied up all right. She felt foxy and fine in her fitted plum blazer thrown over a white blouse with black tailored pants. Her stilettos were a little high—but hey, give a girl pretty shoes and she can walk on water. Carefully applied lipstick matched the blazer perfectly. She was back in control, pleased that the preschool meeting had gone so well. Wanting an apple tree incorporated into her logo, Rosie was happy with Abby's preliminary sketches.

Now Abby was dealing with two annoying men. Levi was already on a roll, skewering her with a censorious stare. "Abigail, why have you brought your boyfriend along? It's highly unprofessional and your focus needs to be on branding my business."

Max answered smoothly for her. "Abby's car gave her problems. I offered to bring Abby to her appointments today."

Levi gave Max a severe look. "Did you get beaten up along the way? What's with the black eye? Abigail needs to focus. Our last meeting did not go so well. She needs to learn how to listen, how to understand a client's vision. I won't tolerate shoddy work."

Max's sudden rigidity didn't bode well for the small fellow, so Abby stepped forward. "Levi, I'm here to make sure that you come away with the right branding. Let's talk about color."

"Don't schmooze up to me, missy. I gave you a list of colors I like. You chose to use them in the most unsettling of ways. At the end of all this, I may have to find someone else as your work is not up to standard."

Did Max just growl? Abby shot him a look, guiding Levi to a table to hash out the designs.

A long hour later Abby climbed back in the truck.

Max paused before turning the key. "That little prick."

Levi Bakal's digs didn't bother Abby. Her work was of a high standard, her customer base was happy, and repeat business was a primary source of income. "It's all good. Levi's a little uppity, but I can deal with it."

"Screw that. Your work is fucking awesome!" Max swiveled in his seat to face her. "You have a natural talent that's unbelievable. I look at those designs, and I think wow, they're masterful. Any client of yours is lucky to be on your books, and don't get me started on your fine art."

Groping for words, Abby reached out and touched his arm. She strived to be a good artist and earn a decent living, but doubts over her talent would creep in. She lived a lonely life, and aside from Lizzy, her diminutive cheerleader, no one ever offered support. Max would never know how much his kind words meant to her.

"Thank you" was all she could say, staring into those piercing eyes.

A moment melted into two moments and then three. Abby eventually tore her attention away from the intense warrior and fastened her seatbelt.

"You look pretty. I'm sorry I behaved like such a dick earlier. You always look beautiful. I was just tired of seeing that drawn look on your face."

"Apology accepted. I needed a few days to re-center myself. That man—at La Coraggio—really hurt me, knocked me mentally and physically on my ass and then finding out…" Abby stopped and bit her lip.

"Finding out what?"

Shaking her head, Abby shifted away.

"Tell me," Max insisted.

"Finding out that I was back to being alone in my corner. To think that I almost trusted you, I'm just as stupid and naive as I always was."

◊ ◊ ◊

Goddammit, Max thought. Talk about breaking his defective heart. He grasped for something to say.

Staring out the window, Abby saved him from saying something he'd regret. "Let's get moving, otherwise we'll be late for the next meeting."

Wayne Jacobs was a damp mess. Max didn't like the man's ruddy countenance; the man was nervous. They sat in a quiet, little-known coffee shop in an older area of Johannesburg. A far cry from the trendy downtown area that was Mr. Jacob's stomping ground and place of business. Wayne looked around carefully before leaning in. "If Blue Corp finds out I'm here, I'm as good as dead." Max raised his eyebrows and Wayne self-corrected. "Well. More fired than dead. In any case, Miss—"

"Call me Abigail."

"Abigail, I cannot work there for much longer. The CEO is determined to drive me out, and I'll leave on my terms, not his." A sweat droplet dripped onto the table and Max looked away, hiding his aversion to the griping man.

"Mr. Jacobs, I'm not sure how this involves me."

"I'm not creative and I'm also technically challenged. Usually, one of the interns creates the PowerPoints for me, but I'm on my own with this." His voice dropped to a harsh whisper. "I'm starting my own company, and I'll need new materials. I need them done quickly. Everything from letterheads to business cards to presentations and of course, a logo. Could we start with a workbook?"

"What do you have in mind?"

Wayne Jacobs suddenly reached into his pocket. With one deft move, Max dragged Abby's chair back—with her in it—and stepped in between, his hand gripping the gun tucked into the small of his back.

"What the blazes?" Wayne sputtered, and Abby jumped up, trying to shove past.

Max reached behind, holding her to his back, not taking his eyes off Jacob's hand. "Whatever you have in your pocket, I suggest you remove it real slow like. Feel free to take your time."

Wayne gulped as he haltingly removed a USB stick, his hand shaking. "Mister, I'm not sure what you think I was hiding, but you're freaking me out."

Shaking Max off, Abby danced around him as apologies

flowed. "I'm so sorry, Mr. Jacobs. After being mugged a few days ago, my boyfriend is still a little jumpy and sees a boogeyman in every corner."

Max gave the other man a slow once-over, assessing the fit of his clothes and his darting eyes. Wayne quaked in the shadow of his looming form. Max wouldn't sit down. Not yet, not until he had a read on the man. "Hands on the table. Why are you so nervous?"

"Because it looks like you're going to kung-fu chop my head off!"

"No. You've been perspiring, looking visibly ill for the last ten minutes. Why the hell are you so worked up?"

"I told you, I'm sneaking out of the damn office—going behind my boss's back."

Max shook his head. "There's more."

"Oh, for goodness sake." Abby rolled her eyes, sat back down at the table and fired up her laptop. "Ignore him, Mr. Jacobs. Is this the folder you need me to work on?" She pointed at her screen.

Wayne's gaze darted briefly to the screen before shooting back to Max. His wet forehead glistened in the light. There was a slim possibility that the skittish executive could be working for, or coerced into working for, Khalid's network. Drugged food on the table or a hidden sniper and Abby would be wiped from existence. Max barely restrained himself from dragging Abby off like a cave dweller.

Donnie's voice came through his earpiece. "Everything okay, boss?" Slater and Donnie were parked across the street. Max gave a subtle signal for "Hold" that only his team would know.

"Mr. Jacobs, what is this?" Abby asked, frowning. Max leaned to the side and glanced at her screen, before returning his gaze to

Wayne's hands on the table. If he reached for a weapon, it would be the last move he'd make.

"That's the material I need you to work with," Wayne answered, distinctly uncomfortable.

"I'm confused; these materials have the Blue Corp's trademark stamp on them."

"It's not a big deal—change a few words, recreate the layout into a new manual, and at the end of the day you'll be well compensated."

Abby shook her head, removed the USB and closed her laptop. "That's a breach of your contract. You're planning to steal their content, almost word for word. I'm sorry, I can't be a part of that."

"Why the hell not? If you do a great job, I'll use you in the future. Besides, who'd know?" Wayne's face flushed with frustration.

Max relaxed, knowing the little turd's worst crime was infringing on a business agreement and not trying to assassinate a target.

"For starters, I would know. I'm sorry but you're on your own. Having an upstanding reputation in the design industry means everything to me. I refuse to have my name muddied by an illegal transgression. I won't replicate company materials." Abby stood and shouldered her bag. "Good luck to you, I hope you find success in whatever you do."

"You sanctimonious bitch!" A pudgy hand grabbed her wrist with surprising speed. Abby yelped as Max reacted. Wayne opened his mouth to say something and instead squealed in pain. Max bent the jerk's index finger back, causing him to let go of Abby's wrist. And then continued twisting, as Wayne fell to his knees.

"You fucking asshole! You touched her?" Now it was Max's turn to steam in anger. He felt Abby's hand on his arm.

"Stop. It's okay. I'm okay! Please stop."

Max shoved the dimwit away. "Don't contact her again, Wayne. If you think your hand is hurting, wait until you see what I can do with your small dick and your two tiny balls."

Grabbing Abby around the waist and watching their six, Max led her to the car.

Slater made some smart-ass chirp in the comms about the turd, but all Max could think of was calling it a day.

Abby sat quietly on the drive home, probably mad at him. Hell. He was furious at himself. Max Andersen had lost his shit in the field for the first time in his long career. He glared at Abby's profile and felt better blaming it all on her; she pushed all his freaking buttons. Never mind pushed, she hammered away like she was banging away at an old typewriter, that was his brain. Yeah, this was so her fault. Next time, Slater could trail alongside her like a freaking lapdog.

"Thank you," Abby said.

Max felt flummoxed. "What?"

"Thank you for being there. For putting that bully in his place."

"Ah, no problem."

"That was pretty funny... 'Wait until you see what I can do with your small dick and two tiny balls'!" Her husky impersonation of Max's voice had him answering her with a smile.

They stopped at a four-way stop.

Abby rubbed her wrist as she pondered. "I'm half tempted to call Blue Corp and warn the CEO about the little weasel working for him. Could I be that mean?"

Max was only half listening. His rage ran back up to a boil as he eyed her wrist. "He hurt you."

"Relax. This is the wrist I broke in Sharjah. It's sensitive— one wrong twist or squeeze and it gets a little sore. Besides, his hand was too sweaty to get a decent grip, it was only greasy desperation. He wasn't trying to hurt me."

Max frowned at her arm. "When we get home, put some ice on it and take a break, maybe watch a movie."

"Yes, sirree."

Once they were home, workaholic Abigail Evans didn't put her feet up and didn't watch a movie. Instead, she was back behind her desk, racing through design ideas. The rest of the week passed uneventfully. Abby retreated into an industrious shell, catching up on design work. When she wasn't working, much to his team's delight, she cooked and baked up a storm. Max sensed that busy energy was a cover for a deep pool of inner angst. In truth, he felt equally on edge.

Friday saw Max on a secure line with Fort Bragg and Washington, negotiating for most of the day. They revised plans and relayed new information on the mercenary cell that they hunted. The following morning, Max called Slater and Johnny in for a briefing. Donnie and Max had sat up for most of the night. It did little to appease the disquiet running through him. One of his favorite quotes, "theories look great on paper until reality scribbles all over the page," kept playing over in his head.

Donnie ran across the way to keep an eye on Abby as he'd already worked through a separate briefing with Max.

As the other two men rolled through the door, Johnny waved a grocery bag in the air. "I picked up sandwiches for lunch, and I got your gummy worms." He threw a packet at Max. "A pain in the ass to find the all-natural, dye-free shit you eat."

"Natural gelatin is good for the joints," Max said as he tore open the bag.

Slater started in with his wisecracks as he wandered to the fridge to grab a Red Bull. "Arghh boss, you made me leave the happy place…to come to the sad place."

Max raised a brow. Slater shoved the fridge closed with his foot as he continued. "What? Evans's place smells nice. There's a beef stew on the stove, and it has cake. This place? Nothing in the fridge and it smells like FAN."

Max rolled his eyes at Slater's slang for feet, ass, and nuts. "Those are probably your dirty socks stinking up the place, and if I find any of those soggy missiles hiding behind our equipment, I'll stuff them down your throat. Now sit your ass down."

"Don't get your Nordic thunder cock in a wad!" Slater threw himself into a seat with a grin.

Pulling up a chair, Johnny addressed Max. "After the briefing and lunch, I'll stop by Lizzy's. Shift work means that I'm only able to meet her some evenings after she gets out of beauty school. We need a new schedule so she's not left unprotected." Max sensed a fine thread of tension running through his teammate.

"We'll get to that after lunch. First, we're running through the updated intel. An informant came through for us." Max turned to projected images on the wall. "Another Somalian canary came forward, contacting AFRICOM."

"A reliable source?" Johnny asked.

"AFRICOM has used him before. Apparently, Khalid is planning that South African hunting trip. He knows Evans is in country."

This was their one chance to take Khalid out. The Sandpiper

had been holed up in an extremist stronghold in Somalia for months. No allied team could get near him. The entire Southern region was under Khalid's control.

"We get one chance. Khalid won't have his al-Shabaab buddies to cover his ass. We'll go over possible scenarios later. I need you all on point."

Max tapped on a photo of Roman Petrovich, a Ukrainian mafia henchman turned mercenary and a high-value target. "Roman is now second-in-command in Khalid's cell. His predecessor died two days ago in a backwater clinic with cerebral malaria."

"Shit, lucky break for the crazy bastard," Slater said.

Roman was indeed a crazy bastard—rumored to have purposely run over his brother with a truck on one occasion and also to have murdered his wife, mounting her head on a stick for burning his dinner.

Roman ran sex trafficking rings in Eastern Europe, over and above his campaign of violence against innocents in East Africa. He was responsible for setting hospitals alight, blowing up food markets, targeting hotels and destabilizing regions for profit. Roman was now second in charge—that didn't sit well with Max.

Max then switched to an image of Viktor Maslov. "As we know, the Russian has been Khalid's bodyguard for the past five years. That hasn't changed. The man does not exactly blend in, built like a tank. Not just any tank, like a freaking M1-J10 Main Battle Tank. He makes Johnny look like a flea."

Johnny grunted. "Give me five minutes in a ring with the Russian bear, and I'll rip his spleen out."

Max's mouth curved up dangerously. "I didn't say he's better than you, just a bit larger. He shouldn't be hard to spot once they step onto South African soil. Mandla has his canaries on the lookout in every suburb and border-entry points."

After the briefing, Johnny unpacked the ham sandwiches, and Slater grabbed bottled waters from the fridge. Max stared intently at Abby's open file as they sat down to eat.

Slater nudged Max's foot. "I get that you're focusing like a laser-beam, but lunch is up."

"Just checking our profiling," Max said as he ran his hand through his hair and rubbed his neck. His teammate read frustration in the action.

"What's up, maybe we can help?" Johnny asked.

Max tore into a gummy worm and leaned back in the chair. "I can't get a thorough read on her. The majority of the time, I'm on point with building a target's dossier. Finding the core of what makes them tick. But she's an enigma."

Slater spoke carefully. "I've read your profiling and agree with your assessment that she's cool-headed, polished, has tremendous self-control, but there's more to her. That's just her armor."

"Tell me what you mean?"

"Well, for one thing, she has an amusing way of looking at the world. Now and then, a little gem slips out of that pretty mouth."

Max bristled at the 'pretty mouth' comment.

Slater continued, seemingly unaware of Max's annoyance. "You wanna hear my theory on that?"

"Go for it."

Taking a swig of Red Bull, Slater dived in. "All her adult life, Evans has strived for control. But it doesn't come naturally to her. She has to work at it and she's got it down—seamless in executing a serene dance through life. Without that iron fist she believes she'd fall over the edge. I bet she was a very different little girl before her father beat her down. Cheerful, passionate, spirited. Now she's stressed. Her life is being turned upside down again. What does a human do under long-term stress? They revert to their base instincts. The past week, I've seen a new quirkiness beneath that cool exterior."

Johnny piped in. "He's right. I spotted something on the monitors the other day." He propped his feet up on the opposite chair, getting comfortable. "Evans polished the furniture in the living room. I suddenly hear a shriek, and she jumps back in full geek-out mode. I can't find the threat."

Max leaned forward, listening intently.

"Then I see her staring with wide eyes at the television, but it's switched off, so I zoom the camera in, and I see an insect sitting on a shelf. Evans starts speaking to it and says, 'Hey, Mr. Mantis. You gave me a fright; I thought you were a grasshopper. What ya doing, buddy?' So I zoom in a little more, it's a praying mantis, just chilling. Then she cracks a joke. 'It's a nice day outside, bug man, why don't you go out and pray?' She slowly grabs one of her sketch pads from the shelf and tears off a sheet of paper and says, 'Now I'm still working through my fear of spindly legs, so be patient while I rescue your skinny ass. Don't you dare fly at me, else I'll be a blubbery mess.' It took her five full minutes to get him out to a leafy bush near her patio." Johnny started grinning. "And get this, her parting shot to the mantis before walking back inside was, 'Don't lose your head, little buddy. Safe sex means wearing a helmet.'"

Max was taking a sip and almost sprayed water over the table, grabbing a napkin as he guffawed with laughter. Johnny smirked in response.

Slater looked around in confusion. "I don't get it?"

Still chuckling, Max replied, "The king of one-liners doesn't get it! Dude, the male praying mantis loses his head after mating! The female eats it."

Max finished the rest of the meal in amused silence as the other men chattered about their new interest in rugby and how it differed to American football. He was just about to stand when Slater took him unawares.

"I studied Abby's medical records last night. Fucking brutal." Intensity rolled off Slater.

Where was he heading with this? "I agree. And?"

"There may be similarities between Nasari and Evans, but they are not the same woman."

Max gathered the sandwich wrappers. "We're not doing this right now."

"I'm just saying; I know you're drawing parallels. Hell, we all are. After Sully's death, it's natural to be overly cautious."

Max sighed. "And your point is?"

"Sharon Nasari came to us with bruising and lashes. As we now know, it was all for show, to set us up. Abigail Evans, on the other hand, the sheer brutality of her attack is off the charts. Extensive internal damage. It was solely about teaching her a lesson that she would never walk away from."

Johnny interjected, "I agree, but what if Khalid broke Evans, threatening retribution if she didn't join him?"

Slater nodded. "It's a possibility. The timeline is off though. Khalid assaulted Evans around the same time as the Black Friday bombing. Sharon Nasari had little detail on Sully's unit. Her cell assumed we were FBI, and after the attack none of our names were leaked. Khalid doesn't know about MIT2, thinking that just the CIA is after him. MIT2 is currently invisible. He'd first need to know his enemy to plant Evans as a lure. On the off chance that he waited this long to ambush us, it's not in his character. Khalid has never been all that careful and is becoming increasingly arrogant. It's just a matter of time before his luck runs out."

"Besides, after Nasari, we won't get caught again," Johnny said.

"Won't we?" Max asked. He enjoyed his team's interplay, getting their perspective on the mission.

"Even if Khalid knew of the existence of our team, he doesn't know what type of men we are. Name how many operators you know who wouldn't give a fuck about her injuries and just see Evans as a means to an end."

"Aren't we doing the same thing?" Max asked.

"Nope, protecting our asset is just as vital as catching Khalid," Slater stated emphatically.

Max nodded. "Good to know we're on the same page. Fort Bragg gave the go-ahead to keeping her in place until Khalid lands on South African soil. I'll continue with the boyfriend ruse. Abby is seeing two clients next week, shopping for art supplies and returning to swimming sessions. Lizzy's birthday barbecue is being held next Sunday at her family home."

Max stared at the whiteboard. They still had zero intel on the attack in the parking lot at La Coraggio.

He tapped Johnny on the shoulder as he rose. "Time to build a roster that includes Lizzy's protection detail. You're going to be one tired mother. You'll be balancing your focus between both Lizzy's and Abby's detail."

Johnny nodded. "Fine by me, casualties of this war won't be happening on my watch. Let's hammer out the details."

Chapter Twelve

Later that afternoon, Max got some shut-eye and had just awoken and was doing push-ups alongside the bed when Donnie poked his head in. "Yo, Batman, as nice as it is to ogle your ripped, bare-naked chest before dinner, I have some news."

Max gave Donnie a rude sign as he bounced up and grabbed a shirt. "A man takes one small nap in twenty-four hours and this is what he gets? What do you have?"

"Omar Salib," Donnie answered with a grin.

"What about him?"

"He's landing in Johannesburg early tomorrow morning. He has a connecting flight to Mogadishu later in the afternoon."

"Great. What's his ETA?"

"0600 hours."

"Excellent. Let's roll out the welcoming mat."

◊ ◊ ◊

This was her cleaning day. Thanks to a combination of anxiety and claustrophobia, Abby took spring cleaning to the next level, deciding to scrub and organize all the kitchen cabinets at eight in the morning. Abby stacked the last of the pans and hefted them into the pot cupboard just before lunch. The next target was the living room. Polish in hand, Abby attacked the coffee table when she heard men at the door.

Max stood to the side, and the man who stood beside him made her blood run cold. He was backlit by morning light but…was Khalid standing at her door? Were these men working with Khalid? Was it all a big lie? A sick game? Abby staggered back. Strong hands grabbed for her as the world spun.

Loud cursing broke through her fuzz. "Head…between legs… Sit her down. Breathe. Abs, breathe." Max's voice cut through the haze.

She felt his fingers at the back of her neck as he pushed her head down. "Kha…Khalid."

"No, honey. I'm so sorry. I should've done this right. It's not Khalid. It's a friend of mine, a work colleague. His name is Omar, he works for the US Government."

Abby felt almost afraid to look up. She trembled like a damn coward.

"Deep breaths, Abs. You've got this."

No. She didn't have this. She didn't have any of this. Her life was a shambled junkyard of pain and shame. She had never felt as helpless as in that moment. Tears leaked as she pulled herself back from madness. After a moment of snuffled breathing, Abby raised her head slowly. For the second time in a matter of days, her cheeks flushed with embarrassment.

The man sitting cautiously on the edge of the chair was as tall as Khalid with a similar build. He had the same smooth, honeyed skin. His haircut resembled the terrorist's stylish cut, but that was where the similarities ended. His face was different. Not as sterile. His nose flatter and his lips fuller. More importantly, his eyes reflected genuine concern.

"You're not him. I'm sorry. I feel so foolish."

He smiled kindly. "Nothing to be sorry for. I do look a little like Khalid. We come from the same town. I'm a distant cousin, but that is where it ends. I've been hunting him for a long time."

He had an American accent with a slight trace of Arabic. Taking a deep breath, Abby stood on quaking legs. Max's hand was at her back.

Extending her hand, Abby said firmly. "Let's try this again. Abigail Evans."

"Omar Salib. It's an honor to meet you."

Max cut in. "Omar has worked with our government for just over twelve years. We've worked together on a few missions for the last six. He's also a good family friend. I trust him with my life. I stayed over with his family on my last vacation. His wife, Aisha, should be on *Masterchef*, her food is that good!"

"Where are my manners? Would you like something to drink, Omar?"

"I'm good. I won't be staying too long. I have a connecting flight to catch."

"No, I insist. How about joining me for at least a cupcake? I baked chocolate caramel."

"Bud, they're incredible. I've had three this morning already," Slater encouraged.

Omar shrugged. "Sure. If they're that good."

Max glared. "Three, bro? Really? You're getting as bad as Johnny! I leave you alone for two seconds."

"And how many have you had, you Finnish bastard? I saw you stuffing your face earlier!"

As the two bantered, Abby quickly plated two cupcakes, one for Omar and one for herself—needing the sugar to calm the jitters. She then grabbed an icy glass from the freezer and poured him a chilled glass of milk. By the time she sat back down, she felt a little more human. Omar grunted with pleasure as he bit down into the thickly frosted cake with a gooey center.

"You're a good baker, Miss Evans! I would say better than Aisha, but she would kill me if she ever found out."

"Thank you and please call me Abby. Do you have any kids, Omar?"

"Three little rascals. All under the age of eight. The youngest is still in diapers, so it makes for a lively house."

"Sounds like a happy home." Abby smiled. The love Omar had for his family was clear to see.

"It is. I'll miss them. I'm gone for two months."

"That's tough." Abby smiled wistfully. "Bet they'll grow like beanstalks when you're gone."

"True. I'll make it up to them with lots of gifts. Gifts and tight hugs are the secret to homecomings." Omar regarded her mildly. "Abigail, I'm sorry to do this, but I need to go over your story with you. I bring a different perspective. There may be something that we've missed. A puzzle piece for finding Khalid. We're always adding to the image that makes up the man. Trying to get to the core of what makes him tick."

Abby played awkwardly with the empty cupcake baking cup, refusing to make eye contact.

Adding to his plea, Omar elaborated, "I never personally knew Khalid growing up, but I knew of his family. His parents are extremely wealthy. Wonderful pillars of their community. Khalid has brought shame upon them with his hatred and greed. His father disowned their son, but it hasn't stopped the destruction wielded by Khalid on our villages back home." Omar sat back, his face drawn with sadness. "He recruited soldiers from our community. Teenagers seeking instant fame. His actions tore apart families. It destroyed mine. When the elders stood up to him, his mercenaries planted a car bomb in the town square. My brother and uncle died that day."

"I'm so sorry." Abby leaned forward and grasped his hand.

"Thank you. I was eighteen at the time and vowed to seek revenge on the Sandpiper. He wasn't much older—Khalid started killing at a young age. My father is a well-known, outspoken civil rights activist who fights for regime change. When his family's life was threatened, we were offered asylum in the States. I now fight alongside my father against tyranny. He writes books, I use laws and guns. Help us catch the man who's haunted both of our dreams. Both yours and mine."

Max squeezed her arm. "We can give you space, Abby. Slater and I will just be outside if you need us."

She still didn't answer.

"If you prefer me to stay…"

"I have a feeling I'm going to be telling it too many times, before that chapter of my life is closed."

"It is what it is," Max replied.

Abby finally looked up into his serious gaze. "I know. I'm just so worn out and drained and angry and frustrated. God, I'm so frustrated."

Abby placed the plate on the coffee table with calculated gentleness before placing her head in her hands.

"Fine," she mumbled, "let's just get this over with." Raising her head, she rallied. "I can do this on my own. Max, make yourselves useful out on the patio and tidy up a little, please. Between John's giant ass shoes scattered in the way and Slater's dirty plates on the outside table—well, it's driving me up the wall. Oh, if you could also water my pot plants while you're at it."

With competent economy, Max grabbed cleaning supplies

from under her sink, closed the door on them and got to work. Abby noticed him keeping a close eye through the glass, as she ran through that black night in Sharjah.

Omar asked many questions. He was kind and patient. Bone-deep exhaustion was all she felt by the end of her narrative. It was easier to talk the second time around, and she felt a little better for it.

Yet after saying her goodbyes, Abby excused herself to take a long shower and to gather herself. She had a mission to complete, one that didn't include the special ops team squatting in her sacred space.

◊ ◊ ◊

Omar sat with Max and Donnie before his trip back to the airport. Max appreciated his spook colleague's assistance on what was turning out to be a labyrinthine reconnaissance mission. Max trusted Omar both in and out of the field.

"She's hiding something." Omar stared unseeingly at the wall as he sorted through his thoughts.

Max didn't like the sound of that.

"But I don't think she's working for Khalid. No one is that good an actress in telling that story. It's personal though. Something happened that night that she's hiding."

"Do you think that's the reason Khalid is searching for her?"

"I think that's exactly the reason. Whatever she has on him will compromise his operations. If it was just about her escaping, yes, Khalid would want to get his hands on Miss Evans, but after three years? It's a little farfetched. Even for a man with a giant ego." Omar stood. "I'll send you a report once I get to Kenya. Max, I'm always available to come and see you if need be."

"I appreciate the offer, I have this handled."

"I know. I have a bad feeling about this op. Be careful, my friend," Omar said.

"I will. *Wadāʿan.*"

"*Maʿa al-salāmah*, I'll keep in touch."

They chatted in full Arabic before they said their final goodbyes. Donnie and Omar slipped quietly out of the door. Max stared down at the monitor. Abby sat on the edge of her bed, combing the knots carefully from her wet hair. She was a tough nut to crack but he'd broken tougher. Max just hoped that their mission didn't go FUBAR before he drilled through that pretty outer shell.

And…yes…his thoughts had taken an uncomfortable turn. He needed to think about anything else than drilling into Abby. Drilling into her with his… Goddammit. It was now Max's turn for a shower. An arctic shower. He yelled for Johnny to take point as he grabbed a towel.

Chapter Thirteen

The rest of the week passed by uneventfully. If they didn't go to blondie's birthday barbecue, it might raise suspicions. Lizzy was Abby's closest friend. Abby would naturally go about her routine, at least until they had a handle on the threat. She was their only link.

Eleven in the morning and the sun was already baking hot. Max dressed casually in faded jeans and a white T-shirt. While waiting for Abby to emerge from her bedroom, he ambled down the passage and paused at her studio. The woman was talented. A new canvas featuring a charging African elephant sat on the easel. The rough sketch already captured the movement and power of the giant mammal. Throughout the busy week, Abby had still made time for her art. Sandals clicked as Abby walked towards him.

"What do you think?"

Abby's deep blue dress blew his socks off, complementing her warm chocolate hair and tanned skin. She'd paired it with tan sandals and a matching belt. The dress flowed casually to the floor and clung in all the right places. The gentle dip of her cleavage peeking through had him working up a sweat.

"Killer dress," he said gruffly.

"I mean about the artwork."

Max looked at her blankly.

"You were looking at my new canvas?"

"Um. It's good. Amazing. You have bucket loads of talent."

"I don't need to be pandered to. I won't be able to improve if people aren't honest with me."

Max leaned towards her, taking in her comforting scent. "Do I look like someone who panders? If I didn't like it, I'd tell you."

Abby nibbled her lip. Did she know what that simple action did to a man? This assignment was hell. Max pushed away from the wall. "Let's go, Abby, we're going to be late."

◊ ◊ ◊

"It's as hot as fucking balls," Max muttered.

"Hot and dry, baby. Just pretend you're in your sauna back home," Johnny said before sauntering away. The men never got tired of the Finnish jokes.

"Screw you, Big Bird!" Max poured a Sprite, loading it with ice.

Lizzy's backyard was a hive of activity; South Africans sure knew how to throw a party. Endless amounts of meats sizzled on the grill, tables overflowed with salads, and the beers were flowing. Max eventually lost track of all the family members. Each person was just as crazy as the last, and it was clear where Lizzy got her energetic nature from. Roars of laughter and good-natured ribbing filled the yard. Lizzy raced past, giggling as one of her crazy cousins threatened to push her into the pool.

She'd merged her eighties vintage vibe seamlessly with current fashion trends, in fitted jeans with a neon-pink belt matched with a striped white-and-pink tank top. Converse sneakers and chunky bracelets finished the look. Her blonde hair was blown out into a fluffy hairdo. Max kept a close eye on the girls as he stood with the men around the grill.

Abby stood amongst the chaos like a beacon in foggy seas. She smiled sweetly at one of Lizzy's jokes. It pleased him that she was relaxing among her friends. She deserved every ounce of joy after all the misery she'd suffered, first at the hands of her father and then that bastard monster, Khalid.

Max couldn't resist walking over and placing a hand on her waist. They were supposed to be newly dating—that was their cover story and he took every opportunity to drive that home. Not that it was a hardship—if anything it felt natural to slide his hand into hers or to stroke her back—it felt too darn good.

Abby ran her fingers up and down his spine as she chatted to Lizzy's mother. Shit, if she kept that up he'd be sporting a giant boner and waving it in her friend's mom's face. What were they freaking talking about anyway? Rose pruning? Oh hell no. That was a sign to excuse himself. Max almost ran back to the grill.

◊ ◊ ◊

The afternoon passed quickly. Good food and good company, however, Abby's focus should be on the endgame, and Max and his team weren't coming along for the ride. Her heart thumped sluggishly. As soon as she had an opening, she'd give them the slip. Josephine Abigail Evans had work to complete.

Abby wandered over to the bar, and Max stepped up, entwining his fingers with hers. Even though this was all an act, she'd gotten used his steady presence and his heavenly touch, but that was a dangerous step towards a place Abby couldn't afford to go.

Max spoke quietly. "Donnie says there's a suspicious car driving around your apartment block. I need to talk to him while

I check the perimeter on this end. Johnny is wrapping up; we'll need to leave soon."

Max moved off into the crowd. John stood at the far end of the yard chatting with Lizzy's father. Abby headed inside towards the bathroom before swinging off into one of the guest bedrooms. Lizzy's house was quiet; all the guests were enjoying the warm weather. She opened a bedside drawer.

Please let it be here. Her hand ran along the back of the drawer, and her relief was immediate. Abby pulled out a disposable phone and switched it on. Her neck felt damp with perspiration as she dialed the memorized number. She moved around to stare out the window. John glanced towards the house, and it wouldn't be long before he came looking for her.

"Shit," she whispered. "Please answer, answer, answer..."

Her contact picked up, and the relief was so huge that she stumbled back on shaky legs.

"Abigail?"

"Is the line secure?"

"Affirmative."

"How are things?" Abby asked.

"Good. We miss you."

"How is he?"

"He wants to see you."

Squeezing her eyes shut, Abby took a deep breath. "It's just a matter of time. God, I miss him so much. I love him so damn much. I so badly want to talk to him, but there are others involved. An American special ops team is watching my every move. I think they're working with the CIA and are talking about sending me to a spook facility. They're after Khalid, and if they get in my way, it changes everything. Plans will be destroyed."

"Oh, Jesus. Are we adjusting our strategy?"

"That's a negative, at least for now, although I'm thinking of disappearing," Abby replied.

"Are you safe? Have they hurt you?" her contact asked.

"For now, I'm as safe as I can be, but I have to go." Abby swallowed hard. "Tell him I love him."

"I will. Abigail, please be safe."

Abby hung up. The phone blurred as tears brimmed.

"You're one cold fucking bitch," Max said from the door.

Oh, God. Before she could turn, he had her wrist in a vise-like grip. Abby tried to twist away, and Max shoved her against the wall. The impact knocked the wind out of her, as his powerful forearm pinned her across the chest. Max grabbed her hair and pushed her head back against the wall. Not exactly hurting her, but she couldn't stop the overwhelming panic. She gasped for breath, staring into glacial eyes.

His body vibrated as he snarled at her. "Stay still. Think about twitching, and I'll end you."

She believed him. His loyalty lay with his country and his men; she was now branded as a traitor and a terrorist.

"Max—"

"Shut it."

"Let me explain."

"Fuck you and your pretty-faced lies." Max shoved his arm between them and wrenched the phone away, tossing it on the bed. His knees pushed her legs apart, and he traced his hand over her body, probably looking for hidden listening devices or weapons.

Her dress draped to the floor and Max worked around the pooling material. Like she could hide an arsenal under her flimsy dress.

"This is crazy."

Max shoved his face into hers. "Shut the hell up."

Still pinning her with his forearm across her chest, he tapped his ear with his other hand. "We've been compromised. Third bedroom down the hall. Now. We're moving out. Slater, we need pickup."

"Max, stop."

He skewered her with a vicious glare. "I'll find you a new buddy to chat with at Gitmo. I'm not interested in anything you have to say, ma'am."

He called her *ma'am. Ouch.*

John slid into the room. "What the fuck?"

"Miss Evans here decided to have a chat with her terrorist buddies, on that." Max nodded to the burner phone on the bed. "Pity that I happened to hear the whole thing. Right, sweetheart? Bag the phone and let's move."

Animosity rolled off John. "Don't draw attention to yourself; it won't end well for your little friends or be conducive to your physical well-being."

Max anchored her to his waist and walked out to the garden. Abby felt John's gun pressed into her back.

Her friend bounced up, and Max stepped forward. "Abby just had a fainting episode. It has to be the heat; we're taking her home."

Lizzy gasped. "Honey, you look as white as a sheet. You could rest on my bed for a little while." Abby reached out; John nudged her in the back.

"I'd feel better at my place. Besides, I might pop into the emergency room if this dizziness continues."

John turned to Lizzy. "Sweetheart, I'll go along just in case Max needs help."

Lizzy fussed worriedly, her bracelets jangling as she stroked Abby's hair. Max shifted.

"Take it easy and enjoy the rest of your birthday, I'll call you later."

Lizzy nodded at Abby's words, tried to give her a delicate hug, and Max pulled Abby away. In under a minute she was sandwiched between Max and John in the back of a black sedan.

"Please let me explain."

"Not a word," John growled.

Abby ignored him and focused on Max. "Five minutes is all I need."

Max's tightly strained voice indicated his struggle to remain calm. "Five minutes will get my team killed. I told you to shut your traitorous mouth."

"They're in no danger, I swear."

"You sold us out to your Sandpiper buddy."

"No. I didn't."

"Khalid roughed you up, to provide the cover for your new life in South Africa. Am I right? In case you're questioned then your sob story stands up. Are you Khalid's little fling on the side?" Max used a girly voice as he air quoted sarcastically, "'How is he? I love him. I miss him. If they get their way, plans will be destroyed.'"

Max then turned in the seat, his face so close that she could see the dark rims encircling those pale irises. "What. The. Fuck. Was. That? You're his little whore, aren't you, Evans?" Abby flinched. *How to kick a girl when she's down.*

Max ran on, his face flushed with rage. "It's time to move out. Let's hope you survive the experience, and your militant friends don't decide to take you out. Your mission is shot to shit. I'll have the truth from you tonight, and let's just say you're not going to like my interrogation techniques."

◊ ◊ ◊

He knew he was losing his shit and he didn't give a flying fuck. Cool as ice Max was now a raving lunatic.

Her reaction wasn't what he expected; she looked at him as if he was daft before shrugging. "You men are all like amped-up rabbits bouncing all over the place; I can't talk to you while you're like this. Where are we going?"

Max glared at her as options raced through his head. He trusted his profiling. If he gave Evans the benefit of the doubt, it could get them all killed.

"Fuck!" Max swore loudly, she jumped, and the two men in the vehicle shot him a worried glance. "Pull over, Slater." He turned to her. "Five minutes and if I don't buy your bullshit cockamamie story then you're done. Understand that?"

"Yes," she replied softly.

"I'll erase you from existence like a dirty smudge if you pose a threat to my team."

"I understand. I screwed up, but I'm not working with any extremists."

Max stared at her a second longer and glanced out the window. "Slater, find the closest secure spot, no boxing in and no audience."

"Sir."

"And make sure we're not being followed."

"Always do." Slater deftly maneuvered into traffic.

The last time Max lost it this badly was when his team had been blown to shreds in the mall bombing. He was always cool and in control in the field, and that was why he was assigned the team leader position. Evans snatched away that control, and he didn't like the feeling.

Tension fogged up the vehicle, making it hard to breathe. The wounded look plastered on her pretty face when he'd manhandled her in that bedroom probably meant she'd had a flashback to the attack at La Coraggio. Max also had a freaking flashback. When frisking her, running his hands over her firm buttocks, his flashback had been of her wet naked body orgasming in the shower, and that angered him.

Screw her; this was her own doing. She gently clasped her hands in her lap. Red marks marred her right wrist, marks he'd put there. Slight tremors ran through her, rippling up the side of his arm.

Guilt weighed heavily. Guilt that he couldn't save anyone. Not Sully, not Mike, none of the victims in the mall attack, not Abigail Evans from herself and, God help him, he couldn't save himself from getting sucked into this mess and dragging his team along with him.

Max glanced at her wrist for the second time. Looking down, Abby saw the red swelling that throbbed in time with her racing heart. Minutes passed as she stared at her still hands, her heart suddenly feeling lighter than it had in years. Max truly cared; the driving force behind this formidable man wedging her into her seat was honor.

Abby had never been this close to someone this fine before. And what she meant by "fine" was a person who displayed integrity, bravery and most of all loyalty to those who deserved it. Stomping all over the scrap of trust he'd bestowed meant that he probably would never believe her, but Abby knew that she could trust him. She'd known it from that first night when he'd comforted her on a cold floor, she was just too stubborn to accept help.

Abby was done with all the secrets, her plans were shot to hell, and she needed expert help. Max stiffened as she touched his leg. That look of contempt would've shriveled most humans. "I'm not hurt."

"What?"

"My wrist is not that sore."

Slater sniggered up front.

"I don't give a shit. If you were carrying a weapon, I would've broken your twiggy arm in a heartbeat." He clicked his fingers.

Damn, he was pretty scary when he was mad; she'd literally almost peed herself. He'd do nicely as her right-hand man.

The setting sun bathed the quiet industrial park in golden light. Sunday evening meant the place was deserted. Slater chose a business under construction, just a shell of a building which hadn't yet had electronic gates installed. There were two exits, one at the front and one around the rear for deliveries. Slater parked around the side of the building near concrete stairs that accessed a side entrance, and Max ordered Abby to sit on them.

Slater remained in the car with the engine running while Max and Johnny took charge of the interrogation.

The industrial park sat on a hill, and the setting sun silhouetted the two men. Both men striking in their own way, John, a colossal mass of muscle and Max, all sinewy strength vibrating with silent energy. His keen eyes seemed calm, but Abby knew better.

Max rubbed a hand over his mouth before folding his arms. A quick scan of the perimeter and he then focused all his attention on her. "Your five minutes has already begun."

She wouldn't rush, this was too important. Bowing her head, she expected Max to push, but instead he waited. John turned his back and kept watch. A small stone bit through the coolness of the concrete and she flicked it out from underneath her awkward seat.

"I told the truth about that night."

"Did you?" Max sneered.

"I never lied about anything, but I left one important thing out. Where do I begin?" Abby rubbed her eyes.

"At the part where you do a good job of convincing us that you're not a traitor to your country." Max looked skeptical.

◊ ◊ ◊

"I left out some details of the physical damage done to me that night and the challenges I'd face."

He'd thought long and hard about that; it was a miracle that she could function at all, yet here she was holding down a job and trying to live a healthy life. Brave. At least that's what he'd thought until she snuck a phone call on a damn burner...

"The clinic in Dubai took evidence photos, did a rape kit, started me on antivirals and gave me the morning-after pill."

Max's stomach always churned with anger when he saw what men on this earth were capable of. He'd come across many atrocities on women during his SF days. Villages raped and pillaged, women mutilated and left to die. They'd rescued girls along the way, but the dead look in their eyes would haunt Max for the rest of his days.

She forged on in a robotic voice. "A security officer stayed by my side the whole time. She held my hand and told me everything would be okay. Her name was Noleen; she was a trained bodyguard assigned to protect any South African dignitaries visiting the UAE. She volunteered to accompany me on the flight to Johannesburg. Noleen and I just clicked, we had this intense connection. She felt like the sister I never had, and I told her things I never told anyone. About that night. About my childhood."

She swallowed back tears. "Noleen listened and made it her priority to protect me."

Max didn't know where this was leading and kept silent. She seemed so lost sitting on the stairs in her pretty dress as the sharp wind blew up wisps of hair. He fought the outrageous urge to sit down next to her and drag those silken tresses off her face. As if hearing him, her hand came up and swiped at the loose strands, tucking them behind a delicate ear.

"I chose to stay in Cape Town for my recovery and rented a beach house from one of Noleen's friends, using a different name. Those were my darkest days, sleeping mostly or sitting on the beach staring at the ocean. One hot day I remember getting horribly sunburned and not even caring, instead welcoming the pain. I didn't bother with my healing wrist and missed doctors' appointments. I wanted to die."

Max would give anything to rip Khalid's throat out. *Savage bastard.*

"Six weeks in and I woke up one warm afternoon needing to use the bathroom but had no energy to move. I'd slept for over fourteen hours. I knew I was depressed but thought abstractly that I was unusually tired. A medical check-up was scheduled for later that afternoon, and I mentioned the lethargy to the doctor. He asked me some interesting questions." Abby looked directly at Max, a distant emotion littering her eyes. "I'd missed my menstrual cycle, and in my emotional state hadn't taken note."

Max took a second for that to sink in and couldn't stop himself from reeling back. What a fuckup.

"God, Abby." What this woman had gone through.

She spelled it out for him. "I was eight weeks pregnant."

Max stood rigidly, contemplating the new scenarios that came into play, fitting the pieces of the puzzle together.

"'Tell him I love him.' That's what you said on the phone. You weren't talking about Khalid or any other man; you were talking about a child. Khalid has a son."

Abby's broken demeanor changed in a heartbeat. "He's *my* son," she spat at him with blazing eyes. "Not Khalid's. Mine! You hear me? Gabe is *mine!*"

"Ab's."

Wrapping arms around herself, Abby unconsciously rocked on the stairs. Unheeded tears rolled down her cheeks. "If you take the morning-after pill within 24 hours, it is about 95% effective. I guess I fell into that five percent bracket. The doctors and my counselor kept saying that it would probably be wise to abort the baby early on, it would be easier for me, for the healing process. That I didn't need to go a day longer like that." She sobbed. "What they meant was a day longer with a monster's spawn growing inside me."

Max stepped forward, and Abby raised her hands. "I thought there was something wrong with me because I considered keeping the baby. I swung between abortion, adoption and the horror of keeping a child who might grow up to look just like Khalid. I had crazy thoughts of walking off a cliff and ending it all."

Ah shit. Max lowered himself gently at the other end of the step.

"Noleen came home for her annual leave and came to visit. I broke down and told her everything. She took me back to her apartment that night, fed me a home-cooked meal and tucked me in. Told me I could only make a decision when I felt well enough. We took long walks, swam in the ocean, and she dragged me to the cinema. Noleen saved me from myself; I felt more human than I had in months. We spoke about the fact that the baby was developing into a unique person who'd be defined as being more than just bloodlines."

Abby played with a piece of gravel as she spoke. "I thought about my father, how his character has never defined who I am. I've succeeded in spite of it."

She was right.

"Noleen said something to me one day. 'Sometimes when you're in a dark place, you think you've been buried, but you've actually been planted.' She'd read it somewhere and liked the quote. That little seed developing inside was my saving grace." Abby etched a flower on the step with the gravel stone. "The moment my life changed was at the first ultrasound. I heard his little heartbeat and heard the sound of innocence." She glowed as she talked of her subsequent visits and of feeling him move for the first time, and Max saw how love could transform a pretty woman into a breathtaking vision of radiance.

"When my baby boy was born, Noleen organized home birthing to stay off Khalid's radar."

"What's his name?" Johnny asked.

"Gabriel. Named after the archangel. He's my angel; he saved us both." Her sweet smile floored Max; her lashes still damp with tears, she was the fallen angel. Her face bathed in golden light made Max's heart turn over in awe.

Suddenly growing serious, Abby grabbed his hand. "I have proof. I buried it in the yard. Birth certificates, ultrasound pictures, photographs. I couldn't risk keeping them in the house."

"Where is he?" Max asked.

"When did you start watching me?"

He raised an eyebrow and kept silent.

"For goodness sake, it couldn't have been longer than five months ago because I had Gabe with me in March."

"We started surveillance in June."

"Once Gabe was born, I knew I had to get on with my life. He was growing up quickly into an energetic toddler. The design work lay up in Johannesburg, and I knew I could earn more money in a bigger city. I moved here around Christmas. I already had an apartment, which I'd bought as an investment while living in Dubai. I tried to keep to myself but one morning in late February, I ate breakfast at a cozy little coffee shop in Edengate Mall while Gabe slept in the pram. The waiter brought the bill, and when I opened it up, a napkin fell out with a warning written in red." She paled as she recalled that fateful day.

Max angled towards her. "What did it say?" Had Khalid reestablished a connection? Was this the comms they'd missed?

"'He knows. Run.'"

"What?"

"The note just said 'He knows. Run.' I knew what it meant. Khalid knew about Gabe, someone was warning me."

"You don't know that," Johnny chimed in.

"I do. Because if Khalid had found us I would've been dead, and Gabe would be with his father. Khalid desperately wants a son to continue his legacy."

She had a point.

"That night, I sent Gabe to a safe place. The worst moment of my life was saying goodbye to my baby. He was nineteen months at the time and very much aware of what was happening, but I knew I wouldn't be able to hide forever, Khalid would eventually track me down, and I've been preparing for that confrontation ever since." Her body stiffened with determination. "If Khalid gets his hands on Gabriel, he'll raise an extremist soldier, the heir to his evil legacy. Gabe will become like his father. He has to be protected at all costs."

Max cupped her shoulders. "Khalid is a powerful man. You cannot hide Gabriel forever."

"He's with Noleen at a safe house. Gabe knows her, she's his godmother and will defend him with her life. The call I made was to Noleen."

"People can be coerced into saying anything. For all you know, Noleen had a gun to her head."

Abby blanched. "We have code words. She would've said something."

Max leaned back on his elbows. "How often do you communicate?"

"This was the first time."

Johnny grunted.

"I wouldn't risk Gabe's safety. I even missed his second birthday." She rested her face in her hands. "It's been seven months since I've seen Gabe. He hasn't seen or heard from his mommy since the day Noleen took him out of my arms."

"You used a burner phone. Where did you get it from?" Max asked.

Abby raised her head and pursed her lips stubbornly.

"Abby, this isn't a game."

She answered reluctantly. "It was placed in the drawer next to the bed."

"Who put it there?"

"Max—"

"Who put it there?"

"Lizzy," she said glumly.

Johnny surged forward. "She's helping you? She knows about Khalid?"

"Kind of…"

Johnny looked keyed up. "What the hell does that mean? She either does or doesn't."

"Lizzy thinks I'm running from an abusive ex-boyfriend. Given how we met, I told her a half-truth."

Now fully invested in the conversation, Johnny knelt on the step, giving her his full attention. "How did you meet?" he asked carefully.

Abby looked directly at Johnny, smiling slightly. "My dear Lizzy never told you, fancy that."

"Lizzy said she'd met you at an art class."

"Well, well. My little friend is more guarded than I thought." Abby grinned. "Your charming interrogation tactics not working for you, buddy?"

The jibe hit home. "Tell me how you met?" The words came out of gritted teeth.

The sky bathed in reds and golds drew her gaze. "When I moved to Johannesburg, I battled to sleep, with recurring nightmares and all. I found a private support group for female victims of violent crimes. We met twice a month."

Johnny quickly stood up, shoving a finger in her face. "You're telling me that Lizzy was part of that kind of support group? Bullshit. Her background check doesn't include any records indicating abuse."

"Easy, bro." Max frowned at Johnny.

"Her father is a wealthy man and has connections. After the trial, he made sure the legal evidence was sealed up. He wanted his daughter to have a fresh start without it following her through life. I guess Lizzy isn't as open as you'd like to think, huh? Maybe lying to her about who you are isn't the best strategy."

"What trial? There's no evidence of trauma, Lizzy is a ray of freaking sunshine and bounces from place to place like a happy Care Bear. She's a goddamn angel."

"It's her story to tell, and you don't deserve to know it, but yes, Lizzy is an angel. An angel who had an abusive boyfriend who choked her and shoved a gun in her face when she tried to leave his evil ass. She'll move heaven and earth to help me out, but that doesn't mean Lizzy deserves any of this. Your deception and lies will destroy her, and she's barely started living again. So screw you, John. Screw you all." Abby turned to face the wall.

"Some abusive fucker tried to kill her? Fuck." Swallowing hard, Johnny turned and walked a small distance away. Max stared at his brother-in-arms. This was getting messy at a rapid rate; Johnny obviously cared more for Lizzy than he was letting on. They were in the damn *Twilight Zone*.

Shifting his attention back to Abby, Max asked, "Is that the only method of contacting Noleen? The disposable phone you've used?"

Abby shook her head. "There's a second phone in Lizzy's spare room, hidden under the mattress. Noleen has both numbers listed. If I call her from any other number, she won't answer."

"Why keep them at Lizzy's place?" Max asked.

"In case Khalid breaks into my house or captures me, I don't want him finding the phones or tracing the calls. I'm just using them to check in."

"Your plan is full of holes. Noleen would have no idea if you were found or killed by Khalid. She'd have little warning."

"She wouldn't need a warning. Khalid would never find them," Abby vowed.

"You believe that? That you wouldn't break under torture?"

"I would never give up my baby. I'd die first."

Max shook his head. "Torture is an ugly game—once the pain gets too much, family turns on family. Terrorists are experts at inflicting pain."

"I'm a mother; I'd die a thousand times over for my son."

"I won't allow it to come to that. Does Gabe carry your last name?"

"Noleen pulled some strings when he was born. We used my grandmother's name. Capello. Gabriel Capello."

Max smirked. "Appropriate."

"What do you mean?"

"Capello means 'Cloak or Cape.' Since you're cloaking Gabe from the world. Well, it's kind of appropriate."

Abby looked at Max blankly and then started giggling. "Well, aren't you a fountain of knowledge." Her sweet laugh caught him unawares; Max smiled and massaged his temples.

"Johnny, did you catch all that?" Max asked.

"Yeah."

"Communicate with the rest of the team. Tell Donnie to retrieve the evidence. Abby, where did you hide it?"

She sighed. "Under the small birdbath at the back of the yard next to the outside water tap. Safe from Khalid if ever any of his men came snooping. The less he knows about my son, the better."

"What will Donnie find when he starts digging?"

"A toolbox covered in plastic wrap. Inside, three waterproof layers encase a large envelope."

"Is the toolbox locked?" Johnny asked.

"With a small padlock."

Johnny moved off, and they waited in silence. Max stood up and stretched. This was what it took to get to the truth. Abby's confession slotted in with the rest of her story. Finally, the pieces fitted seamlessly. Every day as a covert analyst, you just get a little piece of the puzzle; you won't complete the puzzle all in one day, it builds up like a soap opera and Abby's soap opera now made sense. Max believed her.

He glanced back. Abby watched him quietly.

"Any more lies?"

She shook her head. "I'm glad we're finally working together."

"Hold up, sweetheart; you've got it all wrong. My team is bringing Khalid down, and you're still heading up north for a debriefing."

The panic flared, closely followed by a stubborn glint. Oh boy. "If I disappear then so will Khalid. Keep using me as bait."

Max shook his head as Abby continued with her crazy talk. "That was the mission I'd formulated with Noleen. With her help and embassy connections, I looked into Khalid's background. We knew he was a criminal, suspected in the disappearance of a couple of women. Noleen taught me how to shoot and covered basic self-defense moves."

Abby pulled her knees to her chest. "I'm not waiting for fate to wrap around me, to rip my child away. I'll kill Khalid; you can either help me or move out of the way."

"You know we can't do either." Max cupped the back of her neck to gain her attention. "And Khalid will exterminate you before you have a chance to harm him. You're the lamb to his wolf. Look, let's take this one step at a time. First, I'll need the evidence, and then we'll decide what comes next. We'll sit down tomorrow and sort this mess out."

The industrial park descended into darkness as they waited for Donnie's confirmation. Johnny decided to walk the perimeter of the building. Slater parked nearer to the gate to watch for any unwanted traffic. Max sat silently beside Abby. She hadn't said too much after pleading her case and offering herself up as bait, staring calmly out into the night. A warm breeze kicked dry leaves across the lot.

"I'm sorry I called you a whore."

She stiffened, angling her shoulders away. "It's okay."

"It was unforgivable of me."

"Max, it's fine."

Max glanced at her profile and noted her wrist tucked snugly into her lap. Technically it was justified due to the threat level, but it still bothered him.

◊ ◊ ◊

"Let me see it," Max said.

"What?"

"Your wrist."

"It's fine."

"Is that why you're cradling it in your lap? Let me see it, Abs."

She placed her hand on his, and he pulled out a flashlight to examine it. Goose bumps broke out at his soft touch. Max squeezed along the inside, and she flinched in pain.

"Shit. I'm sorry."

"It's not your fault." Her smile shook.

"Yeah, right." Max ran his thumb up her arm, checking the tendon.

"This is the wrist I broke, remember? You probably just twisted it wrong, it's never healed fantastically."

"I should've remembered, especially after what happened with Wayne Jacobs."

Bumping his shoulder, Abby said, "You thought I was a bad guy and did the right thing."

"Ice this as soon as we get in. It may come as a surprise to you, but I don't purposely hurt women."

Her mouth turned up at one end. "Unless they're suspected terrorists about to blow up the world."

"Yes."

The pain in his voice sat heavily in the intimate space.

Max continued, "There've been times when I've killed women. Female extremists armed with RPGs, disabling a mother with a baby strapped to her back and a bomb strapped to her front. It's part of the job. Violence in combat eats away at every soldier, and if you're not careful it can fill you with bitterness and hate."

"You're doing a job that many men aren't brave enough to do. I'm sure you were justified every time."

He smiled sadly. "Every time."

They sat in the dark, and his body heat seeped through the thin dress, slipping through her defenses. Max still examined her wrist, and his bent head brushing lightly against her arm. Warmth trickled like honey from her stomach, settling between her legs. Abby sucked in a quick breath.

"Is it still throbbing?" he asked.

"What?"

"Your wrist?"

His thumb traced circles. There was definitely throbbing happening, just in a different spot. The energy in those hands matched his clever eyes. The open hunger she saw reflected her own. For this one moment, shrouded in the dark, all she wanted was to touch him.

◊ ◊ ◊

Max ran a hand down her throat and lightly traced her collarbone with his thumb. Abby gasped, and his eyes shot to hers. Her lips were just inches away, and his hormones raged like a damn teenager's. A loud vibration cut through the night—his phone, but shit, what the hell just happened with Abby. Max leapt to his feet and took long strides, putting distance between them. Air would be good. Donnie's name popped up on the screen.

"What have you got?"

Donnie sounded upbeat. "It's all here, Evans even saved the napkin from the coffee shop. There are detailed accounts of her son's birth including all his identity documents and a handful of family photos of mom and the baby."

"Is everything secure?"

"Yes, sir. I'm back at base."

Max hung up just as Johnny strolled around the corner.

"Her story checks out. We need to get her secure. Khalid is after his heir, and he'll take out anyone that gets in his way, including and especially, the mother of his child."

Max led her to the vehicle. Abby smiled shyly, but Max shut her out. He couldn't afford pretty distractions no matter how hard his dick got. Touching her was a mistake. He'd been chasing Khalid for a long time, and nothing would get in his way.

Chapter Fourteen

The ringtone indicating Mandla Nkosi's call pushed Max to jump out of the shower and snap up the phone. Mandla wouldn't call without a damn good reason.

"How are you, sir?"

"I'm sitting on some interesting news and pondering how this might affect our plans. Where are you?"

"Back at our base."

"Do you have eyes on the woman?" Mandla asked, putting Max on edge. It had been two days since the barbeque and all seemed quiet.

"One of my men is with her, and one is watching her place. What's happened?"

"It may not be much, but I like to keep a close eye on what goes on in my country, even if it is all the way up on the northern border."

Northern border. Were Khalid's men filtering in from Zimbabwe or Mozambique?

Mandla's baritone voice continued, "Kris Muller's anti-poaching team was ambushed two days ago. Poachers shot at the five-man squad and the rhinos they were protecting. Kris Muller was the only survivor."

Max swore as he grabbed a towel. "Do you think it's related to Khalid?"

"Rhino poaching is carried out by criminal gangs, sometimes linked to extremist groups with sophisticated multinational networks. Al-Shabaab funds its activities through elephant and rhino poaching. As far as I know, Khalid is linked to gunrunning but isn't linked to any poaching networks. More than 120 Rhinos have been killed in the last 200 days, which is tragic for our people and our animals. The poaching syndicates are well organized and well-funded."

"Who funds them?" Max asked, rubbing the towel through his hair.

"Wealthy businessmen. Illegal wildlife trafficking is one of the world's top criminal activities."

Something didn't sit right. Would Khalid target Kris Muller to get to Abby?

"I need details on the attack. Was Muller injured?"

"His left arm was grazed by a bullet, nothing serious. He's heading back to Johannesburg," Mandla replied.

"Send me the details." This wasn't good. Muller was a potential distraction. Abby already felt guilty for lying to Kris about what happened to Megan in the UAE.

◊ ◊ ◊

Reading a book on the sofa, Abby greeted Max with a smile. John yelled out a greeting as he rooted around in the kitchen.

"Are you eating again, bro?" Max asked.

"None of your business, hoe."

"Make me some muesli. I haven't eaten breakfast."

"Make your own damn birdseed," John grumbled. "I'm heading to Lizzy's soon."

Max sat on the edge of the sofa. "Are you enjoying your book?"

"It's an interesting book. *Irena's Children*." She flashed the cover, then paused. "You know what I'm reading, of course you do."

"I haven't researched it as I stalked you on camera if that's what you're referring to." Max smiled.

"It's a novel about a woman who rescued thousands of children by smuggling them out of the Warsaw Ghetto in World War II."

"Sounds heroic," Max said.

"I've just started, seems good so far." Abby paused. Max seemed different, more reserved if it was possible. Reserved and distracted. "What's wrong? Have you heard something?"

His eyes shot to hers. "What makes you say that?"

"You seem stiffer than usual. Is it Khalid? Has he found me?"

"No, but I spoke to HQ back home. They're understandably charged up about Khalid having a son and want Gabe's location."

"They won't get it. None of you will. I trust you to an extent, but the risk of a leak is too great."

"We can offer greater protection than you currently have. There are safe houses and teams trained for this."

"How many of those teams have been killed protecting a high-value asset? Isn't that what you'd call Gabe? Khalid isn't some low-level criminal, he's an international terrorist with global connections. Two people know where my son is, and I'm one of them."

"We'll talk later. I have other news."

Abby could see from the determined glint in his eye that Max wasn't letting this go, but the wary look that replaced it had her on edge. "Max, you're making me nervous."

"Kris was ambushed two days ago while guarding three rhinos."

Shock slammed in and Max quickly reassured her. "Kris is okay. Bullet grazed his arm—lightly grazed—and he's shaken up, but he's doing good."

"Thank God," Abby said, closing her eyes in relief.

"Is his team okay? The rhino?"

"They didn't make it. Kris was the only one to escape. He went back to the vehicle to grab more water when the shooting started. Kris used the Land Rover as cover and returned fire but was outnumbered; he drove out for help. By the time he returned with enforcements, the poachers were gone, and his men were dead."

Abby squeezed her eyes shut from the horror. Those poor men were cut down in the prime of their life, doing an honorable job. She was so tired of wicked people thinking they had a right to kill and maim others, assuming they were superior to all else on earth. Kris had survived this. He had survived.

She might have betrayed Kris, but she could at least comfort him. Max was gauging her reaction. Abby ignored him as she got up to retrieve her phone.

John leaned against the opposite sofa arm, legs crossed as he ate a sandwich. A large slice of cake teetered vicariously on the edge of his plate.

"What are you doing?" Max asked her.

"What do you think I'm doing? Texting Kris."

"Texting Kris what?"

"Why is that any of your concern?" she demanded.

"This could be a trap."

"What the hell are you talking about?" Abby reached into her handbag.

"Khalid knows that Kris is your friend. If he's been tracking Kris, he could have hired mercenaries to kill the team, knowing Kris might contact you for support."

Abby paused. "Do you think that's the case?"

Max stared at the floor, saying nothing.

Continuing, Abby said, "Because I trust you to give me the right advice, to have our backs. If you tell me not to contact Kris, then I won't. I don't have to like it."

"It complicates things," Max replied.

"Or maybe it makes things simpler? Khalid will finally make a move, and we'll be ready. We can get this over with, and I can be with my son."

Max looked up sharply. "Don't be naive. It's not going to be that straightforward, not in any scenario, so get that out of your damn head. Even with my team as backup, Khalid is a dangerous man with resources and weapons. I'd love to get my hands on him—hell, I'd like to see the bastard coming, but that may not be the case, even with all our intelligence at our backs. My best hope is to keep us all in one piece and hope there aren't any additional casualties caught in the crossfire—like your friend, Kris Muller."

The psychological burden Max carried to keep everyone safe wasn't lost on Abby. He seemed driven to shield those weaker than himself while hunting evil anarchists.

Abby felt inconsiderate and careless. "As usual, I'm dragging innocents into the mix. I should've learned my lesson by now, especially after getting my best friend killed in Sharjah."

Max grabbed her hand, squeezing it hard. His light eyes drilled into hers with an intensity that took her breath away. "Don't you fucking go there. You are not responsible for Meg's death, not even remotely."

She opened her mouth to reply but Max cut her off. "Megan was a well-trained operative who knew what she was doing. It was a tragic thing that happened to her, but Jesus! It happened to you too. You're the innocent here, you and your sweet baby boy. If I hear garbage coming out of your mouth, then you and I are going to have a serious problem."

His vehemence tore her up. His passion in her defense was gallant, but she still felt answerable for that night because she'd caved at Khalid's fateful job offer and Meg was dead.

"Max is right." John leaned over and plonked his empty plate on the coffee table. Abby had forgotten that he was in the room. "Constantly blaming yourself isn't doing you any favors. It's self-serving and coloring your vision."

"Self-serving!" Abby glared. "I'll give you self-serving. No more cake for you Johnny boy, get your smelly carcass off that armrest and vamoose!" She shoved his startled massive frame towards the door. "Out now."

"You're not kicking him out!" John yelped as Max grinned in amusement.

"Max has better sense than to call a girl 'self-serving' and besides, he takes up less space in my living room compared to your clumsy ass."

"Clumsy!" John's bewildered expression had Max breaking out into a full out laugh.

"You heard the lady, Big John. Hustle your fat booty out of here now that you're done stuffing your crumb catcher—"

"Fat booty, my ass! Screw you. I'm Dwayne Johnson shitting hot."

Abby giggled as she shut the sliding door. John glared at them through the glass, making them hoot with laughter.

"Hey, Icelander. This isn't over. You'd better sleep with one eye open; I'll be coming for you."

Max gave John the finger as Abby pulled the curtains shut.

"Dwayne Johnson shitting hot, did he just say that?"

Max grinned. "He surely did."

"I feel bad that I called him fat. He's far from it."

Max laughed. "You didn't call him fat. You called him clumsy. I called him fat."

"True. I'll make it up to John and bake some chocolate chip cookies."

"Keep that up, and we'll all end up with giant booties, waddling around with chocolate crumbs decorating our shirts as sugar soars through our veins."

Abby chuckled at the mental image.

◊ ◊ ◊

A slight dimple graced her right cheek. Its appearance was a rare occurrence. Max itched to know what would lighten that load. He'd find out, technically gathering more intel—Max couldn't protect Abby without knowing everything there was to know about her. Nothing personal.

Keep telling yourself that, Andersen, just keep repeating that mantra.

He allowed Abby to use a burner phone to text Kris. The game ranger was back in town and resting up for the rest of the day, so they agreed to meet up the following afternoon at a coffee shop. Slater could scope out the location beforehand.

Handing the phone back, Abby said, "I need to weed the yard. Want to help?"

"I don't know much about plants. I might kill the things by looking at them, but if you trust me with your bug-infested babies, then why not."

Abby snorted. "Bug-infested. What kind of operation do you think I run here?" Her eyes sparkled with humor.

"The organic kind. I see you, Miss Evans, with your earth-friendly sprays and your little tomato plants, tucked in the corner."

"I also have green peppers and a whole pot of herbs."

"Well excuse me, Miss Fancy Pants." Max tucked a lock of hair behind her ear, and his hand paused. Her cheek felt soft beneath his fingers; he itched to pull her in for a bone-melting, tongue-melding kiss.

"Umm... Speaking of fancy pants, I need to change into gardening clothes. I'll be right back." Abby's husky voice pulled him out of his reverie.

Shit a dick. Sucking in air, he went to the fridge to grab a cold juice, while Abby changed clothes.

"What the hell is this?" She stormed down the passage and held one of their surveillance cameras out to him.

Max sipped his pineapple juice. "Where did you get that?"

"In the freaking bathroom! The bathroom, Max!"

"I understand you're upset—"

"You're damn right I'm upset! Oh God. You've seen me on the toilet! In the shower! Oh crap."

"You were a suspected terrorist. We install cameras everywhere. Now we use them to keep you safe."

"In the bathroom? What? In case a giant poop wrestles me down the toilet?"

Max tried to hide a grin.

"This is not funny!"

"We're professionals and do this a lot. No one is ogling you. The men on my team know better. We allow for privacy while still keeping a handle on things."

"Oh! So, what you're saying is that you're just like a gynecologist? Seeing people's private bits is just another day at the office!"

"In a sense. I'll tell you what, I'll remove the surveillance from the bathroom. That's the best I can do for now."

"Gee, thanks! Where else are they hiding? In the bedroom?"

Max nodded once in reply.

"Guess I'll be changing in the bathroom from now on. No cameras in the damn bathroom!"

Reaching out, Max said. "Abs, this isn't permanent, it's just until we catch Khalid."

She shrugged him off before cringing. "Oh God! The shower. Two weeks ago..." Her face flamed.

"Come with me." Max took the camera from her and placed it on the counter before taking her hand and leading her to the bathroom. Once inside, he closed the door and turned on the shower, then placed a damp face towel over the second listening device behind the sink before turning to her.

"No one can see us or hear us. That day...after I left you in the kitchen..." Max stopped to take a breath. He ran his hand over his face. "Dammit to hell. I can't believe I'm saying this."

Abby waited for him to sort out his thoughts.

"I wanted you so fucking badly. I wanted to mount you on the dishwasher and shove my dick deep inside."

Her eyes widened.

"It's the first time in my long ass life that I've ever considered crossing a line. That I've ever felt anything for a target and it scares the hell out of me. I've served my country for over ten years and never compromised a mission. I know you don't believe me, but I would never have taken you to bed. I planned to pull you in for questioning, the day after our date."

"Where are you going with this?" Abby asked.

"After I left you loading the dishwasher, I took over the surveillance. I was alone in the room when you had your shower."

Abby's face reddened as she looked away.

"I deleted it from the recording feed. I was the only one that saw you."

The room felt charged as shower steam fogged the mirror. Abby's chest rose and fell rapidly. When she finally looked up, she asked, "Did you watch?"

Max was done with lies when it came to her. "I initially turned away." He swallowed. "But then you screamed my name." He pulled her face back to his. "You were so fucking beautiful."

Their harsh breathing echoed through the small space. Slipping hands around his waist, Abby stood up on her toes and kissed his neck. It wasn't a chaste kiss. It was an open-mouthed, tongue-swirling, teeth-nipping kiss that nearly buckled his knees.

"Fuck, Abs." Max stood like a statue as she nibbled the side of his mouth.

"I love your bottom lip. It's so damn sexy," Abby whispered, before nipping it gently. Max shoved her against the tiled wall.

"Don't play with me," he growled, dragging her yoga pants down, and rubbed her mound with the heel of his hand. He captured her moan in his mouth as an index finger sank into her tight heat. His thumb rolled back and forth over her clit. "You're so wet. Is that for me?"

"God. Max."

Slipping a second finger in, Max scissored both before slipping them out…then in again.

"I remember everything about that shower. The way your tits

rubbed against the tiles. How you squeezed your nipple while rubbing your clit with your other hand." Max's thumb pressed down, and she spasmed around his fingers. "Were you thinking of my hands touching you like this?"

Abby whimpered.

"Say it, say you were thinking of me finger fucking you like this." He curved upwards towards the top of her passage, applying pressure, finding and stroking the spongy spot he'd been seeking. "Wrap your legs around me baby."

Abby kicked her pants free and did as he asked. Max sat her on the edge of the sink, his hand working her between them as he sucked on her earlobe.

"Oh God. Yes."

Max pressed hard into her heat. Abby came apart, and Max covered her mouth with his. Her body spasmed around his fingers. He freed his hand and stepped between her legs, rubbing his clothed cock over her entrance. He wanted her so badly, his hands shook. Stepping out of the bathroom was the right thing to do, they'd been in here too long.

Max dragged his mouth from hers before stroking a thumb over her lips. "Get your gardening gloves on; I'll meet you out front." With Herculean effort, he stepped away from a dazed Abby straddling the sink and slipped out the door.

◊ ◊ ◊

The following day, Kris Muller hadn't contacted Abby, even after she'd messaged him with a place to meet. If they had not heard from Muller in the next twelve hours, Max would reach out to Mandla to check on his whereabouts. Max knew that Abby was worried, and he distracted her by asking for a painting lesson. Max was no Michelangelo, but at least his palm tree looked like it was supposed to.

Pleased with his progress, Abby leaned in. "You have a natural understanding of perspective. I like that you're analytical in the way you divide the painting up and the way you look at lines. With a little practice, you'll be a decent landscape painter."

"Decent, huh?" He winked. "Lucky me."

Such proximity to Abby had been torture. He only had himself to blame for landing in the hot seat. He'd complimented a landscape sketch she'd left on the kitchen counter, saying that he wished he could draw. Abby took that as a challenge and hustled him into the art studio for Art 101. Now as she leaned over his shoulder, her breast rubbed his back and her sweet-smelling hair tickled his neck.

"Watch how the shadow of the palm fronds fall; you'll need to get that same angle in the painting."

After one of Max's past assignments, he'd had been lucky enough to visit Zanzibar, where he'd snapped some incredible beach photographs. He used one of those images as a reference for his first work of art. Except all he could concentrate on was Abs's sweet ass curves as she moved around him. *Concentrate, Andersen. Freaking shadows. We're painting a freaking shadow.*

Slater's voice chirped in his ear. "Sorry to interrupt the scene from *Ghost*, but we have a problem. Donnie's on his way over."

Max was already on the move. "What kind of problem?"

"Kris Muller's at the front gate."

"Muller's at the fucking gate?"

"Timothy told him that he has the wrong address, no one by the name of Evans lives here. Ranger boy, however, is determined and is calling the burner phone."

Abby followed anxiously, skidding to a stop as Max rounded on her. "Does Kris know where you live?"

"What? No. I deliberately kept it from him. After what happened to Meg, I wanted him to move on. If he knows where I live, he'll insert himself back into my life."

"Well, he sure as shit knows. He's squatting in the cul-de-sac."

Donnie unlocked the sliding door and swung it shut as he gave Max the ringing phone. "Do you want Abby to answer it?"

"Hell's fire." Nostrils flaring, Max handed it to her. "Find out how he knows your location."

"He's my friend. Should I let him in?"

"Ask him first, then we'll decide." The phone stopped ringing. Abby called back and put it on speaker.

"Yer security dude at your complex won't leth me in! What the hell Cwicket. Fucking acting like I'm some stalker!"

"He's drunk," Abby mouthed. "How do you know where I live?"

"I followed you."

"What? When?"

"When ya drove homey wif that headache. I was wurried for yer."

"Kris, hold on a second."

"Anyfing for you, sweets."

Abby covered the mouthpiece as Max grabbed Donnie's arm and marched him to the spare bedroom.

"He followed her home. Did you not see him trailing behind her, behind you!"

"Jesus. It was a short drive—a couple of blocks, and he probably hung way back. Abby was driving real slow that night—with her migraine—there was a whole train of cars behind us."

"Who's the fucking professional in the room! For shit's sake, Don."

"Sir, I screwed up."

Max thought for a second. "Let's keep him close; I need a better read on Muller. We also need eyes on his residence in case Khalid tries to get to Abby through him. The poaching incident put Muller's name in the news. This complicates the shit out of things, plus he's in a bad place and a potential grenade."

Abby stood where Max had left her, mouthpiece covered and clutched to her chest. Still and calm, among a sea of unknowns.

"It's up to you, Abby. Let him in or send him away. Either way, we'll work around it."

Abby thought for a second before uncovering the phone. "Kris, you're drunk. I'm not letting you drive home." She gave him her apartment number, hung up and then dialed Timothy to let him in.

◊ ◊ ◊

Donnie had already left. "You need to go," Abby said to Max.

"I'm not leaving you alone with him. You said it yourself, he's drunk."

"He'll be fine. I've known him pretty much all my life. He's like my brother. He's just shaken up by the ambush."

"Abs."

"You're a few feet away and can hear every word. Kris needs me."

"I don't like it."

"Seriously, save the slaying of my dragons for another day. This is one hassle I can deal with. I'll sober him up with strong coffee and bucket loads of water, then he'll crash on the couch for the night. Now go!"

She ran down the porch steps, leaving Max to fume—the obstinate man was now a hulking statue in her doorway. It didn't help that Kris was in a bad way. The sour stench of liquor made it hard to breathe. "Jeez, Kris, did you drink a whole brewery?"

Kris stumbled, almost dragging her down with him. Her knees buckled as she led her inebriated friend up the garden path. Oh, the irony.

Judging from his slurred speech, he wasn't remembering any of this by the morning.

"Ag. My loverly Creekit... So damn bootiful... I got a gift for yur..." Kris pressed his hot face into her neck, and she stumbled up the stairs.

"Please don't let the gift be vomit. Jesus, turn your head away. I mean it. You stink, Krissy!"

Muller whined. "You used to call me dat when we were kiddies... I lick it when you say my name...Kwissy. Kissy. Kwissy."

Oh brother. Muller laughed hysterically as she shoved him onto the sofa. He groped at her, and she wrenched herself out of the monkey grip.

"Ouch, watch the arm. Wait! I got sumfing to show ya..."

Max moved to the side. Abby didn't need a 'told you so' and ignored his scowl as she dragged Kris's heavy legs onto the cushions. Anger vibrated off Max's hard body as he paused in the entrance.

"Go, Max, it's all good." Kris handed her his car keys and a wadded-up napkin. A backward glance told her that Max was gone. At least she only had one obstinate male to deal with.

"Who was that?"

"None of your business. I'm brewing some coffee. Now lie back and behave."

Kris gave her a sloppy salute. "Open my gift, Cwicket! I wrapped it meself! In the napkin! Open it! Open it! Open it!"

"I don't have time for this." Abby pulled the napkin apart, and her breath froze.

◊ ◊ ◊

Max was halfway back to their unit when Abby's earsplitting scream pierced the air. *What. The. Fuck.* Buzzing in his head blocked all else as he threw himself at her front gate, ripping out his gun and racing up the porch steps. If Muller had laid a fucking finger on her... The sliding door sat open.

"Max! Dial it back! Dial it back, dude! She's okay." Slater's voice in the earpiece cut through the panic.

At the last second, Max concealed the weapon, barging into the room. Abby scooted back towards the opposite couch. The look of terror made him want to rip the laughing bastard's face off. Had Muller touched her?

Her eyes were glued to an object on the tiled floor. All Max saw was a napkin. Something large crawled out of it—a half-dead cricket. Abby looked at it like it was Satan. It half limped towards her, and she shrieked in fear. Muller guffawed even louder.

Max scooped up the offending insect and quickly dispatched it outside. The poor creature had lost a couple of legs and was suffering. He returned to kneel next to Abby's frozen form. He tucked her hair behind her ear and gently stroked her arm. "You okay, Angel?"

It was unlike Abby to be scared of anything, and her reaction surprised the heck out of him.

"Abs, look at me. It's gone. You're fine. It's just an insect. It can't hurt you."

She whispered so softly that he had to lean in. "I have a fear. It's silly. Ortho... Ortho... Orthopterophobia." Her voice shook.

That would explain it. His calm and brave girl was afraid of an insect. He barely stopped his mouth from twitching in amusement. It wasn't funny to her. It had been a hot spring day.

"Where did the cricket come from? Did it hop in?"

Abby shuddered at the word *hop,* which made him want to smile again. Her eyes narrowed. "Kris knows about my phobia and tortured me with them as a kid after one got stuck in my hair. He brought it as a gift!"

"You was funny, Cweekit! Your face… I found it outside yer gate. It was fate."

Max rose, wanting to punch Muller. Abby scrambled to her feet, trying to push Max towards the door. He planted his feet instead. *Son of a bitch.* Donnie's voice chirped a warning in his ear.

Kris stretched out. "Relax, bru; it was a jokey joke."

Abby almost launched herself at Kris. "How could you! You should damn well know better, plus you hurt the poor thing. That's damn cruel."

Anger was much better. That terrified look in her eyes freaked Max out.

"You need to get ova it. You harped bloody on about confronting yer fear for years. It's just a cricket for my crickety cricket."

"You know I hate being called Cricket. It's not damn funny. It was never funny, not the first time and not any of the other times either."

The fact that the bastard had done this before pissed Max off.

"But you lurve me anyway."

She gave Kris a dirty look. "I'm done. It's late." Eyes blazing, she turned to Max, jabbing him with a slender finger. "You, go home." She swiveled to Kris. "Not another peep out of you. I'll give you a water bottle and a warm blanket. I don't want to hear a sound from that sofa until morning."

Kris started to whine but shut it when Abby shot him a dark look.

Max pulled her aside. "Are you okay?"

"Just dandy."

"Lock your bedroom door."

She huffed. "Kris is fine…"

"He's an ugly drunk who's mentally in a bad place, so lock your damn door."

"Fine. Now move your concrete ass out of the way and leave me in peace."

Max jabbed a finger towards Kris. "Lay a finger on her, and I'll snap it in half like a fucking twig!"

It was a futile threat. Muller's head lolled back, and his mouth hung open. A gravelly snore filled the room.

Chapter Fifteen

Eight in the morning saw Abby making Kris breakfast and kicking his smelly ass off the sofa. Max hadn't taken his eyes off surveillance of Muller.

When the ass-hat stirred in the early hours to use the head, Max gathered himself. Leaving the bathroom, Muller turned towards Abby's room instead of walking back down the passage to the sitting room, pausing at her closed door for over a minute. Both men stood immobile in the night. One readying himself to make the biggest mistake of his life and the other readying for retribution. Finally, Kris backed away. *Good move, asshole.*

Abby walked Muller to the door as Max ate the last of his yogurt.

"I'm sorry, my sweets. Last night shouldn't have gone down like that. I was an idiot," Kris said with a remorseful tone.

"You did act like a bit of an asshole. You cannot drive drunk; you'll endanger others."

"I'm going through a tough time. They all died. Why did I survive?"

"I don't know, but I'm here to help. If you're having a rough day, don't reach for the bottle, just call me. Maybe you need to see a therapist?"

"Maybe. I'll think about it." Kris pulled her in for a rough hug. "Don't disappear on me again, swear that you won't."

Muller held on like a damn limpet.

"Go home and rest. We'll have dinner sometime, I'll call you."

Kris left. Slater followed. Max headed over. Misty rain dampened the air. "Soliloquy to the Frogs" played in the background. Her head rested in her hands. Max used a detector to scan the place for electronic bugs, a standard practice when a new individual entered the space. Finding nothing, Max sat down on the sofa, as close to Abby as he could get, shoulders and thighs touching.

Glancing sideways at him through her fingers, Abby mumbled, "You look like shit."

"Are you okay?"

"Nope." Leaning her head back, Abby sighed.

"This song helps a little? I notice you play it often."

Abby smiled. "It was the only song that Gabe would fall asleep to. His fwoggy song. God, I miss him. It hurts so much at times that I can barely breathe—every day I ache for my baby boy. Then my dearest friend in the world comes over, and I barely recognize him, wanting him gone. I'm a bad mother and an even worse friend."

A tear ran down into her hairline.

"Your situation isn't normal. You're doing your level best to save the people you love. To save your future, short-term sacrifices will be made. You're the bravest person I've ever met."

His heart turned over at her watery smile. "You think I'm brave?"

"As brave as a mountain lion. I also think you're exhausted, so have a nap, then tonight is a Lizzy night."

Her eyebrows furrowed. "What's a Lizzy night?"

"It's when your tiny, happy friend comes over and we watch movies and guzzle popcorn. What's not to love?"

Wiping her tears, Abby stood up and stretched. "Only if you promise to also get some rest. Did you stay up all night?"

"Damn right, protecting you from fiery dragons, and all that." Max headed for the door.

"Watch that rain doesn't rust up your shiny suit of armor," Abby called.

"You're hilarious, Abs," Max called back as she sauntered down the passage.

◊ ◊ ◊

Lizzy's squeals of delight squeaked through the monitors' speakers. Max wandered towards the front room where Donnie watched Lizzy throw herself into Abby's arms like they were long-lost sisters reuniting.

"She's an enthusiastic little thing, ain't she?"

Max concealed his weapon in the small of his back. "She grows on you."

Watching a douchebag all night had screwed with his mood. With little to no rest, his head pounded. It was going to be a long night. He grabbed a gummy worm on the way out.

"I can't believe Johnny actually allowed Lizzy to drive him over in this." Donnie flipped a camera. A bright yellow Beetle convertible sat in Abby's guest parking. White flowers decorated the sides—even the taillight covers were cut-outs of daisies.

Max grabbed a couple more worms. "Yep, we can't let him live it down."

"Have fun on your double date." Donnie winked at him.

"It's all business."

"Sure it is."

"Abby is showing strain. It's good for her to have a girlfriend around, take her mind off the fact that she's bait for a jihad extremist."

"She's missing the kid. Emotion can lead to rash decisions."

Donnie's comment riled Max up. "I know how to do my job. Do yours, keep an eye out for any unwanted visitors."

Donnie swiveled back and forth in his chair. "Well aren't you a little ray of pitch black."

"Screw you." He was an easy mark and Donnie riled him up without breaking a sweat.

Abby's sliding door sat open. Johnny was sprawled across the largest sofa, snoozing like he was on his daddy's yacht. Drifting chatter indicated that the girls were down the hall. Max kicked Johnny's leg. Hard.

"What the fuck, dude!"

"Napping on the job."

"I'm not napping. It's more like a horizontal life pause."

Max snorted. "Horizontal life pause, that's your defense? The door is wide open! Let's just invite ISIS and all their fucking friends in."

"Chill the hell out, ice-hole. It's not my fault you sat cross-eyed all night. Besides, I heard your loud ass stomping over here."

"You wish. What are the women doing?" He retraced his steps to slide the security gate into the locked position.

Johnny settled deeper into the couch. "Lizzy's changing into something more comfortable and Abby's grabbing a couple of throws."

Visions of watching *The Notebook* while snuggled under a fluffy blanket made Max want to poke his exhausted eyeballs out.

He collapsed onto the opposite sofa, feeling like a bear shot in the ass. His expression must've given him away.

"Don't get bent out of shape. You're the one who planned this torturous movie marathon."

"I don't care. Wake me up when it's over." Something scrumptious was cooking in the oven, smelled like chicken. Maybe Max would stay awake long enough to wolf it down.

"The hell you are! Never leave a brother behind! I'm going to kick your scrawny ass if you do."

Abby wandered in and threw a blanket at Max's head, aiming the next one at Johnny. "Make yourselves useful and switch on the telly and that DVD thingy. I never know how to operate it."

Grinning to himself, Max grabbed both remotes. Abby was so right, in the three months he'd watched her, she hardly ever watched the television, preferring to hibernate in the art studio. Lizzy bounced into the room and Max's jaw dropped. Mother of God. What in heaven's name was she wearing? Johnny grinned in surprise. There was no way Max could keep his trap shut.

"What in the hell is that?

A light blue baggy one-piece thing decorated in white snowflake designs engulfed her petite frame.

"It's cold and rainy so I wore a Onesie." Lizzy pirouetted in a circle.

"A one what?"

Abby laughed. "A onesie. It keeps her whole body warm, including her toes."

"You look like Alice in Wonder-freaking-land!" Max said, screwing up his face.

Abby chuckled. "I think it's the black headband along with that pale blue color."

Lizzy touched her stretchy headband holding back the crazy

blonde curls and gave an exaggerated curtsy.

"Just call me Alice. And don't diss the headband, it keeps my hair out of my face."

Johnny stretched his leg out and tapped her with his giant foot. "Lizbug, you look adorable."

Lizzy grinned crazily, picked up a grocery bag and pulled out *Taken*.

"That's my cool as shit girl!" Johnny grinned.

"I love dude movies! *Predator* and *The Accountant* are next!" Lizzy threw down the bag.

Smoothly lifting the DVD out of Lizzy's hand, Abby said, "First you're playing us something on your guitar while I grab the snacks from the oven."

Johnny sat up. "You play the guitar?"

Lizzy backed up. "Yep, but nope, I think I'll take a pass. I've changed my mind."

"Lizzy also sings. She has the voice of an angel. It's her secret weapon." Abby winked.

"I haven't played in forever. I'm not sure I even know how!"

Abby tugged at her friend's curls. "You've sung for me, it's incredible."

Lizzy rolled her eyes. "Dingbat, that's different, I'm allowed to screw up with you."

Johnny entwined his fingers with hers. "I dig it. I'd be honored to hear you perform, but you don't have to do anything you don't wanna do."

Lizzy sighed. "One song."

"Five songs," Abby countered.

"Two songs."

"Three…and I'll make your favorite hot chocolate laced with cinnamon cream."

"Son of a beach ball! You drive a hard bargain. Fine, get Whitney and I'll grab my guitar pick out of my bag."

Max frowned. "Who's Whitney?"

"My guitar. Named her after Whitney Houston, 'cause she has some pluck to her."

Johnny pulled Lizzy into his lap. "My crazy flower child."

"I'm not a flower child! I'm an eighties child, with a bit of nineties thrown in." Lizzy sighed dreamily. "I'd have given anything to be a groupie in the eighties." Max chuckled. What an oddball.

Lizzy sat cross-legged, her guitar resting on her dainty lap. "Since we're all currently living it up in South Africa, my fellow Americans, I guess I'll start with Toto's 'Africa.' This one makes me want to go on a weekend game drive into the African bush."

The guitar playing was masterful, but once Lizzy started to sing, the whole room was stunned into silence. Her voice was a shining wave of joy. Her passion for the music was reflected in her angelic face. Goose bumps broke over Max's skin when she sang a Lana Del Rey song. Johnny's eyes were glued to the petite blonde. Abby smiled lovingly at her friend, looking happy and proud. It was a good moment.

As tired as Max felt, he enjoyed the evening and found himself laughing out loud at a few of the girls' antics. Johnny nodded off halfway through *Predator* and Lizzy followed shortly after, her head resting on his broad chest.

Max glanced over as Abby stretched. Her hair was scooped into a messy bun—the way girls liked to wear their hair these days—and it made him want to unloosen the knot and run his fingers through the heavy waves. She wore yoga pants with a soft grey T-shirt that clung to her in all the right places.

"Do you want anything to drink?" Abby asked as she stood.

The whispered words seemed pointless as the other two snoozed through *Predator* bedlam.

"Nope. Are you off to bed?"

Abby snagged a knitted blue throw and headed across to the kitchen. "I need fresh air, you're welcome to join me."

The back door led into a narrow lane that ran down the backs of the apartments. A high wall separated her lane from the entrance road into the complex. It reminded Max of the cobbled streets that ran between houses in Europe. Just wide enough to fit a small table and some chairs. Abby occasionally ate her breakfast out here. Although they had cameras monitoring the lane, Max didn't like it. A great spot for an ambush, but Max didn't sense any danger. Besides, Donnie was watching from across the way.

Abby balanced herself on a wrought iron chair, pulling her knees to her chest while tucking the throw around herself. Iron scraped on stone as Max dragged a nearby chair closer. The skies had finally cleared, and the chill in the air felt good.

"Can you hear them?" Abby asked softly.

Max stiffened, alerting himself to possible dangers. "Hear who?"

"The crickets. One of the first signs that spring is here."

A couple of crickets chirped softly in the distance. "Does the chirping scare you?"

Abby looked at him as if he was daft. "Why would that scare me?"

"I just thought that since you were afraid—"

"Afraid of them jumping on me. When I was eleven—on the farm in Botswana—I played in the shade of the front steps on a warm summer's day. A giant cricket jumped down the back of my shirt and it wasn't just any cricket, it was an Armored Bush

Cricket that's native to Southern Africa and is common in Botswana. It has sharp spines and thick armor and I couldn't reach it as it fought for its life, like a thorny branch shoved down my back. Once it was caught in my hair and scrambled up against my neck, I was a goner, screaming and screaming for help. Everyone, including Kris, thought I was just being a drama queen, eventually my mom saw the huge beast. They cut a chunk out of my hair to remove the fat cricket and it squirmed and scratched the entire time."

Abby rubbed her arms with the blanket. "It took six months for my hair to grow out. Every time I felt the shorn hair, I was reminded of that spiny giant cricket crawling on my skin and the terror stuck, becoming a lifelong fear. I'm not afraid of crickets chirping. I actually think crickets are kind of cool, from a distance."

Her eyes sparkled in the moonlight. "Did you know the intensity of their chirps depends on the temperature? The warmer it gets, the more frequently they chirp? In China, crickets are a symbol of good luck."

Max smiled. "I did not know that."

They paused to listen to the night. A cold breeze swept up the narrow passage and Abby tucked her socked feet in.

"I heard you rescued a praying mantis the other day."

"The damn cameras." Abby rolled her eyes.

"You're not afraid of a praying mantis? They kind of resemble crickets."

"They do, but they're fragile enough that I can control the ickiness factor. Their legs are so delicate. I make a point of studying insects, especially anything that looks remotely similar to a cricket, to overcome my fear. Familiarity negates fear—besides, I've faced real fear and violence—an insect could never hurt me that badly."

Before her dad tried to mold her into the perfect daughter, before Khalid mauled her, Max got the feeling that Abby had been a bundle of bright energy. The small glimpses of her animated side lurking beneath the surface was a stark contrast to the composed mask that Abigail Evans presented to the world.

"How do you cope with what you've endured? How do you heal?"

Abby blinked away sudden tears. "Some days are rougher than others. I keep busy. Swimming helps, it washes over scars and I pretend that I'm whole again."

The foreign lump in his throat took Max unawares; her self-soothing statement kicked him in the gut. Abby was damn easy to love, and her dickhead family should have protected her, they should've loved her better.

"I've had enough therapy to last a lifetime. It's all about taking baby steps. Learning to sleep in the dark again. Being in a room of strangers for the first time after the attack was a big step. Going on a first date."

"You've dated since?"

"I dated a lovely man about a year ago, really kind and gentle. It would've been ideal except he was possibly the most boring man on the planet, all he spoke about were feet. George was a podiatrist. We dated for two months." Abby rubbed her socked feet. "With the help of a great therapist, I worked through my intimacy issues and the scars from the rape."

"You mean you were, um…with this George…" Thinking about her with another man had Max tensing.

"We were never in love, but he never judged me. If I'd never dated, the damage would have won, and I'd never let another man touch me. Thanks to his patience, I overcame much of the horror. George was what I needed at the time." Abby glanced at

Max. "Relax, shortly after we broke it off, George fell in love with one of his patients. They're happily married with a kid on the way."

Max didn't know what to think; warring emotions had him frozen in his seat.

Abby shifted awkwardly. "When Khalid hurt me…I was a virgin. Violence was all I knew. I was determined to experience kindness in the bedroom. It's only been three years but I don't want my future husband to have to deal with all the repercussions of the rape."

"God. Abby."

"I'm just like any other girl. I want a normal life one day with a man who loves me, who doesn't just see a damaged soul."

"I've been groping you like I'm a teenage boy. I'm sorry."

Abby turned to him and grabbed his wrist. "Don't be. For the first time, I've wanted to grope someone back." Her thumb stroked his arm and the air heated. Abby stared at him with hunger, trust and so much more.

Max opened his mouth to promise her a world he wasn't sure he could give, when she suddenly let go, settling back in her seat.

"Enough about me. What are you afraid of? What would a big, bad soldier fear?"

It took Max a second to answer. "I'm big and bad, am I?"

Abby smiled. "Sometimes. Hell, much of the time."

Max leaned in. "If I'm the bad wolf, then where is your red cape?"

"Not sure, Mr. Wolf, but I do have a snazzy blue throw."

Max roared with laughter.

Chapter Sixteen

La Coraggio was packed, Max and Johnny sandwiched Abby on the bench. Max pulled a dollar bill out of his wallet and folded it into a sword shape as Lizzy chattered away on the other side of him. Abby had initially sensed his impatience with her bubbly friend when they'd first met, but Max now saw the girl beneath. Intelligent, kind and courageous.

His mouth turned up as Lizzy made a silly joke, but Abby was thoroughly absorbed in his sexy hands folding with confident precision. His long fingers so capable. Capable enough to take away life or to protect it. Well-trained hands decorated with a few rough calluses and light scars. Feeling them run down her back or stroke her arm always resulted in goose bumps.

Max stroked her calf with his foot; who knew that the game of footsy could be so damn sexy? The small paper dagger was waved in front of Lizzy, who snatched it up. He needed to smile more often. He had the sexiest smile, and combined with those piercing eyes, the result was heart-stopping.

Kris made his way through the crowded patio and Max turned serious. Abby hoped they'd form a bond and now was as good a time as any. Kris could occasionally act like an ass, but his heart was in the right place. Besides, the past couple of weeks had been torture for her friend. Seeing your teammates blown away by poachers. Max should know how that felt, to lose a teammate. Abby rose to greet her friend.

Kris pulled her in. "I'm sorry," he whispered, "about the other night. I'm a complete idiot."

Abby tried to extricate herself, but Kris held firm. She tamped down the urge to shove him away; Kris was like a brother and oldest friend rolled into one.

"Have you been drinking?"

"Just one beer. I swear."

"I'm worried about you."

Kris drew her head in, and she felt his lips against her ear. "It goes both ways, I'm yours, you need to know that."

That was an odd thing to say.

"You look beautiful by the way."

Abby smiled her thanks. Heated stares greeted them as Kris pulled her into the chair next to his, causing Max to stiffen. After all-around introductions, Kris slouched back, slinging an arm over the back of her seat. The sudden silence had more of a deadly feel as opposed to uncomfortable, although Abby could happily tick both boxes.

Kris was no match for Max's stone-washed glare in the mini staring match that commenced. The stillness running through Max caught Abby by surprise. It was the trained soldier in him but needed dialing back, if they were to keep this pretend-couple subterfuge thing going.

◊ ◊ ◊

Mature, Max thought as he read Muller's wrinkled T-shirt: *Game Rangers do it in the bush.*

Judging from the bloodshot eyes and flushed cheeks, Kris was juiced up again. Max knew he should be more understanding. PTSD varied from person to person. Hell, after the Black Friday bombing, Max had suffered nightmares and cold sweats.

Kris spoke up first. "All these Americans at the table… You're making me feel like the bloody foreigner in the room. So, Max. Abby tells me you sell tactical gear, shoes and shit?" Muller's trembling fingers toyed with his car keys.

Max smiled benignly. "Yeah."

"What brands?"

"Arc'teryx, Mechanix Wear, Crye…" Max said.

"Interesting." Muller gave Max the once-over. "You look like a fit kind of guy."

"I work out."

"Did you serve?"

"Sure."

"Good for you. That's honorable. Navy? Army?"

"Army."

"See a lot of action?"

The undefined intensity rolling off Muller put Max on edge. It was clear that he saw Max as a threat.

"I worked on the back end. A security specialist of sorts."

Abby cut in. "Max was a programmer for the military. He helped secure facilities, Stateside."

"So, you were a geeky security guard, and now a traveling salesman who's seeing my girl."

Max raised his brows. "Your girl?"

"We have a history. She's like my—"

"Sister." Max threw in.

Kris bristled. "You hurt her and I'll bliksem you."

"Understood." Max's eyes glanced down at Muller's fingers resting on Abby's arm.

"And I'll beat the shit out of you too, if you keep getting touchy with my woman."

Abby shifted forward as another stare off commenced. Visions of snapping Muller's fingers ran through Max's skull. Muller glared back a while longer then stretched, pulling his hand back.

Bingo, don't fuck with the alpha in the room.

Lizzy's cheery voice piped in. "Fantastic! Now that we have that sorted out, who's having what? Kris? Can I get you a menu? Anything to drink?"

◊ ◊ ◊

Once everyone had ordered, Abby tried to relax. Kris told John about various species of African giraffe and how numbers had dwindled due to habitat loss. Max punched out of the conversation, instead locking Abby in with an unblinking stare, like a hawk zeroing in on a piece of meat. He was definitely out of sorts. Well, tough toodles, these men needed to grow up and get along.

Lizzy paid little heed to the men's conversation. Abby followed her friend's gaze to the dessert display. Lizzy and her sweet tooth. Her transparency was heartwarming in this harsh world, even after all she'd been through. Deceit ate away at Abby.

When this was finally over John would leave her friend in the dust, and there was no guarantee that Abby would be there to pick up the pieces. In fact, there was a real possibility that Lizzy would never forgive Abby for injuring her heart. Another casualty of her war-torn life. Abby wanted to rush over and beg forgiveness for being a deceitful bitch along with her shifty band of liars.

Her male friend's deep voice drew her back to his profile as the waiter placed antipasti platters on the table. Kris was awfully good looking. Lizzy and Kris could make a beautiful couple. She loved them both dearly and who knows. Maybe in the chaotic future that lay ahead, they could turn to each other for comfort. A city girl and a country boy. Or perhaps not, they might end up killing each other. A chuckle escaped.

A shoulder nudge from Kris had her glancing up. "What are you giggling at?"

Her mouth still curved into a smile, Abby shrugged. "Nothing."

"Liar, your clever brain latched onto something. What gives?"

Sitting forward, she decided to throw it out there. A test of sorts. She was most interested in Big John's reaction and watched him out the corner of her eye. He definitely liked Lizzy. If he turned out to be the biggest dick of them all and crushed her friend's heart, well it wouldn't hurt to plant a seed for the future.

"Tell us," Lizzy said, nibbling on a bruschetta.

"Before you and John started dating, when I first ran into Kris at the mall, I had a crazy thought." Abby paused for effect, looking at Lizzy and then at Kris. "Wouldn't it be wild if my two best friends—two people I adore most—eventually got together."

"What do you mean?" Lizzy asked, looking confused.

"You know, you and Kris?"

There were horrified expressions all around. John's grip on his water glass tightened. Nostrils flaring, he stared at the table. Now wasn't that interesting.

Lizzy laid down her fork. "Sweetness. Seriously. You know I'm with John." She spoke slowly like Abby was daft.

"It was a silly thought, don't mind me."

"Really stupid!" Lizzy huffed.

Kris snorted. "Blondes are so not my type. You can keep her, big man."

Then Kris whispered furiously in her ear. "What the hell was that?"

"When last did you go on a date? I'm just kidding, but you need to find someone nice." She met his livid gaze.

"Pass the Balsamic, I don't have time for little girls and their shit. Besides I get plenty of action from game ranger groupies who just want a quick fuck in a tent."

Abby's mouth fell open as she handed over the vinegar. "I didn't just hear that... Kris, you need someone good in your life."

The sudden flat look in Kris's eyes chilled her. "I had someone. She died, remember? But of course, you remember, because you were there. Or were you? What really happened that night?"

Abby looked away...into Max's intelligent eyes zeroing in on the conversation. An awkward three-way moment charged the air.

Kris focused on slicing up the caprese as he spoke. "That was a mean thing to say. I love you, and I know you want what's best for me. I'm an arse at the moment and taking it out on you."

Abby allowed the guilt to flow, wanting to scream out her frustration at the world.

She was drowning. Screwing things up with her dearest friend, who was now a royal mess. Missing her son so badly that it tore her apart, not to mention fighting for her son's freedom and life. *Don't lose it, Abigail Evans. Suck it up.*

"Buck up, Cricket, have some of this buffalo mozzarella. It's amazing." Kris nudged her plate towards her. "Remember that flight to Rome? You worked that layover and I bummed a ride.

We bought all those Italian meats and cheeses and had a picnic on the Spanish Steps. This mozzarella is almost as good."

"That was a great day. And I fell in that fountain," Abby said with a watery laugh.

"Because you were trying to get an impossible photo, you almost dragged me in! I need more pepper." Kris stood and walked to the next table as Abby wiped a drying tear.

Max placed a second paper sculpture on the table and scooted it across. He knew what she was going through and God bless the man, he was trying to help. She gently picked up her new addition to Gabe's paper frog collection. Max already made three frogs over the past few days and they were all different, this looked like a bullfrog—the man had talented fingers.

"You did those?" Kris pointed at the paper sword and frog as he sat back down.

"Sure."

"That's hectic, bru. What do they call that shit? Oregano? Oro…"

Abby reached forward and picked up the tiny dagger. "Origami."

"Sounds like something my grandmother would do."

John froze with a fork halfway up to his mouth.

Max shrugged. "Different strokes."

"That must really help your game?"

"Excuse me?"

"I bet chicks eat up that shit. Make them teeny, tiny flowers on the first date, and next thing you know, you're popping their sweet cherry."

John shot a warning glance towards a motionless Max. Abby kicked him under the table.

"What fancy shapes can you make? Are you like those balloon

guys who can pretzel a balloon into some kind of functional car? Let me extend a challenge. I name something, then you make it."

"Name it," Max said.

Tapping his index finger against his jaw, Kris pretended to think of an object. Abby wanted to bash him upside the head. This wasn't the side of Kris she knew best, he was generally an easy-going guy. They hadn't seen each other in years. There was a brittleness to Kris's demeanor, a bitter edge that she'd never seen. She was partly to blame. A dead girlfriend would forever taint that initial innocence and the recent massacre of his friends didn't help. Sourness was now his sword, and it was currently aimed at her pretend boyfriend.

Kris pulled out his wallet. "Why don't we use South African currency, how about a two hundred rand note?" The money landed on the table. Worth about fifteen dollars. "At least your teeny artwork would have some value once you're done…"

"This is ridiculous." Abby tried to snatch the money back from the table and Max stopped her.

Kris smiled. "What to make? What about a cricket for my little cricket? Can you make it jump? Put some spring into its little paper legs?" He used his hands to manically action his words. "That way it can jump into all sorts of nooks and crannies."

Kris's bouncing hand jumped into Abby's cleavage and Abby shoved his hand out.

Max pushed back from the table. "I'm done. I'm seriously done. I'm using the head."

Abby jumped up as he headed inside the bistro.

"Ag, shame. Someone's a little sensitive," Kris said.

John excused himself. "I've got this."

Max let the blowhard get to him. He paced the small unisex bathroom as the door swung open.

"Is Slater watching the girls?" he asked Johnny.

"Yep. He's at table seven. What the fuck, bro? Muller is wasted, you know better than to engage."

"Not a word. Not a goddam word," Max said.

Johnny looked at him like he was a stranger and not a brother on his team. Max knew why—he was always as cool as a cucumber yet some snotty game ranger tipped his lid off. Usually he psychologically controlled every room, but sadly not today. He pulled apart the last fifteen minutes, trying to find the trigger point.

He was comfortable with who he was, the origami was a quirk and he didn't give a fuck about the ranger trying to poke fun. Max could easily kick his ass. Muller couldn't dream up the shit that Max had seen and done. There was no need for a pissing contest. This was about Abby. Muller wanted her. It was plain to see, yet it wasn't the jealousy driving Max's rage. The minute Muller stepped in and took rough liberties with Abby, Max's temper began to rise. What made him angrier was that she allowed Muller to get away with it. Kris ramming his hand down her blouse had been the final straw.

"Kris wants her."

"And that's our problem how? We're here as a lure for Khalid tonight, not to tango with an idiot game ranger. Get your shit together and let's do the fucking job."

Johnny left Max to get his shit together, and Max thought he'd done a fine job—until he stepped out, running headlong into Abby's sweet body. Abby pulled him back into the bathroom before locking the door.

"Kris is going through a tough time. He knows he's a jerk."

"Stop defending him. We'll talk about this later."

"No, we'll talk about it now. You've had a bad attitude ever since Kris walked in. You didn't even try to play nice."

"Jesus, woman."

"You sat there like a wet blanket, skewering him with sulky man glares, and after all he's gone through!"

"You're defending him after he shoved his hand down your shirt!"

"He just saw his teammates being murdered in front of him. If anyone should understand that, it's you."

Now he was royally pissed. "Don't ever compare me to him. We're nothing alike."

"Max—"

"Fuck it. You want to know why I'm pissed? Because you allow him to walk all over you. He had his damn hands everywhere, you allow him to touch you and push you the hell around." Max grabbed Abby's shoulders. "Do you let him take advantage because of guilt, or have you always let him touch you that way?" It was jealousy pushing his rage but Max couldn't stop. "How far would you let Muller go?"

"You have some nerve. You have no right to tell me who touches me. Let go of me!" Abby kicked him in the shin.

Max crushed her lips to his. Passion fueled his temper as he ravaged her mouth. Abby moaned, and he ran a thumb over her rib cage, stroking beneath her breast. His other hand lifted her onto the ledge of the sink. Her legs wrapped around his waist as he ground against her. She mated her tongue with his, and his dick saluted in response. Dragging up her blouse, he thanked the gods for a front-clasping bra. Her perfect nipple peaked in his mouth. God, he could suck on it for hours.

"We're doing it again," she moaned.

"Doing what?" Max asked as he worked his way to her other breast.

"Getting raunchy in an impossibly small bathroom. It's our thing."

Hard counters and cold tiles weren't exactly conducive to canoodling. Max needed to make an effort to seduce her in a comfier spot. His mouth paused, and he stroked both nipples with his thumbs. Eyes closed, Abby looked like a wanton queen as her head fell back in ecstasy. *Mine.* He went cold thinking of Muller's hands touching her, but what right did Max have, telling her who to be with? Abby wasn't his woman. It was all just a pretense.

Johnny was right, they had a job to do and Max was screwing things up. His dick needed distance. Touching the flawless Miss Evans fogged up his brain.

◊ ◊ ◊

Max's mouth felt so damn good. *Good* wasn't the word. Orgasmic, mind-blowingly, freaking incredible. Abby's warm throbbing body was like honey in his arms. Coming apart in a public toilet, under the skillful touch of this rock-hard warrior. She closed her eyes as desire-laced blood pounded through her veins. Deliberate thumbs stroked her hard nipples then... nothing. Magical hands very suddenly pushed her away. She opened her eyes to his rigid back as he ran those delicious hands through his hair.

"Max?"

"Fix yourself up, Abby. I'm not fucking you in a public bathroom."

"Excuse me?"

"I'm not fucking you. Period."

"Is that what we were doing? Fucking."

Max looked over his shoulder with icy eyes. "We're not having this conversation."

Slipping off the granite counter, Abby pulled down her shirt. Anger and hurt balled in her throat. "Because I thought it meant a little more than that."

"I'm here for a specific reason, and I can't let anything get in the way."

"Of course not. What was I thinking? The first man I could actually trust—care about—and it turns out he's just like the rest. Looking out for himself and everyone else."

"Abby." His voice sounded hoarse.

"I don't need your pity fucks. You and your team can go and jump in a big man bastard lake for all I care." Abby pushed past.

"Jesus, Abs." Max swung her around.

"Get your hands off me." The big lout wasn't listening.

"You're an angel. You're freaking pure and sweet. I've never done this before—been so close to an asset. You're all mixed up in this case and it's screwing things up."

"I don't care," Abby said.

"I just need time. Let's sort through this later."

"Max. I don't play games. It's already too complicated, and I want simple. If you can't give me simple, then you have no right to touch me." She felt like she'd run a mile.

Max rubbed circles on her arms with his thumbs. "I care about you."

"Well, don't. I'll only destroy you and your precious career. Now go. I'm a big girl and need a minute to put my big girl panties back on."

◊ ◊ ◊

The bistro was quieting down. It was late and time to wrap up a screwed-up night. Max wasn't going to pretend to be civil, which was a-okay because right at this moment, Muller seemed to be ignoring him, focusing on Lizzy instead.

"Lizzy Liz. Abby's new friend. Here's my number." He scooted a business card across the table. "In case you wanna give my number out to some friends—it's Kris with a K."

Lizzy ignored the card. Johnny pushed it back with a deliberate and large finger.

"You're really pretty."

Lizzy smiled awkwardly. "Thanks."

"Your sweet accent reminds me of my girl."

There he went with the "my girl" thing again. Max gritted his teeth.

Kris continued, "So Lizzy, how long have you lived in South Africa?"

"Since I was twelve. My mother is from California, my father grew up on the South African coast. My parents met when he consulted for a mining project in San Diego, way back when."

"Now, it makes more sense. So how did you meet Abby?"

Lizzy lied well. "An art class. We were both Americans and I invited Abby to join my Facebook Group—Americans in Jo'burg."

"You're also an artist?" Kris asked.

"No."

"I didn't think so. Let me guess. Bouncy blonde, Californian roots. You're a hairdresser?"

Sarcastic fucker. Max wanted to wipe the grin off Kris's face, and by the look of it, Johnny wanted to rip his head off. This was going south quickly. There was more to Lizzy than people thought. Max was just as guilty of prejudging her based on her initial sparkle. He'd delved deeper into her background since they'd discovered her past. A survivor who had fought her way out of an abusive relationship. She hid the damage well; PTSD was indeed a bitch. Lizzy was working toward a nursing degree before her fiancé savagely snapped. Due to the trauma, she'd dropped out of college. Max had little doubt that she would eventually get her life back on track. Lizzy had recently enrolled in a beauty school, but her confidence had taken a violent hit and she seemed lost, putting on a bubbly face to mask the anxiety.

Max glanced at Lizzy as she answered Muller's question. "Massage therapy."

"Do you give 'happy' massages? Give a squeeze, get a squirt?"

"It's time to go, Lizbug." Johnny reached for her hand.

Eyes sparking with anger, she shook him off. "You know nothing about me."

Max stretched across the table. "Lizzy."

She silenced him with a glare and swiveled back. "We're not stereotyping or anything but go ahead, Kris, let me know what you really think?"

Muller grinned like a hyena. "Let's see… I'm guessing you have a rich daddy? Apple of his eye? You collect stuffed toys and display them on your bed. Probably a little high maintenance."

The whites on Johnny's knuckles were showing.

"How on earth did you come up with that?" Lizzy asked.

Kris nodded to the chair next to her. "Your Louis Vuitton bag is draped on its very own chair."

"Holy cow! My mother gave that to me four years ago for my twenty-first birthday, and for your information it's the only designer bag I own."

Kris ignored her. "Sweetheart, don't talk kak, no man likes a spoiled little rich girl." He turned to Johnny. "Good luck, bru, I bet her last boyfriend nearly strangled her to death to get away."

Oh. Hell. No. Max shot towards his friend as Johnny launched across the table, barely managing to get between them. Max's typically laid-back buddy morphed into a rabid dog. Did Muller know about Lizzy's past? Or was that last phrase just a coincidence?

"Calm down. Fucking breathe." Max pulled Johnny farther aside. "Look at me, Johnny. Calm the hell down. You're causing a cluster fucking scene."

His teammate took a moment before switching into a more familiar operator mode. Thankfully due to the later hour, the audience was minimal. Slater ambled past before retreating into the shadows.

Abby yelled out, "Get out now!"

Max turned, not sure who her ire was directed towards.

Abby pointed to the door. "Now, Kris."

"Are you serious? That jaw breaker attacked me and tore my freaking shirt!"

"I heard what you said to Lizzy."

"I'm sorry. I'm a fokking idiot." Kris stepped towards her, desperation now leaking from his pores.

Abby moved back, and Max stepped between. "She's done, buddy. I suggest you leave."

Kris tried to touch Abby and Max sidestepped, shoving him back.

"Cricket!" A high-pitched whine.

Have some pride, Max thought.

Abby stood firm. "I know you're going through a tough time, but that's no excuse, I can't help you. I can't even look at you."

Kris stiffened, and Max readied himself. "Don't be stupid. Walk away, buddy."

"I'm not your buddy, and you know what? Fuck you, Josephine. You can use your middle name and hang out with all your new kak-ass friends, but I know who you really are. A sad little girl with fucked-up daddy issues."

Max stepped forward. "Out now, before I pound you into the floor."

Kris turned, sauntering out. Kris Muller was becoming a big ass complication, and Max had a bad feeling that this wasn't close to being over. He turned to Abby and she walked into his arms.

"Ding dong, the dirt-hole is gone," Johnny said as he met Max's grim stare. Lizzy lunged for her hand bag like a frightened rabbit. John reached for her as she leapt back.

Sensing her friend's distress, Abby let go of Max. "Sweet pea, are you okay?"

"I have to go."

Johnny tried to embrace her. "I'll take you home, angel."

Lizzy yelped in a shrill voice. "Don't come near me. I need some air. Max, can you give John a ride home?"

Max nodded.

Clutching the VW keys tightly, Lizzy made her escape. Johnny tried to go after her.

"I've got this." Abby stepped forward. Johnny's distress convinced Abby that she was doing the right thing. "If I talk to her, promise me that you will do right by my friend. Come clean and tell her why you're really here."

"I'm planning to tell her."

"Do you want to be with her?" Abby asked.

Johnny looked sideways at Max and nodded. "After this mission is wrapped up, I'm planning on taking vacation time, I'll return to South Africa to see her."

Max swore. "And you were going to tell me this when?"

Abby poked Johnny in the chest. "You're good together, if you can get off your deceitful butt and do right by her. You seem to be a good man, but that won't stop me from kicking your ass if you play games with her heart."

"Yes, ma'am."

Abby raced to catch up with her friend and Max trailed behind, sticking to the shadows.

"Lizzy!"

Tears streamed down her friend's face. "I can't be with him. This was a giant mistake."

"Tell me what's wrong."

"Didn't you see the violence?" Her wild fear was apparent to Max. "I thought John was my defender against all the brutality that we've seen, that we've experienced."

"He was protecting you."

"And one day when he turns that violence towards me…"

"He wouldn't do that."

"How could you know?" Damage from Lizzy's past ran her life.

"Oh, Lizzy." Abby hugged her tightly.

"He's just like the rest. Men with their filthy tempers are all the same, wanting to destroy everything around them."

"That's such bullshit, and you know it."

"The hell it is! That's the reason why you isolate yourself from the world."

"I've been wrong. Happiness doesn't exist in a singular bubble, never touched by life's realities." Abby grasped Lizzy's hands. "What about your dad?"

"What about him?"

"He loves you to the moon and back. Has he ever hurt you?"

Lizzy shook her head.

"He adores you, and your mom and would commit violence to defend his family."

"That's different."

"John is nothing like Ivan," Abby stated.

Lizzy flinched at the mention of her former fiancé's name.

"In therapy you once mentioned that Ivan was all darkness, you instinctively knew that his soul was damaged, the first night you met him. You ignored those instincts."

"Ivan felt wrong from that first moment," Lizzy agreed.

"What about John?"

"What about him?" Lizzy asked.

"Is he darkness or light? When you first met him, did you want to run away or towards him?"

Lizzy scrunched her nose as she sank back against the driver's door. "He's a mix of both I guess." Her shoulders drooped. "I only ever wanted to run to him. Until tonight."

"Tonight, you've questioned your instincts. I'm not saying John is perfect—no one is—but he'd never hurt you physically."

"I thought I was getting back to normal. That everything was fine. I'm not fine though, I'm damaged and stupid and—"

"You're brave and strong and it takes time."

"Did you tell Kris about Ivan?" Lizzy asked.

"I'd never do that!"

"His strangling comment seemed weird."

Abby folded her arms. "It's a generic insult. I've barely spoken to Kris since we've reconnected."

"Don't confide in that man, I don't like him."

"Liz—"

"I don't know how you ever became his friend. He's cruel and mean spirited."

"He's lost and hurting. He wasn't always like that."

"People don't change all that much. You believe in what you want to see. Trust me, I did the same with Ivan."

Abby tucked her arms in tighter. "It doesn't matter, that friendship is over."

"What about John? Did you say something to him? His reaction was a pretty extreme one to the 'generic insult.'" Lizzy air-quoted.

"No, sweet—"

"Because I don't want John's pity. He can never know."

"He wouldn't look at you that way."

"I can't take the pitying glances my parents shoot my way when they think I'm not looking, and he'd do the same." Lizzy jangled her car keys before unlocking the Beetle. "I have to go. Thanks for standing up for me tonight."

"What can I do?"

"Nothing. I need time to myself."

"Call if you need anything." Abby nudged her. "For you, I killa the bull."

Lizzy smiled at their obviously private joke as she climbed into her bright yellow car. "Well for you, I killa the bullfighter and save the bull."

Abby chuckled. "Text me when you're safely home." She waved at her friend's disappearing convertible.

Max stepped up. God, she made him feel things. Hopeful things that could tear apart his carefully constructed world.

Abby turned to him. "I lied to her again—about John not knowing."

"You didn't have a choice."

"That's just it. I do have choices and I'm done with all the deceit, especially when it comes to us. I don't belong in your military world, hiding whatever this relationship is. You're messing with an asset and risking your career. This flirting thing is over—once your mission is wrapped up we'll go our separate ways."

Those words were demolition to his soul.

Chapter Seventeen

Back at base with Abby locked in for the night, Max gazed at the monitoring station, recalling the girls' conversation. It maddened him that there were fucking monsters out there who inflicted such lasting damage on women.

At the same time, seeing his tough woman comforting her friend filled him with pride. Despite Abby's last words to him, she felt like his woman. What an effing screwup the night had been. First dealing with Kris "the dick" Muller and then discovering that Johnny was also emotionally invested in an asset. His team was falling apart, and Max was the rebellious leader doing the damage along the way. The sooner they wrapped up the assignment, the better, then hopefully they could screw the brains out of their chosen women without having to deal with the guilt.

Abby wandered out to sit on her patio in the dark, and there was too much physical space between them. He was always watching. Max was so tired of the watching. He wanted to be touching, always touching.

He traced her image on the screen. She looked so sad; losing a lifelong friend would do that to you. He wanted to unravel all the bandages wrapped around her heart and rescue her and her baby from the terror. Unravelling the hurt wasn't his job. He was expected to hand Evans over to the agency, wrapping this mission up with a nice little bow. Except he didn't want to do that. He couldn't. Abby was no longer a job. She hadn't been that since he'd discovered her innocence.

Donnie surprised him from behind, and Max pretended to adjust the screen for a better angle before grabbing the nearest file.

Donnie sank into a nearby chair. Equipment hummed softly in the quiet space. "Did I ever tell you about my wife?"

Donnie never spoke of her. She'd passed away from breast cancer a year before and it had nearly killed him. Donnie was still fairly new to the team, only just a year with them. A year that saw less action in the field then they were used to, but there was no doubt that David "Donnie" Wilson, also a former Green Beret and their 18Fox—the intelligence specialist—was in for the long haul. Donnie's reserved shell was hard to slip through, but once you got to know him, you had a loyal dog at your back.

Max didn't know what to say and Donnie continued. "Not about how she died—you all met her when she was ill—I'm talking about how we first met."

Max shook his head. All he knew was that she was French. He'd met her once briefly, when Donnie joined the team, just over a year ago and by then she was terminally ill. Too weak to stand, connected to IVs…frail and so vulnerable. That horrifying and helpless journey that ultimately led to the loss of Donnie's wife, scared the hell out of Max.

"I never speak about how we met. I should, but it's our own special adventure and no one else's business."

"Donnie, you don't need to—"

"I met Sophie in Mali, when I was an MLE, providing additional security for embassy employees in Bamako."

MLEs were small teams of Special Ops guys stationed at US Embassies to gather intelligence and assist in counterterrorism operations. They were usually drawn from Green Berets and Rangers, as well as Navy SEALs, marine and air force units. Max held huge respect for those small teams, who operated in a similar capacity to his own four-man unit.

"Sophie worked as a translator, also providing support by befriending the locals and reinforcing our informant network. The instant I saw her I knew I wanted her. I convinced myself that we'd screw each other till we could barely stand and then walk away. But that ain't me. Some soldiers may find a warm bit of pussy in a foreign country to pass the time, but I've always focused only on the mission, looking for a hometown girl whenever I returned Stateside."

Max did the same. All work and no play made for a really lonely existence, but a James Bond lifestyle never appealed, and screwing random strangers in third world countries could potentially lead to crazy STDs.

"I loved Sophie from the first moment I saw her, sounds corny but it's the truth. I avoided her whenever possible and almost got away with never touching her, that would've been the biggest damn mistake. One night, Sophie introduced us to an informant at a local market. We were targeted by insurgents. It took every ounce of skill to get our four-man unit out of there. Five of us walked out of the embassy that morning, but only three of us walked back in. Two of my teammates were airlifted out."

"*Perkele,* I'm sorry, man."

"Yeah. It sucked. Jesus. When Sophie was safe, I threw her on the bed and marked her as fucking mine. When my contract was over, I applied for leave and went back to Mali to propose.

We got married…and buddy, I had the best year of my life. My wife was so freaking beautiful." Donnie smiled sadly. "Sophie found a small lump under her left arm while in the shower, on the morning of our first-year anniversary." He swallowed, his voice rough. "That was the end of our hiatus."

Max squeezed Donnie's shoulder, allowing his friend a moment of mourning.

Donnie cleared his throat. "The point I'm making is this. Regardless of work conflicts or moral quandaries, Sophie and I made it work, because we loved each other. Sophie wasn't a distraction, she was the real deal."

"Abby's not a distraction either."

"Bullshit. Me and the boys know you'd never place the unit in jeopardy. We trust your judgment regardless of what option you choose, but where you are right now? Questioning yourself. Questioning your instincts. It's dangerous for all of us. Make a decision and act on it."

"Aaah. Fuck it." Max leaned back in his chair. "I care about her a lot more than I should, and I won't stand back and watch her walk away."

"Then don't. She's not Sharon Nasari, you know that, right?"

"What the fuck, Don! I know that."

"We know that too, it's as clear as day. None of us trusted Sharon. Sully was fooled, but you weren't the only one who figured her for being a viper in the grass."

Life was short and damn cheap. Max refused to spend another moment without Abby by his side. He stood, staring at the monitor as she headed indoors. "I'm heading across the road."

Donnie yawned. "I'm going to get me some coffee. I'll keep an eye on things. If a certain listening device behind a certain dresser happens to malfunction, I'll write a report."

Max nodded as he rounded the chairs.

"And Max, take your mobile with you, just in case."

◊ ◊ ◊

The epically dismal day was over, which included losing Kris once and for all, a horrid fallout with Max and, as always, Abby missed her little angel. Just to feel him in her arms, to snuggle into his chubby neck and smell that sweet smell. Oh God. Her baby. Logically she knew she was doing the right thing by protecting him from his monstrous father, but it was tough. She'd cried more this past month than her whole life combined.

Wrapped up in her softest robe, Abby sipped warm milk laced with honey as she headed to bed. A sudden noise almost made her drop the mug. A dark shadow with ghostly eyes slipped through the sliding door.

Max.

"Are you trying to give me a heart attack?"

He pulled her cup from nerveless fingers, his eyes ravaging her face. As she tried to speak, Max shook his head and firmly led her to the bedroom, closing the door and locking it. Was something wrong? Had Khalid made a move? Max walked over to the dresser, staring at the small Nike statue before running a finger down its side. He seemed pensive, and she kept silent.

"I monitored your movements for months. Every day I watched you glide through the water like some kind of water sprite. Like you were born to it, and I couldn't look away. Were you a siren luring me to my destruction or my lighthouse in the storm?"

Abby didn't like that insinuation. He meant *siren* in that Sharon Nasari kind of way.

"When I saw this statue in your bedroom, I felt uneasy,

drawn to its alluring beauty. A calm deity in the face of the storm, standing steadfast in destructive winds." His thumb ran over a wing. "Men are drawn to your calm; you're the eye of the hurricane. Even my team has fallen at your feet, wanting to slay your dragons and to protect you."

He had the analogy all wrong. She wasn't the eye of the tempest. She was the storm, wiping out everything in her path, destroying the lives of those she loved.

Abby stirred. "You're comparing me to a monstrous sea nymph—a siren with a flayed soul that sits on a heap of decaying bones and lures any mortal who sails by with a bewitching song. You may be right."

"Baby, no—"

Abby took the statue from Max. "When I worked for the airlines, I'd bid for Parisian trips. As soon as we landed, I raced for the Louvre, standing in those long lines for hours. Once inside, I'd head straight for this statue. It's an immense work of art, sitting at the top of a wide staircase. I gazed at it for hours, studying and sketching it from every angle. A woman leading her own course. Fighting the elements. Winning the battle. We'll never know what the full statue looks like. The Nike lost her head, hands and feet, yet, she's still strong, confident and victorious. Everything I always wanted to be."

Max stroked her hair. "You're closer to that than you will ever know."

"Maybe." Abby gently set it down. "I need her by my side, even if it's just a tiny replica occupying a small spot on my dresser. It's a reminder of my fight for freedom." She wrapped her robe closer before turning his way. "What are you doing here?"

Max knelt next to the cabinet and pulled a listening device out from behind. He walked into her bathroom and placed it onto the counter, covered it with a heavy towel before closing the door. They were now alone.

"You just lost one of your best friends."

"Is this what this is? Checking up on me? I'm not as broken up about it as you might think." Abby climbed onto the bed and sat cross-legged, pulling a pillow onto her lap. "Kris and I have been moving in opposite directions for a long time. I pretended it would be okay, but guilt played a role."

"You have nothing to feel guilty for, Abs. You were a victim, you could never have saved Megan."

"I know. I guess I felt guilty about lying to Kris. I just couldn't bring myself to tell him the truth about that night, and I realized tonight that I don't trust him with my past."

Max stepped forward. "What do you mean?"

"I guess I trust him with certain things, but not with my heart. Does that make any sense? He was such a mischievous kid. I thought he'd grow up to be this incredible man. I put him on a pedestal for so long." Abby shrugged. "He has gaps in his soul. Does that sound weird?"

"It doesn't."

"Don't get me wrong. I'm proud of what Kris has become. A fearless conservationist protecting our endangered species. He's just so twisted inside. So immature…almost mean. Did I make him that way?"

"Abby."

"Did Meg's tragic death or me deserting him harden him so much?"

"Don't put this on you." Max sat on the side of the bed and grabbed her hand. "I guarantee that he always carried that mean streak. Maybe it just wasn't that prevalent when you were kids."

She nodded sadly.

◊ ◊ ◊

Max gazed at her delicate profile as she played with the corner of the pillow. He could watch her for days. Hell. He had been watching her for days. He would never get tired of it. Her fine skin was slightly flushed from the shower. Damp tendrils fell from a messy bun, clinging to her lovely neck. Hunger surged as he imagined running his lips over her warm skin. Nibbling that perfect earlobe as he buried himself inside her.

"Not to mention his ridiculous T-shirt," Abby said.

What were they talking about? Right, Muller the douche.

"Game Rangers do it in the bush?" Max said.

"A juvenile shirt for a juvenile boy."

Enough about Kris Muller. They'd wasted too much time on the ass. Max stroked her knee. "I want to apologize for things I said to you."

Abby smoothed the pillow. "You made a valid point. You need to focus on the job and on your future, we both need to. I have to save my child from a monster, and you have to do the job and go home."

"What if I don't want to go home, at least not without you?" Max said, tracing her neck before rubbing her earlobe.

He laid bare the tempest of emotions, not hiding anything and Abby sucked in a breath. "Don't play games."

"This is not a game, it's incredibly complicated even if everything goes according to plan."

Abby frowned. "What do you mean? You'll get Khalid, and I'll have my Gabe back."

"You'll be taken in for a debriefing where your story will be examined." Max rubbed a hand across his eyes.

"I'll be interrogated."

"No, sweetheart, you'll be questioned. You're now just a person of interest."

Abby looked scared, and Max pulled her in. "I'll be there every step of the way."

"You'll be reassigned."

Max kissed her. "I'm not going anywhere. You're my only priority. No more ignoring this thing between us. I want to touch you, stroke you." He ran fingers up her arm. "Feel your skin against mine as we screw each other's brains out." He whispered hotly in her ear, "I want to make achingly slow love, and then fuck you hard and fast."

She moaned.

Max pulled back, cradling her head in his hands. "Every cell in my body is yours, tell me to stay." It wasn't exactly a declaration of love, but he put his heart out there for the first time in his existence.

Abby's calm eyes stared deeply into his and they pooled with tears. "Leading me on would be cruel. I have no room for light in my life, at least not at the moment."

"Ah shit, Abs. Don't say stuff like that, you're breaking my heart."

"This whole romance thing is new for me," Abby said as she pulled his hands into her lap.

With a crooked grin, Max said, "For me too. I'm a workaholic and will probably mess it up—I'm an ass like that—but would never intentionally hurt you, and I'll fight for whatever this is."

Abby grasped his hand. "There's too much happening in my life at this moment. My head feels like it's rolling around a cotton candy machine coated in sticky webs."

"That's okay, you've handled more than most people

including hardened soldiers."

"If you can handle one overwhelmed woman, I want to be with you."

"Well, when that woman hints that she tastes like cotton candy, a guy's gotta investigate."

Abby jumped to her knees. "Are we really doing this? Gland to gland combat?"

Max barked with laughter as he swept her up into his arms, then threw her back onto the bed.

"Move faster, Mr. Big Bad Wolf, what are you waiting for?"

In a flash his phone and gun landed on the dresser, followed by his shirt. Max shucked off cargo shorts while pulling out a condom as he stumbled back towards the bed. As he placed it on the bedside table, Abby ran her gaze over him as Max grabbed the throw off the bed, cloaking himself and diving on top. He pulled apart her robe.

Abby laughed. "What are you doing?"

Max poked his head out. "Don't you know? Operators do it in the dark…"

She sniggered as he ran hands down her waist. His bristly cheek brushed against her stomach before spreading her legs and planting kisses on the inside of her thigh. Her muscles shivered in response as he pulled a pillow down to slip under her ass. A hint of coconut drifted from the soft linen.

"Mr. Operator, you move damn fast."

"I can do fast, and I can do slow, now prepare to be ravaged slowly by my manly tongue," Max growled.

"Do your worst. I surrender to your particular set of skills."

Max delved into her core. Abby surged up, and he grasped her ass with one hand as his tongue circled her clitoris with slow strokes. He slipped in a finger, stroking and circling. Abby's low moans pushed him to increase the pressure ever so slightly. She jerked in response, thrashing with need. So damn beautiful and she tasted so good. His dick brushed against the mattress, feeling like a rock between his legs. Her tight pussy lightly pulsed. As it slicked up, Max slipped in another finger, separating her folds and sucking gently on her clit while caressing her sex. The angle of her ass meant that his upward strokes were long and firm, rubbing the front inner wall of her pretty cunt.

"Oh God. Max. Oh God."

Abby spasmed around his fingers, thrusting off the bed. Her ass cheeks clenched as the orgasm rocked her to the core. Max couldn't take his eyes off her glorious face. Drops of liquid leaked from his swollen dick, as her pussy clenched around his hand. His fingers remained inside, and he blew gently on those hot, wet folds.

When her body was lax, Max started to lick her lightly, purposely softening his tongue, taking his lazy time and enjoying her taste. Abby squirmed, and he draped a forearm over her flat stomach to hold her in place and increased the pressure of his mouth ever so slowly. Her toes curled into his sides; he nibbled at her folds as Abby tried to arch her back. He gently pushed her back down. The silent space heightened her raspy breaths. He listened intently, paying attention to what she liked. Every time her breathing picked up, he repeated the action.

Abby thrashed her head from side to side. Twisting his still embedded hand, Max started stroking again. Her tightening passage made his cock jump.

"Max. Holy. Hell." Her eyes met his, and he felt like a fucking god. Every lick, every suck and he saw the need flashing in those green eyes. He fucked her soaking wet pussy with his fingers, while latching on with his mouth and sucking hard against her clit. Every cell of his being kept pace. His mind, his fingers, his tongue, and soon it would be his cock.

Abby focused on his eyes, Max knew she could read his deep carnal thoughts. *These folds are mine. I will suck you off whenever I feel like it.* He sucked harder. He pulled out and thrust in. *My hot dick will stroke your tight, throbbing pussy.* She got the message and her eyes grew wild. Powerful spasms rocked her uncontrollably.

Max pulled his fingers out, grasping her ass, he raised her up, licking and moaning into her wetness; the vibration set off more spasms. Jesus, she was sensitive. If he didn't bury himself soon, he'd disgrace himself.

Max pushed the blanket off, grabbed the condom, quickly sheathed himself and settled over her limp body. He stared into her jade eyes. Reaching down, he continued to caress her wet center. In time, her sleepy eyes widened with pleasure. His other hand stroked her temple.

Abby's face was inches from his, and her gaze connected with him so powerfully that it robbed him of breath. Intimate minutes passed by as he took in every detail of her face. The tiny freckle above her upper lip, the inner golden rim of those mossy eyes. He swore he could see into her very soul.

Abby was the light in his life, it wasn't the other way around. Max swallowed hard and circled her passage with a firm stroke. Abby moaned in response. He eyed her sexy lips before capturing her mouth in his. She tasted like honey. He sucked at her bottom lip before plunging his tongue into her sweet mouth. His fingers were coated with her juices as he eased them out, slowly nudging the head of his cock into her entrance.

His thumb ran over a small scar on her thigh, and the reality of their situation came slamming back. He loomed over her like a beast, not taking any of her past experiences into consideration.

"Please don't stop."

"Honey—shit—what you've been through."

Abby stroked his cheek. "This is different. It's pure and amazing. It's just the two of us."

"Jesus, Abs." He couldn't move. Abby grabbed his hand, guiding it to her breast. "Touch me with every part of you."

He leaned down and sucked on her dusky nipple. She arched into him, nudging the tip of his shaft into her wet core. Shit, that felt good. Grabbing his ass, Abby opened her legs wider and pulled him towards her, steadily driving his dick home. It was freaking heaven.

He settled back over and looked into her eyes. "How does it feel?"

She smiled up at him. "Full. You're kind of large."

"It doesn't hurt?"

Abby wiggled. "I like it." She bit her bottom lip as she stroked his brow.

Face to face. Core to core.

"Wrap me up in you, baby," Max growled.

He pulled out and drove back in as Abby cried out. She twined her legs around his knees and kept her hands on his buttocks as they found a slow rhythm. His intense eyes never left her face. Observing for any sign of fear or discomfort. All he saw was his woman's pleasure.

"Abby—"

"Don't stop. Oh. God."

Max crushed his mouth to hers, devouring her escaping scream, groaning and thrusting like a madman, burying himself to the hilt as his cock pulsed. He felt her everywhere. Her hot, tight pussy milking him, her vanilla hair, her soft skin. His seed seemed to explode from the base of his cock and he let himself go, moaning into her wet mouth.

◊ ◊ ◊

Cocooned under his strong body, Abby was surrounded by musky leathered essence. Her protector. The first man she truly cared for thrust powerfully into her and it was all too much. Pleasure tore through her. She clung to his shoulders as Max drove deeper, claiming her with a primal groan, thrusting out his own volatile release. Time slowed as she spiraled down feeling his warm breath on her damp neck.

He finally rolled to the side, pulling her with him. "Are you okay?"

"Oh, hell yes. I think you literally blew my head off."

"Well, I sure hope not 'cause that's the prettiest head I've ever seen." He kissed her temple before running for the bathroom for a quick clean-up. He brought a warm washcloth back for her. Once they were done, Max spooned her, giving her ear a playful nip.

"You like my ears."

"What?"

"You're always touching or nibbling my ear. It feels nice."

"They're prettily shaped, with delicate folds. I can't resist touching your lovely helix." Max licked the tip of her ear. "And your dainty auricle." He traced his tongue down. "And your charming lobule." He bit her earlobe before sucking on it. "And, God. I love the way you smell. Like soft sunshine and warm skin."

"You say the sweetest things sometimes," Abby said as she stroked his hand on her breast.

"Only sometimes?" Max muttered.

"Well, yeah. You still have to maintain that big, bad operator reputation."

Instead of laughing at her small joke, Max tensed. "I swear on my life, I'll never be mean to you. I'll protect you from all the shit in this world, and that includes my own shit."

Abby tried to turn to him, but he held her tight. "I know that."

"I hope so. Not all men are like your father, and no matter how much baggage I bring home from the job, no matter what I do out in the field, I would never take it out on you."

"Do you think I don't know who you are? You're a good man, with a noble heart." She held up her hand. "I get that you deal with evil stuff in your line of work, and I'm sure you've done more than your fair share of killing, but your moral code is in place."

Max was silent for a moment before saying, "I'll make space in my life for us. You, me and Gabe. It won't always be easy, with my line of work. I'm often deployed, and you'll need a little patience along the way."

"Patience, huh?" Abby turned and pushed Max over onto his back. She ran her hands down his stomach, trailing kisses down to his already erect member. "You might need a little patience with me... I've never given a blowjob before and reckon I'll need some encouragement."

◊ ◊ ◊

Max's eyes widened at her words. Then her heavenly lips wrapped around him, doing an incredible job of sucking him off. His hips thrust upwards as Abby fingered his balls with one hand. Her tongue swirled around his tip before her mouth sank down all the way, and then up, and then down. Forget patience, if she kept that up, he would be a goner by the two-minute mark. *Good golly, Miss Evans.* He groaned in pleasure as her mouth did naughty things. One mind-blowing orgasm later, he drifted off to sleep with bad girl Evans wrapped in his arms.

Chapter Eighteen

A flushing toilet jarred him awake. The faucet ran and then Abby made her way back to bed in the dawning light. Max pulled her close, warming her chilled limbs.

"It's cold out there," Abby said, burrowing under the covers. "If you need to pee, I suggest you hold it until the sun comes up."

"I'm perfect just where I am, spooning your pretty ass."

Abby snuggled in deeper, doing naughty things to his dick but he sobered quickly when his thumb ran over the scarred ridges branding her back.

"You can talk about it and I won't splinter into a million pieces. I've lived with that scar for the past three years. It's been part of my therapy and it's now part of my soul."

"Knowing what he did fucks with my head, I can't imagine how you feel," Max said.

"It doesn't matter how I feel. It's not going anywhere; the damage is permanent. I've thought about covering it with a tattoo."

Max traced the seared skin. "What kind of tattoo?"

"Not sure yet. I'll know when it's time."

Max shifted down and kissed the scar. Obviously

uncomfortable, Abby rolled to her back.

"You know everything about me. Tell me something about yourself. Something that's not a lie."

Max traced her collarbone. "Not everything I told you about my family was a lie. I may have fudged over where they actually lived, but the essentials were in place."

"So you grew up in a small town ranching family?" Abby said.

"Maybe not so small town. I'll give the full rundown before you meet the clan."

Abby turned to face him. "You want me to meet them?"

"I very much want that," Max said. Her pebbling nipples fascinated him and he ran a thumb back and forth over a dusky tip.

"They might not like me. I've had a strange life, and I've never met someone's parents before."

Running his hand along her stomach then up her arm, Max said, "I love that you're different, your past has shaped who you are. So has mine. I was the strange kid growing up."

"Don't talk baloney. Like any alpha male, I bet you controlled the playground."

"I wish. The other kids thought I was weird. I was born in Colorado, to Finnish immigrants. Much of our family still lives in Finland and Sweden. We traveled to Europe often when I was a kid, my mom often got homesick. I spoke Finnish, German and Dutch at a young age, and loved languages. By the time I entered the military, I spoke multiple languages and have learned more since. I'm what's called a polyglot. Technically I'm almost a hyper-polyglot, an individual who speaks a dozen languages or more."

"That's incredible. How many do you speak?" Abby asked as Max kissed the side of her breast.

"Eleven—including Arabic, Portuguese, Urdu, Russian, Swahili, Somali and Hausa." He noted her goose bumps as he paused to suck the curve of her bosom, so he repeated the action with an added tongue swirl.

She sighed. "Because of the Dutch, I'm sure you have a handle on the Afrikaans language?"

Max settled back into the pillow. "It's fairly similar to Dutch. I also learn differently. Teachers at school thought I may be slightly autistic. Turns out I process things non-conformably. I didn't fit in with the other kids—even with my siblings—my white-picket-fence family battled to connect with me."

Abby rolled over and stroked his chest as she listened.

"I was an active child like my brothers but wasn't socially normal, preferring to isolate myself. I finally figured out the act of normalcy in my teenage years and made new friends. Much to my mother's horror, I was a little rebel except it was all an act; I just learned how to hide the freak in me."

"Don't ever call yourself that," Abby said.

"I don't mind the term now, back then it was a different story. Joining the military was my way of proving I was a typical badass. Funnily enough, my skills were highly sought after in Special Forces units and still remain extremely useful for my career."

"Do you miss your family when you're away for such long periods?"

"Sometimes, but they lead a different life. Their world consists of livestock, Sunday lunches and church…and having tribes of babies. I can't always connect. The best part of my job is exploring new cultures, traveling across continents, whereas they've settled into a different rhythm, a clan of homebodies I have little in common with. But I love and would die for every one of them, even if I'm still the weirdo of the bunch."

Abby stroked his jaw. "I know that travel bug well, it bit me in the ass as a teenager. Maybe it's meant to be. Two exotic nerds colliding and getting their freak on."

"Hey." Max laughed. "Who's calling who a nerd. Don't lump me in the same category as you, Miss artsy fartsy Nike wannabee."

"Oh. Now I'm the only nerd in this bed. Scoot your hunky butt over, I have a shower to get to."

"If you wanted more bathroom action, Miss Evans, you just had to ask. Lead the way, sweet cheeks."

That tender moment—Abby grinning as they stumbled across the room—nearly stopped his hardened heart. Max wanted to snatch up this foreign practice and make it routine, but Donnie's text message scratched up those rose-tinted glasses.

We have a problem. Be here in five.

◊ ◊ ◊

The somber mood in the room put Max on edge as he walked through the door. "What's happened?"

"Nothing good, boss. We're done here."

"What are you talking about? SITREP."

"Khalid isn't coming to Johannesburg. He has his hands full back in East Africa. There's been a split in his Somalian cell. His second in command, Roman Petrovich, went on the run with some of Khalid's faction. Khalid is hunting them down."

This created major complications.

"You have confirmation?" Max said.

"An informant delivered video footage of the fallout between the two groups. Shit went down at an Al-Shabaab training facility, in the Bakool region."

"Do we have positive identification on Roman and Khalid in the video?"

"It's shaky and grainy. A side view of Roman firing on Khalid's soldiers and a shadowed image of Khalid taking cover behind a structure."

"I'll need to see it."

"Affirmative. I spoke to HQ. Our analysts believe this shake-up will tie Khalid up for at least the next twelve months as he loses control of his small empire. Rumors are that Khalid has retreated deeper into Al-Shabaab territory. Locating his son will be put on his back burner until he's regained control. We'll be reassigned, most likely heading to Nairobi after the debriefing."

The Sandpiper had, yet again, slipped through their grasp. It would be months before they got a handle on his shadowy whereabouts. Abby and Gabe were back in limbo, at the whims of the US Government and could end up anywhere.

Johnny threw down the file. "Son of bitch is as slippery as a slope filled with good intentions."

"We go over the new intel with a fine-tooth comb. Grab a coffee and let's do this."

The prospect of telling Abby made Max feel ill. She deserved a normal life, not one with years on the run.

◊ ◊ ◊

All the men were gone, and they'd never left her alone before. Slater initially replaced Max on guard duty, and then thirty minutes later, a grim-faced Slater walked out the door. It felt all wrong.

Sitting nervously at the breakfast counter and playing with her yogurt wasn't doing Abby much good. Relying on others to plan her fate didn't sit well. The sudden isolation was also getting to her. How had she gotten so used to having the big men around? Was she safe?

Feeling vulnerable, Abby checked that the doors and windows were secure and wandered back to the sitting room. For the first time in forever, she switched the television on. The background noise felt comforting. She soon lost interest, was staring vaguely at the wall when Max turned the key in her door. The three other men filed in behind. Judging from the looks on their faces, Abby wouldn't like what they had to say.

"I told the team about us," Max said.

And that wasn't what she was expecting.

"I told them I'm not leaving your side. Until you're safe, I'll go where you go."

Slater stepped to the side. "You're family, Abby. We're here for you every step of the way."

That sounded dire.

"What's going on. What's changed?"

"Khalid won't be looking for Gabriel."

"What are you talking about?"

Max spoke up. "The Sandpiper's network is falling apart, there's dissension in the ranks. Khalid Al Juhani is in Somalia. Around sixty of his soldiers are dead. Killed in a shootout at a training range. It's estimated that half of his three hundred fighters have joined up with Roman Petrovich, a high-ranking member of his cell."

Donnie leaned against the wall. "Khalid is fighting for survival so finding Gabriel is his last priority."

"What you're telling me is—"

"We're wrapping up the mission. We'll be heading out in a couple of days, back to East Africa."

This wouldn't ever be over. Cowering underground was

always going to be their life. Her son would never be free of his father, Abby was back to fighting this all on her own. Only when Max lifted her up did Abby realize she'd sunk to the rug.

"I'm right here, baby."

"No, you're not. You have a job to do."

Max tried to lower her into an armchair. "I'm not going anywhere."

Abby shoved him away. "You don't have a choice. Would you give up your career to go into hiding with me?"

"If I have to. You're my responsibility. You and Gabe."

"That's such crap, your entire life has been about your job. You haven't even met Gabe, the son of the man you despise most in this world. The son of the man who killed your friend."

"Don't do this," Max ground out.

Bitterness came rushing out. "You'll despise him. He has his father's eyes, and his hair. All thick and curly."

"I've seen Gabe's photos, I know what he looks like," Max said carefully.

"Why do that to yourself? Saddle yourself with a scarred woman and her Al Juhani son." Right at that moment Abby despised herself. Max looked ready to throttle her. "Don't look at me like that. You know what I am."

"How dare you color yourself with that crock of shit. All of us standing in this room know who you are and don't need to build you up by kissing ass. You're a strong woman and a damn good mother, however it's clear what you think of me, I'm obviously a waste of your time."

"I never freaking said that! What are you talking about?"

"You think that little of me that I don't have the capacity to love an innocent boy. That I won't treat him like he's my own?"

"I don't know what to think. I don't know what normal is,

this whole being with someone forever and building a white picket fence. It's moving so quickly, I need a minute here!"

"Yes, ma'am, and you've got it." Max turned to walk out.

"I won't ruin your life over this, you've worked too hard to get to where you're at. I'm a destroyer of lives."

"That's where you're wrong. My life is better with you in it— sadly you don't feel the same way." Then he was gone.

Slater walked past and swatted her on the arm. "That was fascinating. All that was missing was popcorn. Now I need to use the head."

Abby threw herself into the armchair.

John headed to the kitchen. "This calls for cookies, what have you got stashed away?"

"Go away. Leave me to wallow in misery."

Cabinets squeaked open. "I'm hoping for chocolate chip."

He was always hoping for chocolate chip. The darn man had eaten her out of house and home.

Abby groaned and rolled to her feet. "Well, you're looking in the wrong place. There's a cookie tin on the counter. If you're going to raid the kitchen, make yourself useful and make me a hot chocolate."

John mumbled something between bites. Besides feeding the beast living in his stomach, Abby knew what he was doing. John was distracting her with sugar, and it worked. God bless the man.

◊ ◊ ◊

The following afternoon, Abby stepped back from the painting, pleased with her progress. So what if she'd been moping for the past twenty-four hours. At least she had an outlet for the heartache. The canvas was the best cure for despondency. Slapping paint onto a white surface was uniquely satisfying, giving her time to think.

Shame pecked at her conscience when she thought back to the harsh words spoken in her epic moment of panic. An apology was needed. Could you buy a man flowers? That might not go down so well in the alpha dojo across the street. Doubtful that they even owned a vase.

Pride kept her anchored to the easel. Maybe she'd paint a little longer. Abby dabbed the brush into a pale-yellow mix and applied a highlight to the elephant's hide.

"That's unbelievable."

The paintbrush jerked, and the paint dab went wild.

"Don't sneak up on me like some kind of shifty ninja," Abby said, cleaning up the mess.

"I'm naturally shifty, get used to it." Max stepped into the room, admiring her work. "Your talent blows me away, that elephant looks like it could charge right at you." He moved closer to examine the delicate brushstrokes.

"He's a beauty. Pity I won't be able to finish him before my life explodes."

"Your life won't explode. I'm there to make sure that doesn't happen."

"You still want to be in the same room as me after I said all those awful things? I thought you'd stay away for the rest of the assignment."

Max eyeballed the detailed hide of the elephant. "You won't get rid of me that easily."

"I was so mean. What I said was horribly unfair and it's not how I see you." Abby waited for a response while Max still stared at the large painting.

Finally, he looked at her. "Give me your hand."

"My hand?"

"I want to show you something."

Abby pulled the dirty apron off and followed Max out to the street. He tugged her towards their apartment.

Abby slowed her stride. "Am I allowed to go in there? Don't you have classified things lying about?"

"It was the big cleanup today, so restricted materials have been sealed or destroyed. All that's left is the surveillance station, which we're utilizing until we leave. We do have some laptops and an iPad lying about if you want to steal one and get one over on me."

"I've gotten one over on you before…with an apple of a different variety."

Max chuckled. "The team will never let me live that down."

Once inside, Donnie gave her a passing wave from his computer. Max pulled her into one of the bedrooms.

A stuffed green frog sat in the middle of the bed. Correction, it engulfed the entire bed.

"Is that what I think it is?"

"Yep."

"How on earth—"

"Gotta love online shopping. There's a place in Johannesburg that makes giant, stuffed—oomf."

Max suddenly had an arm full of woman. Abby clung to him like a monkey, planting a giant smacker on his lips.

"Do you think Gabe will like it?" Max managed to get out between kisses.

"Are you kidding me? He'll adore it. Thank you, thank you, thank you. When did you order it?"

"After our movie night."

Abby pulled his head down for another long kiss. His tongue mated deliciously with hers. He pulled her closer, his erect cock nudging against her stomach. She reached down and stroked it through his cargo pants.

Max groaned. "This is the best thank-you I've ever received. Hands down."

"That's the best gift I've ever been given," Abby countered with another stroke of her thumb.

"Interesting. I think I have myself a low-maintenance woman."

"I'm your woman?"

"As long as you'll have me." Max took his time pillaging her mouth before muttering. "As much as I'm enjoying your incredible hand fondling me, we'd better slow it down. The Hardy Boys are probably lurking around every corner."

Abby gave his heated member one last stroke before stepping back. "Where does this leave us, Gabe and I?"

"It leaves you both with me. It just takes planning."

"Ever heard that saying, 'The best-laid plans of mice and men often go awry'?"

"Well, you're not a timid mouse, and I'm a tier one man."

"Tier one?"

"It's a military term. I've run over our options and there are two viable scenarios."

"Well, that's two more than I have," Abby said. "I cannot leave Gabe where he is and Noleen needs to get on with her life. She may be his Godmother, but she's done way more than she should ever be expected to. What's the first scenario?"

"We all fly to Cape Town, secure Gabe and then probably head to Camp Lemonnier in Djibouti for the debriefing before heading Stateside. I'll take three months' worth of vacation time—"

"Hold it. Three months, are you insane?"

"I have accrued vacation, a load of PTO days I've never used."

"What about your team or your next mission?" Abby asked.

"MIT has procedures in place for an individual team member who needs to take leave. Another team leader would stand in." Max wandered over to the window, staring at nothing in particular. "I'd use the time off to set up a safe house with rotating security teams. Once I've secured the both of you, I'd head back to Africa to hunt Khalid and make it a priority to put him out of commission."

Abby sat on the bed and pulled the giant frog into her lap. "Rotating security teams. You mean like bodyguards?"

"That's exactly right. They'd be men I know or have personally vetted."

"That sounds ridiculously expensive, especially if it takes time to eliminate the threat. How could we afford that?'

Max looked sheepish. "Remember when I said my family owns a ranch? Well, the ranch is more like a large farm, it's actually a number of large farms in Colorado."

"How large are we talking?" Abby asked warily.

"Spanning over 120,000 acres of land. One of the largest cattle ranches in the US. My family employs 70 people. Their total worth is more than $1.1 billion."

Abby stared at him as if he'd grown two heads.

Max continued, "I've never been involved in the business, but my dad insisted on giving me 15,000 acres. Selling just a third of that would secure a safe house with all the trimmings and no limits on security measures."

"You're not selling your land for us."

Max leaned forward and stroked her neck. "It's my land, and I can do with it what I want. I've never had much use for fancy trappings. Using the money to protect us is the easiest decision I've ever made."

"I come with baggage. I'm a single mother on the run from

one of the most dangerous men on the planet. How can you want this?"

"I've never been afraid of unbeatable odds. If I were afraid, I wouldn't be doing this job. Stop underestimating your value and start fighting for us. Fight with me by your side."

"What is the other plan? Scenario two?" Abby asked instead.

"You're a stubborn wench." Max kissed her palm. "I'm not a fan of this option, but it's your decision. We collect Gabe, have the debriefing. You'll be presented with the option to be placed in WITSEC—Witness Protection. You'll disappear into the system. I'll continue tracking Khalid with every tool at my disposal. Once he's eliminated, I'll return to the States to find you."

Abby paused in stroking the frog's tummy. "How on earth would you find us?"

"I have a high-level connection in WITSEC," Max said.

"Why don't you like this plan?"

"Because your safety will be out of my control and I'd be trusting strangers with your life. WITSEC has been compromised in the past. It's rare but it happens. Anyone can be bought. Families threatened. By the time I found out, it would be too late."

"I trust our lives with you. Let's go with the first option." Gabe's safety came first. Abby refused to examine the second reason—spending more time with Max. She stood up and placed the frog back on the bed.

Max pulled her in for a tight hug. The safest place she'd ever known was in his arms. Forgetting the terror, Abby tucked her head into his neck.

"That's not even the biggest challenge we have," Max muttered into her hair.

"What's the biggest challenge?" Abby asked, snuggling in.

"Squeezing that fluffy green monstrosity into my luggage."

Chapter Nineteen

Two large suitcases and a carry-on bag. Abby stared at the packed luggage sitting in the corner of her room. That was all she could carry into their new life. Going back to the place she'd started out in this world felt terrifying; the last time she had been in the States was at the brash age of seventeen. She'd loved her time in South Africa. It was time to move on and new adventures started with a first step…and Djibouti.

Abby asked Lizzy to come over that evening. It was time to tell her friend the truth and to say their goodbyes. Lizzy wouldn't like the revelation, it could be the death of their friendship. A grim byproduct of the circumstances, but Lizzy needed to be warned she was a link to Josephine Abigail Evans that Khalid may uncover down the line.

Gruff voices drifted down the passage. The men gathered in the kitchen, making sandwiches from a dinner spread Abby had laid out earlier, and she dug in with gusto. Max was on the phone and hung up as Abby bit into her freshly made sandwich.

"We're meeting a colleague from a joint agency at Aroma Café at six pm. You'll come along for the ride. While I meet with our contact, Slater and Donnie will sit with you."

"Is that the coffee house near the gym?"

"Yes."

"You don't want me to stay here?"

"We've packed up the surveillance equipment and I'd feel better if we stick together as a precaution. When we've wrapped up the meeting, we'll talk to Lizzy and outline the potential risk to her safety. Are you all packed for the morning?"

Abby mumbled a yes between hungry bites. The past twenty hours were a whirlwind of wrapping up her business and packing the rest of her safe world into a storage unit. Leaving the artwork was challenging but she could always send for them. Maybe if Lizzy wasn't too mad, she'd keep the keys to the unit and look after Abby's things. A private plane down to Cape Town had been arranged and they were leaving in the morning.

"You'll give me Gabe's location once we are airborne and security is locked down," Max said.

"Thank you for understanding. I know it's grating for your team not knowing his whereabouts."

Max agreed. "I get that you're a mother who'll do anything to safeguard her son, but it makes me antsy not knowing where we're heading. Khalid's cell is in ruins, less than twelve hours ago he was sighted in Somalia and that's the only reason you've not been strong armed into giving up the address."

Abby grabbed a handful of salted chips. "How does this work? Do we rent a vehicle once we've landed?"

"No, baby. I'll have a local team on standby, standard protocol for such a high-valued asset."

Abby finished her meal as the men ran through the game plan for the next twenty-four hours. All she thought of was holding her son in her arms and the future safety of her friends. Gabe might be just an asset to the US Government, but he was her entire world.

"What about Kris?" Abby said.

"What about him?"

"He'll need to be warned. Khalid knew of our friendship in Dubai. If he tracks Kris down, he could torture him for information."

◊ ◊ ◊

Max gave Abby his full attention. "Kris worked for the sheikh on his game farm. Did he ever work for any of the sheikh's friends? How well does Khalid know Kris?"

"Max, you did a background check on Kris when he was in Dubai. You know where he worked."

"I know his history, but you may have picked up on something."

"I kept to myself. They moved in the same circles. Khalid was closer to Meg. Obviously, I had no idea that she was inserting herself purposely into Khalid's life."

"Would Kris have stayed in touch with anyone from Dubai after he left?"

"It's doubtful. Kris is a nomad and hates the setting-down-roots thing."

Something about that statement bothered Max.

"Do I need to warn Kris?" Abby asked again.

"We'll call him once we're Stateside. I'm not dealing with his theatrics today." Max zipped up his go-bag and grabbed his Smith's sunglasses.

Mandla had requested to meet with developing intel before MIT2 left. It was inconvenient but Mandla Nkosi was a valuable ally who'd arranged the transport to Cape Town. MIT2 would leave on good terms. Max wouldn't relax till they were safely on the final leg to MIT headquarters in North Carolina. That could still be weeks away.

"Are you ready, Abs? We're moving in ten."

Abby tidied the kitchen before grabbing her purse.

An uneasy feeling took residence in Max's gut on the quiet drive over to the strip mall. The men did a comms check and secured their weapons. They'd stacked an additional arsenal of firepower in the trunk. The mission was wrapped in Johannesburg, but Max couldn't shake the edginess as he glanced at Abby's profile in the back. Cool and collected, in Converse sneakers, skinny grey jeans and a white shirt she'd layered with a fitted leather jacket. His Italian girl next door, even if she had her own ideas about their future, she'd always be his girl.

Along with his security detail, Mandla sat near the entrance with a good view of the surrounding area. Slater and Donnie steered Abby to a sheltered table inside the cafeteria and out of view. Her high ponytail swayed as she sauntered to the back. Abby turned and shot Max a small smile, and he smiled in return knowing he'd fallen for his secretive siren and would take apart mountains stone by stone if it would make her happy. Max forcibly focused on his compatriot, joining Mandla at his table while Johnny stood just outside the entrance.

"So, you're leaving sunny South Africa. I'm not sorry that Khalid Al Juhani was an elusive bastard, no operative wants an extremist crossing their borders."

"Our team would have relocated or exterminated him," Max said.

Mandla added sugar to his tea. "I prefer to do my own cleanup. No offense to brawny American powerhouses such as yourselves, but I'm capable of cleaning my own house."

Max shifted his chair to face the entrance. "I appreciate your assistance and the bird provided for our Cape Town trip."

"I'm not done, I have new intelligence on one of the

background checks you requested." Mandla's phone buzzed and he glanced at the number before taking a sip of Earl Grey. "I need to take this, it relates."

◊ ◊ ◊

"Why is there never any soap in public bathroom dispensers?" Lizzy grumbled as she pumped a trace of foam out before washing her hands. She'd stopped in at Aroma Café for a bathroom break and to grab a smoothie. Thanks to a canceled class, she could squeeze in an aerobics session at the gym next door, before driving to Abby's place.

She wore her new neon pink leg warmers, matching headband and grey sweats. Lizzy paused to study her reflection, trying to tame her curls. She looked almost happy. Hopeful. That's the word she was looking for; her gentle giant made her feel hopeful and she'd see him later. John had no clue that she was a virgin. Ivan hadn't been her first—she'd wanted to wait till the wedding night, besides it hadn't felt right—but with John, it was too right.

The fondling sessions drove her insane. Lizzy wanted to do wicked things and knew he wanted the same, yet the times that she got carried away, John slowed them back down. Not tonight, an old *Snow Patrol* shirt wouldn't cut it. She needed something sexy, like a blue baby doll or maybe neon pink? Next stop after gym class, lingerie shopping at the mall. Fluffing her hair one last time, she swung open the door, heading for the counter to pick up the fruit smoothie she'd ordered, and she saw Abby.

Lizzy wanted to yell out but paused instead. The two well-proportioned strangers sitting at the same table were way too familiar with her hermit-like friend. Lizzy stepped back into the shadows. The slightly shorter man with a goatee had his back to the bathroom. The other was way too good looking, with bedroom eyes and a sensual mouth. Abby said something that made the hottie laugh and he touched her arm with easy familiarity. Lizzy felt bothered by the scene.

Abby never socialized outside Lizzy's group of friends, just meeting with Lizzy was a push for her reserved friend. A customer stood up behind Abby, bumped into her chair and shoved her forward. Both men moved smoothly as Abby grabbed for the table. The quieter man reached for a gun concealed in the small of his back. He kept his hand at the ready, analyzing the threat. The other man stood guard between Abby and the clumsy patron, easing back down once the customer had passed.

Why would Abby be hanging out with armed men? The dimpled male model casually touched his ear, speaking quietly. Movement at the door caught Lizzy's eye. John stood at the entrance, hands folded, looking like an unyielding stranger. Was he talking to someone? John adjusted something in his ear. *Holy strawberries!* Was John talking to that other man with some type of earpiece? Were they communicating with each other, like in the movies? John's electric gaze swung in their general direction, landing on the bronzed god before flicking Lizzy's way. Unwelcome surprise briefly registered, then John shot her a phony smile.

Lizzy was an uninvited guest in a duplicitous game. John advanced, and his puerile smile faltered as she stepped back, her agitation registering in his deceitful brain. He said something to Abby as he walked past, and Abby stood, moving towards Lizzy as if she were a spooked deer. Lizzy regarded them both warily.

Abby halted a few feet away. "Sweetie, what are you doing here?"

"I could ask you the same thing."

"I'm not sure what you mean?"

"Who are those men?" Lizzy nodded towards the table.

"They're my work colleagues," John said.

"Armed work colleagues who have business with Abby. You weren't even sitting with them."

John and Abby exchanged a loaded glance, which pissed Lizzy off. "Whatever game you're playing, leave me out of it." Lizzy stepped past and Abby grabbed her hand.

"We'll be heading back to my place shortly. Can we meet there to talk for a minute?"

"I'm not going anywhere with you, not until I know what's going on. I have an aerobics class in five, but this feels more important."

John pointed to an empty table behind the other men. "What do you want to drink, angel?"

"I ordered a juice, it's at the till."

Abby eased down next to her as John retrieved and paid for the drink. Lines bracketed her strained mouth.

"You've been lying to me," Lizzy said.

"I have. It's complicated. There are bad people after my son and I need protection."

"Gabriel's father?"

Abby nodded.

"How does John tie into this?"

Before Abby could reply, an older man stepped up to the table.

"Miss Evans."

Abby looked surprised. "Mr. Bakal, what a coincidence."

◊ ◊ ◊

Max watched the foul-up from a distance. John was doing damage control in a public arena and the itch between Max's shoulder blades wasn't helping. This meeting needed to be terminated. He scanned the parking area and neighboring restaurants for potential threats as people went about their daily business. Perhaps he was overreacting, but he'd never been this invested. The personal stake embedded in his heart was the lovely brunette sitting across the room, messing with his focus. Max shamelessly eavesdropped on scraps of Mandla's conversation. Mandla enquired on an interrogation of a suspect.

Levi Bakal walked into the café. Grand fucking Central Station today. The turd beetle made a beeline for Abby and Max gave his team the heads-up.

Somebody upstairs must have a grand sense of humor, Abby thought as the tiny man started in on her. "The bakery across the road makes the best bagels. Have you tried them? I'm waiting for a fresh batch to come out the oven."

"Hello, Levi, no, I have not."

"I was killing time when I saw you walk in. I'm so glad I spotted you. Thank you for sending all the artwork. The logos are wonderful, but still not what I need. The excuse that you're leaving town for an extended vacation is unacceptable."

Lizzy gasped. "You're leaving? You never told me that!"

Abby had only just sent Levi the email. John's disapproving look told her that she'd made an error in judgment by mentioning her plans, even if it was just to a grouchy little man. She felt bad for Levi. She'd felt bad for all her clients, pushing to wrap up as many projects as possible before she left. Once settled in America, Abby would send the non-urgent artwork over a secure line.

Abby started to talk when Levi cut in. "The least you can do is change the colors on my logo. Red and black won't work, I want gold and dark brown."

Abby kept the exasperation out of her voice. "Gold and dark brown isn't a wise choice. It'll look too similar to the UPS logo."

"Nonsense, I bought new wallpaper and it'll match perfectly. I have a sample roll in my car."

"Levi, I can't finish the logo for you."

"Please, Abigail. I can't afford to hire someone else and I'm pumping a lot of money into this bakery. Just adjust the color scheme."

And there it was. The guilt soiling her skin. The crusty gnome gave her such a hopeful look and dang it. "Where's your car?"

His eyes lit up. "Just outside, the red one parked to the left."

The old station wagon wasn't that far from Max. Abby could check on Levi's new color palette and still be visually within reach.

"Abby," John said with a warning.

"I'll be back in a minute."

Lizzy shoved her drink away. "Golly gee! What's a minute in the big scheme of things when you're leaving for an extended vacation? It sounds awfully permanent to me." Sarcasm laced her words.

"I've got this," John said. "Don't wander off. Stay close."

Lizzy looked like a stubborn fairy. "Actually, I've changed my mind. I don't want to hear a thing from either of you."

Abby escaped the loaded silence, following Levi out to his car. Max gave her a WTF stare as she walked past. One of the men must've communicated. Max relaxed a smidgen, but not by much. He glanced at the red car. Abby could relate, what a fudge up.

"Did I interrupt something?" Levi asked.

Abby ignored the question. No need to mention the impending friendship implosion. Lately, it seemed to be her thing.

Levi opened his trunk, temporarily blocking Abby's view of Max. Glancing down and expecting to see a roll of wallpaper, all she saw was a spare tire.

The trunk was empty.

Horror replaced confusion when Levi rammed a gun into her back. "If you move or scream, your pretty blonde friend will be the first to die. My colleagues will then target your boyfriend and his CIA friends. Shift slightly so your friends can see you and not get suspicious. Laugh at something I say. Keep your eyes on the trunk."

Abby did as he asked. "What are you going to do with me?"

"Nothing except hand you over, then my job is done. A florist's van will pull up next to us and you'll climb in. If you don't, our men will open fire. Now smile."

Abby played along, thinking of a way to warn Max.

"I played the part well, a whiny little baker desperate for your services. I may look Jewish, but I'm from Khalid's village."

"You work for him?"

"Khalid is an honorable man that you should never have crossed; you'll die for your sins. A bitch that hides a son from his father deserves a gruesome death."

◊ ◊ ◊

Clear as day, Abby walked out of the café with Levi Bakal.

Max's earpiece came alive with Donnie's voice. "They're walking to Bakal's car to see his new wallpaper. The red car, forward and to the left."

Max spotted it one aisle over. Abby's design company was

closed for business so what the hell was she doing? "Donnie, I want you out there. Do a loop to our vehicle, pretend to get something and then pull her back in."

"Copy."

Donnie walked out. Mandla hung up on his call and immediately started talking to Max, who listened with half an ear, uncomfortable with Abby out in the open. Levi spoke. Abby smiled as she glanced into his trunk.

"...we caught the poacher trying to jump the border," Mandla said.

"I'm sorry, I didn't catch that," Max said.

Mandla delicately picked up a biscotti and dipped it into his tea. "Customs captured one of the poachers responsible for the ambush on Muller's unit. He tried to cross the border into Zimbabwe yesterday evening, rhino horns hidden in food crates. One of my associates just completed the interview and the bastard cracked like a soft egg."

Donnie closed the door to their truck, two lanes over and circled towards Abby's position.

"The poacher gave up the syndicate?"

"He gave us a name. A familiar name."

Max's blood chilled. "Who does he work for?"

"Kris Muller. It was a setup. Muller got his own unit killed. Either for the horns or perhaps they started asking questions. Apparently, Muller's operation extends all the way up into Kenya, and get this, the poacher identified Roman Petrovich as a silent partner in the syndicate."

Max launched himself over the trellis, even before he saw the flash of white accompanied by the screech of brakes. A van pulled alongside Abby. "Muller's dirty!" Max yelled into his comms unit as he pulled his weapon.

◊ ◊ ◊

Johnny tried to break up the silence. "Lizbug, we're trying to protect you."

"Go eat soap! I don't know who you are, and I honestly don't give a freaking fuck."

"That's not true, you do give a fuck, and so do I. This matters. It matters that you know the truth about me, it matters that you know how I feel about you."

"'The truth about me.' Those are the exact words my ex used. Everything was a giant lie."

"Don't ever compare me to Ivan."

"You know about him."

"Abby told me he hurt you, but she never gave details."

"Did she now? What a stand-up friend."

"Abby loves you, please don't do this."

Lizzy's reply was lost as Max surged to his feet. A flash of movement to Johnny's immediate left drew his attention. Johnny threw Lizzy to the floor, her landing brutal, his narrowed focus on the patron training a weapon on his tiny woman. Gun already drawn, Johnny squeezed off a shot, providing cover for Lizzy.

Ignoring her dazed expression, Johnny dragged her towards a rear exit. Had Max yelled that Muller was dirty? *Fuck*.

Johnny communicated with Slater. "Heading to the rear with the second asset."

Slater scrambled for cover behind a concrete pillar. "Check. Visual on a black sedan with additional insurgents."

The black vehicle mounted the curb. Assailants poured out and opened fire on the structure. A nearby vase exploded as bullets rained down on them.

Johnny yelled at Lizzy. "Move! Now. Stay down."

The son of a bitch who'd taken Johnny's round square in the chest staggered towards them, taking aim at Lizzy for a second time. Fucker wore a bulletproof vest. Johnny calmly squeezed the trigger, hitting him between the eyes. He then swiveled, eliminating a second target as Slater took out two militants before coldly cleaning up the rest. Mandla's men lay down suppressive fire and Johnny hustled Lizzy out the back door.

◊ ◊ ◊

Levi Bakal had a gun on Abby, waving it around as he wrestled her towards the three men spilling from the white van. Max fired his first shot, blowing the small man off his feet. Two masked men shoved Abby into the back of the van. Max took out a second militant taking potshots at Donnie and then shot a third, all while clearing his path to the accelerating vehicle. Continual gunshots echoed behind Max. The fuckers had ambushed the café in a diversionary attack. All that mattered was getting to Abby. Max propelled himself through the van's door before it slid closed.

"Squeeze the trigger again and I'll blow her fucking head off!" Roman Petrovich held Abby firmly against his chest, a pistol shoved up against her jaw.

Two men aimed AK47s at her head. A fourth man in the passenger seat trained his weapon on Max. Petrovich was on South African soil—which according to their intel was not possible, but informants could be paid off and photographs doctored. They'd been fed fake intel from Somalia.

He weighed up his odds. Khalid needed her alive but she could still get caught in the crossfire. The men tried to steady themselves as the van lurched around corners, fingers too close to their triggers. Max handed his gun to the man behind him.

"Nicely done. On your knees. Hands behind your back."

Max followed orders as they trussed him up and destroyed his comms. Finally, Roman restrained Abby's hands before shoving her on the floor. She burrowed into Max's side. The small move wrenched his heart. He'd failed her. Their saving grace could be the embedded tracker in his arm, a standard requirement for covert agents on Mobile Intelligence Teams. But he wouldn't rely on the device. He didn't need guns to kill; his hands were just as lethal. Retribution for touching Abby would be brutally swift.

Chapter Twenty

The rear door opened onto an alley. Johnny pulled Lizzy behind him as he cleared the area, leading her away from the café. The chatter of fire dropped off. The now infrequent pops meant that the threat was under control. She lagged behind.

"Move, Lizzy, we're getting out of here." Johnny adjusted his earpiece. "Slater, do you read?"

"Copy. Terminated eight tangos. No new unknowns located in the area. What's your location and status?"

"Both unharmed. Moving around to the right side of the building. I'll need to evacuate Goldie. Status on Max?"

"Status unknown. Donnie gave chase," Slater said.

"Did you just call me Goldie? Because I'm blonde?"

"We're not doing this right now."

"Not that you're being a sexist jerk-face or anything." She huffed.

"Goldie, because you look like Goldie fucking Hawn when she was young. We use aliases so the targets don't get a bead on you. Now move your sweet ass, princess."

"I'm not going anywhere with a two-faced beast waving a gun around like he's used it his whole life and don't call me princess."

Her wobbly voice indicated shock, a natural reaction given the circumstances.

"You want to stay back here, in the alley, be my guest. Let's hope we took out all the bad guys." Johnny eased his head around the side of the building.

He stepped back and Lizzy—careful not to touch him—stumbled out of the way. "You just blew that man's head off. Inside that place. I think I'm going to be sick."

"Since he was aiming for you, I chose to save your life and eliminate his."

Now on her haunches, Lizzy eyed his weapon like it was a viper.

"Don't freak out, I'm not here to hurt you, I'm here to protect you." Johnny stepped towards her and Lizzy flinched. The small act was a shit grenade to the plexus and Johnny swallowed back his frustration.

Donnie checked in. He'd lost the van. Max and Abby were in the wind.

"Is Abby okay?"

"I have no idea. This is a clusterfuck. Stand up."

Lizzy stood, clutching her side.

"Dammit, have you been shot?"

Johnny pulled up her shirt. Dark bruising marred her midsection. "Goddammit!"

"I banged up my side when I fell."

"You mean when I threw you to the ground. Shit, I'm sorry Lizbug."

"I'm not your Lizbug. I'll never be that to you again."

"It shouldn't have come—"

"It's over, John. How are we getting out of here?"

Johnny ignored the hurt, concentrating on keeping her safe. "I'll examine your ribs more closely when I'm able. Where are your car keys?"

"In my backpack. It's still in the coffee shop."

"Slater, I need Goldie's car keys, her rucksack was left at my last location."

"I'm on it. We've been advised to vacate the area before local enforcement arrives. Stay where you are. I'll meet you around the side."

"Affirmative."

Mandla wanted them gone. Having American operatives tangled up in a terrorist shoot-out would mess up everyone's day on a global scale.

Donnie pulled into the lot. Johnny thumped Slater on the back, glad to see his friend in one piece.

"I'll take Lizzy home and set up a temporary base," Johnny said.

After handing Lizzy's gym bag over, Slater circled to the driver's side. Donnie scooted over, pulled out his laptop and immediately searched for Max's signal as they pulled away. Slater and Donnie were going hunting.

A groan just inside the shot-up café had Johnny turning. One of the attackers was still alive. The dick maggot needed to be questioned.

"We'll handle it," Mandla said, stepping up beside him.

"I need two minutes with the man," Johnny replied.

"We don't have two minutes."

"Then one minute and thirty seconds. I'll question him in the bathroom."

Mandla groaned and gestured to his men. "Make it quick. I need to know if it was one of my men that set us up. I'll watch the girl."

"Johnny? What are you doing?" Lizzy's eyes were wide in her pale face.

"Give me a minute. This man will keep you safe."

Johnny hated leaving her, but Max's life was on the line. Mandla's men dragged the mercenary into the small bathroom and dumped him on the floor. The man swore in Afrikaans, pain making freckles stand out against his ginger complexion.

"You're a South African, so what the fuck are you doing working for terrorists?"

"Fok you. I'm not saying anything."

Johnny knelt down, applying pressure to the bastard's shot-up knee. "I'm short on time. Answer my questions and you live, choose not to and you'll sacrifice yourself for a man who'll be just as dead as you are within the week."

Mr. Freckles screamed, vomiting on the white tiles. Johnny shifted out of the way and placed a gun to his head.

"How did you find us? Did you follow us here?"

"No. We followed the blonde woman."

John stiffened as his trigger finger twitched. "Why?" he growled.

"We planned to take her. It was dumb luck that the Evans woman turned up."

John swallowed the rage. "Why target the blonde?"

"My boss couldn't get near Evans, she always had men with her. We suspected her boyfriend was more than just a fuck. From the way you all move, my boss thought you were CIA. He was going to use Lizette Steyn to lure Evans away." Freckles whimpered in agony, trying to straighten his leg.

"It wouldn't have worked. Where are they taking them?"

"I don't know."

Johnny made a move and Freckles scrambled back. "I swear, I was only hired three days ago. I can give you the location of the abandoned warehouse that was our original meeting point, but they cleaned out the place."

"Who do you work for?"

"They'll kill me if I talk."

"I'll kill you if you fucking don't. Who the fuck do you work for?"

"He called himself Roman—that's all I know."

Johnny holstered his weapon and stood. He squeezed out some soap and washed the blood off his hands before speaking to Mandla's men. "Text me the warehouse address and any other information that you squeeze out of him. The piece of shit is all yours."

◊ ◊ ◊

They pulled out just as local police descended. Shivers racked Lizzy's tiny frame. She refused to look at him, huddling against the passenger door. Johnny turned up the heat as he negotiated the busy streets. Talking to her would be a waste of time. Percussive trauma meant that she wasn't thinking clearly. Hysteria would run the show.

There were no signs of a tail, but Johnny wasn't taking any chances. Evasive driving added to the journey time. Five minutes from her parents' home, Lizzy stirred, digging around her backpack. Hands shaking, she pulled out her phone.

"Who are you calling?"

"My mom." She sounded like a scared kid.

"You cannot speak to anyone about this. My team is not supposed to be here. Too many people's lives are at risk and pulling your parents into this is not wise."

"What is this that I'd be pulling them into, and who the hell are you? I stumble into a network of lies and discover that my best friend is the ringleader surrounded by a gang of Spartans. The biggest and baddest swine of them all is the man that I've fallen in… Never mind. None of you give a flying squirrel's nuts about me and all I want, right at this fucked-up moment, is a bear hug from my mom." The last part of her tirade was stuttered through a barely intelligible mess of tears.

Johnny pulled into an empty lot, slammed the car into park, and pulled Lizzy into his arms as she sobbed out the shock. They sat that way for some time before Lizzy wiped at her eyes.

"Who has Abby?"

"I don't know, Lizbug. I'm going to try my level best to save her. Save them both. She's with Max, and he's the best-trained man I know."

"Is he your best friend?"

"He's my best friend, my teammate, and my brother all rolled into one." Johnny stroked fingers through her soft curls.

"Did you torture that man, in the bathroom?"

"No, angel. I asked a few questions, that's all."

"Is he still alive?"

"I left him that way, which was fucking hard."

"Why?"

"It's complicated. He wanted to hurt you, and for that he should die."

Lizzy tried to pull away, Johnny held on. "Did Abby ever tell you where her son is?"

"No. Why won't you tell me who you are?"

"You've already come to your own conclusions. I work for a black ops team, we're here without full permission from the South African government and cannot be exposed."

"So, in other words, I can't be the rat. I'll have to keep my mouth shut." Lizzy twisted away and resettled back in her seat.

Johnny felt the loss. "Saying something could get good men killed and Abby needs us here, to extract her."

"Then why are you still here, with me, and not with your team. I gather it's to make sure I don't open my blabby mouth, rather than out of concern for my well-being."

"That's not true, your safety comes first. I'm not comfortable taking you home, the men who attacked us may know where you live."

Lizzy hefted her bag onto her lap, holding it like a shield. "Take me home, and I don't ever want to see you again. I won't tell a soul about you or your operation. I would never dream of endangering my friend, but I need to get as far away from you as possible. You've endangered my family, and that makes me so mad, I want to claw your damn eyes out."

"When this is over, I'll be back to see you to sort out this mess between us."

"I don't want you coming back, I don't want you. Period. I had one violent liar in my life, and that's one too many."

Johnny stared at Lizzy's profile before shifting the car back in gear. His stomach felt like lead. This grim day was beyond recall. He focused on the one thing he could control, doing his job and finding the assholes who took Max.

Lizzy stalked into the empty house without saying a word. Her parents weren't home. Johnny checked the security, grabbed an ice pack and checked out her injury. No broken ribs but she'd be damn sore. He located an Advil equivalent in the bathroom cabinet and poured her a sugary pop drink.

"I'll tell my family that I fell down the stairs. Text me an update on Abby. Lock up on the way out, you know the drill."

Lizzy took the supplies to her bedroom and shut the door. Walking away was hard, but there was work to be done. He'd sort out their mess once this was over.

Donnie checked in with lousy news. The white van was

found abandoned in a railyard an hour north of Johannesburg. The signal from Max's transmitter stopped relaying at the train tracks, which meant it was now purposely jammed. Johnny then contacted Mandla for a warehouse location to set up new comms. Mandla promised to designate a trusted two-man team to watch over Lizzy.

Three of Mandla's men met him at a designated warehouse, providing state-of-the-art equipment. In no time, Johnny made a call on a secure line to their Deputy Director at MIT Headquarters. Aside from the ass roasting, they were given the green light to track Max to Khalid. For JSOC, rescuing Max and capturing Khalid took precedence. Max was valued as a two-million-dollar super soldier due to the extensive training he'd received over the years. The agency wanted him safe.

Extracting Evans was a secondary objective. Johnny would follow orders but placed the rescue of Evans and her son as an equally vital mission. They didn't have much time; once Khalid knew the location of his son, he'd eliminate any witnesses. The team technically should fly to Cape Town and start the search from there, but that could mean sacrificing Max. Khalid wouldn't take Max along for the ride.

Currently, it looked like they were being transported inland, farther up north, which made little sense. North of Johannesburg lay the city of Pretoria. Beyond that, there were some small towns, safari lodgings, but little else. Where would they go? Private land. Johnny would bet his life on that.

If Muller was involved, he'd likely purchased property on South African soil. Johnny contacted Mandla and then his handler, looking for any links to real estate in the Polokwane area, and the territories that lay to the west of the Kruger National Park.

◊ ◊ ◊

A fucking container. They were in a container truck; clever bastards weren't taking any chances. The steel box blocked any signal transmissions. The stifling shell was pimped out with iron shackles, welded to the sides and to the floor. An ankle and wrist were both secured, rendering him ineffective. They'd fastened Abby to the opposite wall. Too far away from him. So far she'd been treated well enough, without any roughhousing, and thankfully they'd given her water.

Max needed out of the metal box for the transmitter to work, a breadcrumb for his team to follow. He estimated their journey time at around the two-hour mark.

"I need to piss."

"Piss in your pants, asshole," Roman said.

"I can do that. Hope you can deal with the smell. It sure is a warm day today, and no offense to the smelly-ass dicks in here, but some of your colleagues are less hygiene conscious then say...the three of us."

Max looked over at the guard in the right corner who reeked of garlic and unwashed duds. The guy stank. It was no surprise that the immaculate Roman gave the man a wide berth; vanity was a bitch.

"Guess the smell of urine will just add to the bouquet."

"Max, please don't," Abby piped up. "I'll throw up. I'm already nauseous." His woman had caught on and was playing the game.

"Well, this should be a sweet-scented ride. She suffers from motion sickness and a swaying steel crate isn't the best cure."

Roman glanced down at his shiny loafers, clearly envisioning a floor covered in piss and vomit. Pulling his gun, he pressed the intercom secured to the wall and told the driver to stop. With sudden ease, he shoved Abby to the floor.

Max lunged, restrained by the damned cuffs. "Get the fuck off her."

Roman ignored Max's rage, straddling Abby as she lay on her back. Gripping her jaw, the fucker shoved the barrel of the gun into her mouth.

"You son of a bitch!" Max scrambled to reach them.

"My beauty, we haven't officially been introduced. I'm looking forward to getting acquainted on an intimate level." Roman rolled his hips.

Max exploded. His savage shouts thundered through the container as he fought against the restraints.

"Calm the fuck down, get out and take a piss. One wrong move and I'll blow her head off, Khalid be damned. I won't die for another man's cause. Oh, and I would hurry if I were you. I'm tempted to play, such a pretty piece of ass."

Garlic Boy uncuffed a panting Max, who envisioned ripping Roman's head off, but the prick's finger rested on the trigger. With little choice, Max hopped out and took the quickest leak of his life as a guard stood watch. Glancing around, Max only saw African bushveld. Acacia trees everywhere. They were traveling in a northeasterly direction. His location would be pinged but had it been worth letting that slime-ball's hands touch Abby?

Max clambered back into the hot box. Once he was secure, Roman holstered his gun and jumped off the truck to make a phone call, too far away to make out what he was saying. Convulsive crying told Max that something had gone down during the brief time he had left Abby. Refusing to make eye contact, she rolled towards the wall.

"What did he do to you?"

Abby shook her head, choking on a sob.

"Honey, talk to me. What did that son of a bitch do?"

Abby remained silent. Explosive fury ate away at his sanity. Any semblance of control he'd achieved over the years was washed away in the eruption. Roman wrapped up his call, climbed in and the truck rolled onwards. Max hadn't known true hate until that moment, vowing that Petrovich would be a vaporized memory in the red mist of the rising sun.

◊ ◊ ◊

The thirty-eight-second transmission indicated Max's position as being near Makopane in the Limpopo region, just off of the R101 freeway. A drone combed the area, along with a contingent of Mandla's men accompanying Slater and Donnie. Their ETA to the transmission site was ten minutes. Searches for properties registered to Muller came up empty. MIT HQ looked at aliases and offshore bank accounts possibly linked to Kris Muller. They were closing in on the fucker. Johnny only hoped that it wasn't too late.

Two of Mandla's best analysts sat with Johnny as they combed through the intel while running through the feeds. Johnny now had the dossier on the poaching ambush and subsequent interrogation.

Noleen Keller was a ghost. The only property listed under her name was thoroughly searched and they'd come up empty. MIT would keep looking.

Slater checked in. "Max's transmission pinged at a pitstop. Tire tracks indicate that they are being transported via a truck. I'm assuming it's a container truck, reinforced to block any outgoing signals. Footprints in the sand tell me that Max found a way to exit by taking a piss. Looks like his boot pattern and approximate size. Two other sets of footprints are visible."

"Which direction is the truck heading?" Johnny said.

"Still northwards. Trouble is that the road forks up ahead. They could travel west towards Botswana or eastwards to the Kruger. Muller's worked in this area. If we find Muller, we'll find Khalid."

Johnny stared at the map, melding Kris Muller's profile with the best tactical shuffle that Johnny would make if he were in the man's shoes. The targets would want someplace remote, away from prying eyes. That crossed the main roads and small towns off the list.

Kris Muller loved the African bush; aside from killing rhino for selfish gain. Kris was also a braggart. Combine those two traits and Johnny guessed that they were looking for a decently sized game lodge with all the trimmings.

"Look for private game lodges in the area. Mid-sized and run by a small contingent of foreigners. Spread out and ask questions. The locals will know who's new to the area."

Johnny circled the territory they'd concentrate on. "Hold on, brother," he muttered. "We're coming for you."

Chapter Twenty-One

When they reached their destination, five guerrillas pulled Abby out and held her separately, boxing her in with AK47s being waved about. Roman stroked a gun across her temple and Max had no choice but to comply. The container was backed into an open door of a large structure, enclosed in thick concrete walls and a solid concrete roof with no windows. Of all his fucking luck, any signal would be blocked by the solid structure.

If it were just him, Max would have already made a move. With Abby in the mix, saying it was complicated was a gross understatement.

Max made his play. "I know where her son is."

Abby gasped, and Max deliberately avoided eye contact. He had no idea where Gabe was but Roman didn't know that. Abby probably wondered if Max had intel on Gabe's whereabouts.

Roman regarded Max warily before handing Abby off. "If he makes any moves, break her arm."

Max didn't plan on making a move. Hopefully, the fake intel would get them on a plane to Cape Town and his team would be on them like white on rice.

"I'm guessing you're some kind of covert operative who knows the value of her son, both to Khalid as well as your country. Why would you give up the location so easily?"

"I'm tired of working for a government who doesn't give a damn about me and I know how you'll extract information from us. The danger pay isn't worth it."

"What are you looking to get out of this revelation?"

"Whatever is on offer. I'd like to walk away with my ass intact."

Roman's body language and lack of interest were worrying. The mercenary ambled over. The designer bush shirt and tailored linen pants he wore looked magazine worthy. Despite baking in a metal container for the past few hours, the puffed-up dickhead looked like he could pose in a Safari photo shoot.

"Give me the address."

A retired SAS colleague lived in the Cape. Two years ago, Johnny and Max flew in for a quick visit. If he led Khalid into his friend's neighborhood, Johnny would catch on and give their British buddy a heads-up. MIT2 could roll out the infidel welcome mat.

"Do you think I'm foolish enough to give you the exact location? You get that when we arrive. He's in the Parklands area on the Western Seaboard." Max was spouting bull-crap, but Abby played along, struggling, calling him a traitor and a bastard. He met Roman's unblinking stare, refusing to look away.

Roman slipped his hands into his pockets. "Playing games will get her killed. For every lie that comes from your Yankee mouth, I'll remove one of her limbs." He turned to his men. "Secure him."

The intel was dismissed out of hand, which made no sense. The terrorists should at least try to verify it. Max sensed a sudden void as he tried to work out Roman's game. More shackles lay welded to the floor. They secured his ankle. Abby wasn't restrained and that bothered Max. It meant they planned to take her from him at some point. Max slid down the wall and Abby backed up against him. No words were said, none were needed. They'd stripped her of her jacket. Her ponytail was a saggy mess; Max pulled out the elastic, burying his nose in her hair, her warm body reassuring him that she was still alive and in one piece.

Two guards stood at the far end, near the rolling shutter doors. The empty concrete cell was devoid of furniture. Max visually scanned the room carefully for bugs and couldn't spot any in the hollow space. There was a possibility that he'd missed one and Max pulled her head to his ear, telling her so.

"Why did he outright ignore the location you gave him?" Abby whispered.

"I don't know, it doesn't make any sense, maybe he sensed it was a play." Max mentally ran over all the angles as he carefully braided her hair.

"You're good at that."

"I have a couple of nieces. I had to learn when I got them ready for school."

"You don't have to tie it up. It's a dusty mess anyway."

"Don't let the bastards see you looking disheveled. We present a strong front together."

"For psychological reasons? Never let them think they've broken you?"

"Exactly," Max said.

"I'm sorry that I got you mixed up in this."

"None of this is your fault." Max placed his lips on her ear. "It's going to be okay. This is what I do, I'm trained to get us out of this."

"You're shackled to the floor by a medieval-looking device."

"True. It's a problem. If only you had a bobby pin tucked

away in those beautiful tresses."

"Sadly not. I'm guessing the next step is torture."

"They'll use me to get you to break. I'm trained to take it; don't you dare say a thing."

"Oh God. I won't let you do this."

"You have no choice. We can't let them get to Gabriel," Max whispered.

Abby turned and clung to him; quiet sobs echoed through the cavernous space as he ran soothing hands down her back. Max waited until she'd calmed to break the news, squeezing her tightly up against him and talking quietly.

"Kris is involved, he's working with Khalid."

"That's impossible, he would never—"

"He would, and he did. I received the intel at the café. He set up the ambush on the anti-poaching team. Kris got his own men killed."

"You're saying that my Kris was responsible for the death of his friends."

Max stiffened. "Your Kris?"

"You know what I mean."

"He must've been recruited in Dubai. Poaching ties to terrorism in Africa, it's a money maker for extremists. Muller has the means and the access."

"But Kris is one of the good guys."

"Stop fooling yourself, you need to be prepared."

Instead of becoming all emotional, Abby stilled. When she finally spoke, Max didn't like what she had to say. "Back in the truck—when you left to pee—Roman said something."

"What the fuck did he say?"

"He ground up against me and whispered, 'Do you like that, sweet thing? I want to ride you so hard.'"

"I'm going to rip that son of a bastard's skull out."

"He said that to me once before."

"Was he in Khalid's home in Sharjah?"

"I never saw him in the Middle East. It was in Johannesburg... He was the attacker at La Corragio."

Max wanted to punch walls.

"By the time you climbed back in the truck, I knew who he was and panicked in the moment. When I finally calmed, I thought things over. If that was a kidnapping, why did Roman take his time toying with me and why were there only two of them? Where were the rest of Khalid's men?"

Max ran over the same conundrum when a small side door slammed open at the far end. Roman along with three guards walked towards them. Max pulled Abby up.

"Khalid will see you now."

Max shielded her. "Don't fucking touch her."

He kicked out, causing Roman to stumble. A follow-up kick to the peacock's balls had him collapsing to his knees. The rest of the mercenaries laid into Max, landing blows. Roman staggered to his feet, kicking Max for good measure before dragging Abby away.

When the pugilists finally let up, Max was left with nothing more than a bloody nose, sore ribs, and a slight concussion. Amateur hour meant Max had effectively blocked the more lethal blows, leaving him mostly unscathed; nevertheless, he played up his injuries, pretending to cower.

A militant with a deep scar running down his cheek knelt to speak. "Next time we'll use a blunt machete to pretty up your handsome face."

All Max focused on was the absence of Abby. That Al Juhani monster now had her and Max was nailed to the floor, as useless as tits on a nun.

"We were trying to be gracious to our guests and offer you food and water, instead, you spit in our faces, but I can be the better man." Scarface gestured towards someone standing in the shadows.

A slight, compact man wearing a traditional tribal shirt and beige pants carried a tray towards them. His shirt marked him as a local man from the Venda Tribe.

Scarface grabbed a piece of bread from the plate and took a sip of the water. "See, I eat it. No drugs. It's clean food."

The men walked away, and the servant placed the tray hesitantly on the ground and unloaded a paper plate topped with bread.

Max spoke softly. "Do you speak any English? I apologize, but I don't speak Tshivenda."

The man looked up in surprise. "You are American, how did you know of my tribal language?"

"Africa has been my place of work for many years. I know of many tribes. What is your name?"

The man looked around before answering. "Mutali."

"Mutali, my name is Max. It's good to meet you."

Mutali handed Max a water bottle. "We shouldn't be talking."

"You work for these foreigners; do you know what they do? They are bad men who build bombs and blow up schools and hospitals, in the name of God."

Mutali dusted off his pants as he rose. "I need the money, the work at this lodge supports my family. We need to eat."

Max pressed on. "The man who owns this lodge will sell out Africa and its people for money."

"I know this, he has a black soul." Mutali looked down at Max's ankle. "I have no key for that."

A guard yelled out for him to get back to work.

Mutali spoke Tshivenda. "*Thakha ndi mulambo, a i lengi u fhalala.*"

"What does that mean?"

"Wealth is like a flooding river, it rises but also goes down quickly. The evil waters in this place will not soak our lands." Mutali moved away.

Max watched the slight man walk out. A possible ally, an angle to be worked. Khalid was going down quickly. That was a promise Max would keep, even if it took his own life to make it happen.

◊ ◊ ◊

In any other circumstances, Abby would have found the game lodge beautiful; instead, the chilled air was infested with a greedy plague. A slight sound to the side of the dust path had her glancing to her left. A kudu bull sat quietly in the grass. Its twisted horns almost seemed to bow gracefully as the huge buck watched her walk by. Two zebras stood behind, their tails twitching in the dusky light.

Stairs swept up to a wooden deck that led to the luxurious main lodge. An infinity pool draped off the side, the water tinkling in the night. The lodge's massive framework held up a thatched roof. Contemporary African art and thick rugs were scattered among leather sofas and dark wood trimmings in the spacious living area.

The overall effect seemed inviting until you spotted the basket of elephant tusks and rhino horn tucked to the side of the roaring fireplace, or the soldiers with assault rifles standing in every corner. Abby had so far counted seven men, aside from Roman at her back.

She was made to stand in the center of the room like a

naughty child as a grandfather clock in the corner ticked away. A Scops owl's call echoed across the valley, bringing tears to her eyes. The loneliest sound reserved for her very own pity party.

When a door finally opened, Khalid Al Juhani swept into the room. "Josephine. It's good to see you again."

Abby said nothing as she looked at the polished worm. Memories of his brutality threatened to bring her to her knees. She locked her legs in place and inclined her head haughtily, as if she were the royal member in the room. Calm snaked around her, settling her in for battle.

He narrowed his eyes. "You now use your middle name. I think Joey is a much better fit."

"Joey was exterminated by a yellow-bellied toad who gets his kicks from raping innocent girls. Abigail, however, will twist your testicles off if you dare to lay a hand on her."

"Brave talk for a whore who was eager to climb in my bed and steal my only son."

"The only thing I was eager for that night was getting away from your filthy hands."

"You have the nerve to hide my heir from me?"

Abby narrowed her eyes. "I gather your wives are still popping out daughters?"

Anger flared. "Shut up whore. Where is my child?"

"There is no child, I have no idea what you're talking about."

Movement from a darkened room to the right had Abby swiveling. Kris rose from an armchair. He'd been watching all along.

"Such an artful liar, my little Cricket." Kris threw a pile of photographs onto the coffee table. Pictures of her and Gabe at a restaurant, shopping in a baby store at a mall, all taken before she'd sent Gabe away.

Khalid picked up a photo of her son—her son, not his—running a finger over his face. "He has my mouth. My hair. You're a hard woman to find. Your antics in Sharjah caused me such headaches. I had to pay off numerous police officials and send out a general missive on your whereabouts, but would never have bothered finding you, until I received a picture of a very pregnant woman at a food market in Johannesburg who looked remarkably like Josephine Evans. I knew that was my child growing in your belly. It took me over two years to find you."

Khalid stepped behind her and ran his hand across her neck, causing her to flinch. "A month ago, when I finally got a fix on your location, Kris told me about your protective military friends. We knew the CIA was onto us. I pretended there was a coup in my organization, leaked photos and used look-alikes. Forced our American enemies to look elsewhere, while I've enjoyed a visit to South Africa's friendly shores."

Khalid only found her four weeks ago? The photographs lying on the table were taken six months before. Whoever took them had discovered her whereabouts long before Khalid. Abby frowned as she ran over the quandary.

Kris's fickle voice cut in. "You sold me out—your best friend in the whole world—for a better life in Paris. Eager to sign away your freedom while whoring yourself out to the wealthiest bidder by sleeping with Khalid. When his seed grew in your belly, you kept it a secret, hiding from the world."

Kris walked over to the bar and poured himself a glass of lemonade.

"Is that what Khalid told you, that I willingly slept with him? Khalid injected me with a drug and forced himself on me. I have the scars to prove it."

Kris flicked a glance at Khalid. "You told me she wanted to

301

bed you, that she got cold feet the next morning about working for us."

Abby beseeched him. "Kris, you know me. I would never do that, I hadn't been with any man before that night. Why would I give away something so sacred to a worm like Khalid?"

Khalid selected a caviar and smoked salmon canapé from a snack display, balancing it delicately on a porcelain plate before going for an avocado shrimp bite. "Like all Western whores, she's lying."

"He killed Meg. I saw him break her arm before they dragged her away. She was trying to help me escape after Khalid drugged me."

Kris spoke carefully before taking a sip of his drink. "Meg was just a bit of crumpet on the side, turned out she was the biggest traitor of all. She worked for the British government. If Khalid hadn't killed her, I would have, and it would have been a slower death."

"You're seriously working with radical terrorists. What happened to the Kris I know, the child who loved Africa and its people? The boy who helped his aunt deliver baby bucks and showed me the beauty of the land."

"Do you think my life was idyllic on that farm? My uncle and aunt adopted me when my parents died when I was a kid. My uncle taught me everything. How to hunt, how to kill and torture animals, how to lay quiet in the tall grass while he played with me for hours. One fine day, as we lay under a tree, I put the monster out of his misery permanently. My aunt thought he'd drowned, would never have believed her ten-year old nephew grew some balls that day."

Abby stared in astonishment.

"Don't look so shocked. Thanks to him, I learned the art of

killing. I grew up and also discovered that the only bucks that matter are the green paper ones. I'm repeatedly betrayed by treacherous women who lie to my face. First Meg and then you. I know nothing about you except that you're a lying bitch who now has the hots for a dirty American soldier. You never even bothered telling me about your son."

"Hundreds of innocent people have died at Khalid's hands. Why are you doing this?"

"Hundreds of people have died at America's hands. Fuck the West and fuck you. Tell Khalid where his son is, and we may let you live."

"Never."

Kris leaned against the counter and crossed his ankles. "How's your blonde friend? Lizzy."

"Don't go there!"

"I have been going there…quite often lately. I think you were onto something. I can't stop thinking about that tight little body, fondling that sweet fig. I might just court her once this is over."

Court her? He was certifiably insane. Abby said nothing; was he trying to make her jealous with his sick words?

"Why don't you eat with us before you go back to that American turd? I have a delicacy prepared just for you." Kris leaned back and lifted a silver lid before shoving the plate under her nose.

The visceral reaction was horror, and it took all of Abby's willpower not to scream in terror as she gazed at the scorched little bodies. Spiny legs, creepy antennae, and roasted thoraxes decorated the plate.

Kris smirked as he shoved the platter closer. "Many tribes in Africa consider crickets a delicacy. Their crunchy bodies are a convenient snack when you have long distances to travel. I insist that you try some."

Abby's pounding heart pumped tingling terror throughout her limbs, blocking out Kris's taunts. Cold sweat coated her brow as she stared down at her worst nightmare. She refused to give in to a panic attack while she stood vulnerable, in a room with two snakes. Pain lanced through her chest as panic attempted to take hold, and she steadied her breathing.

Tiny dead insects. That was all that they were. Dead and tiny. Another minute passed as the trembling in her limbs slowed. The fear began to diminish when compared to the loss of her son or seeing Max hurt.

Abby grabbed a handful of the critters and shoved them in her mouth, wiping the evil smirk off Kris's cruel face. She fought the urge to gag as she chewed on the thorny meal and her triumphant swallow was a giant "fuck you."

Abby grinned manically. "Yummy. Tastes a little nutty, like eating sunflower seeds."

She'd done it, faced her fear of a harmless insect and for a moment, she was invincible. Screw these two power-hungry dip-shits, playing their stupid games. They might have the ability to kill her, but Josephine Abigail Evans was their siren song, lulling them with the calm before shredding them to tiny pieces.

Kris narrowed his eyes before pulling her in for a bruising kiss. His grinding teeth split her lip as he pulled her up against his length. "And now you taste like cricket. It's getting me all hard."

Abby kicked him in the shin and Kris shoved her away.

Khalid placed his plate on the coffee table before delicately wiping his hands on a napkin. "This reunion is riveting, but I have business to attend to and need the location of my son. If you refuse to talk, I'll spend time getting to know your tough boyfriend, and you're welcome to watch."

Abby swiped at her mouth. "He knows nothing, I swear, I've kept him in the dark."

"Debatable, but it doesn't matter what he knows. He's just a tool to open that luscious mouth of yours." Khalid popped a bite into his mouth. "You have a good chef, Muller. I'm half tempted to steal him from you."

"Wait until you try the stuffed venison. I shot the impala this morning in honor of my valued guest," Kris said.

"I appreciate your hospitality, I'm looking forward to dinner. First let's get unsavory business out of the way. Roman, get the equipment."

Khalid grabbed her arm and marched towards the door. Abby shot Kris a pleading look as he ambled alongside.

At the top of the stairs, Kris spoke up. "Khalid, let me try first. Give me twenty minutes alone with them. I guarantee an answer."

Khalid paused. "This way is a lot more fun."

Kris pulled him aside. "I have a relationship with her. If it doesn't work, then let the games begin."

"Fine. I'll have my dinner, but I want answers by the time I'm done."

Khalid turned to Abby. "Twenty minutes is the difference between having a live male companion or a tortured lump of flesh chained to the floor. It's your choice." The Sandpiper took a deep breath of fresh evening air before ambling back inside.

Chapter Twenty-Two

Abby's swollen bottom lip had Max on his feet.

He pushed a water bottle into her hands. "Drink and eat the bread."

Two men followed behind. Muller the douche and Roman the prick.

"Who hurt you?"

"I'm okay. It's you I'm worried about."

"Who touched her?" Max asked Kris.

"I may have got a little amorous while cuddling up to my cricket, she's such a hot little pocket."

"Muller, if it wasn't personal before, it sure is now. I'm going to rip out your spleen."

"I'm sure a spook like you could. Try anything and I'll shove my Alfred Khuzwayo up your arrogant ass, before pulling the trigger." Kris waved an AK47 around.

Max assumed the term *Alfred Khuzwayo* was the local slang for an AK47.

"Try it," Max growled.

The two men faced off. Kris grinned. "I have more important things to deal with than some Yankee dickhead."

Kris nodded to Roman, who yelled in Arabic for the two

guards to leave. Once the four of them were alone, Kris focused his attention on Abby. "We need to talk."

"I'm not telling you anything, you can go to hell."

"We've been watching you for a long time. By 'we' I'm not referring to Khalid."

Max then figured out Muller's game and squeezed Abby's hand. "Kris was the one who slipped you the note on the napkin, back in February."

Kris bowed. "Guilty as charged. I was trying to warn you. Khalid's network was closing in on your location, and I'd hoped you'd take the hint and disappear. Instead, you sent away the brat and continued squatting in Johannesburg."

"But you work for Khalid?" Abby said.

"The man is like a father to me but lacks ambition. I'm expanding my operations, when I heard that Khalid was hunting for you, we needed to find you first. I still love you after all your lies and deceit, I fucking love you."

Roman walked up beside Muller, Abby shot him a dark look. "Roman is in on this?"

"He's my new business partner."

Max didn't like this treacherous turn of events. "The business partner who attacked Abby in the strip mall parking lot."

"We were trying to spook her into leaving the country. Roman had to make it realistic."

"Realistic, huh? Was a nasty head wound, concussion and sexual assault what you were aiming for?" Max asked.

"He got a little carried away. Joey, why didn't you leave?"

Abby drank the water, wincing as it hit her split lip. "Because I'm tired of running and my name is Abigail, not Joey and not Cricket."

"Well. ABIGAIL. You've got us in a real tangle, and it's now up to me to save your lying ass."

Abby tightened the water cap with shaking hands. "Were you actually drunk when you came to my house or was that just part of your act?"

"I temporarily fell off the wagon. Watching over you—seeing you again—made me feel all nostalgic. You make me weak, and I don't like it."

"None of that was guilt, for getting your team killed, or butchering a highly endangered species?"

Kris folded his arms. "The unit got in the way of my business operations and needed to be eliminated. Rhino horn is a lucrative income."

When Max first assessed Kris, he'd thought he was a sociopath. He was wrong. Muller was so much more. A textbook psychopath. Callous, yet charismatic. Manipulating others with charm and mimicking feelings to present as "normal" to society. Organized in his criminal thinking, displaying little emotion, even under situations that most would find horrifying. He was keenly aware that what he was doing was wrong but didn't give a damn.

Max tucked an ill-looking Abby in a little closer. "What do you want, Muller? Get to the point."

Roman glanced at the closed doors. "We don't have all day, tell them."

Kris smiled at Abby. "It's a win-win situation. Small sacrifices will be made but everyone walks away from this alive, and your son will be safe."

Abby now had a handle on the newly revealed Kris Muller. "I'm guessing that you'll benefit from this the most."

"You could benefit equally and have a good life. It's up to you."

That statement had Max's spidey senses tingling. "What do you want with her."

Kris's entire focus was on Abby's reaction to his next words. Max wanted to shut the conversation down. When Muller moved into their space, it took all of Max's restraint not to smash his pretty face.

"13 Willow Avenue, Somerset West," Kris said softly.

Abby buckled, a low moan escaping. That had to be the location of Gabe. Fuck.

"After you handed your son off, one of my men followed your friend to the safe house in Cape Town. She was careful and used evasion tactics, but my man was better. If you don't agree with my terms, I'll have no choice but to reveal the location to Khalid."

Abby pulled out of Max's arms, pummeling Kris in the chest as she sobbed. "You were my friend. I trusted you. Don't you dare touch my baby. Please, Kris, I beg you, don't take my child."

Kris shook her. "Fok! Stop the fucking drama."

Max launched himself as far as the ankle cuff allowed before yanking Abby back.

Roman aimed the M4 carbine at his head. "Would everyone just calm the fuck down. We have eight minutes left before Khalid requires an answer."

Muller stepped quickly out of Max's range. "Here's my offer, and I'd examine the alternative before turning it down. I'll give Khalid a different address in Cape Town. Cricket, you'll accompany us. Once we arrive, a team will be waiting for Khalid and ambush the arrogant prick, removing him from the equation. You and I will then leave the country to start our new life together. I've built the perfect ranch, farther up into Africa. You'll love it. I've based the design off my auntie's farm in

Botswana. Do you remember how you loved the wraparound porch and the sunny kitchen?" Kris's eyes glowed as he spoke.

"You're fucking crazy," Max said.

Kris ignored him, outlining details of the plan. "There are conditions attached. I don't like children, so your bratty kid needs to remain where he is. Permanently. One day you'll have my babies, and that will be different. It'll be my seed in your belly."

Max furiously shoved Abby behind him. "You sick son of a bitch."

"If you do this, I'll guarantee that your son will be safe. He can grow up in South Africa, far away from his father's legacy."

"You're insane if you think Abby will fall for that."

"Both of them will be safe, and Khalid will be dead. Problem solved."

Abby finally spoke, "What about Max?"

Max twisted around. "This is a sacrificial game that I won't allow you to be a part of."

"If you let Max go, I'll consider your offer."

Max grabbed her shoulders. "Abs, I won't allow you to do this."

"I don't need your permission."

"We can't just let him go," Roman reasoned. "Khalid won't allow that."

"Just give Max the key and allow him to escape," Abby said.

"We're not idiots. He'll come straight for you."

Max ground his teeth. "Damn fucking right, I will."

"The best I can do is have a man release him after we've left. We'll tell Khalid that we're executing him. Hopefully, Khalid won't want to do the honors himself."

Max didn't believe that for a second. Due to the connection

Max shared with Abby, Kris would remove him from the equation.

"I need a moment alone with Max before I give you an answer."

"Two minutes is all you get. If you choose to stand with the American spook, then I'm done with you. I'll withhold the location of your son until the torture is over. Khalid's a cruel bastard. I doubt either of you will be recognizable by the end of it."

The door banged closed behind them. Max knelt down to pull at the leg iron riveted to the floor, working on it whenever possible. His torn ankle showed the effects.

"The shit-holes knew what they were doing. This fucking thing is anchored to hell and goddamn unpickable."

"Max, talk to me."

"What do you want me to say? You've made your decision, giving yourself over to that slithering dick-wad. Fuck!" Max pulled the manacle, his muscles screaming with strain. "Fuck, fuck, fuck!"

Abby knelt, laying a hand on his arm. "I won't let them torture you. Once I'm gone, you'll find a way to escape without my safety hanging over your head. The team can't be far off. Please rescue Gabe. Once he's safe, then search for me."

"How are you so damn calm?"

"Because for the first time in my life, I trust someone else to have my back and I know you won't give up on us."

Letting Abby go wasn't an option. "Baby, don't do this, please. We can't be separated." Max was now begging and didn't give a damn.

"I have no choice. They'll tear you to pieces and Khalid will still find Gabriel. I have to go with him. I can save you." Abby stroked his neck.

Max shrugged her off and stood up. "Bullshit. You're not fighting for yourself or for us. You're taking the easy way out and that's not the woman I know."

Abby hugged him. "I trust you to find me."

Max removed her arms. "The way you've always trusted Muller, the brother you've never had?"

"You didn't just say that."

"If things don't work out, then at least you're not alone. You'll be sitting in Muller's sunny African kitchen, knowing Khalid has been exterminated and that your son is safe."

"How can you think that of me? That I'd use others to—"

"Use others to stay safe. Choose the path of least resistance. Isn't that what survivors like you do, find that escape?"

"You're not thinking clearly. I love you."

Max looked as shocked at the declaration as Abby was, but rage rampaged over the sweet confession with little care to the consequences.

"Keep telling yourself that as Muller's wife, enjoying the spoils of war."

◊ ◊ ◊

Abby slapped him. Max swore and turned away. With her world tearing apart, all she could take with her was a last look at Max's frigid back. Choking down the screaming hurt, she said, "All those flowery words you spouted about fighting by my side meant nothing."

"Evans, you're not at my side. You're at Muller's side."

"I won't be for long. I'll find a way to escape or to kill him, and I will kill him."

"Taking a life isn't easy and he's your childhood friend."

Running her fingers down his back caused muscles to freeze,

but Abby took no heed. "Be safe, my wolf."

She pressed a last kiss to those frosty muscles before walking towards the men stepping through the door.

"You have a deal."

Kris pulled her to his side. "Let's give Khalid the fake address before heading out."

◊ ◊ ◊

What did he just do? Fear tore away control as Max threw himself towards their disappearing backs. Rabid threats for Muller's demise came screaming from his lips. The manacle shredded broken skin but never halted Max's continued efforts to get to Abigail.

"Kill him," Roman said.

Abby screamed, launching herself at Roman. "We had a deal! Don't touch him!"

"Your boyfriend is too dangerous. Shut the hell up before Khalid hears you."

"Max!"

Roman smothered her screams, dragging her away.

Kris turned at the door. "Guess you lost both your life and the girl. Sorry for you, buddy."

"Roman will sell you out!" Max yelled at Kris. "Deceit seeps out of his black heart. Whenever he looks your way, he fucking hates you."

"You're wrong," Kris said. "There's a large bundle of cash coming his way, and more to follow."

"That asshole is playing you like a chump."

Kris turned towards Max. "I never take a man's last words seriously. They stem from desperation and fear."

The fear wasn't for himself, it was for Abby. He'd spoken the truth. Roman was a snake who'd destroy Muller, and Abby would get caught in the crossfire.

Kris paraded up to Max like a vain cock. "You'll be shot in the head knowing you've failed at your job and you've failed her. Joey's mine now. Think about that in your last kak-ass moments. I'll keep her around for a couple of years and when she's lost her pretty mojo, I'll bury her in my backyard."

Max blocked out the prick's taunts as Scarface and his two sidekicks walked over with suppressed M4's. If they got close enough, Max could take one target out and acquire the weapon. Survivability sat below the ten percent mark. He'd faced crappier odds before—well, maybe not this crappy, but his homicidal rage might tip the scales.

Kris broke in. "Not in here. I don't want a blood-soaked floor, that's a bugger of a stain to clean up. Take him into the bush; the vultures will clean the carcass. Keep your distance. He's a lethal bloody bastard."

"Yes, sir."

"Lock up the place and pay off the staff. We'll meet over the border in a few days." Muller left to join Khalid.

The crappy odds were now happier ones. Max allowed himself to be freed. The men were cautious, having no idea that they'd just become chickens in the coop and Max was one bloodthirsty fucker. They shoved him up a hill. The opposite direction to the house. Then down a path, crossing over a cattle grid and into the bush; arguing over the best spot for an execution. Max slowed his gait, listening for closing distance. A couple more steps and he'd make his move.

An unknown gunman burst from the surrounding brush and fired at the men. Max dove, twisted and tripped up Scarface's legs. He gripped the M4, wrestled it from the brute's hands, then slammed it upwards into the asshole's nose. Scarface went limp. One shot to the face and Max realigned his sights on the second mercenary, who staggered back under the stranger's fire. A double tap from Max and the man fell dead on impact. The third target groaned in the sand with a gaping chest wound. Max pointed the assault rifle at the lone ranger.

"I'm with you, don't shoot!"

The man looked Indian or Pakistani.

Mutali emerged from the bush, stepping between bodies, before slashing away at the dying man with a machete. "This is Rashid. He is my good friend."

"Thanks for the assist, buddy." Max rolled to his feet before checking the M4 and the dead men for ammunition. He had to get to Abby.

"You're from Pakistan?" Max asked Rashid in Urdu.

Rashid shouldered his weapon. "My parents came from Karachi, I grew up in Johannesburg. Mr. Muller came to our local mosque and hired five of us to work on his farm. We had no idea that he worked with these extremists until it was too late. Men like him give Islam a bad name."

Gunshots from the east caused Max to pause. He switched to English.

"How many of you are there on the property, fighting Muller's men?"

"Ten staff members. We have machetes and guns we've stolen from the guards."

"I'm going after them. Where is that gunfire coming from? Are those your men firing?"

"I doubt it. Most of the staff are at the lodge. It's coming from the road that leads out. It splits, if you go right, you'll head to Mr. Muller's private airstrip. Turning left will take you ten kilometers towards the main freeway."

"Thanks. I need a phone."

Mutali dug in his pocket and handed Max an old Samsung.

"I'll replace the phone once this is over. Is there any coverage?"

"Only on the main road. Do you need any backup?" Mutali called to Max's back.

"No, look after your people. My team will be rolling in shortly. Don't shoot at them."

"What do they look like?"

"Nasty mothers like me."

Gunshots continued, indicating Abby was caught in a firefight. Max hotfooted it, not allowing the ankle to slow him. Mercenary thugs ran through the shadows, hindering his progress. Max encountered and eliminated three bogies before approaching the front gate, but by then it was too late.

◊ ◊ ◊

A burst of rounds kicked up around the van. Khalid literally sat on Abby, smashing her into the floor mat and yelling at the driver to move as his minions piled in. The escalation of violence began when they were making their way to the transport parked near the entrance of the lodge.

Abby had ignored their hasty withdrawal, instead fighting and straining her ears for the round that would obliterate her world, killing her brave Max. It was all her fault, she'd tried to save him and failed. He was right. She was a Sharon Nasari, luring friends and lovers to the rocks of her sad existence, smashing lives along the way.

When the gunshot came, Abby jerked before stumbling in a haze of pain. The volley of distant pops that followed had her holding her breath. Something had gone wrong, or in her case, right. Max might still be alive and fighting back. Abby bent over with her hands on her knees, sucking in mournful breaths. *Please be alive. Please be alive.*

Khalid paused to listen and yelled commands in Arabic; men scattered. Some ran back towards the lodge; the remaining men hustled her towards the vehicles.

A bodyguard unlocked a Jeep. Kris turned away to redirect two guards, Abby spotted the fleeting look exchanged between Khalid and Roman, a Judas Kiss that pushed Kris out of the circle of trust. Roman readjusted his grip on his Glock, and in a split second, Abby chose the side that was lesser of the two evils.

"Kris! Watch out!" Abby screamed as Roman raised his pistol, splitting the Al Juhani-Muller alliance for good. Kris dove sideways, getting nicked in the arm as opposed to the head. Men scrambled to choose sides as shots were exchanged. Kris scurried off. Abby was shoved into the vehicle with Khalid landing roughly on top.

Now the Jeep mowed down guerrillas as it bounced wildly towards the exit. Roman was an excellent shot, ruthlessly eliminating anyone who got in the way. More of Khalid's men piled into a second van, then they bolted for the airstrip.

◊ ◊ ◊

Two vehicles roared away as Max broke into the paved clearing. Bodies littered the road. An engine screamed, and a Ford pickup smashed its way out of a shed, aiming directly for Max, who dove to the side. Bullets slammed into the ground as he scrambled for cover behind the abandoned guard house. The vehicle drifted around in a skid, Muller's face at the wheel, flashed in the moonlight. Taking aim at the ranger, Max's bullet slammed into

Kris's shoulder. The truck swerved violently before accelerating out of the grounds, heading left towards freedom.

Only one sedan remained with a shot-out windscreen, but thankfully the keys were still in the ignition. Max pulled a dead mercenary from the driver's seat and grabbed the dead man's R4 rifle as an additional backup weapon.

Pulling onto the sand road, Max prayed he'd be in time. A call to Johnny confirmed that the team were ten minutes out, too late to provide support in grounding an aircraft. Max immediately gave up Gabe's location. Mandla's Spec Ops unit in the Cape could evacuate Gabriel and Noleen before Khalid got to them.

Two miles of bone-jarring driving and Max smashed through the brush at the end of the runway just as the jet ascended. Engines roared, the landing gear retreated. Max raced onto the tarmac, yelling at the plane's retreating form. He skidded to a stop and dialed a number with shaking fingers.

Black night was all that remained, consuming his sanity.

Slater answered on the first ring.

"Where the hell are you!" Max shouted.

"Three clicks away."

"Three clicks too fucking late, we're all too fucking late! I'm parked on Muller's airstrip. Move your damn asses!" Max hung up and stepped out into the darkness. He cradled the large rifle as he sank to the ground.

How had the mission that mattered most turned into such a clusterfuck? Two years of working seamlessly as a team and this was where they'd ended up? Losing valuable hostages in the field.

Abby's value was all wrapped up in Max. He couldn't survive without her, yet he'd pushed her away when she'd needed him the most. As team leader and her protector, the blame lay squarely at his feet.

Chapter Twenty-Three

Fifteen minutes after takeoff, Abby had to delay Khalid and his four guerrillas. There were too many of them to take on herself, especially with a limited knowledge of self-defense. If she guessed correctly, the flight was only eighty to a hundred minutes of flying time. *You can do this, girl. Take what you know about aircrafts and formulate a plan.* A history of extensive flight safety training might just give her an edge.

Two of the four guards were buckled in their seats. One man in the lavatory while Roman stood near the cockpit. Khalid tapped away on his laptop, seated towards the front of the aircraft on the plush seats facing the cabin. The cold bastard behaved like an ordinary businessman on a work trip. The guard seated opposite Khalid was buckled in. Abby was positioned in the back row, on the left side of the aisle.

Viktor sat across the aisle from her. The gargantuan Russian was the one who'd broken Meg's arm that fateful night. Ignoring his shoulder-holstered gun, Abby spotted an ankle strapped piece, exposed as Viktor's cargo pants rode up his leg.

If she could get to that weapon she could shoot Khalid, a rooted fantasy that would be suicide. She was outgunned. The old pre-Max Hansen Abby from a month ago would have jumped at the chance to sacrifice herself for the greater good. The new post-Max Hansen Abby wanted to live, even if he never forgave her.

Abby refused to think about those last angry words fired in her direction. Did he really think that badly of her? She'd been trying to save him and all he saw was a self-serving bitch. No. That was just ugly desperation pulling them apart. Abby was determined to stand with her fierce warrior, and the time was now.

She glanced at the window to the left. They were on a Gulfstream G150. She was trained on Airbuses and Learjets—they were her old friends—but she'd flown once before on a Gulfstream. This was a roomier aircraft than most private planes with six plush leather seats taking up most of the space. Four facing forward and the two front seats facing the cabin. The windows were small and round.

Her plan formed. The estimated altitude was twenty-five thousand feet. Shooting out a window would cause an immediate decompression. With luck, the unbuckled men would receive injuries as they were thrown around the cabin on an emergency descent. The pilot would drop rapidly to a safer altitude to avoid oxygen deficiency, and then divert to the closest airport for an emergency landing.

Khalid would find a way to get to Cape Town but delaying them as much as possible bought Max and his team precious time. Abby had solid faith that Max had used his Jason Bourne skill set to escape, and it was time for them to catch up on Khalid's head start.

Viktor was not an attractive giant, with his crooked nose nestled between beady eyes. Abby ran eyes down his steroid-soaked body, noting his position as he dozed with legs stretched out. No one paid her much heed, thinking she wasn't going anywhere. Wrong. She was about to go somewhere called ape-shit. Hurricane style.

Unbuckling the seatbelt without drawing unwanted attention was the next step. Abby slipped as many fingers between the metal bits as she could and pulled the clip handle slowly. A dull click barely registered. She subtly repositioned herself. Moving fast was essential and her aim had to be accurate. This was going to hurt; Khalid's retribution would be a bitch.

Abby dove for Viktor's feet, grabbing the ankle-strapped gun. Mercifully it slid out on contact, and it helped that the safety clip was located on the trigger. Swiveling, Abby aimed at the window as Viktor lunged forward, pulling his primary weapon. He moved incredibly fast, shifting the gun towards her head. His seatbelt restricted his movement as he tried to twist in the chair.

One of them had to die and it wouldn't be her. Abby swung the gun around and pulled the trigger. The bullet traveled upwards through the bottom of his jaw, exploding out the back of his head. Viktor's brains splattered across the ceiling, a horror she'd never erase. Abby re-shifted her aim to the window. One shot, two shots and her aim was true.

The cabin erupted into chaos as men fumbled with seat belts, tripping over themselves. Roman rushed up the passage, with a teammate following close behind. Abby threw the gun away and raised her hands. Roman ripped her upwards into the aisle. Her head bounced off the back of the seat in front. Pain ripped through her neck, but all Abby focused on was one glorious sound—the cracked window sucking out whistling air.

Roman threw her face forward into the aisle, and she scrambled to her knees and reached over the seat, grabbing a seat belt and wrapping it around her wrist. A knee slammed into her ribs. Abby nearly vomited but held on, knowing what was coming. Sure enough, a huge bang echoed as the window blew out. Roman's startled eyes met hers as Abby pulled in a deep, yet painful breath. She had approximately twenty seconds to get to an oxygen mask before hypoxia set in.

Time slowed as men dove for safety, grabbing for anything as air tried to suck their bodies out. Roman was nearest the blown-out window and held onto an armrest. Carts broke free in the galley. A coffee cup flew past only to be pulled out into the atmosphere. Oxygen masks finally dropped down, bobbing frantically in the wind-torn cabin.

As the aircraft descended into a nose dive, screaming men flew backwards, their bodies battering the rear bulkhead like tenpins scattering. Gravity pulled Abby up the aisle, her legs floating as she clung to the seat belt. Securing herself and grabbing the oxygen mask flapping about was her primary objective. Desperation tore at her lungs but there wasn't any oxygen to be had. Agonizing pain ripped through her body, indicating damaged ribs. Eyes tearing, Abby clawed her way into the seat. Once latched in, she pulled on a mask and took her first breath, keeping the dizziness at bay.

Moans rolled through the cabin. Abby smiled at Khalid, who sat buckled in with a mask settled over his smoothly handsome face. There would be retribution if the look on his face was anything to go by. His white knuckles clutched at armrests and his eyes spat with fury. It was foolish, but she couldn't resist goading him. She'd waited too long for this moment and would rather die than let this monster touch her son.

Abby pulled the mask up and mouthed the word, "Oops" before settling back and donning a cloak of control.

Once the plane landed, Khalid stood up and sorted out the

bedlam. One dead. One broken wrist. Roman fared well with just a gash marring his manly forehead. Abby wished he'd been cabin-whipped into oblivion, but he still looked as smooth as hell.

Stomach churning, Abby watched them drag the Hulk's almost headless body up the aisle, tossing it in the rear galley. She'd done that, blown the back of a man's head off. Blood spray still dried on her forehead and she trembled in morbid shock. Max had warned her about taking a life. She'd gone and done it and couldn't look away. The metallic smell of blood coated her lungs.

Abby glanced up vacantly. Roman grabbed her hair, the seatbelt strained in protest and her poor ribs were cracking in two.

"You killed my comrade, now you will fucking die." Roman slammed the butt of his gun into her cheek. Pain exploded. He reared back again.

"Enough!" Khalid's voice cut through dizziness, Roman didn't pause, instead grinding the muzzle against her forehead. Warm blood trickled down her face.

With a flat look, Roman adjusted his stance. "Close your pretty eyes, it's time to clock out."

Abby had taken it too far and now she would die. She closed her eyes, not because the douchebag asked. She needed to see what mattered most. Max was holding Gabe. He'd go to the ends of the earth to rescue her son. They could have been an actual family; her little family who would never be together in this life. How badly she wanted that. Growing up in constant loneliness had isolated her soul in cynicism. With Gabe, she'd thought her family was complete. Max shattered that image, replacing it with something so much better. That dream would be snuffed out, along with her fragile life.

"I said enough!" Khalid stepped closer. "If you kill her, I'll be very disappointed. I need her alive to find my son."

"You know where your son is!" Roman shouted.

"And what if Muller's wrong?" Khalid swore in Arabic. "You take orders from me."

Roman's finger stroked the trigger slowly. "Khalid had his turn with you, but it's my turn next, I've been waiting a long time." As he shoved her roughly back, Abby smiled.

Her dazzling life included a sweet baby boy and a strong man by her side. Max would annihilate anyone who got in his way. Abby had just turned the tables, outfoxing Khalid, and the arrogant fool didn't even know it.

◊ ◊ ◊

The helicopter landed just north of Johannesburg at Lanseria Airport. Max leapt onto the runway, followed by Donnie, Slater, and Anton. Go-bags were provided as they raced to a private aircraft, fueled and ready for takeoff. Mandla Nkosi and Johnny greeted Max at the bottom of the stairs. Johnny dude-hugged him before breaking the news. "Khalid hired additional help. We didn't get there in time. Our drone saw five men entering Noleen's safe house. They're holding them hostage until Khalid arrives."

Mandla grabbed Max's bag. "My six-man team got there as quickly as they could but we were too late."

"For fuck's sake. Do those mercenaries know your men are watching?" Max asked.

"My unit is keeping a low profile. They commandeered a vacation home across the way."

That gave them a good site to work from, but Gabriel was now also Khalid's captive, and that messed with Max's head.

Mandla stepped in his way. "There's more."

"Unless it involves miraculously getting to Cape Town before Khalid, there's no time." Max pushed past, but Mandla's next words stopped him in his tracks.

"Twenty minutes ago, a private jet matching Khalid's rental made an emergency landing at Kimberley Airport."

Max turned slowly. "What kind of emergency landing?"

Donnie placed a hand on his shoulder and Max shrugged it off.

Making his way past Max up the stairs, Mandla called out, "I'll explain onboard. With luck on our side, we may just get to the Cape before Khalid does. This is the delay we need."

"Why aren't we heading to Kimberley?" Ignoring the throbbing ankle, Max motored up the stairs. "What the fucking hell happened?" He wouldn't pander to Mandla and his goons. Max was grateful for their help but needed intel, and if Mandla wasn't a team player, then he was dead weight.

"Grab a drink of water, you need hydration, and we'll need to patch up that foot."

Max wasn't interested in grabbing a drink. For the first time in his career, his skin crawled with panic. If Khalid or his fucked-up band of merry men had harmed Abby in any way, Max would gut them alive. Roman worried him most, they needed more intel on the sick bastard.

"SITREP now! What the hell happened in Kimberley?"

"I have an informant who's a Chief Engineer at Kimberley Airport," Mandla said.

Max cut in. "You have informants everywhere. Get on with it."

Mandla raised an eyebrow at Max's rude tone but continued, "A Gulfstream matching the description requested an emergency landing. After landing, the pilot wouldn't allow airport personnel to board the jet. My man, however, got close enough to hear the altercation between airport security and the people on board. It looked like a decompression. A blown-out cabin window. Someone caught a glimpse of blood in the cabin."

Max's stomach dropped.

"Was anyone injured?" Slater asked.

"They couldn't get close enough to confirm injuries, but my informant detected a nasty smell wafting through the door. The telltale mix of blood and feces."

Signs that a recent death occurred. Someone died onboard that aircraft, it could very well be his beautiful Abigail.

"What's the flying time to Kimberley?"

Mandla raised his hand, but Max barreled on, "What are you waiting for? Let's fucking move!" If he raised his voice, he didn't give a flying fuck.

Johnny tried to calm him back into his seat. "We're too late for Kimberley, by the time we get there, Khalid will be gone. Cape Town is the only option, and if we leave now, we might just beat them to it."

"Tell the pilot to get us the fuck out of here," Max snapped. Ignoring his men's careful glances, Max clipped the belt, hands shaking. It wasn't going down like this. Worry combined with a lethal need for vengeance seared a hole in his gut.

Mandla spoke carefully. "If Khalid gets there first, I could give my unit the green light to engage. Or I could have a welcome party meet them when they land."

"And if Evans gets killed in the crossfire? There is no way that you'll be risking hostages' lives without MIT2's boots on the ground."

"They're an excellent team, all former SF boys."

"If that little boy or his mother gets hurt because some cowboy operator is trying to save the day, I'll kill him, and you'll be next on my hit list. Your men will stand down."

Mandla nodded before turning to the cockpit.

Donnie slipped into the adjacent seat. "Stop shitting blood, buddy. You can't run around like a Rambo banshee on meth. We need to take Khalid alive."

Max gritted his teeth so hard, he thought his jaw would crack. "Someone died on that aircraft. One unarmed woman against five armed thugs. You do the math."

"It wasn't Evans."

"You don't know that."

"Our girl has spunk and moxie and an incredible brain. I think she caused the decompression. She knows we're on their tail and that was no accident."

"What if it got her killed?" Max's eyes burned.

"It may have. But we can't let her down. She's doing her part, and it's now our turn. Mr. 'Cool as Ice' Max needs to come out and play—if for no other reason than to save that little boy."

"I fucked everything up, saying stupid-ass things to her that were untrue. She went with Muller to save me, and I basically told her that she was a selfish bitch looking after her own ass."

"That's fucked up. Why would you say that?" Donnie asked.

"In our line of work, we're used to seeing people screw others over to save themselves. We deal with selfish cowards all the time who sell out and betray their loved ones. I jumped to conclusions, thinking she chose Kris over me. He has a measure of control over her."

"Abby would never do that. Especially knowing what Muller's capable of. She'd never choose his black soul over the ones she loves."

"I know that! Being chained to the floor made me go insane. I couldn't stop her hurt or the fear and instead of making it better, I made it worse. Stupid jealousy could've got the woman I love killed and God, do I love her. I love her so damn much."

Slater squeezed Max's shoulder from the seat behind. "We're here for you, brother. The first step is getting to Cape Town. After that, when we've kicked dickhead ass and she's safe and sound, then you can grovel for forgiveness, Finnish style—build her a longboat or a sauna or something."

"Screw off, Slater," Donnie said. "Find a bottle of Axe spray to drown in." He opened his laptop as the plane took off. "Let's get to work. I'm pulling up an aerial view of the address."

Max closed his eyes and took a steadying breath. Time to do his job, and failure would not be an option.

Chapter Twenty-Four

The landing was rough. Fourteen miles per hour winds rocked the aircraft. A Cape windstorm descended on the city, and fifty mph gusts were predicted within the hour. Thanks to Mandla's contacts, they'd secured a private landing strip on a wine farm near Sir Lowry's Pass—thirteen clicks out. With lights and speed on their side, they were looking at a nine-minute drive. Khalid's jet had landed at Stellenbosch Airfield twenty-eight minutes before them but had a longer commute of twenty-one kilometers.

Praying that Khalid hit traffic, Max's team raced for Somerset West.

Mandla gave Max the stink eye. "Never mind a windstorm, we'll be driving into a political shit-storm if you get exposed. There'll be more than just my reputation on the line if you go berserk."

"We look like berserkers?" Slater smirked.

"Not so much you, but the look in his eyes tells me otherwise."

Max didn't like the jab and told him so. "This is my operation, my men, and Khalid is my responsibility. If you get in my way, a political shit-storm will be the last thing you'll worry about."

"Easy, sir. We're on the same side, but my men's safety is my first priority, and you've had a taxing twenty-four-hours."

"I'm just peachy." Max gave him a feral grin.

Five minutes out and they received the news that Khalid had arrived ahead of them. Frustration at the setback had the men on edge as Mandla called his team.

◊ ◊ ◊

Salty winds whipped Abby's face as Roman shoved her through the front door. The sparsely furnished safe house still spoke of home comforts. Two sofas stood in the right corner with a brightly covered handwoven throw draped over the side. An old wooden wall unit held a small television and a couple of knickknacks. Drawn curtains added to the ominous tension. A humble dining table sat on the left side of the open-plan living area, where Noleen sat with Gabe in her lap. Two burly men stood guard on either side. Two more men were watching soccer on the telly in the dim living room.

Ignoring the guns pointed her way, Abby rushed to her confused son's side. Gabe stared up with wide eyes. She'd sworn she'd kill Khalid before he touched her son and she'd failed. He buried his head in Noleen's shoulder, clinging like a crab. It was a natural reaction. Noleen had been his entire world for the last six months. Still, Abby felt the pain of rejection.

Khalid knelt in front of the pair, reaching out to his son and stroking Gabe's face. He spoke softly to the terrified kid, who hid his face in her friend's shirt. Eventually Khalid gave up, joining the squad of terrorists and issuing commands in Arabic.

Abby ignored them. "Have they harmed him? What about you?"

Noleen shook her head. "We're fine, but sweetie, look at your face…" She reached out to touch Abby's torn-up cheek.

"My ribs are even worse, but I have a lot of fight left in me. Khalid won't take him away."

"No, Khalid won't."

Their exchanged look indicated that the emergency plan was now in effect. Khalid assumed that Noleen was just a nanny, an intentional mislead on Abby's part. Noleen was a highly trained bodyguard, an expert in hand-to-hand combat and a kung fu master. One level away from the title of sifu.

With a snuffle, Gabe finally reached out to his mommy and Abby pulled him in. He'd grown so much in the past months, no longer a baby but now a little boy. Rocking her son and kissing his neck, Abby knew she'd die rather than hand him over. When the time came, she wouldn't have a choice. Having faith in Noleen's plan was one of the toughest choices she'd ever made. Her life for Gabe's.

Khalid switched to English as they discussed their plans with the rest of the guards. "We'll take the trawler northwards, up the coast to Lambert's Bay. Is the plane ready for us?" he asked one of the local mercenaries.

"Yes, sir. It'll take you over the border into Botswana. I have men waiting for your arrival at a private landing strip, a hundred miles from Gaborone."

Khalid turned to Roman. "You'll remain behind to do cleanup."

Abby knew what that meant. Eliminating the women.

Roman stroked himself. "The bitch will pay for killing my brother-in-arms. I'll drive over the border and meet you in two days. Sameer will stay with me." He gestured to one of the bodyguards, the one who'd been eyeing Noleen furtively.

"Fine, but don't attract attention. The less time we spend in this country, the better."

Roman's obscene grin signaled the moment of reckoning. "It's time to say goodbye to the brat."

Abby fought like a tigress, but the trained thugs made quick work of prying Gabe out of her desperate arms and smothering her high-pitched wails.

"Shut her the fuck up. The neighbors will hear." Khalid now held her little boy.

Roman landed quick blows before clamping a brutal hand over her mouth. She was no match for his practiced strength.

"Play some music and drown the bitch out."

Sameer selected a music channel, pushing up the volume. Heavy metal blasted through the speakers. Khalid took the remaining men with him.

Sameer slammed the door shut and turned to Noleen. "Time to draw my sword. Wanna taste?"

Roman chortled as he dragged Abby down the passage, spotting a bedroom to the left and tossing her onto the bed. Agony spiraled through her side. Regardless of whether Max came, it was a fight for survival, and she'd save Gabe or die trying.

◊ ◊ ◊

Max grabbed Mandla's shoulder. "Do they have a visual of Evans?"

"Affirmative. Along with Khalid and three of his men."

Max huffed out a breath. Abby was alive.

"She's been injured," Mandla continued.

"How badly?" Max waited impatiently for Mandla to relay information.

"Mobile but hobbling, she also has a facial injury."

Sons of bitches. Max knew in his gut that Roman was

responsible. He'd pay. They pulled into a side road, grabbed the equipment and hustled the two blocks to the back of the house, where Mandla's men were squatting.

Max took charge. "Let's get comms set up. Khalid won't be staying long. Three hostages and nine targets. USSOCOM wants him alive, but if he poses a direct threat to any of the hostages, he'll be eliminated. Hostage rescue is our first priority. Khalid Al Juhani will eliminate the two women—Abigail Evans and Noleen Keller—and take Gabriel Capello with him."

The teams worked together seamlessly, running through schematics and breach scenarios. As it was an urban environment, they chose to use suppressors to keep from attracting attention. Mandla's team would serve as backup, forming a cordon around the house to stop squirters—targets trying to make a run for it. Heat signatures indicated eight bodies in the front area including the hostages. Two targets in the backyard and two more flanking the building.

The tempest howled angrily, echoing the restlessness rippling through Max as he shouldered a Vektor R5 rifle. Gale force winds could pose a problem for Slater's skill set when taking out targets on the perimeter, and the sniper set up as close as possible without attracting attention. The teams moved in position just as Abby's frantic screams cut the air. Max's heart clenched as he surged forward. Death metal music suddenly blared from the house. The thumping music whipped through the turbulent air as the front door swung open.

"Move now. Go, go, go."

Ten steps down the path and Khalid walked into an ambush.

Slater's sniping skills took out two of the three targets flanking Khalid with potent accuracy. Anton took out the third. The *slit-slit* sound of his suppressed weapon was lost in the wind.

Confirmations via the headset told Max that the four men on the perimeter were taken care of. Abby was still in the house with Roman, and the thought made Max ill.

Desperation had Khalid immediately shielding his head with Gabe's tiny form, a knife to the baby's throat. Max was closest to the pair. Gabriel's big brown eyes found his, and Max's heart lurched. He shut down the rush of emotion at the child's strange calm. His immediate connection with the tyke added to his resolve.

Khalid kept shifting position, waving the kid in front of him like a basketball.

Max craved a clean shot. "It's over, Khalid, your men are dead. Hand the kid over."

Slater's voice came over the comms. "Wind is screwing with accuracy. No shot."

"Get out of my way or the boy is dead!"

"You'd kill your own son?" Max shouted over the wind.

"If I have to, he'll be a casualty of war, and I will be in Jannah."

Max doubted the terrorist would grace the pearly gates in any realm after the atrocities he'd caused.

"Murdering your child won't get you there." The fucker wouldn't stop moving, and sand whipped at open skin. Gabe squeezed his eyes shut against the blustery assault and started to cry.

Gothic music expanded for a beat as the front door opened. Max tensed as a flash of grey drew his attention. An agile-looking woman crept down the stairs towards Khalid's back. This had to be Noleen, a younger version of Halle Berry with long hair pulled back into a braid. Interference could get Gabe killed, yet she moved with the grace of a big cat, a wicked knife clutched in her right hand.

"Still no shot," Slater muttered. Max had the same challenge. Both men were accurate marksmen—you had to be at their level of training—but weather conditions combined with Khalid's smart shielding efforts were delaying a trigger pull.

"Who's the wannabe Sarah Conner? Is that Noleen Keller?" Johnny muttered.

"Affirmative," Donnie growled.

Gabe's cries were lost in the wind as Khalid chanted, psyching himself up for death. This was getting tight, and Max lasered in on any opening. Noleen stepped to the right and defanged the serpent, expertly slicing through tendons and ligaments above Khalid's elbow. His knife hand dropped uselessly as he lurched, still trying to hold onto Gabe with his other arm.

Slater pulled the trigger, marking Khalid with a clean shot to the head as Max lunged to catch the kid. Little hands clung as Max rushed the toddler out of harm's way, shielding him as he ran. Donnie stepped forward.

Max thrust the tyke at him. "Get him in the Toyota."

Donnie secured a crying Gabe in the back of the fully armored vehicle. Max grabbed Noleen's arm. "I need Abby's exact location."

"Back bedroom, second to the left. I don't think he knows you're here."

None of the tangos got a shot off, and the team's suppressors combined with howling winds gave them the surprise factor.

"I'll find her. What about the other target?"

"Sameer. If he's not dead, he's close to it. I sliced him up and knocked him out, in the front room, to the right."

Max spoke as he ran. "Donnie, cover the kid. Johnny, I need you to have my six, Abby's injured, she'll need a medic."

The pounding music provided cover as Max eased open the

unlocked door. He forced himself to stick to training protocol and not charge down the dark passage. Movement to his right confirmed the second target was still alive. A crimson trail marked the asshat's progress towards the door. Sameer's bloody hands fumbled for an ankle-holstered weapon, his hatred evident as he spotted Max. A bullet to the throat silenced the fucker, the soft thump of his head hitting the floor the only indication of Max's presence, just as an agonized moan rose above the music.

Abby. Murderous rage fogged up Max's focus as he cleared the passage, heading towards his woman.

◊ ◊ ◊

The only makeshift weapon in the austere room was a clay bowl situated on the bedside table. Abby lunged for it, as Roman pounced onto the mattress. Grabbing the lip of the bowl, Abby smashed it into the side of his head, causing him to collapse as the ornament exploded.

Roman moaned as Abby scrambled off the bed. Due to her injuries, she moved far slower than she'd have liked, as though she were wading through quicksand. She crawled to the door, the swaying room and the hammering music added to the disorientation. She had to get to Gabe.

"You fucking bitch."

Pain ran through her scalp as Roman grabbed her hair, swinging her towards the bed. The defensive skills Noleen taught her were no match for combative training, and before she knew it, Roman straddled her on the bed, blood dripping onto her chest from the slash across his temple.

"Time for some schooling. Lesson number one, don't fuck with my face." Roman drew out a long, thin knife. "I got this as a gift, from your brother, Kris. A Frank B. Nine-inch Italian stiletto."

"He's not my brother," Abby gasped.

"No. He'd like to be a lot more. He wants to fuck you like I'm about to, but the only thing of his that will ever slide into you will be this knife." Roman shifted his hips; nausea rolled as he sliced open her shirt.

"That looks painful." The stiletto ran over the dark bruising decorating her side. "I gave that to you. Makes me so hard, knowing that I'm marking you in every way and no one will hear a thing."

In a blink of the eye, he sank the blade into Abby's shoulder. The shock of pain made her gasp for breath.

"I chose well, avoiding any major arteries, so we can enjoy the maximum amount of time together." Roman twisted the knife and Abby keened in agony, floating in a haze of pain.

Shifting his weight, he unzipped his pants. "How about I introduce you to my other sword before we continue getting to know each other." The evil look in his flat eyes twisted her to the core.

Dirty rain slammed against the rattling window, rising above the music with determined anger. The tempest called to her and Abby turned her head to the raging storm that spoke to her delirious mind.

"You're a beautiful woman. I'll be the last thing you see on this earth."

He had it wrong. With superhuman strength, Abby arched her hips. Roman jerked back. Her good arm reached for the handle of the knife, and she yanked it from burning flesh, twisting it and burying it in Roman's neck.

Shock registered on his handsome face.

"I am the storm," she whispered. "And the last thing you'll see on this earth."

Roman grabbed her throat, squeezing as he wheezed through gurgling blood. Her energy was centered on his monstrous face when it exploded like a melon. Time slowed as the fine spray clouded in the filtered light. Blood suddenly slapped against the wall like crimson paint thrown on a canvas.

Abby's gaze stayed transfixed on that wall as a black shape moved across her vision before dragging a large weight off her legs.

Someone yelled over the metallic sounds pounding through the room. "Abs, baby. Oh God. Abs." Gentle hands pushed hair from her face, still she stared at the Jackson Pollock wall. Fingers pressed against her neck. "Someone turn that damn music off!"

Another voice cut in. "Sir, has Petrovich been neutralized?"

"Damn straight. I shot the fucker in the head."

"Do you have a pulse? Max, move your determined ass out of the way. Find where all that blood's coming from while I check her vitals."

"Looks like he jabbed her just under the collarbone."

The wave of pain in her shoulder was accompanied by intense pressure. That got her attention and her eyes focused on the two alien beings looming over her.

"Stay with me, baby. I've got you." Ghostly eyes shone through yellow goggles. It was Max pressing on her shoulder, not an alien. Men wearing tactical gear knelt on the bed.

"Gabe. Where…is…my son."

"He's safe. Don't talk, Abs. Just rest. I'm sorry, I'm so goddamn sorry."

"Saved…us. Saved my son?"

"He's safe and in one piece. Forgive me baby, I'm so fucking sorry."

"Need to see Gabe."

"Shoulder," the other GI Joe barked, and Max swapped positions to the other side.

"Stop Khalid."

"Consider him stopped. Permanently. Noleen and Slater took him out."

"You sure?"

"Yes, baby. I saw it with my own eyes."

"Keep her still, I need to get this bleeding under control."

She recognized GI Joe number two as John, who worked with an efficient urgency. The fire in her shoulder expanded as his latex-gloved hands dug in, causing her to cry out.

Max stroked her hair. "Hold on, baby, it's going to be okay." His tone hardened as he turned on John. "Jesus, she needs some freaking drugs."

"Once she's stabilized. You know the drill, hold your damn horses and get the IV running."

The two men worked quickly, finally loading her onto a stretcher.

"I'm giving you something for pain," John said as Max turned away, speaking into his comms.

"Not yet, need to see my baby first."

◊ ◊ ◊

Mandla met Max at the door with a contingent of men. All the tangos were accounted for. The protection detail was a precautionary measure that Max was comfortable with. To say that he was on edge was an understatement, more like blowing apart at the seams. Entering that room and seeing Roman straddling Abby's broken body, her sightless eyes staring straight ahead, had sent him over that edge. Neatly blowing Roman's head off had been a smooth reflex that removed the threat, but

Max craved more time with the asshole. The luxury of drawing out Petrovich's demise would have sat well after what he'd witnessed. That brief moment of thinking he was too late, that she was already dead, would stay with him forever.

"Police units are on the way." Mandla hustled them to the barricade of vehicles.

"Abigail Evans needs urgent medical care. I won't risk her health for an easy exit," Max shouted over the wind.

"If you're exposed in my country, your superiors and my government won't be so understanding, and your careers will be toast. We'll take care of Evans; your team needs to disappear now."

Max halted. "I won't leave her here! Khalid's remaining cell members may seek revenge, and Muller is still at large."

Mandla crossed his arms and grunted. "I thought you might say that. Lucky that I plan for all scenarios involving crazy Yanks." He nodded towards an armored van pulling onto the block. "An ER doctor and paramedic are waiting for you. My plane can fly you into Namibia. I'm aware of your contacts at that German clinic in Windhoek; they're on standby."

Max nodded to his team, and they moved into action. Max grasped Mandla's hand before pulling him in for a quick hug. "Without your help, we couldn't have saved them. You're a good man."

"Not as good as you might think, without my help, I could never take credit for killing one the most notorious terrorists on the planet."

Max chuckled as he slapped Mandla on the back. "Enjoy the moment, but I somehow think that no one will get the credit. Pretty sure the public will be led to believe that this was just a local drug sting of sorts."

"I'm thinking more along the lines of poachers. Now get moving, cowboy. I can hear the cavalry approach."

Sure enough, sirens sounded over the howling wind as Max clambered into the back of the vehicle. It was a tight fit, even with Slater and Donnie following in the Hilux.

Noleen sank to the floor next to Abby's cot, Gabe reached for his mommy and Noleen tucked the sniffling toddler under her friend's uninjured arm. Abby soothed her baby as best she could as the doctor checked her injuries. Max's stomach turned as he gazed at her abused face. Her left cheekbone would need X-rays; the swelling indicating a possible fracture.

Two fragile beings that were the center of his world lay on the floor of a van, unaware of the challenges they still had to face. So fracturable in this moment, but Max had little doubt that Abby would come out fighting every step of the way. He'd be by her side regardless of whether she wanted him there or not, through the nightmares and the impending PTSD. She deserved better than a man who'd turned his back on her in that concrete cell, who hadn't saved her from Khalid's wrath or shielded her from that sick fuck Roman.

He might not be worth her love, but he could no longer watch his woman from a distance. Climbing over seats and grumbling bodies, Max finally held her hand before stroking the back of Gabe's head. Abby's drugged eyes found his, and Max smiled into those mossy depths as she drifted off to sleep.

Chapter Twenty-Five

Windhoek, Namibia.

By American standards, the German-run health facility was up to code. By African standards it was the Ritz Carlton. The floors were clean, walls freshly painted, it was well stocked and seemed organized. None of that alleviated the tension running through Max. They were still situated in fucking Africa, where he was relying on foreign medical staff he knew jack shit about to perform surgery on Abigail. Two hours had gone by and still no word. The nursing staff were giving Max a wide berth after he'd hounded them for the past hour.

"The speed walker in the room is screwing with my mojo," Donnie mumbled, slouching on the lone couch.

Slater worked on a crossword puzzle in the corner, his legs propped up like he was on summer vacation. "Agreed. Sit your ass down. You're fucking with my concentration and wearing a hole in that ugly ass carpet."

"How long does it take to stitch up a shoulder? It's been too long," Max grumbled as he sat down.

Donnie re-situated himself in a more comfortable position. "Don't forget the chest and zygomatic X-rays to check for fractures to her face and ribs, so calm the hell down."

Five minutes later, Donnie was snoring away and Slater stood up to stretch, eyeing Max's tapping foot. "I'm grabbing some coffee; do you want anything?"

Max shook his head. Coffee was the last thing he needed. What was wrong with him? He needed air, not this balmy African air, just a deep whiff of frigid Colorado air to clear his head. Was he having some kind of nervous shitting breakdown? He eyeballed the exit before observing Noleen heading his way. She eased down next to him.

Max didn't feel like making conversation but had to ask. "Where's Gabriel?"

"Down for a nap in an empty ward. Your giant teammate is watching over him."

"Thanks for helping us to save him."

"I didn't do it for you."

"You have a German accent," Max noted. "Outside the safe house, in that wind, I thought it was a heavy Afrikaans twang, but no, it's definitely German."

"My father is German. My mother is Xhosa. I went to boarding school in Germany, before returning to my motherland."

"I've read your file. I didn't realize how quickly you assimilated in Munich." Max switched to German, but she cut in.

"I prefer English." Before he could reply, Noleen skewered him with a militant look. "Your charm won't work on me, and I'm not afraid of you."

"Excuse me?"

"You may intimidate the doctors and nurses and even your teammates, who are tiptoeing around your testy ass, but I won't back down."

Max quirked a brow. "From what?"

Noleen didn't answer right away, just gave him an assessing stare. Max stared right back.

"Does she mean as much to you, as you mean to her?"

"Who? Abby?" Max asked.

"Yes, Abby. Who else? I saw the way she looked at you in that van. She loves you and that fucking sucks."

The protective-friend routine irritated Max. "You don't like that she's in love with me."

"Cut the bull. Are you going to do right by her? Because a moment ago you were about to cut and run."

"Run exactly where? This is my mission, and my team is situated a few feet away. What I'm about to do is rip someone a new asshole if they don't update me on her status."

"Abby will be fine, she's been through worse."

"I know what she's been through, lady, believe me, and the last two days haven't exactly helped."

"Are you kidding? Thanks to you, Khalid is no longer a threat. You saved Abigail and our little angel."

"I fucked up. I let them touch her again. I swore I'd never let that happen, she trusted me to keep her safe and I screwed it up. She deserves better."

Noleen let out a rather unladylike snort. "Gotta love those SF egos."

"What does that mean?"

"I worked in embassies for over ten years, alongside operators and their swollen heads. Dedicated career military who loved the ladies, promised them the world and then left them in the dust."

"Bitter much?"

Noleen ignored the jab.

"The whole family thing is pretty huge and they're both

worth it. I want the whole package. The loving and promising thing I can do, I'm not going anywhere," Max said.

"Good. It just takes practice and even then, you'll still have sucky-ass moments. That's called being human."

Noleen stood to leave. Max ordered her back down. "I was going to do this after Abby woke, but we might as well get it out of the way while twiddling our thumbs. Wait here."

Max ignored her wary curiosity and retrieved a recording device from his pack. Noleen wouldn't be accompanying them back to the States, and Max needed her statement. Donnie rolled to his feet and pulled up a chair. They questioned her on the day's events before Max narrowed down on her history with Abigail. There were some anomalies in her story that he needed resolution on.

"When Abby turned up at the South African Embassy in Abu Dhabi after the attack in Sharjah, you were assigned as protection detail, and even escorted her all the way to South Africa."

Noleen folded her arms. "That's correct."

"Why were you assigned?"

"I was the only female bodyguard in residence."

"Why did the embassy feel the need to assign her protection?"

"Did you read the report? What they did to her was barbaric."

"I agree, but it was her word against his—him being a wealthy local—yet it was kept under wraps and she was smuggled out of the country." A slight nostril flare indicated that Max was on the right track. "Your embassy knew of Khalid's suspicious activities. I find that surprising since the only agencies who had him under surveillance were MI6 and the CIA."

Noleen bit her top lip before carefully replying. "Just because South Africa isn't the biggest player on the espionage chessboard doesn't mean that we're not in the game. Southern Africa is under an emerging threat as extremists seep down from Central Africa. Any intel that comes our way is carefully taken apart."

"Who gave you intel on Khalid?"

"I'm not giving you a name. A British contact, a good friend."

"My agency won't be happy with that."

"Take it up with the South African Ambassador. It saved Abby's life."

"You took her to your home in Cape Town, where she lived for a time. When Gabriel was threatened, you quit your job to look after him. Why would you do that for someone you hardly knew?"

"We had an immediate connection, like we'd met in a previous life. Call it crazy, but I couldn't walk away. Josephine— Abby—was a broken mess and had no one. Besides I'd just finished battling my own small crisis and wanted to pay it forward." Max frowned, and Noleen elaborated. "Six months before we met, I won the battle with ovarian cancer. Stage one— we caught it early—but nevertheless, it made me question my purpose on this planet."

"Are you still sick?"

"I've been cancer free for three years. When Abby gave birth and moved back to Johannesburg, I worried for them. Gabe is my godchild. When Abby said that Khalid may have found her, I knew I could save our child. I've had some lucrative assignments in the private security sector. Financially, I'm comfortably situated, so taking a sabbatical to guard Gabe was a no-brainer."

Max picked up on the "our child" comment. He felt like scum for pushing but needed to know all potential threats to Abby's happiness, both real and imagined. "You'd give up everything—including your life—for a baby that's not your own?"

Noleen's eyes glistened. "He's my godson. I don't have a family, he's the closest thing I have."

"And you'll have to say goodbye. Are you comfortable handing him back, after all that's happened?"

She choked on a sob. "He's safe and back where he belongs. Wherever they end up, I'll visit. As the godmother, I've done my job."

Johnny ambled down the passage holding a squirming kid. Max switched off the device, and Noleen rose.

Her voice sounded hoarse with emotion. "Those dark months that Abby spent recovering, she never smiled or laughed. Not once. Then Gabe came along, and she reserved her smiles for him. Today was the first time that I saw her light up for someone else. That moment in the van when she looked at you, I saw the girl she once must have been, so full of trust and love. You're a lucky man."

Max turned his head away, gathering himself.

Johnny handed Gabe over to Noleen. "This little tyke has been hopping around for the last ten minutes, refusing to sleep."

"Don't give him to me," Noleen said. "I need to use the head. Pass him over to the grouchy boss man."

Johnny grinned and deposited the energetic bundle into Max's arms. "Good luck, bro. I need a break."

Turned out that Max didn't need luck. The cheerful little boy snuggled in like he'd belonged there all his life. Max walked Gabe around the clinic, stopping to show him the "fishies" in the tank and pausing to look at the "pretty flowers" in a vase. After Max paged through a *National Geographic*, showing Gabe the "growly lions," the kid finally fell asleep, cradled in his lap. Max retrieved the provided baby blanket, covering the both of them and settling into an armchair. Gabe curled tiny fingers around Max's thumb and in that moment, looking down at the little cherub, Max was a goner.

He stroked Gabe's soft curls, the color of Abby's hair, and stared at the tiny eyelashes resting on fat cheeks. "I'll make it right, buddy. No one will hurt you or take you away from your mommy ever again."

A quick clearing of a throat signaled the arrival of the doctor and an update on Abby's condition.

◊ ◊ ◊

Abby woke to two very different male snores. One loud and raspy and the other sounding like a squeaky puppy. Max lay stretched out on the chair, balancing a snoring Gabe like a football in his lap. The comical pair had her giggling, a sound she promptly regretted as a pain lanced through her chest.

Max was by her side in a flash, tucking Gabe under his arm and stroking her hair. "Easy now, baby. Shallow breaths, you'll be okay."

Abby breathed through the pain before grasping his strong hand in hers. Max laid a sleeping Gabe by her side.

He described her injuries, one cracked rib, a badly bruised cheekbone and a stitched-up shoulder wasn't a bad outcome considering she'd gone head to head with international extremists and survived the bloody war. A nurse then kicked him out, fussing over her vitals for the next thirty minutes. After that, the doctor traipsed in, followed by the warrior Asgard gang, needing a debriefing on what had gone down after Max and Abby were separated. Noleen then settled by the foot of her bed.

All of the excitement wore her out. All she'd wanted was quality time with her son and to have a simple conversation with Max. When they were finally alone, Abby drifted off into oblivion only to wake the following morning feeling like she'd been dragged through a hedge backward by a raging stallion, who tossed her to the ground, trampling over her tender body with giant hooves.

"Ouch," she groaned without opening her eyes to the throbbing ache that was her body.

Max yelled for a nurse, and when one walked into the room a minute later, Abby heard the irritation in his voice as the attendant rifled through charts. "She's in pain. Stop fannying about and get her something."

Abby grinned inside. "Fannying about" was a British saying she'd adopted in South Africa. Max had obviously inherited the verbiage from her, and it sounded damn cute coming from him. She heard the poor woman scurrying around like she was about to get shot. The man was formidable, and she sympathized. No one wanted to be on the wrong side of that frosty glare.

Max spoke softly in her ear as he traced it with his thumb in that touching way. The muttered sweet nothings and the occasional kiss on her forehead kept her eyes closed. At some point, she'd need to put her big girl panties on and emerge painfully from her cocoon. A girl needed to pee and freshen up before facing a room full of tall warriors, and one adorable kiddo who needed attention. Besides, she needed to scrub the terror of the past couple of days off her skin.

"Where's Gabriel?"

"With Noleen in the cafeteria, having his breakfast. That kid sure can eat."

"He does love his food. There's not a fussy bone in his little body. I need him with me."

"You need to rest. You've been in the hospital for fourteen hours; your body hasn't even begun to heal."

"Stop making a mountain out of a damn molehill. I'm getting my shit together, and I'm starting with a shower."

Ignoring the protesting alpha male in the room, Abby climbed onto wobbly legs before an unkempt Max with five o'clock stubble pretty much carried her into the bathroom. The nurse hovered close by as she negotiated through painful ablutions. A toothbrush, underwear, new pajama set, and a hairbrush sat on the counter. Looking at the mirror came as a shock; half her face was swollen. Butterfly stitching stood out starkly on pale skin.

When Abby was done, Max helped her back into bed. He'd retreated into that remote shell, the clandestine operator mode that made him seem like he had the world on his shoulders.

Abby reached out for his hand, and he grasped it tightly. "How's the ankle?"

"I'm on pain meds, feels fine."

"You look exhausted. How much sleep did you get?"

"Very little. I was on the phone with Washington and HQ for half the night."

His calloused hand enveloped hers. Abby examined his fingers, running a thumb over his broad palm. It felt so good to touch him again. The temptation to crawl into his lap and hibernate for the next decade was strong. She craved this man, regardless of the solitary look in those polar eyes. The loaded stillness built as she waited for Max to say what was on his mind.

He finally spoke. "I screwed up. And—"

"That's the fourth time I've heard that in the last twenty-four hours. Do operators apologize after all their missions?"

A flash of uncertainty flitted across Max's face.

"Last night Noleen told me that she'd screwed up by not rescuing me from Roman before saving Gabriel. I told her what she already knew. Gabe always comes first."

"You had it under control. Shit, you stabbed Roman in the fucking neck. I pray there'll never be a next time, but if there is, pull the knife out immediately. With that move, he would've bled out in seconds."

"You took care of him with the head shot."

"We both took care of him, and I should've got there sooner."

"Slater snuck in after the doctor left, to tell me that he'd screwed up by not taking Khalid out quickly, something about the wind screwing with accuracy. Like I would want him to risk an unclear shot with Gabe in the mix."

Max stroked her arm. "Slater's timing was faultless."

"Exactly. Oh, and John says he's screwed up with Lizzy. I'm not debating that one, we've both burnt that bridge. And then there's me. I must've screwed up a dozen times in the last couple of days."

"Granted, that stunt you pulled on the aircraft has given me grey hairs, but it gave us time to catch up. You are so brave, it blows my damn mind."

"I did kick altitude ass! I also killed a man."

"I know, Abs. You didn't have a choice."

"I can't talk about it, not yet."

"At some point, you'll need to."

Abby gave him a halfhearted fist pump. "Yay, more therapy." She paused before tackling the elephant in the room. "So how have you screwed up?"

"What I said, in that concrete prison, was way off base. To think for even a second, you'd elope with Kris to save yourself was absurd. I don't blame you, if you never want to see me again."

Abby took a breath. "It was ridiculously way off base. I told you that I love you. I don't love easily. You were anchored to the floor like a circus animal, watching me slip away, so I get it. Words shouted in fear would never extinguish what I feel for you."

Max did his soul-staring thing with freaky eyes as Abby drew the back of his hand to her lips and kissed his knuckles.

"Did your accusations hurt? Yes. I kept running over what you said, but you were in a bad place, physically and mentally. We both were."

Max pulled his hand back to tuck a curl behind her ear. "I acted like a dick to the one person who means the most to me, and I stayed behind while they broke you."

"I'm not broken. For the first time in years, I was no longer afraid. I was in control and whole again. My only fear was that they'd hurt or kill you. When I woke up yesterday I felt incredible. I went head to head with a heartless terrorist and came out on top." She giggled. "Like I'd completed the most difficult triathlon on the planet. Hell, I actually ate a handful of darn crickets!"

Max smiled. "Let me guess, you feel like Wonder Woman."

"Actually, the nerd in me feels like the *Nike of Samothrace*."

Max ran his lips over hers. "Just two nerds colliding and getting their freak on."

"I like the sound of that." Abby wrapped her good arm around his neck.

"Easy there, Nike. No freaky stuff is happening until you're properly healed."

"Gosh darn it." Abby patted his cheek playfully. "So, what's next, once I'm mobile?"

"We still travel to Camp Lemonnier. That's the hard shit. You'll be taken in for questioning." Max must have sensed the panic. "I won't leave you, and I'll make every arrangement in my power to keep Gabe safe. You're more of an asset, rather than a suspect."

"How long will it take?"

"Anywhere from a couple of days, to a week or even a month."

"And then?"

"And then we get to start our life together."

"Are you sure you want this?"

"I fucking love you. I love that you're smart and funny. I love how your creative brain works. I love your independent and down-to-earth attitude. That mix of passion and serenity that runs through your veins fascinates me. And I'm just going to say this, your son is freaking adorable. I want to be the best role model for him. I want the hard shit and the happy shit all rolled into one."

Abby ran her hand over his brow. "Well, you certainly know how to make a girl all gooey inside."

"Abs, it won't be easy. I'll be deployed for months at a time. I'm a military man, and love what I do. When I am home, I may not always be the perfect partner, I'm bull-headed, and can be a bit of a loner. I'm bossy at times, but willing to learn. I give you full permission to kick my ass when I drop the ball."

The bossy remark had Abby grinning. "I'm not so sure about two bossy nerds stepping on each other's toes."

Max kissed her jawline and slowly made his way down to her neck. God, he was so incredibly good at that. He nibbled her ear. "Is that a yes, Evans?"

"That's a 'hell yes!' Hansen."

Max paused. "It's actually Andersen. Erik Andersen at your service."

"Well, Mr. Andersen, are you as good of a kisser as Hansen is?"

"Mmm. Debatable. As long as you rest those ribs, I'll let you be the judge. Tell me if this hurts your sore little cheek."

Kissing Max for the next twenty minutes was blissful torture. His expert tongue gently plundered her mouth, leaving him visibly hard and her frustrated.

"This is going to be a long couple of weeks," Abby sighed.

Max slid a hand under the blanket and found her clit, stroking it once, then twice before whispering in her ear. "Think of it as foreplay. I'll touch you every day, until we're both ready to go insane, then when you're healed, I'm going to fuck you so thoroughly, with my mouth and my dick, that you'll be coming for days."

With a quick kiss on her nose, Max was out the door. Well, that took her mind off the aches and pains. Abby grinned at the ceiling. That sounded like fun, and *fun* wasn't a word she'd ever used to describe her life. No more stormy shadows, it was all breezy sunshine on the road ahead.

Chapter Twenty-Six

Johannesburg.
Four weeks later.

That damn dog wouldn't be able to fight its way out of a paper packet, never mind protect his Lizzy. Johnny watched her mom's little rat dog take a shit on the sidewalk, before his blonde beauty bent over with a poop bag to sweep up the steaming parcel. Johnny paused to take in the spectacular view that was Lizzy's incredible ass. Perky butt cheeks shaped beautifully by faded skinny jeans. Her retro outfit included a Michael Jackson "Thriller" T-shirt, silver sneakers, fire-engine lipstick and a bandana holding back curls.

Where was she taking the ankle biter? There were no parks nearby plus she carried a bright red handbag. Not the wisest choice on the streets of Jo'burg, yet she wandered down the street like she was strolling through Central Park. Granted, it was a suburban area, but it wasn't safe. Lizzy dropped the bag of rat droppings into a neighbor's garbage can, then wiped her hands with a wet wipe. Her phone beeped and she fished it out of her bag, pausing to type out a message.

"Woman!" Johnny wanted to yell. "Pay attention to your

surroundings!" Finally, she pocketed the phone before continuing on the walk.

As Lizzy rounded the corner, Johnny turned the car on, following from a safe distance. He'd landed a few hours before. This was a personal trip—he'd rented a vehicle before heading for her parents' home, arriving about the same time as she slipped out of the front gate.

A couple of blocks later, Lizzy walked into a strip mall parking lot, heading straight for a food truck parked in the corner, before buying a hotdog and a Coke. She sat on an outdoor bench that had seen better days. The Chihuahua was on the receiving end of some intermittent meaty titbits, as she scrolled through her social feeds.

Johnny turned the engine off. It was time for the talk. The one needed to tie up loose ends. The conversation he prayed would keep him centered in her world. Clammy hands were a new experience for him and he swiped them over his jeans. *Suck it up, dickhead, and make this right.*

Johnny opened the door and paused.

Two scooter ass punks sidled up to Lizzy. Greasy-haired teenagers with pants sitting halfway down their legs. One of the dickbags, donning a hooped nose piercing, propped his foot up on the seat next to her and leaned in. She folded her arms defensively. The other, with blue-tipped hair, bent over to pick up the dog.

Johnny slammed the car door, flexing his muscles as he zeroed in, marking the ringleader. Definitely Mr. Nose Candy, who was now gesturing wildly in her face.

A split second before he stepped between her and the juvie, Lizzy's wide eyes registered shock.

"Back off. Now!" Johnny barked.

"What are you doing here?"

Johnny's only focus was establishing a safe perimeter.

"What the hell, dude!" The punk straightened.

"I said BACK THE FUCK OFF."

The teenager stumbled back, his surprise evident before quickly recovering his bravado. "Who the hell are you?"

"None of your damn business." Johnny flicked a glance at the second kid still holding the highly-strung rat. "Give her back the dog."

"John, don't be an ass, Curtis lives on my street."

"You know these punks?"

Lizzy moved to stand next to Mr. Nose Candy aka Curtis. "Yes, they're on summer vacation for a couple of weeks. They've come home from boarding school."

"Why were you arguing with Curtis?"

"He was supposed to mow our lawn on Sunday and he didn't show up. So guess who was the plonker, who ended up having to do all the work!" Lizzy glared at Curtis.

"I'll make it up to you. I swear it."

"My father and I will not be paying for the yardwork you're doing on Saturday. If you don't show up, I'll be having a little chat with your old man."

Johnny hid a smile. She sounded like a real schoolmarm.

"Yes, ma'am."

"And are you back to smoking weed?"

"No. I'm trying real hard. By the way, thanks for the tech gig, I'm working the eight o'clock shift tomorrow."

Lizzy gave him a brief nod. "I'll see you on Saturday. Now, if you'll excuse us, I need to talk to this beef bazooka in private."

Curtis snickered as the two boys ambled away.

Johnny folded his arms. "Beef bazooka, really?"

357

Lizzy knelt down and tethered the pooch's leash to the table leg. "I was going for Hulk Hogan, but that seemed mean, even coming from me."

"What did he mean by a tech gig?"

"What's with you suddenly being all up in my business? Oh, I forgot, that's your thing, inserting yourself into other people's lives without their permission."

Ouch.

"What did he mean, Lizzy?"

"It's no great secret. I work from time to time on cars with my dad. Curtis wanted to learn more about mechanics. I got him a part-time job at a local mechanic shop." Lizzy gathered the hotdog packet and napkin before throwing it in the bin.

"I didn't know you worked on cars."

"There's lots you don't know about me. What do you want?"

"Just to talk."

"You flew halfway across the planet to talk. I was okay with just the text you sent, after rescuing Abby. I'm glad she's safe."

"She misses you."

"The moment she lied to me, our friendship was over."

"She was trying to protect her son and you at the same time."

"Yet I landed smack bang in the middle of a shootout."

"We all messed things up when it came to you."

"Story of my life." The bitter edge was hard to hide and Lizzy turned away, concealed emotions smacking Johnny square in the chest.

"I love you." There. He'd said it. It was out in the open. Again.

When Lizzy didn't answer, he continued, "I've thought about you every day since I saw you last. I can't get you... get us...out of my head, and I worry about you constantly. You live in a dangerous city. I'm shit scared that you'll be hijacked or hurt, and I'll be thousands of miles away."

He stepped up to her delicate back, daring to stroke her shoulders with his broad hands. She smelled like sun-kissed peaches and hope.

Lizzy moved away. "In two weeks I'm leaving Johannesburg, so you don't have to worry." Sarcasm laced her words.

"Are you moving to Cape Town?" It was a slightly safer option.

"I'm leaving the country."

"You're going back to the States?"

"Nope."

Hairs on the back of his neck stood to attention. "Where the hell are you going, London?" He knew she had an uncle in the UK.

"Kenya."

"What the fuck will you be doing in Kenya?"

"Can you please watch your language?"

"Answer the fucking question." Lizzy's reticence in not answering had Johnny's shit barometer dinging away. "Lizzy, talk to me."

"I need to find myself, and I can't do it here. I need a fresh start."

"You're an American citizen. Go to America, there are multiple states to choose from."

"I want to be a flight attendant. Abby mentioned her flying career once and it sounded so glamorous. I'll get to travel and explore new places."

Shit, there weren't any topnotch international airlines based out of Kenya. There was certainly nothing glamorous about the state-run airline. "What the hell did you do?"

"I have a job with a private security contractor called JetHaven. They provide specialized and tailored services to accommodate VIP, diplomatic and crisis flights."

"I know what they do." Johnny wanted to punch something and paced wildly before turning on Lizzy. "Let's start with the residing in East Africa thing. Kenya is one of the thirty countries that the DSS deems high-threat nations. That means it's rife with terrorism. It's an extremist hotspot."

Lizzy shrugged. "I'm used to living in high-risk areas. It can't be all that different from Jo'burg."

"It's a lot different. Now let's talk about the asshat cowboys that run these private diplomatic airlines. They have little consideration for your safety and will not hesitate to fly into danger zones. One of those private airlines was recently exposed for smuggling weapons into war-torn areas, most of those weapons landing in the wrong hands."

"I heard about that, but JetHaven is different. It's run by one of my father's good friends, Ethan Matthews. He's ex-military and wants to make a difference."

"All these egghead executives who run these clandestine military transport gigs are ex-military. Let me guess, he's a billionaire with nothing better to do than to pretend he's in the high-stakes protection game."

"I don't like your tone, and nothing you say to me will change my mind. It's done and I'm going."

Johnny squeezed the bridge of his nose, not liking the surge of possessiveness that washed over him. It served no purpose. "Are they sending you on a training course?"

"For five weeks. They have a facility in Nairobi."

"You'll be transporting VIPs and diplomats into hot spots like Afghanistan and Iraq."

"I'm aware of that. Our routes include over twenty destinations."

"I cannot believe that your father referred you to Matthews."

Lizzy looked uncomfortable. "He didn't. He's pretty mad that I'm going. I ran into Ethan two weeks ago at a charity event."

The rat dog began to yap. Lizzy bent down to untie him. "I need to go."

"Let me drive you home."

"That's not necessary."

"Fine. I'll just follow you real slow in my car."

The look on her face had his stomach sinking. Johnny knew what came next. He'd expected this; still it made him ill.

"Whatever you came for, I can't give it to you. I'm trying to keep my head above water while swimming down a giant shit creek that is my life."

"Lizzy, I'm so goddamn sorry that I lied. That I didn't tell you sooner. If I could take it all back—"

"This isn't about us. I was in trouble long before you came along. I need space, maybe I'm running away, but it's what I need to do."

Johnny dug out his wallet before handing her a card. "That's my international number. If you ever need anything…" He couldn't finish the sentence; walking away from her would break his heart. Her sudden tears didn't help, and he ached at the hidden turmoil briefly exposed to his searching gaze.

Lizzy nodded before pocketing his details and wiping her eyes. Johnny led her to the car. The drive was a silent one, the only sound being the small panting beast perched on Lizzy's lap. Too soon they were at her gate. Johnny's grip on the steering wheel could bend steel.

Lizzy turned to him. "You're a good guy. You deserve

someone great in your life. I hope you find peace."

Jesus Christ. She was giving him the friend-zone speech.

He didn't say anything, instead choosing to look straight ahead. What was there to say? He felt her gaze on his profile. One car drove past, then two. Still, she stared.

Finally, Lizzy kissed him on the cheek. "For what it's worth, I loved you too."

The door slammed shut, the finality of the action searing a hole in his chest.

Loved. She'd said *loved* not *love.* Past tense meant that she'd moved on and Johnny was no longer part of the equation. He swore, punching the steering wheel before reaching for his phone. He'd be heading back to the airport, to fly out to the team in Ethiopia, but first he needed to make a call.

"It's Johnny Cane, I need a favor. I need a background check on an Ethan Matthews, he's the CEO of JetHaven. I want everything you have on him. Everything. From what brand of cereal the ass-crack buys, to how long he takes to fucking piss in the morning." Johnny paused. "Hell, yes, it's personal. If this prick is dirty, I want to know about it."

He might not be a part of Lizzy's world, but Johnny could damn sure keep her safe.

Epilogue

Utah.
Four months later.

Max pulled into the drive. It was good to be home. He'd sold a generous acreage of his land in Colorado and decided to purchase the luxury log cabin in the mountains near the Snowbasin Ski Resort in Salt Lake City. Utah was a safe place to raise kids where they could comfortably live off the grid. Close enough to the city yet tucked away in their own slice of paradise. Abby loved the snow, trying out snowboarding and then skiing. As spring weather set in, she'd taken Gabriel on a couple of hikes in the Wasatch Mountains. Max couldn't wait to join in.

The recent three-month deployment he'd just flown in from, meant that he'd spent little time with them since settling down to family life. Max thought back on their journey after leaving the clinic in Namibia all those months ago. After arriving in Djibouti, a bunch of suits met them on the tarmac. Max refused to be separated, stating that the mother and child were under his protection during her de-briefing. His relationship with Abby almost got him kicked off the unit and Max would've accepted that fate. Thankfully, the removal of Khalid Al Juhani and

Roman Petrovich, superseded his involvement with an asset. After she'd been cleared, Max set up Abby and Gabe in Utah – before re-deployment with his unit in Nigeria. He'd just returned from Lagos where they had assisted MIT1 and the Nigerian military in their campaign against Boko Haram to rescue sixteen school girls from the nest of nine Islamic militants hiding in the jungle.

MIT still searched for Kris Muller. Max had definitely shot Muller at the lodge—he recalled the blood spray as the bullet slammed through Muller's shoulder—yet there was no sign of a body or medical treatment. Either he'd bled out in a ditch somewhere, or Muller's powerful connections came through for him, and he was recovering in some extremist rat hole. The bastard was nowhere to be found.

Sitting on his doorstep had him smiling. Max needed a break and the team needed time out. He worried about Slater, who showed signs of a PTSD burnout. Johnny wasn't faring much better. The now somber warrior stayed behind in Africa. Max bet that the distraction came in the form of a feisty blonde firecracker. Max had returned from Nigeria six days ago, and Abby had no idea that he was back in the States. His passenger was the reason for his evasiveness. Locating him had been a challenge.

"Are you ready for this?" Max asked.

"I don't think I'll ever be ready," his companion replied.

A burly older man walked briskly down the drive towards them. Bill Taylor. A former marine who was now a security specialist Max had on retainer whenever he was deployed. Abby and Gabe were still vulnerable to an attack from Khalid's splintered cell. The chances were slim, but Max wasn't taking any chances, especially with Muller going AWOL.

Max climbed out and shook Bill's hand, pulling him in for a hardy back thump before leaning in the truck window. "This is Bill Taylor, he'll show you the way. Give me time to break the news. Are you sure you want to do this?"

The man nodded resolutely.

The open-plan living area was quiet and the kitchen empty. The only evidence of occupants were two cereal bowls drying on the dish rack and a tower of vanilla cupcakes stacked on a plate. Max nabbed one and headed up the stairs towards the distant voices.

They were in the far room he'd converted into a sunny art studio before he'd left. His two angels squatted in the middle of the room on a floor covering, slapping paint on a square canvas partially masked with lines of tape. He paused in the doorway, watching the project unfold. Both rascals were decorated with paint smudges and he couldn't love them more.

Gabe squealed in delight as he squished a tube of paint. Abby promptly lunged. "Easy on the paint blobs, little man."

Max grinned. "He's following in his mommy's footsteps."

Abby jumped at the gruff voice before rushing into his arms. His arms tightened as Max breathed in a familiar coconut scent. "You feel so good," he said as she looked up, her heart in her eyes. This was home.

"What in blazes are you doing here, baby? I thought you weren't due back till next week!"

"I thought I'd surprise you." Max pressed his mouth to hers, reveling in her taste. God, he'd missed her. He plundered her soft mouth, reluctant to pull away.

"You taste like vanilla," she said wiping his lip with her thumb.

"That's what you get for displaying freshly baked goods on

the counter." Max bent down to sweep little Gabe up in his arms. "Hey, baby boy. Have you had fun with your mama?"

That innocence hugging him so tightly cleansed his soul, and Max choked down emotion. He'd bonded with Gabriel in the six weeks they'd had before leaving for Nigeria. Max bounced him up and down; the kid had grown in the last three months.

Gabe touched the operator's facial fuzz he'd grown in the field. "Wolfman!"

Max laughed. At least it was better than "Fwogman," a name bestowed on him whenever he'd made Gabe a paper frog. Gabe had blurted out the damn nickname in front of his team, who found it amusing that he'd been pretty much called a SEAL. He wasn't living that down anytime soon.

Ten paper frogs sat on the windowsill next to Gabe's crib. When Max gave the youngster his first origami frog—the one he'd made at La Coraggio—Gabe handled it with gentle awe. Every morning the tyke insisted on saying hello to the row of frogs, bestowing a kiss on each one of them with a squidgy finger. The gentle ritual got to Max every time, a behavior completely out of character for a rowdy toddler. The kid was still obsessed with amphibians, and a trip to the frog exhibit at the local aquarium seemed imminent.

"I have something for you." Max produced a gift from behind his back, helping Gabe to open it.

It was a color-changing frog night-light. Gabe's eyes lit up. After the traumatic events in Cape Town and adjusting to his new life, he had trouble sleeping. Max hoped the night-light would help...

"Say thank you," Abby prompted.

"Love you!" Gabriel shouted. "Fank you."

Abby gathered the paintbrushes and headed to the basin.

"You're welcome. Love you too, little man." A tiny hand grasped at his beard as Max paused, choosing the right words to say to his woman.

She chatted away; he barely heard what she was saying. "Give me a second to clean up. Do you want some lunch? Did you eat on the plane?"

"I went to Pensacola before I came here," Max said.

Abby turned. "You had a meeting?"

"No. This was personal. I brought something back with me and I'm not sure how you'll feel about seeing it. About seeing him."

"What do you mean?"

"I've probably stepped way over the line and I'm pretty sure you'll be pissed. If you feel uncomfortable in any way, I'll press the reset button and he can stay in a fancy hotel in Salt Lake City, and you'll never have to see him again."

Abby put down a paintbrush. "You're scaring me."

Max tucked a curl behind Gabe's little ear before swinging him around.

"Don't get all drawn into our son's cuteness factor. Look at me and tell me what's happening."

"Our son? Did you just say 'our son'?"

"Isn't that what he is?"

His eyes burned as he tried to get the words out. "That's what I want him to be, both legally and in spirit."

"He's always been yours, even before you ever met him."

Max stepped up to his beautiful Abigail as she leaned against the basin, laying a kiss on her temple. "How is it that you always say the sweetest things, and how is it that I'm always cornering you against some kind of sink."

Juggling Gabe, he brushed his thumb over a smudge of paint

on her cheek. "I want to be doing this for the rest of our lives. I was going to wait till tonight, but this feels too right." Max suddenly knelt, balancing Gabe on his knee.

"Be my wife and I swear, I'll be the best husband and father to this incredible kid. The luckiest day of my life was when your dossier landed on my desk, and when I saw our little boy—calm just like his mommy in the face of danger—I knew I'd die a thousand times over to keep you both safe. I love you both so much." He kissed the top of Gabriel's head before wrestling a ring out of his back pocket. It was his late grandmother's engagement ring. Slightly old-fashioned but a classic beauty, just like Abby.

After leaving Africa, he'd taken Abby to Colorado to meet his family. They all fell in love with the serene woman and her lively two-year-old. When Max pulled his mother aside, telling her that he wanted to marry Abigail Evans, she'd entrusted the one-carat white-gold ring to him.

Abby stood frozen.

"Abs, I know you're a quiet one, but your silence is seriously killing me."

"Yes. Heck yes!" Abby sank down; happy tears and sweet kisses filled the room as Max slipped on the ring. Gabriel's oohs and aahs over the shiny thing on mommy's finger had them all giggling.

"It's so beautiful." Abby clutched her hand to her chest.

"It was my grandmother's. She was fierce and gracious and down to earth, just like you."

Abby stroked his face. "I hope to do her proud, Erik "Max" Andersen."

"My sweet Nike, I think you'll be just fine."

He pulled his new family onto his lap, giving Gabe noisy

raspberries in his neck, making the kid giggle before tickling his soon-to-be wife. The floor covering crinkled as Abby rolled away, laughing while threatening to empty their dirty paint water over Max's head.

◊ ◊ ◊

"Abby Wabs."

Those two words uttered from the doorway broke into the sacred moment, shattering her world. The man standing in the door had to be a mirage. An awful yet divine hallucination that had her falling back against the wall. Her head buzzed as Max's supporting arms pulled her against him.

Abby shoved away, needing space, and clambered up, dusting off her jeans. Only one man had ever called her by her middle name when she was a kid, and the familiar nickname made her heart thump. "Grandpa Noah!"

"My baby girl. God. You look so much like my Lucy, back when we first met." He stepped forward and Abby raised a hand. He looked just as solid as he did all those years ago. Far less hair and additional wrinkles didn't change that face she knew too well. A face she'd seen in her dreams for too many nights as a child. Visions of Noah sweeping in and rescuing her from the hell that was her young life. But he never came, not once.

Anger rose through misty tears. "You're alive."

"Yes, honey."

"You never came for me."

"I did."

"Liar!"

"After I left, I stayed with friends in Florida for a few months. I felt tormented, knowing that I'd left you with them."

"You should have felt that way."

"If I'd known how bad it had gotten, how dogmatic Jimmy had become... I went back four months later but you were already gone."

"You came back?"

"Yes. But you'd disappeared, and it took me months to track you down to Northern Idaho. By the time I got there, I found out that Jimmy took you on a trip to Africa."

Abby remembered that trip. Their first visit to the sunny continent when Jimmy scouted for possible church locations.

"I waited for days—weeks—but I was out of money and needed a job. Construction work paid the bills. I fell in love with the site manager's sister; we got married in Idaho. Her name is Sylvia. We moved to Pensacola for work, but I never ever stopped looking for you." Noah's lips trembled as he tried to formulate his next words. "Years later, I found an online article about Jimmy and his church and flew to his new location and confronted him. They told me that you were dead, that my grandchild ran away and was killed in a car accident. I was shattered and didn't want to believe it, but Jimmy even had a tombstone erected in your honor."

Abby sat down heavily on a nearby stool. "The lying SOB."

Max knelt to stroke her back. "I'm sorry, Abs. If it's any consolation, that sick monster lost out on the best thing he'd ever had, an amazing daughter with an incredible heart. If I ever lay my eyes on him..."

Noah stepped forward. "Max found me in Florida and gave me the third degree for abandoning my granddaughter. I deserved his harsh words." He wiped a shaking hand over his brow.

Max cut in, "When I heard Noah's side of the story, I knew you needed to know the truth, his truth. You can't go back to a new beginning, but at this moment, you can start with a new middle. It's your decision and regardless of what you decide, I'll be standing beside you."

Abby took it all in. She raised the courage to ask the question that had been on her mind for all those years. "Jimmy told me that it was my fault that you left. That I destroyed our family with my willful ways."

"My son is an evil piece of shit. How could he say that to a little girl? You were the only light in that dark house, and I should never have left you there."

"You never wanted to leave me?"

"Never, baby girl. There hasn't been a day that's gone by that I haven't thought of my sweet granddaughter. For years I thought you were dead, then Max came along, and I could breathe again. I should have found you sooner, I should never have given up."

In a heartbeat, Abby was in his arms. The familiar woodsy scent had her sobbing on his jacket.

"I think it's time for a catch-up," Max said. "I'll brew a pot of coffee." He carried their chattering munchkin down the hall, leaving Abby alone with her grandpa for a soul-healing hug.

Later that evening, Abby stood in the kitchen, stirring a beef stew while eyeing the dreaded carrot cake cooling in the corner. Turned out that Gabe loved it equally as much as his daddy. She mock-shuddered, but she'd bake it for the men in her life; they were worth it. Her world was detangling into shiny newness.

There was still heartache. Lizzy refused to reply to any of her emails or phone calls, but Abby wouldn't give up. Gabe still needed therapy, both of them suffered from nightmares, which would eventually lessen with time. On the plus side, Noleen arrived in less than a month to spend time with her godson, while applying for a transfer to the South African Embassy in California. With luck on their side, Gabriel's other mommy could be just a short flight away. Abby couldn't wait to see the woman who'd become like a sister to her.

Abby ladled meaty stew over the bowls of steaming rice. A shout from the living room had her glancing up. The men were gathered around a game Max had brought home, a noisy game of Feed the Frog. Noah was in the lead, competing to feed the most flies to a moving frog. Max helped Gabe to gobble a bug and they shrieked with laughter. Abby's life had come full circle, back to the lively home of her youth. Granny Lucy would be awfully proud of the merry scene and if Josephine Abigail Evans had her way, this would be the new norm.

Truly beached, no longer battered by endless storms. Her new life had grown strong-ass roots, watered by love and warmed by healing laughter. "Dinner's up!" she yelled. "Move those butts! And the last one to the table gets the smallest slice of carrot cake."

The End

Make sure to pick up "Stain on the Earth," the next installment of the Mobile Intelligence Series. Find out what happens in Johnny and Lizzy's story!
Stain on the Earth (MIT Book#2) is available for pre-order here: https://www.louisedawnauthor.com/books/

Peshawar, Pakistan

Lizette Steyn disengaged the slide, pulled up the door handle and swung the aircraft door outward. Frigid air swept in and she barely repressed a shiver. "Freezing fudge buckets," she muttered before greeting the ground agent at the top of the stairs. The miserable structure that was Bacha Khan International Airport looked archaic—with all the developing nations Lizzy had visited in the past five months—that was saying a lot. Peshawar, the wild west town of Pakistan, felt as cold as a dead man's nose.

"Well isn't that just grand," Brianna muttered, stepping out of the wind. "All I bloody packed was a vest and a T-shirt."

Lizzy refrained from rolling her eyes. The other two Cabin Attendants had as much sense as two rolling hamsters. Brianna, a hardy Irish girl who started flying for JetHaven around the same time as Lizzy, was a workhorse in the Cabin but loved to go on partying benders the minute they arrived at the hotel. Then there was Suzie. This was Lizzy's first flight with the high-maintenance Capetonian. Thanks to her lax attitude onboard, Lizzy and Brianna worked their asses off. She didn't mind. Suzie was still new to the job, although Lizzy doubted she'd last out the month.

Had she ever been that juvenile? The last six months affected her in so many ways. Lizzy now felt like a mother hen, especially with Tweedledee and Tweedledum whining behind her.

"How hectic is this weather! Aren't we supposed to be in the Middle East? It's a desert."

Lizzy turned to Suzie. "You'll need to get into the habit of researching weather conditions on future flights. Early March is barely spring in Peshawar. It snows in Afghanistan in the winter and we're east of the border."

Suzie rubbed her goosey arms. "But we're nowhere near Afghanistan!"

"Hun, where do you think Peshawar is situated?"

"Um. Somewhere in Asia?"

Lizzy gave up on the conversation and readied herself to greet their disembarking passengers. They carried a smaller contingent than they were normally used to, thus utilizing a smaller Airbus—The A318 Elite.

The six male passengers looked somber as they gathered their sparse belongings. Definitely a team from an American three letter agency, Lizzy thought. Possibly CIA, FBI or NSA. Throughout the flight the hardened men had kept to themselves, shut in the boardroom at the front of the aircraft, only pausing for the breakfast service. Lizzy worked on a number of clandestine flights that flew into high risk regions. She'd also ferried diplomats and their families, military personnel and news correspondents. After some gruff thanks at the door, the men drove away in a black Hilux into the early morning light.

The crew bus pulled up and Lizzy covered her hair with a scarf before teetering down the wet stairs and dragging her trolley bag to a seat. She was the first onboard the musty coach and settled her tired ass on a window seat in the middle of the bus. Brianna popped up through the door. "We have a twenty-four-hour layover. I'm heading into town after I've cleaned up. I hear the Khyber Bazaar has the best Persian rugs. On her last flight to Peshawar, Jane got a fierce Pakistani Persian that is fucking unbelievable."

Jane, a fellow crew member, was an interior designer wannabe. Indigenous knick-knacks drowned out her Kenyan apartment, and it smelt like a damn Brazilian rainforest. Lizzy had no inclination to replicate the "jungle-style Zen" that Jane strove to create.

"Sweet cheeks, you should know better than to venture into Peshawar on your own. There are travel warnings in place for good reason. I'm going to hibernate in my room, order room service and watch the first Bollywood movie that I come across."

"Oh, come on," Brianna said as she tossed her suitcase onto a seat. "That hotel isn't even a two-star, never mind a three-star. The last time I stayed in Peshawar, I thought one of those stinky ass street donkeys wandered into my room, and then figured out it was just a fucking cockroach the size of a damn stallion. You really wanna spend your afternoon in a cockroach motel? Plus, you know what Captain Stuart is like, he'll be knocking on your door in no time trying to drag you down to the bar for a virgin martini."

Brianna had a point.

"Besides, Suzie is coming along. It's her first layover and the girl needs to live a little. It's not like we're going out on the lash! It's a dry town. Hell, not even the hotel has a mini bar!"

"Tell me about it, doll," Suzie grumbled as she swung herself across from Lizzy. "I need a tall glass of Chardonnay, like ASAP."

Yip. Good luck with that. Lizzy swiped lip balm over dry lips. "Just chill, you'll be back in Nairobi by tomorrow night."

"Thank fuck!" Suzie sighed. "A white wine followed by a macchiato. At least Kenya has stunning coffee."

Kenya was the base of operations for JetHaven and all the flight crew lived in Nairobi. The private security contractor provided specialized and tailored services to accommodate VIP, diplomatic and crisis flights across Africa and the Middle East.

The bus driver's brief glance reflected disdain at the girls' antics.

I feel you, buddy. Lizzy thought as they waited for the cockpit crew to disembark. She felt herself caving in to the whims of dee and dum. Apparently, there was a fabric bazaar near the Khyber area. Lizzy could grab some pretty materials and keep an eye on the girls at the same time. First, they'd need scarves and a cover up.

◊ ◊ ◊

The rickshaw dropped them off in Clock Tower Square. Brianna scurried into the first rug stall and the other girls followed. The locals seemed friendly and the store owner immediately offered them a traditional green tea. Lizzy loved the sweet tea native to Pakistan and she gladly accepted. Suzie turned her nose up and Lizzy quickly drank it to ease her companion's faux pas. Lizzy brought her digital Canon along and snapped photos along the way. The expensive camera was a gift from her father on her last birthday and she loved it, thinking maybe someday she'd write a travel book.

The narrow streets crammed with wares were an overload on the senses. Donkeys clattered amongst bearded men in turbans selling their textiles. A Pakol hat maker tried to sell her a hat as she dodged a moped bike. The decaying Sikh architecture littering the gray and brown streets were fascinating. Unstable wooden buildings stacked together in grimy colors. Wires, phone lines and old Bollywood signs hung from above. She snapped away.

Brianna couldn't find the right rug for her apartment back in Kenya and the day wore on. After they'd left the third bazaar, Lizzy put her foot down.

"Sadar Road!" she yelled at a driver as they climbed in yet another taxi.

"Apparently they have the best Kebabs and Fried Fish. I'm not doing this without food in my stomach, plus I need to buy some fabric, so your Persian rugs need to wait."

"I could eat a reverend mother," Brianna said. "Lead the way. We'll rest our asses while you buy your materials and shit."

Lizzy left the girls at the café and bought a mix of bright fabrics in the square. She returned to Suzie giggling at something Brianna said.

"Asses up. We need to finish this gig. I'm running out of steam and need a hot shower."

Brianna pulled a face. "We're checking out that donkey."

Lizzy turned to see a mule with its front hooves flailing in the air. The overloaded cart strapped to its tiny frame pulled the poor beast off its feet. Lizzy's heart clenched at the cruel sight, and she turned away.

Brianna lurched to the side, her phone swaying erratically. "I need to snap a photo." Suzie guffawed with laughter.

Something was definitely up. The girls were acting sillier than usual. Suzie swayed as they got up. They linked hands and stumbled ahead of Lizzy. Brianna dragged Suzie's scarf off her head before trying to strangle her with it. Where they drunk? Or high?

"I'm too racked to look at anything else," Brianna yelled over her shoulder. "Let's head back to cockroach city."

They lurched into a shadowed alley and Lizzy ran to catch up. "What's going on?" She grabbed Brianna's arm. "You're acting crazy."

"And you're acting like a Muppet. What's wrong with a bit of fun?"

Lizzy smelt alcohol. "You've been drinking."

"Relax, we smuggled a few minis off the plane. We've even saved some for you!"

Brianna opened her satchel. At least twenty unopened bottles rolled around inside.

"Are you freaking crazy!" Lizzy's screech met their disappearing backs as Suzie dragged Brianna down the alley. If the local police found alcohol on their person, it could mean imprisonment, there would be zero leniency for westerners. Respecting laws in other countries was essential to the job.

"Don't be a party pooper. This looks like a shortcut to the taxi rank. Beat you there!"

This wasn't good. Lizzy hesitated. Then she ran down the empty alley to catch up. Rounding a corner, she came up empty. The girls were gone. She should leave their stupid asses and head back to the hotel. A distant giggle led her up a hill. The roads were quieter on the back end of the bazaar. A shrouded woman watched from a doorway before shaking her head. A couple of kids paused to stare as she hurried past. Lizzy rushed past a fenced hedge, an iron gate leading to manicured gardens hung open. Brianna's shriek came from behind the hedge. Stepping into the private park, Lizzy called out to the women in a whispered shout. When no-one answered, she made her way off the path towards a rustling thicket.

"BOO!" Suzie jumped out, staggering sideways in a fit of giggles.

"Son of a bucket!" Lizzy stumbled back. "Where's your silly sidekick?"

"Trying to untangle my scarf. It got caught up in a rose bush."

"For Pete's sake, lead the damn way."

Rounding a tree, Lizzy looked up and slowed. A towering mosque stood centered in the gardens, gleaming in the midday sun. Arabic yelling had her glancing back down and she slammed to a stop. A group of men surrounded Brianna as she held the scarf to her chest. Her handbag lay on the ground, glass bottles lay strewn across the grass. One of the men grabbed Brianna's sleeve and Lizzy leapt into the fray. "Leave the bag. Let's move."

The angry crowd quickly doubled in size and men screamed in Arabic. The horde shoved the two girls amongst them. Someone grabbed Lizzy's hair, she screamed in terror. Bruising hands tried to tear them apart and Lizzy hung onto Brianna like a leech. If they were separated, they were done for.

Her screams were met by a slap to the face, as the growing swarm of men shoved her to the ground. Panicked regret turned to what could've been, as an image of John came to mind, then dissipated amongst the rabid shouts of violent men.

Stain on the Earth (MIT Book#2) is available for pre-order here: https://www.louisedawnauthor.com/books/

Join my newsletter to find out first about my latest releases, giveaways, sales and free books.
http://www.louisedawnauthor.com

Acknowledgments

Siren in the Wind will always have a special place in my heart. I lived with Abigail and Max for a long time before putting them down on paper. This book fought for visibility through my immigration adventures, saying goodbye to loved ones, settling in a new country and starting a life with new friends. I hope you enjoyed it as much as I loved writing it. Thanks to my wonderful family for always being my rock through the good times and the bad. My loyal friends and beta readers—Jenn, Summer, Jolene—You girls rock! Randy and the two Dereks—you know who you are—thanks for the informative conversations and for answering my endless questions. Any mistakes we'll blame on artistic license ... Lastly, thanks to my editors, Deborah Nemeth and Joan Turner at JRT Editing. I worship at your feet. My cover artist—Syd Gill—is damn amazing and I can't wait to see what she does with the rest of the series.

Louise Dawn writes heart pounding romantic suspense. She's also a corporate trainer in Utah. Louise loves travelling and has lived in many countries before choosing the States as her home. Her passion is reading and writing fast paced stories simmering in romance. If you enjoyed this book, consider leaving a review. It's appreciated by authors both new and established.

Chat with her on Facebook @
https://www.facebook.com/authorlouisedawn

Follow her on Twitter @
https://twitter.com/louisedawnwrite

Or check out her character's developments on Pinterest @
https://www.pinterest.com/louisedawnwrite/boards/